# KEEPER
## OF THE
# LOST CITIES
### NEVERSEEN

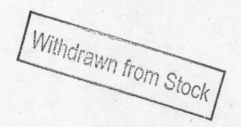

# Also by Shannon Messenger

The KEEPER OF THE LOST CITIES Series

*Keeper of the Lost Cities*
*Exile*
*Everblaze*
*Lodestar*
*Nightfall*
*Flashback*
*Legacy*

# KEEPER
## OF THE
# LOST CITIES
## NEVERSEEN

## SHANNON MESSENGER

**SIMON & SCHUSTER**

First published in Great Britain in 2020 by Simon & Schuster UK Ltd
A CBS COMPANY

First published in the USA in 2015 by Aladdin, an imprint of
Simon & Schuster Children's Publishing Division

1 3 5 7 9 10 8 6 4 2

Simon & Schuster UK Ltd
1st Floor, 222 Gray's Inn Road
London WCIX 8HB

www.simonandschuster.co.uk
www.simonandschuster.com.au
www.simonandschuster.co.in

Simon & Schuster Australia, Sydney
Simon & Schuster India, New Delhi

A CIP catalogue record for this book is available from the British Library.

PB ISBN 978-1-4711-8944-9
eBook ISBN 978-1-4711-8943-2

Printed and bound by CPI Group (UK) Ltd, Croydon, CRO 4YY

MIX
Paper from
responsible sources
FSC® C020471

For my readers.
I love you more than Silveny loves Keefe.
*mallowmelt and custard bursts for everyone!*

# PREFACE

SOPHIE STUMBLED BACKWARD, SCRAM-
bling closer to her friends as a cage of neon yellow
flames erupted all around them.

Heat licked across her skin and smoke choked
her lungs while the Neverseen moved forward, their black
cloaks gone, disguises abandoned.

There would be no more hiding.

The Neverseen shouted insults and warnings that Sophie
tried to focus on, but her mind was too fixated on other words.

*Trick.*

*Trap.*

*Traitor.*

The last word made it impossible to look one of the figures in the eye.

Another betrayal.

Another lie.

Sophie was done with all of it.

She reached for her pendant—the sign of the swan carved into cold black metal curled around a piece of smooth glass. She still didn't fully understand the reason the Black Swan had given it to her. But she knew enough of its power to realize it was their best chance.

She held the glass into the fading rays of sunset, letting the searing beam of white light refract toward the flames of Everblaze.

It was time to fight fire with fire.

# ONE

"WE HAVE TO GO," FITZ SAID, bursting through the doors of Everglen's upstairs guest room.

He found Sophie sitting alone on the edge of the giant canopy bed, already dressed in some of her old human clothes.

"I thought we were waiting another hour?" she asked, glancing out the window at the endless black sky.

"We can't. The Council is already convening to vote on our punishments."

Sophie took a slow breath, letting the words pulse through her veins, steeling her nerves as she reached for her purple backpack. It was the same bag she'd used when she'd left her human life nearly a year earlier. And now she would use it again to leave the Lost Cities.

"Is everyone ready?" she asked, proud of her voice for not shaking. She also resisted the urge to tug out an itchy eyelash.

This was not a time for nervous habits.

It was time to be brave.

The Council had vowed to punish anyone associated with the Black Swan—the mysterious organization responsible for Sophie's existence. But Sophie and her friends knew the real villains were a group called the Neverseen. Fitz, Keefe, and Biana had even tried to help the Black Swan catch the rebels on Mount Everest. But the Neverseen guessed their plan and turned the mission into an ambush. Sophie had discovered the trap in time to warn her friends, and they'd escaped with their lives—and managed to capture one prisoner. But they'd each broken numerous laws in the process.

Their safest option now was to flee to the Black Swan and go into hiding. But Sophie had mixed feelings about getting up close and personal with her creators. The Black Swan had tweaked her genes to enhance her abilities as part of their Project Moonlark—but they'd never given her any clue as to *why*. They'd also never told her who her genetic parents were, and Sophie had no idea if she'd finally have to meet them.

"'Bout time you got here," Keefe said as Sophie followed

Fitz down the twisting silver staircase. He stood next to Dex in Everglen's glittering round foyer, both of them looking very human in hoodies and dark jeans.

Keefe flashed his famous smirk and patted his carefully mussed blond hair, but Sophie could see the sadness clouding his sky blue eyes. During their confrontation with the Neverseen, Keefe had discovered that his mother was one of their leaders. She'd even attacked her own son, before fleeing to the ogre capital and abandoning her family.

"Hey, no worrying about me, Foster," Keefe said, fanning the space between them. He was one of the few Empaths who could feel Sophie's emotions rippling through the air.

"I'm worried about *all* of you," she told him. "You're all risking your lives because of me."

"Eh, what else is new?" Dex asked, flashing his dimpled grin. "And will you relax? We've got this! Though I'm not sure about my shoes." He pointed to his soft brown boots, which were a typical elvin style. "All the human ones Fitz had were too big for my feet."

"I doubt anyone will notice," Sophie told him. "But I guess it depends on how long we'll be around humans. How far away is the hideout after we get to Florence?"

Fitz smiled his movie-ready smile. "You'll see."

The Black Swan had taught Fitz how to sneak past Sophie's mental blocking and view the secret information hidden in her brain. But for some reason he wouldn't share what he'd learned. All Sophie knew was that they were headed to a round window somewhere in the famous Italian city.

"Hey," Fitz said, leaning closer. "You trust me, don't you?"

Sophie's traitorous heart still fluttered, despite her current annoyance. She *did* trust Fitz. Probably more than anyone. But having him keep secrets from her was seriously annoying. She was tempted to use her telepathy to steal the information straight from his head. But she'd broken that rule enough times to know the consequences definitely weren't worth it.

"What is *with* these clothes?" Biana interrupted, appearing out of thin air next to Keefe.

Biana was a Vanisher, like her mother, though she was still getting used to the ability. Only one of her legs reappeared, and she had to hop up and down to get the other to show up. She wore a sweatshirt three sizes too big and faded, baggy jeans.

"At least I get to wear *my* shoes," she said, hitching up her pants to reveal purple flats with diamond-studded toes. "But why do we only have boy stuff?"

"Because I'm a boy," Fitz reminded her. "Besides, this isn't a fashion contest."

"And if it was, I'd totally win. Right, Foster?" Keefe asked.

Sophie actually would've given the prize to Fitz—his blue scarf worked perfectly with his dark hair and teal eyes. And his fitted gray coat made him look taller, with broader shoulders and—

"Oh please." Keefe shoved his way between them. "Fitz's human clothes are a huge snoozefest. Check out what Dex and I found in Alvar's closet!"

They both unzipped their hoodies, revealing T-shirts with logos underneath.

"I have no idea what this means, but it's crazy awesome, right?" Keefe asked, pointing to the black and yellow oval on his shirt.

"It's from Batman," Sophie said—then regretted the words. Of course Keefe demanded she explain the awesomeness of the Dark Knight.

"I'm wearing this shirt forever, guys," he decided. "Also, I want a Batmobile! Dex, can you make that happen?"

Sophie wouldn't have been surprised if Dex actually could build one. As a Technopath, he worked miracles with technology. He'd made all kinds of cool gadgets for Sophie, including the lopsided ring she wore—a special panic switch that had saved her life during her fight with one of her kidnappers.

"What's my shirt from?" Dex asked, pointing to the logo with interlocking yellow W's.

Sophie didn't have the heart to tell him it was the symbol for Wonder Woman.

"Why does Alvar have human stuff?" she asked. "I thought he worked with the ogres."

"He does," Fitz replied. "Or he did before you almost started a war with them."

Fitz said the words in a light, teasing way, but the truth behind them weighed heavily on Sophie's shoulders. They'd be in a *lot* less trouble if she hadn't ignored the rules of telepathy and tried to read the ogre king's mind. She'd known it was a dangerous risk, but she'd been desperate to know why the ogres had snuck into the Sanctuary and hidden one of their homing devices in Silveny's tail. The rare female alicorn wasn't just essential for the survival of her species, she was one of Sophie's closest friends. If only Sophie had known that ogres' minds could detect Telepaths—even genetically enhanced Telepaths like her. She hadn't learned anything useful, *and* she'd nearly voided the elvin-ogre treaty and started a war.

"But that still doesn't explain why Alvar has human stuff," Sophie reminded Fitz. "Ogres hate humans even more than elves do."

"They do," Fitz agreed. "But these clothes are from years ago, back when Alvar used to go out looking for you."

"He did?" Sophie asked. "I thought that was your job."

Fitz was the one who'd found her on her class field trip about a year earlier and brought her to the Lost Cities.

It was the best thing that ever happened to her.

Also the hardest.

Fitz smiled sadly, probably remembering the same thing: the moment she'd had to say goodbye to her human family. He was the only one who really understood what she'd lost that day, and she couldn't have gotten through it without him.

"I started searching for you when I was six," he told her, "after Alvar started his elite levels and wasn't able to sneak away from Foxfire anymore. But my dad searched for you for twelve years, remember? I couldn't go on secret missions when I was a toddler."

"What a slacker," Keefe interrupted. "I totally could've pulled that off. But then again, I'm Batman, so"—he draped an arm over Sophie's shoulders—"I could be your hero any day."

Dex pretended to gag, while Biana stared at Keefe's arm around Sophie.

"Aren't we supposed to be leaving?" they both asked at the same time.

Sophie pulled away from Keefe as Alden called "Wait!" from the top of the stairs. His elegant cape swished as he rushed to catch them. "You can't leave wearing your registry pendants."

Sophie grasped the choker around her neck, hardly believing she'd overlooked that essential detail. The pendants were special tracking devices from the Council. She wondered what other important things she might be forgetting. . . .

Alden pulled out a pair of sharp black pliers and said, "Let's start with Fitz." He spoke with the same crisp accent as his children, but his voice sounded weak and wobbly.

Fitz flinched as Alden cut the thick cord and the crystal pendant clattered to the floor.

"Whoa. This just got real," Keefe whispered.

"Yeah it did." Fitz traced his fingers across his now-bare neck.

"Are you okay?" Alden asked Biana, who was clutching her pendant in a white-knuckled fist.

"I'm fine," Biana whispered, lifting her long dark hair to expose her necklace.

Alden hesitated only a second before he sliced through the silver band. Her pendant landed next to Fitz's, followed by Keefe's.

"Yours will be trickier to remove," Alden reminded Dex and Sophie.

The Council added extra security measures after the Neverseen used their pendants to convince everyone Sophie and Dex had drowned instead of been kidnapped. Both of them even had trees in the Wanderling Woods—the elves' equivalent of a graveyard—from the funerals their families had held.

Alden's brow beaded with sweat as he pried at the thick metal until the cords broke free. "I'll need to remove your nexuses, as well," he said, pulling out a dime-size disk.

Sophie sighed.

Another very important detail she'd overlooked . . .

A nexus was a safety device meant to hold their bodies together during light leaps, but the force field it created could be tracked.

"I guess I didn't plan this running-away thing very well, did I?" Sophie mumbled.

"It's not the kind of thing one can plan for," Alden reassured her. "And do not expect yourself to think of *everything*. You're part of a team now. Everyone works together and helps."

The words would've been a lot more comforting if her "team" hadn't forgotten the same important things—though Fitz, Keefe, and Biana were already nexus-free. Their concentration strength had reached the required level. Dex was almost there too. The meter on his wide blue cuff had less than a quarter of the way to go.

When Alden pressed the tiny disk against it, the level surged to full.

"I've been tempted to do that myself," Dex admitted as he slipped the nexus off his wrist. "But I didn't want to cheat."

"Wise choice," Alden agreed. "Having the ability to do something does not mean it's the safest course of action. It also does not give us permission to break the law."

"It does when the law is stupid," Keefe argued.

"I wish I could disagree. But look at where we are." Alden gathered their fallen pendants and tucked them into his cape pockets along with Dex's nexus. "There was a time when I believed in the infallibility of our world. But now . . . we must rely on our own moral compasses. Right here"—he pressed his hand to his heart—"we know what is necessary and true. You all must hold to that and let it guide you through what lies ahead. But I've let myself get sidetracked. Sophie, let's take care of those nexuses."

Thanks to Elwin, her overprotective physician, Sophie had to wear one on each wrist. He'd also locked her nexuses so they couldn't unlatch, even though both of her meters were full. She'd faded several times during leaps—one of which had nearly killed her. But that was before the Black Swan had enhanced her concentration and healed her abilities.

Still, Sophie reached for the Fade Fuel she wore around her neck in case of emergencies. It hung next to her allergy remedy, both vials tucked safely under her T-shirt. She hadn't needed either elixir in weeks, but she felt better having them. Especially as Alden produced a twisted silver key and unlocked each of her nexuses.

She stopped him as he examined her third black cuff. "That's one of Dex's inventions."

"I call it the Sucker Punch," Dex said proudly. "It releases a burst of air when you swing your arm, so you can punch way harder than normal."

"Very clever," Alden told him. "And a good thing for you to have. Though, Dex, I'm hoping you've learned the dangers of inventing new weapons."

Dex's shoulders drooped as he promised that he had. Dex had built the painful ability-restricting circlet that the Council had forced Sophie to wear, not realizing it would be her punishment for what had happened with the ogre king.

She nudged him with her elbow and smiled to remind him that she'd forgiven him. But he kept his eyes fixed on the floor.

"I think that takes care of everything," Alden said. "Though you all must remember to look out for one another. Fitz and Biana, share your concentration with Dex when you're leaping. And Keefe, I want you to help Sophie."

"Oh, I *will*," Keefe promised with a wink.

"We *all* will," Fitz corrected.

"Hey, I can take care of myself," Sophie argued. "I'm the one bringing us to Florence, remember?"

The blue leaping crystals all led to the same place in each Forbidden City, which would make it easier for someone to follow them. So they'd be teleporting to Italy, an ability only Sophie had—thanks to a surprise side effect of the way the Black Swan had altered her DNA.

"All of you can take care of yourselves," Alden said, "but you are stronger when you work together. You must also have a leader to keep the team organized, so Fitz, since you're the eldest, I'm putting you in charge."

"Hey, wait a minute," Keefe argued, "he's only older by a few months."

"Uh, by 'few,' you mean *eleven*," Fitz corrected.

Dex snorted. "Dude, you guys are *old*."

He glanced smugly at Sophie, and she blushed, hating that she'd been thinking the same thing.

Well . . . she didn't think Fitz and Keefe were *old*, but they were definitely older than her.

She'd guessed that Keefe was fourteen, which would make Fitz at least fifteen—but they could be even older than that. . . .

It was hard to keep track of age in the Lost Cities. The elves didn't pay that much attention to it, thanks to their indefinite lifespans. In fact, Sophie had no idea how old any of her friends actually were. No one ever mentioned their birthdays. Maybe that meant Sophie wasn't supposed to care about age either—but she was very aware that she was only thirteen and a half, and the difference between her and the boys felt *huge*.

"Hey, I'm the one who knows where we're going," Fitz said. "So I'm in charge, and . . . I guess we should probably head out. Though, wait—what about Mom? Shouldn't we say goodbye?"

Alden glanced at Biana. "Your mother has to take care of something at the moment. But she told me to tell you she'll see you soon."

Fitz didn't look very satisfied by that answer. But he didn't argue, either.

Alden turned to Sophie, not quite meeting her eyes. "I . . . offered Grady and Edaline a sedative a few minutes ago, and they decided to take it. We feared what would happen when they actually had to watch you leave. So they told me to tell you that they love you and that they left a note for you in your backpack."

The lump in Sophie's throat made it hurt for her to nod, but she forced herself to do it. Grady and Edaline were her adoptive family, and she hated leaving without seeing them. But she doubted they were strong enough to handle another tearful goodbye, given everything that had happened.

They'd lived in a deep fog of depression ever since they'd lost their only daughter, Jolie, to a fire seventeen years earlier. And now Sophie had discovered that Brant, Jolie's former fiancé—who Grady and Edaline had been caring for as if he were part of their family—had been the one to set the fire that killed her. Brant had been hiding that he was a Pyrokinetic—the elves' only forbidden talent—and joined the Neverseen because he hated living as a Talentless. But when Jolie discovered his betrayal and tried to convince him to change his ways, he lost his temper and sparked the flames that accidentally took her life.

The guilt and grief had left Brant dangerously unstable. He'd even tried to kill Grady and Sophie when they went to confront him. Grady had been so furious, he'd used his ability as a Mesmer to make Brant burn off his own hand. Sophie had barely managed to stop Grady before he went too far and ruined his own sanity. She'd also had to let Brant escape in order to get the information she needed to save her friends.

"All right, we've lost enough time," Alden said, pulling the five of them close for a hug. "Remember, this is not goodbye forever. It is simply goodbye for now."

15

Sophie felt tears slip down her cheeks as Fitz asked, "Do you want us to let you know when we get there?"

"No, I cannot know anything about what you're doing. None of us can."

"Do you think the Council will order memory breaks?" Sophie whispered.

"No, the Council will not sink to that level. Plus, they know we are too prominent and powerful. It is simply wise to be cautious. I promise there's no reason to worry."

Sophie sighed.

*No reason to worry* were Alden's favorite words. And she'd learned to never believe them.

"Come on," Biana said, pulling open Everglen's shimmering doors.

They tromped down the shadowy path in silence.

"I never thought I'd say this," Keefe said, "but I really miss having Gigantor tagging along with us."

Sophie nodded, wishing her seven-foot-tall goblin bodyguard was healthy enough to join them. Sandor had been thrown off an icy cliff during the ambush on Mount Everest and broken pretty much every bone in his body. Elwin had assured her that he'd be okay, but Sandor had a long road to recovery before him.

*Not as long as the road we're about to travel,* Sophie thought as she spotted Everglen's enormous gates through the gloomy night. The glowing yellow bars absorbed all passing light, preventing anyone from leaping inside.

"Time to run," Alden whispered.

Teleporting only worked when they were free-falling, and the bluffs they needed to jump off were beyond Everglen's protection.

Fitz wiped his eyes. "Tell Mom we love her, okay?"

"We love you, too, Dad," Biana added.

"And don't let the Councillors anywhere near my family," Dex begged.

"You have my word," Alden promised. "And I won't let them near Grady and Edaline, either."

Sophie nodded, her mind racing with a million things she wanted to say. Only one really mattered. "Don't let Grady go after Brant."

Alden took her hands. "I won't."

Everyone looked at Keefe.

"Tell my dad . . . that I've been hiding his favorite cape in a closet on the twenty-ninth floor. But don't tell him the door is rigged with gulon gas. Let him find that out on his own."

"Is that really all you want to say, Keefe?" Alden asked.

Keefe shrugged. "What else is there?"

Alden wrapped Keefe in a hug and whispered something in Keefe's ear. Whatever it was made Keefe's eyes water.

Sophie's eyes did the same as Alden opened the gates.

The five friends stared at the towering forest and locked hands.

Slowly, together, they took the first step into the darkness. They'd just crossed the threshold when a cloaked figure stepped out of the shadows—not a black cloak like the Neverseen wore.

A diamond-encrusted silver cloak.

The style worn by the Councillors.

# TWO

I T'S OKAY," A FRAGILE VOICE PROMISED AS
the figure threw back her shimmering hood. Blond ring-
lets cascaded around the beautiful, familiar face of a
weary-looking Councillor Oralie.

Her pink-jeweled circlet was noticeably absent as she told
them, "I came here on my own."

Alden lowered his hand, which was holding a melder—a
small silver gadget that caused instant, painful paralysis. "How
long before the others arrive?"

"Not long. Bronte and Terik are still arguing, but they will
gain nothing. There is too much fear and fury clouding the others' reason." Oralie trailed her graceful fingers across her arms,
shivering in the moonlight. She was an Empath, like Keefe and

his father, and Sophie had never seen her look so pained.

"What will their punishments be?" Alden asked.

Oralie lowered her eyes. "Dex and Keefe will be suspended until midterm and placed under constant chaperone. Fitz and Biana will be suspended for a week and given a month of Sanctuary service—"

"Wait a minute," Dex interrupted. "How come they get off easier?"

"Their family holds a tremendous legacy in our world," Oralie reminded him.

The Vackers were practically elvin royalty. They had more relatives in the nobility than any other family. Meanwhile, Dex's father had never manifested a special ability, and talent was all that mattered in the Lost Cities, not wealth or skin color or age. The elves considered it a fair way of separating people. But Sophie wasn't sure there was any fair way to separate people. Those without abilities couldn't join the nobility, and if they married anyone except another Talentless, it was ruled a "bad match." Dex's mother had married Dex's father anyway, but the scorn had haunted Dex his whole life.

"So that's how it is?" Keefe asked. "Now that we know the truth about my mom, my family's garbage?"

"Not *garbage*," Oralie corrected. "But your father has been removed as an Emissary. The Councillors do not trust that an Empath could be completely blind to his wife's betrayal."

Keefe blinked several times, then barked a loud, cold laugh.

"Well, I guess I can't say my mom never did anything for me. I almost wish I could be there when you break the news."

Title and stature meant everything to Keefe's father, often at the expense of kindness and love toward his son. So Sophie could understand Keefe's rejoicing—but she was surprised to feel a sliver of sympathy for Lord Cassius. In one night he'd lost his wife *and* his beloved title. And in the morning he'd discover his only son had run away.

"What about me?" Sophie asked. "What did they decide for my punishment?"

"That is still the subject of much debate," Oralie said quietly, "but most likely they will banish you to Exillium."

Sophie couldn't decide which part of that sentence was more terrifying. She knew nothing about the mysterious school called Exillium, but she'd been told many times that she did *not* want to go there. And to be *banished*?

Sure, she was running away—but banishment sounded so permanent.

"Exillium is relegated to the Neutral Territories," Oralie whispered, "a part of our world far too dangerous for you to visit. Especially now."

"Why especially now?" Alden asked.

"The ogres are stirring—at least, that is what I fear. Which is why I came to give you this." Oralie snapped her fingers and a small glass sphere appeared in her palm. Sophie hadn't realized Oralie was a Conjurer.

"Your cache?" Alden said, taking a step back.

"Actually, this is Kenric's," Oralie corrected. "He gave it to me, before he . . ."

She didn't say the final word, but it cut deep all the same. Councillor Kenric had been one of the first Councillors Sophie had met, and he'd quickly become one of her favorites. He'd been warm and kind and quick to smile, and had always taken her side. But he'd been murdered a few weeks ago, during Fintan's disastrous healing.

Fintan was the Pyrokinetic who'd trained Brant for the Neverseen. He'd suffered a memory break for his treason, but had managed to protect his secrets. When Sophie discovered she could heal minds, the Council ordered her to heal Fintan, and during the healing, Fintan had found the strength to spark an inferno of Everblaze.

Sophie had managed to grab Fitz and Oralie and teleport to safety—but Kenric had been lost to the flames. Sophie's only consolation was that Fintan died in his own blaze.

Oralie took Sophie's hand, placing the cache carefully in her palm. Seven glittering stones were set inside, each a different color.

"Kenric made me promise to give this to you if anything happened to him," she whispered, "to make sure you'd be protected."

"Does that mean he suspected his life was in danger?" Alden asked.

"We both did. Though I should've done more to help." Tears slipped down Oralie's cheeks. "I should've done so many things."

Councillors weren't allowed to marry or have children, in order to remain impartial in their decisions. But Sophie had seen a connection between Kenric and Oralie and suspected they'd been in love. They could've resigned from the Council and chosen to be together, but for some reason they'd kept their lives separate.

"He believed in you," Oralie said, tracing a soft finger down Sophie's cheek. "He told me you were the spark of change our world needed. So keep his gift close, and if the Council catches you, use his cache to buy your freedom. Do *not* let them send you to Exillium. You must also take this." She handed Sophie an Imparter, a small silver square that worked like a video-phone. "It cannot be traced or tracked—and I'm the only one you'll be able to contact with it. This way we have means to contact each other."

"What if the Council discovers your involvement?" Alden asked. "They will surely see this as treason."

"Sometimes rebellion is the only course of wisdom. As all of you well know." Oralie turned back to Sophie, and her mouth curved with a word. But by the time it slipped from her lips, it had changed to, "I must go."

She raised her pathfinder to the moonlight and glittered away before Sophie could blink.

"Now *that's* what I call mysterious," Keefe said. "Foster, you should be taking notes. And who else wants to play with this cache thingy and see what it does?"

"You will do nothing of the sort!" Alden told him. "And you must not let anyone know you have it—I wouldn't even tell the Black Swan. Our world could crumble if that cache fell into the wrong hands."

"Really?" Sophie asked. It looked like one of the cheap marbles she used to play with as a kid.

"The object itself is not the danger. It's what the cache contains. What do you think the biggest threat to our world is?" Alden asked.

"The ogres?" Sophie guessed.

"Actually, it is knowledge," Alden corrected. "Information holds unimaginable power, and some things are too dangerous to be known—even by the Councillors. So they lock the most disturbing secrets away before having them erased from their minds. They're called the Forgotten Secrets, and they are stored in what you hold there. Each Councillor vows to guard their cache with their lives. Oralie has taken an enormous risk by giving this to you. She's also given you our world's most valuable bargaining chip."

Sophie rolled the glinting marble around her shaking palm, tempted to give such a huge responsibility back. But she owed it to Kenric to protect his gift. Plus, Oralie's vague warnings had made it sound like she was going to need it.

"Come on," she told her friends, shoving the cache into her deepest pocket. "We should get to the Black Swan."

She reached for Fitz's hand, and Keefe took her other hand. Biana clung tightly to her brother, leaving Dex to choose between Keefe and Biana.

"I won't bite," Keefe told Dex. "Ow—but no need to get squeezy!"

None of them looked back as they sprinted into the trees. They wove around fallen branches and gnarled roots, making so many turns Sophie feared they were lost, until her ears picked up the telltale whoosh of waves. The forest parted a few steps farther, revealing a steep ocean bluff.

"I'm going to open my mind to yours so you can *finally* show me where we're going," she told Fitz.

"I don't have anything to show you," Fitz said. "I just know we're supposed to start at the Path of the Privileged."

Sophie dropped Fitz's hand. "I have no idea what that is. And what do you mean by 'start'?"

"That was the first instruction," Fitz said.

"Instruction?" Sophie asked. "Or riddle?"

"I guess it could be a riddle," Fitz mumbled. "But I didn't think they'd do that this time."

"Dude, have you met the Black Swan?" Keefe asked.

"I know," Fitz said. "But I figured for something *this* important they'd be clear."

Sophie backed away so she wouldn't be tempted to shove

Fitz off the cliff. "Okay"—deep breath—"what *exactly* did the riddle say?"

Fitz handed her a scrap of paper where he'd written the complete message.

> Take the Path of the Privileged
> Past eyes that watch eternal, and blood
>     turned precious.
> Seek the tower that would not yield for
>     the next steps of your journey.

"Get anything from that, Foster?" Keefe asked, reading over her shoulder.

"Of course not," Sophie grumbled. "Why didn't you tell us about this earlier so we could've done some research?"

Fitz tore his hands through his hair. "I'm sorry. I guess I messed up."

"And you didn't see anything else?" Keefe asked him. "You searched Foster's mind for a while."

"Only a few minutes," Fitz argued.

Keefe grabbed Fitz's wrist and pressed his fingers against the exposed skin. "Hate to break it to you, but I can tell you're hiding something."

"Empaths," Fitz grumbled.

"Just keeping you honest. So spill. What did you see in the Mysterious Miss F.'s mind?"

Fitz turned to Sophie, and even in the dim light she could see the red flush in his cheeks. "I *might* have seen some other stuff—but it wasn't really thoughts. It was more like . . . feelings."

"Oh?" Keefe asked as Sophie's stomach filled with bubbling lava. "Does that mean you—"

"We're wasting time!" Sophie interrupted. "The Council could be here any second, and I still have no idea where we're supposed to be going."

"Okay," Keefe said, following her as she stalked to the edge of the cliff. "So . . . we still need to go to Florence, right? The Black Swan told you that?" When Fitz nodded, Keefe asked Sophie, "Doesn't your photographic memory have a few pictures of the city tucked away?"

She *had* seen pictures of Florence, but . . . "That doesn't tell us where we go after that."

"We'll figure it out. And once we do, we'll all smack Fitz a few times and tell the Black Swan to knock it off with the lame, non-rhyming riddles. In the meantime"—Keefe grabbed Sophie's hand again—"we're doing this thing!"

They'd barely locked hands before Keefe pulled them off the cliff's edge.

# THREE

KEEFE LAUGHED WHILE EVERYONE screamed and thrashed as they plummeted toward the ocean. "Wow, what a buncha babies. Don't worry, Foster's on it."

His confidence melted some of the fog in Sophie's head—enough to let her focus on the energy rushing with her adrenaline. She shoved the force out of her mind and thunder cracked the sky, sending them crashing into the void.

As they drifted with the darkness, Sophie imagined a picture she'd seen of Florence: *Marble churches. Red rooftops. A golden river lined with colorful buildings.*

She homed in on her favorite landmark: the Cathedral of

Santa Maria del Fiore. Thunder clapped again, splitting the blackness with blinding light.

They slipped through the glowing crack and tumbled into a crowded courtyard, crashing into a marble wall and collapsing in a pile.

"Still gotta work out these landings," Keefe groaned as he scooted out from under Fitz.

Sophie was much more focused on the pain in her head as hundreds of voices sliced through her mind. Human thoughts broadcast like radio waves, even with her impenetrable blocking. Luckily, she'd learned how to shield her mind by imagining an invisible barrier around her head.

Fitz rubbed his temples, clearly doing the same thing, but she refused to return the weary smile he gave her. Now they were lost in a Forbidden City and it was all his fault.

"It smells weird," Biana said.

"Probably human pollution," Fitz explained. "I don't remember it being this strong, though."

"Me either," Sophie said. The air felt thick in her throat, and it had a bizarre caramel smell. Not at all what she'd expected for the land of pasta and garlic.

"So, are we invisible?" Dex asked, watching the crowds milling around them. "Or are they just more interested in that big domed thing." He pointed to the famous Duomo across the courtyard.

"Probably both." Fitz removed a small black orb from his

satchel. "My dad gave me an obscurer to help us stay hidden."

The gadget bent light and sound in a limited radius, camouflaging anything inside.

"Are you serious?" Biana asked. "Then what was the point of these ugly costumes?"

"It's called being careful," Fitz told her.

"Plus, I get to be Batman!" Keefe added. "But I'm done with the jacket. Why is it so hot here?"

"Too many people, not enough trees," Fitz said as he took off his scarf and coat, leaving him in a rather tight blue T-shirt.

Biana ditched her sweatshirt, revealing a yellow screen-printed tee. "I liked that this one had a few girls," she told Sophie, pointing to the group shot of the X-Men. "Even if they have super weird hair."

"Uh, there's a guy who has blue fur all over his body, and you're focusing on the girls' hair?" Keefe asked. "And hey, that clawed dude's yellow shirt might be as tight as Fitz's!"

"Jealous?" Fitz asked, flexing rather impressive muscles.

"Shouldn't we try to figure out where we're going?" Dex asked, shoving his sweatshirt into his satchel and hugging his skinny arms against his chest.

"Probably," Keefe agreed. "But first—what is *that*?" He pointed to the drippy ice cream a family was devouring. "Whatever it is, I want some!"

"I think that's gelato," Sophie told him. "And forget it."

"Actually, I think it's a good idea," Fitz said.

Keefe leaned closer to Sophie. "In case you were wondering—*that* is why he's my best friend."

Sophie sighed. "Even if we had time, how would you pay for it?"

Her friends were used to buying everything with their birth funds—a special account set up when they were born, with more money than they could ever use in a lifetime. But it was useless outside of the Lost Cities.

"Won't this stuff work?" Dex asked, pulling out a wad of crinkled, colored paper. "I had it left over from when we were in that other Forbidden City after we got kidnapped."

Paris and Florence *did* accept the same currency, but . . . "We don't have time for gelato!" Sophie said.

Keefe draped his arm around her shoulders. "Foster, Foster, Foster. *Live* a little."

"You know he's going to keep pushing until he gets what he wants, right?" Biana asked.

"Fiiiiiiiiiiiiiiiine," Sophie mumbled. "Give me the money. I'll be right back."

"We're coming with you," Dex said.

"Uh-uh. I'm going to have to be visible to buy something. And together we'd be way too conspicuous."

"But we're in costume!" Biana argued.

"Yeah, but you guys will still stand out. I mean . . . look at you. You look like models."

"Wait, is Foster saying she thinks we're hot?" Keefe asked.

"I think she is." And the huge grin dimpling Dex's cheeks was practically beaming.

Sophie wanted to deny it, but the truth was, elves were *way* prettier than humans. Even Dex with his messy strawberry blond hair was ten times cuter than any human boy his age.

"I'm just saying you guys will draw a lot of attention," Sophie said. "Especially since you don't speak Italian."

She pointed to two portrait artists sitting in the shade of the Duomo, waving their hands as they talked. As a Polyglot, Sophie could tell they were discussing their favorite soccer teams. But the rest of her friends only spoke the elves' Enlightened Language. Fitz knew a little English from his time searching for her, but that wouldn't get him far in Italy.

"Sophie's right. The less we're all seen, the better. But *I'm* going with her." Fitz handed Keefe the obscurer and snatched some money from Dex. "No one wanders off alone."

"Fine." Sophie was still mad at him, but they also needed to talk.

"I can't believe we're wasting time on this," she said as Fitz followed her through the crowds of tourists. It was so strange to see gray hair and wrinkles and glasses and canes after so much time around the ageless elves.

"I get that we're in danger," Fitz said. "But *that's* why I thought this was a good idea." He scooted closer, lowering his voice as they passed a group of girls ogling him. "I mean . . . aren't you worried about how everyone's holding up? Biana seems really nervous, doesn't she? And Keefe is *barely* keeping it together. I'm sure Dex has to be freaking out too. So if gelato makes them happy, don't you think that's worth it?"

"I guess I hadn't thought of that," she admitted. "But still, we'd have more time for things like gelato if you'd told me what the Black Swan's instructions were before we left and let me work on solving the riddle."

"I know. I'm sorry. I wasn't trying to drive you crazy. I was worried you'd sneak away without us if I told you."

The thought *had* crossed her mind—several times . . .

"I just want to keep everyone safe," she mumbled.

"I know. So do I. And yet we're both making it worse. So why don't we stop trying to do it all on our own and start acting like a team?"

He held out his hand, and Sophie reluctantly shook it, feeling slightly gleeful when the ogling girls gasped.

Her smile faded as she remembered the other subject they needed to cover. "So, um . . . if we're really going to be a team, don't you think you should tell me what you saw in my mind?"

"I didn't see as much as you're probably thinking," Fitz said carefully, "and I couldn't understand it, anyway."

"What does *that* mean?"

"It's hard to explain. I ended up in this crazy place Mr. Forkle called your emotional center. Now I get why Keefe's always talking about how intense your emotions are. It was super overwhelming."

"And that was where you were when Mr. Forkle said, 'Remember this place. You may need it'?"

Fitz nodded. "He didn't say why, though."

"Of course not." That wasn't how Mr. Forkle worked. He was the only member of the Black Swan she'd met in person, but she still knew nothing about him. Even his name was a fake human identity he'd created to disguise himself as her next-door neighbor.

She wanted to ask Fitz more, but she'd spotted a small gelateria at the end of the alley.

"Think we should ask the shopkeeper if she knows about the Path of the Privileged?" Fitz asked as they peeked through the windows.

"I doubt she knows," Sophie said. "But it's worth a try."

Her mouth watered as they made their way inside and studied the shiny bins heaped with sculpted mounds of colorful gelato. Every flavor looked amazing, so Sophie took the shopkeeper's advice and ordered five cups of the *melone*.

"Okay, I don't know what's in this," Fitz said as he took a heaping spoonful, "but it might be better than mallowmelt."

Sophie wasn't sure anything could beat the gooey cookie-cake thing elves made—but the gelato *did* come pretty close.

"Can you think of anywhere that could be called the Path of the Privileged?" Fitz asked the shopkeeper, his accent even crisper with the English words.

When the Shopkeeper didn't answer, Sophie repeated the

question in Italian, adding, "It's for a school assignment. Our teachers have us doing a scavenger hunt, and that's one of the clues they gave us."

"I bet your teacher wants you to learn on your own, not let adults do your work for you," the shopkeeper said, wagging her finger. "But since you at least spoke to me in my language, I will tell you that your teacher probably means the Vasari Corridor."

As soon as the woman said the name, a dozen different facts clicked in Sophie's memory. The Vasari Corridor was a historic walkway the Medicis had built between their palaces, so they could move through the city without having to walk among their people.

"Can you tell us how to get there?" Sophie asked, paying for their gelato as Fitz gathered the cups for Keefe, Dex, and Biana.

"One of the entrances is across the Arno, near the grottos at the Palazzo Pitti," the shopkeeper told her. "The other is at the Uffizi Gallery. But there's no point walking to either. All landmarks are closed today because of the fire."

The sweet melon flavor turned sour on Sophie's tongue. "What fire?"

"Late last night, at the Palazzo Vecchio. It breaks my heart. All that precious history lost because of some selfish arsonist."

# FOUR

I T HAS TO BE BRANT," SOPHIE WHISPERED as she watched the firemen rush around the Piazza della Signoria.

They'd ignored the shopkeeper's warnings, using their obscurer to slip past the police blockades. The fire hadn't killed anyone, and it had been extinguished before it spread to other buildings. But the famous Palazzo Vecchio's stone walls were blackened and crumbling, and the clock tower was leaning more than the Tower of Pisa. The crowds behind them were crying, and Sophie understood their grief. She'd felt the same way the day she watched the elves' capital city of Eternalia consumed by Everblaze.

"That wasn't the building we needed, was it?" Fitz asked

as they jumped out of the way of two firemen. "I thought the entrance to the corridor was in some place with a weird name?"

"The Uffizi," Sophie agreed, pointing to the arched building next to the ruined palace. "But the police have closed all the landmarks, and an obscurer won't fool sensors and alarms."

"Well, I don't think we should stay here," Fitz said. "The Neverseen could be watching."

"How do you know it's them?" Dex asked. "Don't humans have fires all the time?"

"Can't you smell it?" Sophie asked.

Keefe sniffed the air. "It smells like burned sugar."

"Exactly. I should've recognized it earlier. That's how the San Diego fires smelled. And Brant set those." She glanced over her shoulder, half expecting to spot a figure in a hooded black cloak.

"But how could it be him?" Dex asked. "He was *super* messed up when he fled to the ogres. He'd lost a hand and, like, most of his face."

Sophie shuddered, trying not to picture Brant's bloody, blistered skin. He hadn't been able to walk on his own—couldn't even reach for his pathfinder. He'd forced her to get it for him as part of their deal to save her friends.

"He survived Jolie's fire," she said, remembering Brant's old scars.

She hoped a few of them were left. He deserved to be reminded of the life he'd destroyed.

"Or maybe the Black Swan set the fire themselves," Dex suggested, "to hide from the Council or something."

"Do they have any Pyrokinetics?" Biana asked.

"I hope not," Sophie said. "But even if they do, why would they burn the place they instructed us to go?"

"Because this place wasn't part of their instructions," Fitz reminded her. "This is the building next door."

"But it still makes it ten times harder for us to get to them," Sophie said.

"Uh, you guys are totally ignoring the much more important question," Keefe interrupted. He pointed across the courtyard to a weathered marble statue. "Am I the only one who's noticed that dude is naked?"

Sophie rolled her eyes. "That's the David."

"I don't care what his name is," Keefe said. "I still don't want to see his stuff."

"I'm with Keefe on this one," Dex jumped in.

"Me too," Biana agreed, blushing bright pink.

"Yeah, why isn't he wearing clothes?" Fitz asked, looking anywhere but at the statue.

"Because it's art!" Sophie said. "Most of the old painters and sculptors did nudes. They were studying the human body or something, I don't know—why are we talking about this?"

"You're right," Fitz said. "We need a plan. Personally, I think we should keep following the Black Swan's clues. Once we get into that corridor, I bet the rest of their instructions will make sense. We just need to figure out how to get past security and—"

"I'm on it," Dex said, heading toward the Uffizi.

Fitz grabbed his arm. "We all have to walk together to stay in the range of the obscurer."

Dex muttered something about "power trips" as Fitz took the lead. They wove carefully around all the firemen and reporters, reaching the entrance of the museum without bumping anyone.

Dex pressed his palms against the stone facade. "You were right about the crazy security, Sophie."

"Can you disable it?" Biana asked.

"Only temporarily. How do we get to this corridor thing?"

"On the upper floor, through a plain, unmarked door." Sophie could see it perfectly in her mind, which felt strange, since she'd never been there.

"Okay, I can buy us some time," Dex said, "but I'm going to have to ruin the obscurer."

"Is that the only way?" Fitz asked.

"No, I thought it'd be fun to make things extra hard and dangerous!"

"Hey," Sophie said, stepping between them, "no time for fighting."

Dex glowered at Fitz as he went back to work, twisting the obscurer apart and tinkering with the gears. He pulled out several cogs and springs and shoved them into his pocket before closing it back up. "Here, Wonderboy. Catch."

Fitz caught it with his mind.

*Telekinesis.*

It was an elvin skill Sophie rarely used, thanks to an epic splotching match where she'd accidentally flung Fitz into a wall. But Fitz clearly didn't share her reservations. He spun the obscurer a few times, probably to annoy Dex, then dropped the gadget into his hand.

"As soon as I open the door," Dex told Fitz, "roll that in. Then we run. Everyone ready?"

Dex didn't bother waiting for a reply before he tapped his fingertips against the lock and the door clicked open. "Now!"

Fitz bowled the obscurer into the museum and it streaked across the floor, blaring white noise and blinding everyone with a flash.

"How are we supposed to see where we're going?" Sophie asked as Dex pulled her into the museum.

"We aren't," Dex said. "But no one can see us, either."

"Ow, I just hit my shoulder," Biana cried.

"Maybe it was on another naked statue," Keefe suggested.

"EWWW, WHAT IF IT WAS?!"

"Will you two be quiet?" Fitz yelled. "Everyone follow my voice. I found the stairs."

They climbed to the second floor, where the light was slightly less blinding.

"Which way?" Fitz asked.

"I think we're supposed to go west," Sophie said. "Everyone look for a green room and a plain wooden doorway."

They walked by it at first, but Biana doubled back and called them over.

Fitz rattled the locked doors until Dex pushed him aside. "Leave this to the experts."

Several agonizing seconds passed.

"Any time now," Fitz said.

"Sorry, this lock makes no sense. Wait—got it!"

They raced into the corridor, and Dex flicked on the lights before turning to latch the doors behind him.

"Whoa, this place is huge," Sophie whispered as they climbed the grand stairway. She'd been expecting a dark, cramped hall, but this really was the Path of the Privileged. The entrance ceiling was gilded and decorated with frescoes, and the walls were covered in priceless paintings.

"Better hurry," Dex said, running to catch up with them. "The tweaks I did to the lock won't last. Plus, I can feel cameras, and it would waste too much time trying to deal with them. The obscurer flash might've fried their circuits, but it's better to keep your head down. And let's get cracking on that next clue."

"Wasn't it the one with the blood?" Biana asked. "If it was, think it has anything to do with this?"

They stopped in front of a cluster of portraits that looked like they'd been burned and pieced back together.

"No. Those paintings were destroyed during a terrorist attack back in the 1990s," Sophie whispered. "I can't imagine the Black Swan would ever call that 'blood turned *precious*.'"

Biana shuddered. "Humans are so awful to each other."

"Uh, didn't a Pyrokinetic *elf* just burn another building earlier today?" Keefe asked.

"Are you saying elves are as bad as humans?" Biana asked.

"I'm saying we're not as different as we should be. Certain elves, especially." The bitterness in his voice made it clear he meant his mom.

"Come on, let's keep moving," Sophie said, then realized they were forgetting a clue. Before the "blood turned precious" they needed "eyes that watch eternal."

Could it mean the portraits staring at them?

That didn't feel right.

Then she spotted a barred round window.

"Is this the one we saw in your memory?" Fitz asked.

"It's hard to tell. The scene in my head was from the other side of the wall. But I just remembered that these windows were called Cosimo's eyes. They were his way of keeping watch as he walked through the city. That's the next clue."

"Great, so *now* the blood part is next?" Biana asked with a grimace.

"Actually, I think I know what that means—and it's not as bad as you're thinking."

Sophie confirmed it a few minutes later when they reached a row of wide panorama-size windows. "Yep, we're on the Ponte Vecchio now. There are a bunch of gold shops lining the bridge underneath us, but they used to be butchers. The Medicis didn't like the smell, so they moved the gold merchants here."

Biana gagged. "I still can't believe humans eat animals. Did you do that, Sophie?"

"Hey—check out that view," Keefe said, saving Sophie from having to answer. "I'll give humans this, they make their own kind of beauty. Even if that river looks pretty brown."

The Arno River definitely wasn't an inviting color, but it was lined on each side by pastel buildings, many with terraces and window boxes, like a scene from a painting. But the panoramic view also reminded Sophie of another less-than-awesome human fact. The windows they were looking through had been added for Adolf Hitler. He'd probably stood right where they were.

"Let's go," Sophie said, needing to get away from the evil in the air.

The elves might have done some terrible things over time—but she doubted they could ever match human monsters like Hitler.

"We must be getting close to the next clue," she said, trying to stay focused. "Anyone see a tower? I'm guessing it's part of the corridor somehow."

"What do you think they mean about it not yielding?" Fitz asked as the corridor made a sharp turn.

Then another.

And another.

Sophie stopped. "I think we're here. Vasari tore down pretty much anything in his way when he built this corridor. But there was a family named the Mannellis who refused to let their building be knocked down. So Vasari detoured the corridor around it, and I think that's what we just did."

Keefe smirked. "Look who knows all the things."

Sophie looked away. Having to wonder if her memories were *hers* made her wish she could scrub her brain.

"The clue said this is where we'd find the next steps in our journey," Fitz said. "Everyone spread out and look for the sign of the swan."

They combed the walls, the floor, the ceiling. Sophie was starting to worry she'd guessed the clue wrong, when she realized a long scratch under her feet had a very distinctive curve.

"Over here," she called, tracing her fingers along the mark. The curve deviated from its design to make a full circle—but she could still tell it was the sign of the swan.

"I feel a latch," Dex said, pressing his palm against the floor. He twisted his hand a few times, miming turning a doorknob, and a quiet *click* made the floor drop away.

They stared at the rusty ladder leading down into the misty darkness.

"Okay, so who wants to climb down into the scary pit of doom first?" Keefe asked.

"I'll go," Sophie said.

"Nope," Fitz told her. "You've almost died enough times. Time to let me take a turn."

"Or you could just be careful," Sophie said.

He flashed his perfect smile. "That works too."

He slipped one leg into the opening, testing his weight on the rung before stepping onto the ladder.

"Once I see what's at the bottom I'll let you know if it's safe." He stepped down another rung. Then another.

The darkness swallowed him on the next step, and Sophie kept one hand poised on the ladder, ready to rush down at the first sound of danger.

After an agonizingly long time Fitz shouted, "All clear!"

"Yes," another voice called—one Sophie would've recognized even if he hadn't started the next sentence with his favorite expression. "You kids took your sweet time getting here!"

# FIVE

SOPHIE HAD ASSUMED THE BLACK Swan would be done with disguises now that they were letting her and her friends join. But when she reached the bottom of the murky tunnel, she found Mr. Forkle looking as shriveled and swollen as ever. His huge belly barely fit between the curved walls, and the cramped space was filled with the dirty-feet stink of the ruckleberries he ate to alter his appearance.

"Not to complain," Keefe said as he stepped into the ankle-deep sludge, "but you guys seriously need to pick some better hideouts."

"This is *not* our hideout," Mr. Forkle said, handing them each a pendant.

They breathed on the crystals, and the warmth activated the balefire inside. The pale blue glow seemed especially eerie, but that might've been because Sophie despised balefire.

The everlasting flames had been Fintan's trademark—until he learned to spark Everblaze. But Sophie was still grateful to have light in the claustrophobic tunnel. Especially when she saw the shadowy path ahead.

"Well, *that* looks fun," Keefe said, pushing Fitz forward. "Lead the way, buddy!"

"Actually, that path only goes to our demolished hideout," Mr. Forkle said.

"So it *was* at the Palazzo Vecchio?" Sophie asked.

"No. That was marked as a decoy. But if the Neverseen found it, we knew it was only a matter of time before they located the real one. So I collapsed our grotto before I came here."

"Where are we going, then?" Dex asked.

"Through our emergency exit." Mr. Forkle licked one of the slime-covered bricks, opening a secret door hidden in the wall.

Sophie gagged. "That's gross."

"It certainly is, Miss Foster. But let that be a lesson. The best places to hide are the places no one wants to go."

He was right about that. The air in the tunnel smelled like eggs mixed with skunk spray, and cold slimy muck rained down on their heads as they walked.

"Do you know how the Neverseen found your decoy?" Sophie asked.

"I swear it wasn't me," Keefe jumped in. "I threw my Sencen Crest into the ocean, and Elwin melted off a ton of skin, so I am aromark free. Remind me to thank my mom for that one, by the way. So awesome of her to let me lead my friends into ambushes."

The sharpness in his tone made Sophie reach for his hand.

"I'm fine," he promised. But he didn't pull away.

"We do not blame you, Mr. Sencen," Mr. Forkle said. "We assume they used Gethen. We'd been holding him here after we captured him on Mount Everest—but don't worry, we've relocated him to somewhere much harder to reach. And we'll figure out what enzyme they're tracking him with so this won't happen again."

"Have you learned anything from him?" Keefe asked, voicing the question Sophie was sure they'd all been thinking.

Gethen was the first member of the Neverseen they'd captured. He'd also been one of Sophie and Dex's kidnappers.

"Not yet," Mr. Forkle said. "His mind is . . . tricky. We'll discuss it more later. Right now, I need to get you to your new homes."

Sophie wasn't sure which felt stranger—trying to imagine feeling at *home* with the Black Swan, or the fact that he'd said "homes."

"Are we going to be living together?" Biana asked, noticing the plural as well.

"Of course."

"Will you be living with us?" Sophie asked.

"No. I live in the Lost Cities. I cannot disappear too long without someone noticing my absence."

"But you lived with humans for twelve years," Sophie reminded him.

"Yes, and someday I'll tell you how I managed to escape anyone's notice."

"So wait," Dex said. "Does that mean we could've met members of the Black Swan and didn't know it?"

"I'm sure you have, Mr. Dizznee. Many of us are fans of your father's store."

Slurps and Burps was the Lost Cities' most popular apothecary. Sophie could understand how a covert group would find their serums handy, since many could alter appearances. But it was strange to think she might've passed the real Mr. Forkle shopping in the cluttered aisles.

And if the Black Swan hid among them, surely the Neverseen did as well. Sophie wondered if she'd seen the rebels in the streets of Atlantis, or if their kids went to school with her at Foxfire. She ran through a mental list of possible suspects— the primary being her longtime rival, Stina Heks—as Biana said, "So basically, you're all two different people?"

"Or three," Mr. Forkle corrected. "Perhaps even four or five. And yes, that can be rather challenging." He lifted his double chin, revealing a registry pendant hidden underneath. "A clever Technopath rigged this to communicate where I *want* the Council to think I am. But it only covers blocks of time."

"Should I have done that to our pendants?" Dex asked.

"No, you five have already drawn the Council's suspicion. Better to sever your ties and seek refuge in our hideout."

"Any chance we'll be leaping soon?" Keefe asked as a blob of slime dripped into his hair.

"We won't be leaping. The ogres have a gadget that can follow the trail of a leap to its source. It's how they restrict entry to their cities and monitor intruders. Now that we know the Neverseen are working with the ogres, we must assume they'll try to track us."

"So we can't leap anymore?" Fitz asked.

"Not here, when they're so close."

The words echoed through the tunnel, turning every shadow into a cloaked figure.

"If they're close, why aren't we going after them?" Keefe asked.

"We fight the fights we can win, Mr. Sencen. Right now, the Neverseen have too many advantages. They're hidden somewhere in the city, likely somewhere with great potential for human casualties. That's why I have our transport waiting downriver, where they'd never think to look."

"Uh, not to ask the obvious question," Dex jumped in, "but why not have us meet you there in the first place?"

"We have reasons for working in riddles, Mr. Dizznee, and

convenience is never a consideration. But the trail you followed was incredibly secure."

"Maybe, if you ignore all the human technology I had to handle," Dex mumbled. "And you're lucky Sophie remembered all those weird facts about Florence."

"Is that what you think it was?" Mr. Forkle asked. *"Luck?"*

Sophie sighed. "Exactly how many weird memories have you given me?"

"As many as you'll need."

"How can you possibly know that?" Fitz asked.

"Very careful planning."

Sophie stopped walking. "Planning for what?"

"Please keep moving, Miss Foster. We do not have time for such discussions."

"You're seriously not going to tell her?" Keefe asked. "Don't you think she deserves to know?"

"She deserves many things," Mr. Forkle said. "But most important, she deserves a *choice*. And in order to give her that choice, she must discover her purpose on her own. There are also things we must keep secret—for her protection and ours."

"Sandor always says that secrets hinder his ability to protect me," Sophie reminded him.

"That applies to you keeping secrets from him. Not the other way around," Mr. Forkle replied. "We must hurry. Our rides won't wait forever."

Sophie glanced at her friends, and she didn't have to be a

Telepath to know what they were thinking. After all the risks they'd taken—all the sacrifices they'd made—they'd been hoping the Black Swan would be more . . . cooperative.

But it was too late to turn back. They had to keep moving forward and hope they could convince the Black Swan to work *with* them.

She clutched the cache in her pocket, glad to know she had a secret of her own as she followed Mr. Forkle out of the tunnel.

The river was empty. No people. No boats. No sign of whatever ride Mr. Forkle had arranged—until he blew into a slim copper whistle. It made no sound, but the brownish water rippled. Bubbles followed, growing larger until a scaly gray-green head popped out of the water.

"Plesiosaurs?" Keefe asked as five more dinosaur heads burst out of the water.

"Eckodons," Mr. Forkle corrected. "Though Miss Foster likely knows them as Nessie."

Sophie smiled, no longer stunned when human myths turned out to be based on reality. The creatures did have long, hooked necks like the Loch Ness Monster, but their noses were a bit more pointed, and long gills lined their cheeks.

"These are the dinosaurs that use sound vortexes, right?" Fitz asked.

"Precisely why I chose them," Mr. Forkle agreed. "They will be slower than light leaping, but faster than many other methods. And the Neverseen cannot track us underwater."

"Underwater?" Sophie repeated as he handed everyone a clear slimy membrane and told them to wrap it around their bags to keep them dry. "How will we breathe?"

"Yeah, I can only hold my breath for fifteen minutes," Dex said.

"Fifteen minutes?" Sophie repeated. "How can you hold your breath that long?"

"It's a mind over matter skill," Mr. Forkle explained. "One very few take the time to learn."

"My dad said the stuffy nobles underestimate it," Dex said. "He made us practice all the time."

"Your father is wise," Mr. Forkle told him. "Nevertheless, you will not have to hold your breath today. I brought lufterators."

He passed them each a T-shaped gadget and showed how they put the longer end in their mouths and let the other piece cover their lips and nose. It felt like sucking air through a teeny straw, and it made Sophie dizzy. But after a few tries, her lungs fell into a slower rhythm.

"Do you have any more lufterators?" Biana asked.

"One is all you'll need," Mr. Forkle assured her.

"I'd still feel better if I had a spare," Biana insisted.

"I can check yours to make sure it's working, if you want," Dex offered.

"No!" Biana said, a bit too quickly. "I'll just . . . wait here and you guys can send someone back for me with another."

"Don't be absurd, Miss Vacker," Mr. Forkle said. "We're all leaving now."

Biana shot Sophie a desperate *Help me!* look, but Sophie didn't understand the problem.

Keefe grabbed Biana's wrist. "It feels like you're hiding something . . ."

"I agree," Mr. Forkle said. "So let's see what it is, shall we?"

"You don't have permission to read my thoughts!" Biana shouted.

"I do not need it if you're endangering us." Mr. Forkle closed his eyes and Sophie knew there was nothing Biana could do to stop him. Even *she* couldn't block him—and he'd designed her mind to be impenetrable.

Biana turned to her brother. "Please, don't let him do this."

"It's already done." Mr. Forkle said, staring at the empty space behind her. "It appears we have a stowaway."

# SIX

**H**OW CAN WE HAVE A STOWAWAY?"
Fitz asked as Mr. Forkle shouted, "Show
yourself!"

Nothing happened for a moment. Then
Della appeared behind Biana.

"Mom?" Fitz said, rushing to tackle-hug her before he
shouted at his sister. "HOW COULD YOU KEEP THIS
SECRET?"

"I made her swear not to say anything," Della explained.
"And I only involved her because I needed to hold on to someone while we were teleporting."

"Why the subterfuge?" Mr. Forkle asked. "Please tell me you
don't doubt our ability to protect your children?"

"Quite the opposite." Della straightened her gown, looking like an ocean goddess in aquamarine silk. "I'm here to join the Black Swan."

The words seemed to dangle, waiting for someone to reach out and grab them.

"Does Dad know?" Fitz asked.

"Of course. *He* wanted to join, but we decided he'd be more useful if he stayed working with the Council. And my talents are far better suited for covert activities."

"Ms. Vacker—" Mr. Forkle started.

"Della," she corrected.

"Your offer is very generous, Ms. *Della*," Mr. Forkle emphasized with a slight smile. "But we already have a Vanisher working with us."

"No one can vanish the way I can. Not even my son—and I'm sure you've heard how valuable Alvar has been to the Council."

She blinked out of sight, reappearing a second later knee-deep in the river. Sophie wasn't sure what was crazier, how fast Della had moved, or how she hadn't caused ripples in the water.

"Impressive," Mr. Forkle admitted when Della reappeared next to Biana and showed how her gown was still dry. "But the question is whether letting you join would be *wise*. Someone as high profile as yourself—"

"Could be an influential advocate," Della finished for him. "When the Council finally comes to their senses, do you think the public will instantly trust you? The Vacker name may have had a few controversies lately, but it still holds incredible influence and power."

Mr. Forkle studied Della. "I see you've already removed your registry pendant."

"I would never put any of you at risk. Plus, I wanted to prove that I'm committed."

"And yet you make the commitment too lightly."

"Do I?" Della's melodic voice hardened. "I've trusted my children—and three others who might as well be my family—to your care."

"Your children's situation is different," Mr. Forkle argued. "We both know we can't leave them to the Council's caprice."

"But I could protect them on my own." Della vanished again, reappearing with a melder pressed to Mr. Forkle's head. "Do not underestimate me, sir."

"You're not the only one with tricks up their sleeve," Mr. Forkle warned her. He tapped his right temple, and Della's arm dropped to her side.

"Are you a Mesmer?" Sophie asked, remembering Grady's similar feats.

"My tricks are more limited," Mr. Forkle admitted. "But the mind *is* more powerful than the body—never forget that."

"I won't," Della said, vanishing the same instant Mr. Forkle collapsed.

She reappeared, balanced on his belly with one of her

jeweled shoes pressed against his throat. He kicked and thrashed, but couldn't throw her off.

"I believe you've proven your point, Ms. Vacker," he wheezed.

She pressed her shoe down harder. "I told you to call me Della."

"Whoa, remind me never to get on your mom's bad side," Keefe said.

"A valuable lesson for everyone," Della agreed, jumping to the ground and offering Mr. Forkle a hand up. "Everyone believes I'm the fragile beauty hiding in my husband's shadow. But I'm far more powerful than anyone imagines."

"I can see that." Mr. Forkle wiped mud off his long black tunic. "But I alone cannot approve your admittance into our organization. All I can promise is to bring the matter before our Collective."

"Collective?" Sophie asked.

"Our ruling order," Mr. Forkle clarified. "Five overseers, each with equally weighted votes."

"So there are four other leaders we've never met?" Keefe asked.

"There are *many* members you haven't met. But that is a good thing. The more people we have helping our cause, the more chance we have of making a difference."

"All the more reason to let me join," Della said.

"Perhaps," Mr. Forkle agreed. "I'll make the suggestion when I speak with the Collective. But first we have a problem.

I did not plan for a stowaway, so we are short one lufterator."

"I can tweak mine so two can share," Dex said, bending his into a Z-shape. He made a few more tweaks before holding up the mouthpiece proudly. "Now it works on each end."

"They'll have to keep their faces very close together," Mr. Forkle noted.

"Foster and I volunteer!" Keefe shouted.

"Uh, if anyone's going to share with Sophie it should be *me*," Dex argued.

"Wait, why do *I* have to share?" Sophie asked.

"Yeah, I nominate Dex and Keefe," Fitz agreed.

"So do I," Mr. Forkle decided. "Keefe, give your lufterator to Della."

"Wait—what just happened?" Keefe asked.

Fitz, Biana, and Sophie cracked up.

Dex fumed as Mr. Forkle ordered him and Keefe to test the gadget to make sure the lufterator still worked. They had to stand so close their noses practically touched.

"Gross," Keefe whined, spitting out his mouthpiece. "The air tastes like Dex breath."

"Keefe breath's just as nasty," Dex snapped.

"But you *can* breathe?" Mr. Forkle clarified.

When they nodded, he ordered everyone into the water. They gasped as the cold soaked through their clothes— except Della, who strode through totally dry.

"Did you know your mom could do that?" Sophie asked Fitz.

"I did," Biana jumped in. "And I *will* figure out how to do it." She blinked out of sight, and when she reappeared her hair was dripping wet and stuck to her face. "It's going to take some practice."

"I still can't believe you didn't tell me Mom was with us," Fitz grumbled.

"Now you know how I felt when you and Dad were busy planning all your secret visits to the Forbidden Cities."

Sophie had never considered how much the search for her had affected the Vacker family. They'd all lived with secrets—and broken the law—for twelve years.

The river grew deeper, and they switched from wading to swimming. Sophie struggled to paddle while holding her backpack, until Fitz reached over and carried it for her.

"Thanks," she mumbled, wishing she could swim so effortlessly. Within minutes he'd reached the elephant-size water dinosaurs.

"Eckodons are friendly, right?" she asked Biana.

"Of course." Biana swam to a purple-toned eckodon and stroked the base of its neck. "See? Totally harmless."

Sophie swam to a blue-toned eckodon and it made a gurgley, growling sound.

"That's how it says hi," Fitz promised, pulling himself onto his green eckodon's back.

Sophie copied him while transmitting *Friend* over and over. Her tweaked genes allowed her to communicate telepathically with animals. She couldn't tell if the eckodon understood—some creatures thought in images or emotions. Still, the eckodon didn't chomp her head off, so she took that as a good sign.

Dex and Keefe, meanwhile, were having a *very* difficult time figuring out how to sit on their eckodon. After several hilarious attempts, they settled for Keefe facing backward with his arms wrapped around Dex, and Dex reaching around Keefe to hug the eckodon's neck.

"You guys look so cute," Fitz told them.

"Dude, your payback is going to be legendary," Keefe warned.

"Lufterators in!" Mr. Forkle called, before Dex could add his own threats.

Sophie took one last deep breath and slipped the gadget into her mouth. She'd barely grabbed her eckodon's neck before Mr. Forkle shouted, "Dive!"

Down, down, down they plunged, all the way to the bottom of the river, where the water felt cold and gritty. Sophie's balefire pendant gave her just enough light to see Fitz as his eckodon swam up beside her. He held out a thumbs-up to ask if she was okay.

She nodded, taking several shallow breaths as he pointed to where Mr. Forkle and Della had taken the lead. Sophie was glad her eckodon seemed to be following on its own, since she had no idea how to steer a plesiosaur.

Fitz stayed beside her, with Biana right behind, and Dex and Keefe a little farther back. The eckodons swam at a steady pace until the shore dropped away and Sophie realized they'd reached the ocean. Then each eckodon stretched out its neck, tucked its flippers, and let out a piercing scream.

The shrill whine was louder than whale song, richer than dolphin squeaks, and powerful enough to part the tide. The sound pitched higher, then lower, swirling the water into a funnel that blasted the eckodon forward like a rocket. Whenever the vortex slowed, the creature cried again, blasting them faster and faster, until Sophie was sure they'd crossed the whole ocean. And maybe she was right, because when they finally slowed the water was tropical teal and swarming with colorful fish.

They surfaced minutes later, floating along a river that cut through an enormous underground cavern. A thin crack split the ceiling, letting in just enough sunlight to bounce off the glinting rock walls. Everywhere the light touched, life had followed, transforming the cave into a subterranean forest. The farther the river led them, the more the cave widened, until all Sophie could see in any direction was the ever-stretching paradise.

"Can you believe this place?" Fitz whispered.

Sophie inhaled the sweet, heady scents: honeysuckle, jasmine, plumeria—plus dozens of other aromas she couldn't recognize. It definitely wasn't the bleak cavern she'd expected after her previous experience with a Black Swan hideout.

"Okay, I am *done* with Dex snuggle time," Keefe announced

as he and Dex's eckodon swam up beside Sophie's. He leaped from his plesiosaur to hers and prodded Sophie's eckodon to swim away from the rest of the group.

"Relax," he said, tightening his grip on Sophie's waist. "I won't let you fall."

That wasn't why she felt nervous. The last time she'd sat like this with Keefe, they were flying with Silveny across the ocean. The alicorn had been carrying them to the Black Swan that night as well. Sophie hoped this time wouldn't end so violently.

Keefe must've been sharing the same terrifying memories, because he whispered, "I will never let my mom hurt you again."

"You didn't *let* your mom do anything, Keefe. You know that, right?"

"You heard what Oralie said. The Council's blaming my dad for not knowing what my mom was up to. But . . . he's not the only Empath who lived with her."

"You told me yourself, you can't feel a lie—only the emotions that go along with it."

"I still wasn't paying close enough attention."

"Why would you? No one assumes their family is evil."

He tensed at the word and Sophie glanced over her shoulder. "Sorry. I didn't mean that."

"Yes you did. And she is. And I should've seen it."

"You can't do that, Keefe. Edaline told me once that hindsight is a dangerous game. The clues seem too obvious when you know what to look for. Believe me, I would know."

She'd replayed her kidnapping—and Kenric's murder—more times than she'd ever admit. And each time she saw more warnings she shouldn't have missed. But she couldn't let herself take the blame. The elvin mind couldn't process that level of guilt. Their sanity shattered under the weight of the burden. She'd watched it happen to Alden over his guilt from what happened to Prentice—an innocent member of the Black Swan he'd condemned to madness and Exile before he realized the Black Swan weren't really the villains. The only reason he could still function was because Sophie had found a way to heal him.

"Please," she whispered, "you have to protect your mind, Keefe. We both do."

"Okay," he said after a painful silence. "So we catch these guys and make them pay for what they've done."

"Can you really do that?" Sophie asked. "I mean . . . it's your mom. I know you think it won't matter, but—"

"It *won't*. She used me. Tried to kill me. Tried to kill my friends—and don't say she saved Biana on Mount Everest—"

"But she did! They would've rolled off that cliff if she hadn't stopped them."

"Right, so she was saving herself, and Biana was lucky enough to benefit."

Sophie wanted to argue, but she could tell it wouldn't help.

Plus . . . maybe Keefe needed to hold on to his anger. Anger was safer.

"If you ever need to talk," she whispered.

"Thanks," he whispered back, so close she could feel his breath on her cheek. His arms tightened ever so slightly, making her heart switch to hummingbird pace.

"Listen, Sophie, I—"

"You're still wearing your Sucker Punch," Dex interrupted as his eckodon caught up with them. "If he's annoying you, just knock him off with a good backhand."

"Man, one second you're sharing your air with a dude, and the next second he's trying to get you punched in the face," Keefe mumbled.

"Isn't that pretty much what everyone wants to do after they meet you?" Fitz asked as he and Biana swam up beside them on their eckodons.

"Keep it up, dude. You're just adding to my list of reasons to punish you," Keefe warned.

Fitz shrugged. "Bring it on."

"You guys are ridiculous," Biana said, staring at the glinting rocks of the cave above them. "Does anyone know where we are?"

"Yes," Mr. Forkle called from up ahead. "Your new home."

# SEVEN

THE DWARVES CALL THIS CAVERN
Alluveterre," Mr. Forkle said as he slowed his
eckodon to let Sophie and her friends catch up.
"Which in dwarven means—"

"The sands of dawn," Sophie translated.

Keefe laughed. "Always gotta show off."

Mr. Forkle ignored him. "The dwarves view this place as a
testimony of our planet's power to re-create itself. Above us is
a barren wasteland of human pollution and destruction. But
look what has surged to life in the safety below, thanks to a
little light and a little peace. The dwarven king brought me here
when I revealed the existence of our organization. He thought
it would be the perfect place for us to make a fresh start."

"So King Enki is on our side?" Della asked.

"He's not against the Council, if that's what you're wondering. But he has felt for some time that the Councillors' methods are not working. Many dwarves have offered their assistance—though at the moment most have returned to their cities. They need time to mourn their friends who fell in the battle on Mount Everest, and to treat their wounded."

Sophie tried to remember how many dwarves had died that day—was it three? Four?

She hated that she didn't know—hated how easy it was to focus only on the people she knew, and forget that there were dozens of others risking their lives for the Black Swan's cause.

Before she could ask how the injured dwarves were doing, Mr. Forkle said, "Here are your new residences."

He pointed ahead, to where an arched bridge with a black gazebo in the center connected two enormous trees standing on either side of the river. Their trunks had been wrapped in wooden staircases that wound up to the tallest branches, where two massive tree houses overlooked the entire forest.

"The residence on the east is for the girls. And the west is for the boys. The bridge in the center has a common area for you to share meals together."

"See, I think a group party house sounds *way* more fun. Who's with me?" Keefe asked.

Nobody agreed—though Dex looked like he *wanted* to. So did Biana.

The eckodons crawled ashore, and Sophie transmitted, *Thank you,* as she and Keefe slid off her plesiosaur's back. Three gnomes popped out of the bushes to greet them, flashing wide, green-toothed smiles and shaking the leaves off their earth-toned skin as they set a bucket of nasty wriggling things in front of each eckodon. Sophie had thought the sludgers she fed Iggy, her pet imp, were disgusting. But these looked like the evil spawn of scorpions and maggots.

"Larvagorns," a gnome with long braided hair said as the eckodons gobbled the creepy-crawlers up like candy. "Believe it or not, the dwarves consider them a rare delicacy."

Sophie was very glad to be an elf. The *squisssssssssssssssh-CRUNCH* alone made her gag.

"I thought we trained animals to be vegetarians," Biana mumbled.

"Only the ones we keep at the Sanctuary," Della said. "It would be pointless to bring them there for preservation, only to have them hunt each other. But those in the wild are free to choose their own diets."

"So these things seriously live around humans?" Sophie asked as the eckodons licked the bug slime off their chops and waded back into the river.

"Technically," Mr. Forkle said, "they live in underwater caverns. And they swim far too fast for humans to spot them or catch them. Still, we make sure they're safe and undetected. And one of these days we will catch that tricky lake dweller who keeps making headlines."

"Keep telling yourself that," one of the other gnomes told him. Sophie assumed the gnome was a "he," since he wore grass-woven overalls instead of a grass skirt like the other two. But it was hard to tell. Gnomes all had the same huge gray eyes and bodies like children. They lived with the elves by choice and were incredibly industrious creatures. More plantlike than animal, they absorbed all their energy from the sun, and needed very little sleep—and even less food. But they craved work and loved to garden, so they traded their harvest with the elves and filled their sleepless days with elvin tasks. Alden had called it a symbiotic relationship, and the longer Sophie had lived with the elves, the more she agreed. The elves cared for the gnomes, and the gnomes worked happily, neither side imposing upon the other.

"I'm Calla," the gnome with the braid told Sophie, "and this is Sior and Amisi. It's an honor to finally meet you."

Sophie fidgeted as Calla dipped an exaggerated curtsy. "It's nice to meet you too."

The other gnomes nodded and turned back to the eckodons, but Calla kept right on staring at Sophie. Her expression was a mixture of awe and curiosity, and Sophie wondered what the Black Swan had told the gnomes about her.

"We'll take your bags to your rooms," Sior—the gnome in

the overalls—said. He grabbed Sophie's backpack from Fitz.

"And we have fresh clothes for you upstairs," Calla added. "Well, for most of you. I didn't realize you were coming, Miss . . ."

"Della. And not to worry, I'm a surprise visitor."

"Should we add a room in the east tree house?" Calla asked.

Mr. Forkle nodded. "Preferably up high, so it overlooks both residences."

"I thought the Collective had to approve me staying," Della said.

"They have to approve you *joining our order,*" Mr. Forkle corrected. "But either way, it would be too risky to send you home. The Council has surely discovered that you're missing. So consider yourself our guest, and a much needed chaperone."

"*Chaperone?*" Keefe whined. "That's going to cramp my style."

"Yes, it is," Della agreed. "Remember, I kept Alvar in line for years."

Keefe sighed dreamily. "Alvar's my hero."

Sophie had only met Fitz and Biana's older brother a few times, and he'd always seemed very polished and professional. But she'd heard rumors of Alvar's wild side before, and knew it had to be pretty crazy for Keefe to look up to him.

"We should have the new room ready by sunset," Amisi—

the third gnome—said. "Though there are fewer of us, so we might need another hour."

"Yes, where are Gora and Yuri?" Mr. Forkle asked. "I didn't see them yesterday, either."

The three gnomes shared a look.

"They . . . have gone to stay near Lumenaria," Calla said after a moment. "In the hopes they'll be allowed to visit the refugees. Yuri had family in Wildwood."

"I did not realize," Mr. Forkle whispered. "I hope good news finds them soon."

"So do we."

Charged silence passed before the gnomes grabbed the buckets and satchels and shuffled off into the trees.

"What's Wildwood?" Sophie asked.

Mr. Forkle sighed. "Is this how it's going to be? Constant questions?"

"Pretty much," Sophie agreed.

"Well, do not expect an answer every time. But Wildwood was where a small colony of gnomes lived. Most of their race fled to the Lost Cities after the ogres overthrew Serenvale, their ancient homeland. But a few gnomes refused to leave and took up residence in one of the Neutral Territories, in a grove not far from the borders of what has now become the ogres' capital city."

"Why are you speaking past tense?" Della asked. "Calla said something about refugees."

"A better term would be 'evacuees,'" Mr. Forkle corrected. "Some sort of plague struck the colony a few weeks back, and forced them to flee. They arrived in Lumenaria three days ago for medical treatment. And that is the extent of my knowledge. The Council has been *extremely* guarded with their information, and at the moment they're allowing no visitors. But I do know that all of our best physicians are working to isolate the pathogen. I'm sure they'll find the cure soon."

Della looked less than satisfied with the answer.

Sophie wasn't thrilled either. "Oralie told us before we left that she thought the ogres were stirring in the Neutral Territories. Does this have something to do with that?"

Mr. Forkle scratched his chin. "Interesting that a Councillor would agree with the theories."

"What theories?" Sophie pressed.

"This is your last question," he warned. "The Wildwood Colony has claimed ogre sabotage for centuries. But they've never been able to provide proof. I'll have to rally my sources and see if Oralie has evidence for her suspicions. In the meantime, please put this out of your mind. You know better than most, Miss Foster, how truly powerful our medicine can be. I have no doubt the gnomes will recover soon. Shall we?"

He motioned for everyone to follow him toward one of the stair-wrapped trees, and they climbed to the bridge that connected the two houses.

He pointed to the gazebo in the center, filled with pots of

vibrant flowers and a round table with cozy chairs. "Since you'll be dwelling in separate residences, we arranged this common eating area. Dinner will be served here—and you're in for a treat. Calla's starkflower stew is life changing. Otherwise, boys are that way"—he pointed to the tree house across the bridge—"and the girls are just above us. I must return to the Lost Cities and be *seen* for a few minutes."

He reached into his pocket and pulled out a vial of green-and-orange-speckled berries.

"So *that's* how you de-Forkle!" Dex said. "I should've guessed it was callowberries. My dad uses them in his anti-inflammatory ointments. They smell like flareadon poop."

"Taste like it too," Mr. Forkle agreed.

"So all we need to do is crush a few of those into your breakfast, and bam! Instant Forkle-reveal?" Keefe asked.

"I've been consuming callowberries for thirteen years, Mr. Sencen. Do you honestly think I wouldn't notice the smell?"

"I dunno—I'm *really* good at hiding things in people's food."

Mr. Forkle ignored him, holding up a black crystal with a purple gleam.

"Does that mean we can light leap from here?" Della asked.

"Only with special crystals, which we will provide if needed."

"What's this 'if' stuff?" Dex asked.

"Yeah, it's not like we're prisoners," Sophie said.

"Of course you're not. But you are *fugitives*. And you came here for our protection. This is how we provide it."

"It sounds like we're going to have to steal that crystal from you," Keefe said.

"You would be very disappointed if you did. This crystal leads to my safe house, where I go to change identities. Anyone who does not know the secret for leaving is instantly trapped."

"So . . . that's it?" Sophie asked. "Here's your tree houses, have some stew and good night?"

"Hardly, Miss Foster. First you must get cleaned up and meet me at ground level in an hour. You all have an appointment with the rest of our ruling Collective."

# EIGHT

THANK GOODNESS THEY HAVE DECENT taste in clothes!" Biana said, twirling in her pale pink gown, which was frilly and ruffled and looked like cupcake frosting with pearl sprinkles.

Sophie was far less excited about hers. The smoky blue dress was dotted with diamonds, like the first glinting stars in the evening sky. But it was so fancy and fitted and screamed *Look at me!*

"Seriously, what's *with* the gowns?" she grumbled. "Aren't we supposed to be fighting rebels and solving conspiracies?"

"Actually, right now we have an important meeting," Della reminded her. "So why not look our best?"

"But why do *we* have to look like pretty pretty princesses when the boys get to wear pants and tunics?"

Della laughed. "Sometimes I forget how much your human upbringing has altered your worldview. Our society has not been plagued by the inequalities you've grown up with. No one views gowns as a sign of our gender's lesser status. We don't *have* a lesser status. So if you truly hate wearing a dress, you can choose to wear anything you'd like."

"Even if I visit a noble city?" Sophie asked.

"Of course. The only mark of noble status is a cape, and even then, some instances do not require them. All of our clothes—male and female—are designed to enhance natural beauty."

"But . . ."

Sophie had been about to ask, *What if someone isn't beautiful?*—until she'd remembered she was talking about *elves*.

"Okay, but isn't parading around like this"—she ran her hands over her jewel-encrusted bodice—"sort of shallow?"

"Surely you know we value knowledge and talent above everything else," Della said. "Beauty is simply a bonus, to make life more pleasing to the eye. And that applies to everything in our world—not just our physical appearance."

She waved her arm around the bright room, which was different from what Sophie had been imagining. There were no jewels or crystals like the elves usually built with. Instead, everything was earthy and natural. Fall-colored leaves had been woven into brightly patterned rugs, which felt softer than dandelion fluff but still made that great crunching sound when they walked. Flowering branches lined the walls, filling the air with the scent of spring. The furniture looked like carefully sculpted shrubs, and garlands of bright summer berries draped from the ceiling. But the most breathtaking element had to be the shimmering waterfall in the center. It trickled from the skylight along twisted icicles, dripping into a pool of frost-covered stones.

Somehow the gnomes had taken the best parts of each season and transformed them into a place that was both elegant and inviting.

"Everything in our world celebrates beauty," Della said proudly. "Why surround ourselves with ugliness when there is wonder to showcase?"

"I guess," Sophie mumbled, fussing with her sash. No matter how many times she tied it, she couldn't get the bow even.

"Here," Della said, knotting it as perfectly as a Disney princess. "This color really sets off your eyes."

"Great," Sophie mumbled. "Just what I wanted."

"Hey, your eyes are what I always hear everyone talking about," Biana reminded her.

"Yeah, because they're calling me a freak."

"That's only Stina and her bratty friends. Everyone else thinks they're striking and unique."

Della sighed when Sophie shrugged off the compliment. "It must've been hard growing up as an elf among humans—and

I don't mean because you're a Telepath, though I know that came with its own challenges. Jealousy is such a powerful force in their lives—and you have so many gifts."

"How do you know so much about humans?" Sophie asked.

"*That* is a story for another time. But I've walked among them, and the reception I received was less than friendly."

"Is that how it was for you?" Biana asked Sophie.

"Everyone pretty much hated me," Sophie admitted. "They'd call me the Freakazoid, or Superdork, or the Special Sophieflake. But it didn't help that I skipped six grades and had a bad habit of reminding teachers to collect our homework."

"It's better here, though, right?" Biana asked.

"In some ways. But I'm also 'the human girl.' And the Girl Who Was Taken. And now everyone looks at me like I'm public enemy number one."

"Well, they're wrong," Della said. "And someday they'll see that. In the meantime, please try to remember that there's a difference between hiding by *choice* and hiding from *fear*. You should never be afraid of who you are."

Sophie fussed with her perfect Della bow, accidentally messing it up.

She decided not to fix it.

"Look—they gave us Prattles!" Biana said, lifting a huge welcome basket she'd discovered. She handed Sophie the silver box with her name on it, then tore into her own, going straight for the tiny velvet pouch tucked among the nutty candy.

Every box of Prattles came with a collectible pin, shaped as one of the various animal species on the planet. Prattles limited the amount of each pin to how many of that creature existed, which meant some pins were extremely rare.

Biana held up her bluish green water-horse. "I've been wanting a Prattles' kelpie forever! What'd you get?"

Sophie crunched on a piece of the candy as she fished out her pin, nearly choking when she saw the silver bird with long, gleaming feathers.

"The Prattles' moonlark," Biana whispered. "There are less than a hundred of those."

And yet somehow the Black Swan had now given Sophie *two*.

The last time they gave her one, they'd been trying to convince her to stop the Everblaze. What were they trying to tell her this time?

She checked for a note and found nothing, but she was sure the pin couldn't be a coincidence.

"Do you *really* trust the Black Swan?" Sophie asked Della, pinning the moonlark through the cord of her allergy remedy necklace before tucking it under her gown's bodice.

"There are many shades of trust," Della said, "and most of them are gray. But I've decided to hope for the best. Do you know why?"

Sophie shook her head.

"Because of *you*. If all their scheming resulted in such an incredible person, that's a cause I can get behind."

She meant the words to be comforting—and they were. Sort of.

They also were a storm in Sophie's mind. A heavy pressure and an ominous rumble, warning of turbulence ahead.

Which reminded her . . . "You didn't look happy with Mr. Forkle's explanation about the gnomes from Wildwood."

Della smiled. "Alden warned me that you're *very* perceptive."

"I have to be. Otherwise no one tells me anything."

"I suppose that's true." She sank into one of the armchair-shaped shrubberies. "Have either of you studied the Wildwood Colony in multispeciesial studies?"

They both shook their heads.

"I guess I should've figured that. I think everyone would prefer the Colony didn't exist. As Mr. Forkle said, the gnomes who live there often blame their problems on the ogres. And the timing of this plague seems especially deliberate. If the gnomes grew sick a few weeks ago, that would mean it started right around the time Sophie tried to read King Dimitar's mind—"

"Wait—it's my fault the gnomes are sick?" Sophie interrupted.

"There's no *fault*," Della promised. "You aren't responsible for the actions of a hostile species."

"Besides," Biana added, "how can ogres control disease?"

Clearly Biana had never heard of 'germ warfare.' And if humans were capable of it, Sophie was sure the ogres were. Lady Cadence, her old Linguistics mentor who used to live with the ogres, had even told her that ogres were experts in biochemistry.

"We have to find out more," Sophie said, running to get her soggy clothes. She couldn't believe she'd forgotten that Oralie's Imparter—and Kenric's cache—were in her pockets before she'd stepped into the river.

"Show me Councillor Oralie," she whispered, wiping water spots off the Imparter's silver screen. Several agonizing seconds passed before Oralie's face appeared in the center.

"Is something wrong?" Oralie asked. "Did you make it safely to the Black Swan?"

"We did," Sophie said. "But I need to know what's happening with the Wildwood gnomes. Did ogres attack them? Is that why you said the Neutral Territories aren't safe?"

"Clearly I shouldn't have said anything," Oralie murmured. "I meant to keep you away from danger, not draw you into our investigation."

"So you *are* investigating?" Della asked, coming up behind Sophie.

"Ms. Vacker," Oralie said. "I suppose I should've figured you'd be there. Alden's explanation for your absence felt rather thin."

"Is the infection at Wildwood connected to me trying to read King Dimitar's mind?" Sophie asked, getting back to the question that was making it hard to breathe.

Oralie let out a sigh. "The situation with the gnomes is far more complicated than you, or anyone, realizes. No single act is the cause for anything—and I cannot tell you anything more than that. But there's a chance the ogres aren't even involved. So far the only tracks we found at Wildwood—besides gnomish footprints—were made by elves."

"Does that mean the Neverseen are behind it?" Biana asked.

"We do not know," Oralie said. "But it's possible."

The idea was too horrible for words.

"This could crush Keefe," Sophie whispered.

"A good reason to keep this information quiet," Oralie told her. "Nothing has been confirmed. The only lesson you must take from this is to stay out of the Neutral Territories. And please don't let yourself carry the blame. Our problems go much further than anything you've done."

Sophie tried to believe her. "Will you keep me updated about the investigation?"

"I'll do my best. For now, I must go."

"Well," Della said, as Oralie clicked away. "I know your minds are flooding with theories, but we need to decide what to do about Keefe. If this is true, Sophie's right, it will devastate him. Do we want to put him through that without proof?"

Sophie glanced at Biana, relieved when she shook her head.

"I think we should wait until we know more," Della agreed, hooking her arms around Sophie and Biana. "For now, let's go meet the Black Swan's Collective."

# NINE

O KAY, I FIGURED YOU GUYS WERE going to be weird," Keefe said, "but I wasn't expecting *this* weird."

Sophie knew she should probably elbow him, but all she could do was stare.

The whole time she'd followed Mr. Forkle to the meeting point—a black pavilion hidden deep in the heart of the subterranean forest—she'd been imagining a group of pudgy, wrinkly elves who ate too many ruckleberries. Instead they found . . . she wasn't sure what.

"Everyone, I'd like you to meet Squall, Blur, Wraith, and Granite," Mr. Forkle told them.

"I know the titles might seem strange," Squall said, "but

we've found it's easier to remember code names when they match the disguise."

A heavy shiver obscured Squall's voice, and she was clearly a Froster. She'd covered herself head to toe in a thick layer of foggy ice.

Next to her stood Wraith—or rather, Wraith's hovering silver cloak. He was a Vanisher and had turned everything invisible except his clothes. His voice sounded distant and hollow as he told them, "Welcome to Alluveterre."

Blur introduced himself next, explaining that he was a Phaser, and could break his body down to pass through walls. But with the right concentration, he could re-form only partially. The effect reduced him to splotches of color and smudged lines and shadows.

It would've been the craziest thing Sophie had ever seen—if Granite hadn't been standing next to him. Granite explained that he consumed a chalky powder called indurite, since his ability as a Telepath couldn't disguise him. The rare mineral caused his body to crystallize and harden, turning him into a talking, roughly carved statue.

He sounded scratchy and gravelly as he said, "We're grateful to have all of you here—including you, Ms. Vacker."

"Della," she corrected. "Surely if I have to call you those crazy code words, you can call me by my familiar name."

Squall's face crackled as she smiled. "Della it is."

"We've been informed of your request to officially join our

cause," Granite said. "And . . . it's a tricky situation. We realize your husband has clearly shown remorse for what happened with Prentice—and that errors occurred on both sides of that situation. Still, there are some among our organization who might find you hard to trust, and we cannot damage our unity."

"But you're accepting *us*," Biana said, pointing to herself and Fitz.

"You have proven yourselves," Wraith reminded her.

"I'm prepared to prove myself as well," Della promised. "I'll swear any oath, submit to any test. All I want is a chance to set the past right."

The Collective turned to each other and Sophie was sure they were debating the matter telepathically. The Council used the same trick, so no one could hear them argue.

"We believe you," Mr. Forkle eventually said. "And are willing to give this arrangement a try. You can swear fealty tonight with the others."

"What exactly does that mean?" Sophie asked, hoping there was no embarrassing ritual.

"It's a simple process," Granite said. "It'll make more sense when you receive your packages. They'll be delivered to your rooms before your bedtime."

"Wait—we have a *bedtime*?" Keefe asked.

"Yes, Mr. Sencen, your curfew will be midnight—and that means lights *out*," Mr. Forkle said. "We also expect you to stay in your separate houses for the remainder of the night. Every morning you'll meet for breakfast, then spend the rest of the day with your lessons."

"What kinds of lessons?" Biana asked.

"Exercises to better prepare you for the tasks ahead. You're all very talented, but you've only begun to hone your abilities. We will mentor you when we can, and when we're unavailable, your rooms have been stocked with books and assignments."

"Or we could, y'know, work on hunting down the Neverseen," Keefe suggested.

"The Neverseen are not a pressing threat at the moment," Blur said.

"You're kidding, right?" Keefe asked. "They're running around starting fires—"

"*One* fire," Granite corrected.

"That you know of," Fitz countered.

"No, Mr. Vacker, *one* fire," Granite insisted. "We have eyes all over the world. If anything burns, we know about it. Just like we were there to extinguish the Florence fire. And now that Gethen has been moved, the Neverseen have disappeared without a trace. We must wait for them to reveal themselves before we take further action."

"Unless they already did something," Sophie said, careful to keep her words vague.

Mr. Forkle cocked his head. "I see you have all kinds of theories."

Sophie backed away. "Are you *reading my mind?*"

"Of course." He didn't sound sorry.

"Does that mean I can poke around your head?" she countered.

"By all means, be my guest."

Sophie ignored his confident smile as she tried to open her mind to his thoughts . . .

Or Granite's thoughts . . .

Or Wraith's . . .

Or Blur's . . .

Or Squall's . . .

"I made your Telepathy unstoppable," Mr. Forkle said, "but that doesn't mean it can't be deceived. Once you figure out what that means, you'll earn the right to hear what I'm thinking."

"That's not good enough!" Sophie snapped. "Just because I'm here doesn't give you the right to invade my privacy."

Mr. Forkle started to argue, but Granite placed a rocky hand on his shoulder.

"If we maintain the rules of telepathy," Granite asked her, "would that make you more comfortable?"

"A little," Sophie mumbled.

"Then consider that our arrangement—and remember that the rules apply to you as well," Granite told her.

*I will still transmit to you on occasion,* Mr. Forkle added, making Sophie jump as his voice filled her head. *But I will not open my mind to your thoughts or hear your reply unless you transmit back to me. I hope this proves that we do consider your wants and concerns. Clearly it's going to take time to adjust to our new working arrangement. But we are on the same side, even if our approaches differ. And since I already saw what you were thinking, let me go ahead and assure you that we are investigating the gnomes' situation, and we have seen no obvious signs of the Neverseen's involvement. The footprints Oralie mentioned—and by the way, you should use that Imparter she gave you very sparingly—belonged to two teenagers living nearby.*

*Why are there teenagers living near Wildwood?*

*Most likely they've been banished. But they were clearly not a threat to the gnomes. So you can let go of your conspiracy theories for the moment. Give us time to investigate properly.*

"We know you two are having a secret conversation," Keefe interrupted. "Care to share with the rest of us?"

"He was just clarifying something," Sophie said.

"Was it about Gethen?" Keefe asked. "You promised to tell us about the interrogations."

"There isn't much to tell," Mr. Forkle said. "Each time I've tried to probe his mind, he was . . . unresponsive."

"So do a memory break," Keefe pressed.

"You misunderstand what I mean by 'unresponsive.' His head currently appears to be empty. There are no thought processes. No dreams. No memories of any kind. I've never seen a defense like it, and I've yet to figure out how to counter it."

"Do you think it'd help if I tried to heal him?" Sophie asked.

"That would be far too dangerous," Granite said. "It's possible his goal is to lure you into his mind and trap you there. Isn't that what Fintan tried to do during his healing?"

Sophie winced at the memory. If Fitz hadn't dragged her back to consciousness, Fintan would've burned her alive without her even realizing.

"But you're taking the same risk when you search his mind, aren't you?" she asked Mr. Forkle.

"I am *far* less valuable than you—as are we all."

"He's right," Squall agreed. "And I'm sorry, but I must get back or someone will notice I'm missing." She removed a frosted purple-black crystal from her crackly cloak and leaped away in a flurry of snow.

"Now, what was I saying?" Mr. Forkle asked, watching the snowflakes swirl.

"You were making excuses for why we can't find the Neverseen," Keefe told him. "Pretty lame ones, if you ask me."

"So you feel it's *lame* to keep Sophie safe?" Granite asked.

"No—but it's lame to not use *me*," Keefe argued. "We know some of the Neverseen are in Ravagog. Give me a green crystal and I'll hunt them down."

"That is the most supremely absurd idea I've ever heard," Mr. Forkle told him.

Sophie had to agree. King Dimitar had taken out her humongous goblin bodyguard with a single punch from

90

his apelike fist. And the ogre who'd grabbed her during the attack on Mount Everest had literally dragged her through ice and stone.

"If they catch you, they'll kill you," she whispered.

"Well then, I guess it's a good thing breaking into places is my specialty," Keefe told her.

"This isn't sneaking into the principal's office," Fitz said.

"I can handle it," Keefe insisted. "And *now* is the time to make our move. The Neverseen are scrambling. We caught Gethen. Brant's all charred and burned. And my mom"—he cringed at the word—"isn't as tough as she's pretending to be. She won't last long with the ogres. She needs gourmet dinners and fancy clothes—and she's horrible with bad smells."

"That may be," Mr. Forkle said, "but you're forgetting that trespassing on ogre land violates our treaty. We cannot spark a war."

"Haven't they already voided the treaty by helping the Neverseen?" Fitz asked.

"King Dimitar is claiming that was done by a band of ogre rebels," Blur explained. "If they're acting without his permission, the Council can't hold him responsible."

"Does the Council honestly believe him?" Sophie asked.

"Besides, aren't we rebels too?" Dex added. "If they caught Keefe, wouldn't the Council be able to give the same excuse?"

"Why is everyone assuming I'm going to get caught?" Keefe asked. "You guys are clearly forgetting how awesome I am!"

"And yet you wore an ogre homing device for weeks with no inkling of its existence," Mr. Forkle reminded him. "I'm not saying that to fault you. Simply to help you realize what we're up against. The ogres have defenses far beyond our knowledge and experience. And as for your thoughts, Mr. Dizznee, you saw how King Dimitar reacted when Sophie attempted to read his mind. How do you think he'd react to someone invading his city?"

Sophie cringed at the reminder of how serious the consequences of that single act had been. She still hadn't shaken her doubts that it was related to the Wildwood plague.

"We cannot be hasty with our efforts," Granite told them. "We must be strategic."

"That doesn't mean we should waste time, either," Keefe argued.

"Do not fool yourself into believing you are the only one feeling impatient," Mr. Forkle warned him. "Tell me, do *you* know the names of the dwarves we lost on Mount Everest? They were Ermete, Irja, and Kun—and Yegor is still in critical condition. They were dear friends and we are anxious to avenge them. But that is not an excuse to take foolhardy actions."

"I know you've all spent months solving clues on your own and disobeying adults," Granite added. "But you must remember *we* were the ones guiding you through that."

"We figured out a few things on our own," Fitz argued.

"Indeed, you did," Granite agreed. "Which is why we're glad to work with you. But we must be a *team*."

"That'd be easier to believe if you guys weren't keeping so many secrets," Sophie reminded them.

"The only secrets we keep are *ours*," Mr. Forkle said.

"What about the memories you stole from my head?" Sophie had two blank spots in her mind. One from when she was nine and had an allergic reaction to limbium—an elvin substance Mr. Forkle must've given her for some reason. The other was from when she was five, and Mr. Forkle triggered her telepathy. She could vaguely recall seeing a boy in elvin clothes disappear—but she couldn't remember who he was.

"Those memories were *mine*," she said. "And you took them and expect me to pretend it's not a big deal."

Mr. Forkle let out another long sigh and turned to telepathically debate with the Collective. As the silence stretched on, Sophie braced for a long "You kids" lecture.

But when Mr. Forkle finally spoke, he said, "Very well. In the interest of earning your trust, would you like your memory back?"

# TEN

SOPHIE HAD TO LET THE SENTENCE slosh around in her mind before the words could soak in. Once they did, something still felt wrong.

"You mean memories, right?" she asked. "You stole two."

"We are only offering one—the memory I know you desire the most."

"The Boy Who Disappeared?" Sophie asked, and the Collective nodded.

Sophie turned to her friends, knowing she wouldn't get a better offer. When she had their approval, she told the Collective, "Okay."

"All right, then," Mr. Forkle said, reaching for her temples.

Sophie flinched back. "Wait—you're doing it now? Since when is anything with you guys ever that easy?"

She glanced at her right hand, where a small star-shaped scar commemorated the time Mr. Forkle reset her abilities. He'd had to give her an entire ounce of limbium and then inject her with a modified human remedy to stop the allergic reaction from killing her.

Mr. Forkle cleared his throat. "Returning memories is a simple process—though you should prepare yourself for the fact that this memory was taken to spare you additional worry."

"I still want it back. Just like I want the other memory." She turned to the Collective, trying to find their eyes amid their crazy disguises. "If you won't return it now, I think I deserve a guarantee that you'll give it back to me eventually."

"You deserve that and more," Granite said. "So we can agree to your term—as long as you understand that *we* will choose when to return the other memory."

Sophie agreed, and Mr. Forkle turned to Fitz. "I'd like to have you assist."

"Why him?" Dex asked. "If you need another Telepath, why not use Granite?"

"Because Miss Foster trusts Mr. Vacker," Mr. Forkle said. "And the two of them have an extremely unique connection. In fact, we're hoping to train them as Cognates."

"REALLY?" Fitz asked, his eyes sparkling.

"What's a Cognate?" Sophie asked.

"An incredibly rare telepathic relationship," Granite explained. "One very few Telepaths are able to achieve. I know I've never found anyone I could partner with."

"Neither have I," Mr. Forkle agreed. "Cognates combine their power through a deep personal connection. It's too early to know if you're truly compatible, but it's worth exploring—especially given the potential we've witnessed. On your own, Miss Foster, you came far closer to reading an ogre's mind than any have before. Perhaps with the combined strength of a Cognate you would find true success—though I'm definitely *not* suggesting you attempt to probe an ogre's mind again. I'm simply illustrating the potential. Your telepathy has proven far superior to even my most optimistic calculations. If you and Mr. Vacker achieve Cognatedom, it would reach another level entirely."

"You want to try it, right?" Fitz asked as Sophie resisted tugging on her eyelashes.

"Of course I do."

"Ha, nice try, Foster," Keefe said. "I can feel your dread all the way over here."

"It's not *dread*," she argued. "It's just a lot of pressure. I don't want to let anyone down."

"You could never let me down." Fitz said something else too, but it was drowned out by the plethora of gagging sounds coming from Dex and Keefe.

"Don't Cognates have to share *all* their secrets with each other?" Biana asked.

Mr. Forkle nodded. "It's how they reach the necessary level of trust."

Keefe smirked. "Okay, *now* I feel the dread."

"A perfectly normal reaction," Granite told him. "Sophie has been alone with her secrets for a very long time. Sharing them so openly is a whole new concept—one, I might add, that I myself have never been comfortable with."

"Yeah," Sophie agreed. "Plus . . . this could be super dangerous—"

"Nope! We're not doing the 'I'm trying to protect you' speech again," Fitz interrupted. "You're not allowed to worry about me anymore—and *I* don't want to have to worry about *you*. That's why I want to do this. A Cognate is a Telepath's ultimate backup. I promise, I won't be mad if it doesn't work out. But isn't it worth trying?"

He looked so adorably excited, Sophie could feel her cheeks blushing.

"Okay," she whispered.

"Wonderful! So come over here, Mr. Vacker," Mr. Forkle ordered. "I want your minds to be connected as I return Miss Foster's memory."

Sophie's mouth went desert dry as Fitz and Mr. Forkle reached for her temples.

"Try to let your mind relax, Miss Foster," Mr. Forkle told

her. "And let me know once you clear the point of trust, Mr. Vacker."

The Black Swan had designed Sophie's mind with a hidden entry point, where her subconscious could pull someone past her mental blocking. Apparently they had to transmit some sort of password to convince her mind she could trust them.

She had no idea what word Fitz used, but he grinned and said, "I'm in!"

"Very good," Mr. Forkle told him. "Her mind is trusting you much faster."

"Of *course* it is," Dex grumbled.

"I'm going to return the memory," Mr. Forkle said. "And it can be a bit disorienting, so perhaps you should hold someone's hand, Miss Foster."

Dex and Keefe both offered, but Biana wrapped an arm around Sophie's waist and had Sophie lean against her.

"On three," Mr. Forkle said.

Sophie braced for pain, but when he got to "three" all she felt was a whisper of cold.

"Is that it?" she asked. "I don't see the memory."

"It takes a moment to register on your consciousness. You should feel it . . . *now*."

Sophie swayed as the memory hit, fighting to get her bearings. It felt like her mind had been dropped into the middle of a movie running on fast forward.

*That's me,* she realized as the scene slowed to a normal pace and she watched her five-year-old self reading on the steps in front of her small square house.

*What book is that?* Fitz transmitted.

*Looks like an encyclopedia. I read the whole thing from A to Z by the time I was six.*

She wasn't supposed to be reading that day. Her mom had ordered her to go outside and play with Bethany Lopez, the first-grader who lived across the street. But Bethany had called her Dorktionary and told her to go spell something. Sophie had just beaten a fifth grader in her school's spelling bee. She didn't understand why everyone was making such big deal about it. Why did it matter that she was only in kindergarten? Why was her principal talking to her parents about having her skip grades?

That was the real reason her parents had sent her outside. They'd caught her listening to their whispered conversation. She'd still heard three words, though: "She's not normal."

Sophie could feel her eyes burn as her emotions synced with the memory. Her five-year-old self hadn't understood why it was so hard to fit in like her parents wanted. She'd been thinking about running away when she'd felt the prickly sense of someone watching her.

She could feel Fitz lean closer as they relived the moment she'd looked up and spotted the strange boy in the blue bramble jersey. He was peeking at her from behind her yard's sycamore tree—or she assumed he was. His head was turned her way, but his face was a blur.

Sophie fought to focus the memory, but the boy remained fuzzy, even as he raised a crystal up to the sunlight and disappeared. *Now* Sophie knew he'd light leaped—but at the time she'd been terrified she'd seen a ghost. She'd grabbed her book and raced for the safety of her house. But her toe caught on the concrete stairs, and the last thing she remembered was the ground racing toward her and a sharp pain in her head.

From there the memory skipped to the part Sophie already knew: waking up in the hospital, hearing thoughts for the first time and crying because she couldn't understand what was happening.

*Whoa*, Fitz transmitted. *The voices feel like knives.*

*I know*, Sophie thought, fighting to shut down the memory. Her mind seemed determined to relive every second.

*I knew it had to be scary, manifesting so young*, Fitz said, *but I never realized it was like that.*

Fitz's hands were shaking now, sharing five-year-old Sophie's terror as she'd screamed and thrashed, begging someone to make the voices stop. The doctors hovered around her, sticking her with needles, checking equipment.

*How long was it like this before you figured it out?* Fitz asked.

*The doctors gave her another sedative,* Mr. Forkle told them, *and while she was out I was able to plant the truth in her mind so she'd understand. I'd tried to do that before, but hadn't been able to reach her while the ability was still manifesting.*

*That makes sense,* Sophie thought. *I remember somehow knowing that I was hearing thoughts. Also that I couldn't ever tell anyone. I'd never felt so alone.*

*I'm sorry,* Mr. Forkle said.

"Uh, are you guys okay?" Keefe asked. "Foster's emotions are spiking all over the place, and Fitz feels . . . weird."

"I'm fine," Sophie promised, shaking her head to clear it. She turned to Mr. Forkle. "But I still can't see the boy's face, or how you triggered my telepathy."

"You were unconscious for the telepathy triggering. And the boy's face is blurry because he was wearing an addler. It's a gadget that makes it impossible for your eyes to focus on the wearer's face. They were very popular during the Human Assistance Program, since humans forget anyone they cannot recognize."

"Why would the boy have one?" Sophie asked. "And who was he? Why was he there?"

"Those are the questions I've been trying to answer for the last eight years. Obviously he's with the Neverseen, but I have no idea how he found you, or why he didn't seem to realize what you truly were. I'm glad he didn't, because I wasn't watching you as closely back then. I hadn't even known you were outside until I heard the neighbor girl shouting that you'd fallen. I ran out to check and found you bleeding and unconscious. When I probed your recent memories, I realized you'd seen an elf and

I was tempted to grab you and flee. But there were too many people watching. Plus, the boy had disappeared, and I hoped that meant he'd crossed you off whatever list he was working from. Still, I decided to move up your timeline just in case. I called 9-1-1 and triggered your telepathy, knowing the head injury would be an excuse to help your mind accept the new ability. I also altered your memory to be sure you'd forget the boy. And then I never let you out of my sight again."

"If you erased the memory that quickly," Keefe asked, "how did Foster write about the boy in her journal?"

"I merely hid the memory at first. I was trying to avoid interfering any more than I had to. But the memory kept resurfacing. Sophie's mind had latched on to the moment to try to understand it. When I caught her writing in her journal, I knew I had to be more drastic. That night I washed the moment completely and tore the page out of her journal."

"So you *did* sneak into my room while I slept?" Sophie asked, feeling especially squirmy when he nodded.

"My job was far from easy, Miss Foster. I had to ready your abilities, keep you safe, and still have you believe you were a regular human girl."

"You failed pretty epically at the last one," Sophie mumbled. "If you'd wanted me to feel normal, maybe you shouldn't have made me read minds—or at least taught me how to block the thoughts I didn't want to hear."

"Believe me, I tried. Certain skills need conscious training, and I couldn't reveal the truth to you yet. So every night I searched your memories and helped your mind set aside anything too upsetting. I also tried to help with your headaches—don't you remember how I was always asking about them? I even gave your mother remedies to try, but I doubt she gave them to you. She wasn't a fan of medicine. She made it clear at her first fertility appointment that she was only there as a last resort. It was one of the reasons I selected her. So many human remedies do more harm than good, and I had to ensure you wouldn't be subjected to them constantly. The few times you went to the doctor, I had to monitor what they gave you and then find ways to undo the damage. I also had to change your records to ensure you looked human on paper—and your hospital stays were even worse. So many files to erase and treatments to adjust. You have no idea what a nightmare it was."

"I might, if you gave me back my other missing memory," Sophie reminded him.

"Nice try."

"But it's not like this memory even taught me anything," Sophie argued. "I still don't know who the boy is."

"Perhaps that will convince you we are not withholding crucial secrets," Granite said.

Or that they picked that memory to return because they knew it was a bust . . .

"And you really have no theories for who the boy could be?" Sophie pressed.

Mr. Forkle heaved a heavy sigh. "In the interests of avoiding further questioning, I will tell you that we've spent many years investigating the children at Foxfire. And we've ruled out every single boy."

"Could you have missed someone?" Biana asked.

"Our methods were *very* thorough. I'm convinced he was not there—and if I'm right, then there's only one other place he could have been."

Fitz figured it out before Sophie did. "Exillium."

"And before you start plotting ways to find the campus," Mr. Forkle told her, "keep in mind that you saw the boy *eight* years ago. He has long since aged out of their curriculum."

"So where do the Exillium kids go when they graduate?" Fitz asked.

"There is no single place," Granite said. "Some earn jobs in the Lost Cities. Others remain banished. Either way, the boy is just as untraceable as the rest of the Neverseen."

"There has to be a way to find him," Sophie said. "Maybe the teachers saw something suspicious, or the Exillium administration kept records, or—"

"I can assure you, Miss Foster, you will find no record saying 'Boy X is a member of the Neverseen,'" Mr. Forkle interrupted. "And the Coaches would be of no help. Exillium is designed for anonymity. Those who attend do not use their names. They also wear masks."

"Sounds like the perfect place for the Neverseen to hide,"

Sophie pointed out. "They could have members there right now."

"I doubt it," Blur said.

"Why not?" Dex asked.

"Well, don't take this the wrong way," Blur said, "but . . . Exillium is for kids."

"What he means," Mr. Forkle jumped in as they all groaned, "is that the Neverseen haven't demonstrated a pattern of relying on children."

"They did once," Fitz argued. "Shouldn't we at least look into it?"

"It's not worth the risk," Mr. Forkle insisted. "Finding Exillium would require breaking into an incredibly secure database."

"I can do that, easy," Dex said.

"Don't get overconfident, Mr. Dizznee," Mr. Forkle told him. "And do *not* attempt it. Whatever modicum of information could be gleaned by searching Exillium's records does not match the havoc that would occur if you were caught."

"Plus, we have far more important assignments for all of you to work on," Granite added. He glanced at the rest of the Collective, waiting for them to nod before saying, "It's time to rescue Prentice."

# ELEVEN

"PRENTICE," SOPHIE WHISPERED, NOT sure what to feel.

Relief?

Hope?

Fear?

Yeah . . . it was mostly fear.

And then of course there was the *shame*—mostly because of *all the fear*.

Prentice had allowed his mind to be broken in order to protect *her*. And healing him was the only way to be sure Alden's sanity would never shatter again.

But . . . Prentice had been trapped in his madness for thirteen years, and his whole life had fallen apart during that time.

His wife had died—faded away during some sort of light-leaping accident. His orphaned son, Wylie, had been adopted. And even though Sir Tiergan—Sophie's telepathy Mentor—had surely been a good father, Wylie was now all grown up, a Prodigy in Foxfire's elite levels, having spent most of his life never knowing his dad.

That was a lot of heartbreak for someone to wake up to. What if Prentice shattered all over again once he faced those cold realities?

"Whatever concerns are causing that crease between your brows," Mr. Forkle told her, "we *do* share them. But we cannot stall Prentice's rescue any longer. He is too important."

"And we're not saying that because we miss our friend," Granite added, clearing his throat several times. "We've also long suspected that Prentice's mind is hiding something crucial. It would explain why he called 'swan song' before he was captured."

"Swan song" was a code the Black Swan used if they feared their life was in danger.

"Prentice used the code the day before his capture," Mr. Forkle said. "I've always wondered how he knew they were coming for him."

"As have I," Granite agreed. "I'd been monitoring Alden's investigations most carefully, and he'd had no suspicion toward Prentice whatsoever. Then Prentice called swan song and suddenly he was arrested."

Della looked away, twisting and retwisting her graceful fingers.

Granite turned to Sophie, his stony eyes almost pleading. "No one is more aware of the risks that come with healing Prentice than we are. But don't you think it's worth it, to find out what happened, and give him a *chance* at happiness?"

Sophie pictured Prentice the way she'd last seen him, locked in a lonely cell, rocking back and forth, muttering to himself, drooling. . . .

"Okay," she whispered, not sure if her heart wanted to race or explode. "But isn't he still in Exile?"

"We're working on a plan," Granite said. "And it's going to take everyone's help. Biana—you'll need to be able to hold your vanish far longer than you currently can. Dex—we managed to get our hands on one of the bolts used on the cells. We'll need you to master opening it quickly and silently. Sophie and Fitz—we'll need your minds at their absolute strongest. So we've prepared notebooks with exercises to further your Cognate training. And Keefe—we have several Empathy books we need you to familiarize yourself with."

"Books?" Keefe asked. "You're giving me *books*?"

"Never underestimate the power of the page," Mr. Forkle told him. "Miss Foster would not exist without the decades I spent researching genetics—and you have just as much to learn about your ability."

"It will take us a few days to make the arrangements for this mission," Granite added. "But when we're ready, we'll need to move quickly. So tonight, prepare your minds to swear fealty to our organization. And tomorrow, get ready to work."

"Well *that* was interesting," Dex said as they climbed the stairs to their tree houses.

Sophie had thought she was too nervous to eat, but when they reached the gazebo in the center of the bridge, their dinner smelled *amazing*. She couldn't tell what was in Calla's famous starkflower stew, but Mr. Forkle was right. It truly was life changing. Every bite felt like home, warming her from the tips of her toes to the top of her head and making her feel safe, happy, and loved.

"Was anyone expecting the Black Swan to be like that?" Fitz asked as he mopped up the last of his gravy with a piece of crusty bread.

"You mean secretive and stubbornly unhelpful?" Sophie mumbled. "I guess I should have. But I'd hoped it'd be easier."

She'd agreed to their plan to help Prentice, and she didn't regret it—but she also didn't believe that should be their only focus. She wasn't ready to drop the idea of trying to find the Boy Who Disappeared through Exillium's records. And she wanted to find out more about the ogres and the Wildwood Colony. But she wasn't sure if it was safe to discuss any plans with her friends. They were in the Black Swan's territory now, so they were probably being watched.

"I do think they might be onto something with the code names," Keefe said as she searched all the shadows. "In fact, after I swear fealty I should have you all call me Emo. Fitz can be Brainwave. Biana and Della can be Blink and Wink. Dex, you're Gears. And Foster? Hmm. That's tricky. . . . Maybe Enigma? Unless you want to be Cognate—or is Fitz the only one allowed to call you that?"

Sophie sighed.

"You do realize you basically agreed to merge your brain with his, right?" he pressed. "You'll be Fitzphie! Or Sophitz! Personally I'd go with Sophitz. Better make it clear *you're* the boss."

"You're just jealous," Fitz said with his best attempt at a smirk.

Keefe shrugged. "Team Foster-Keefe will always be cooler."

"Yeah, but Sophitz will be unstoppable," Fitz said, pushing back his chair. "I can't wait to start training tomorrow."

Sophie tried to feel the same way, reminding herself of all the important reasons she'd agreed to the Cognate thing. But her brain kept circling back to Biana asking, *Don't Cognates have to share all their secrets with each other?*

She was sure Keefe could feel her panic. But instead of teasing her, he said, "So, when are you going to tell me what you guys are hiding? Something about the gnomes, right—don't think I didn't notice all those nervous glances."

Biana couldn't have looked guiltier. "We . . . just wanted to make sure it was true before we said anything," she mumbled.

"And it's good we waited," Sophie added. "Mr. Forkle gave me better information."

She explained their worry about the elvin footprints outside the Wildwood Colony, and how two teenagers made them, not the Neverseen.

"So . . . you thought you had evidence that my mom was *poisoning gnomes* and you decided not to tell me?"

Keefe looked so betrayed, Sophie wished she could think of something better to say than, "It turned out to be nothing."

"That's still not cool. We're going to find out a ton of awful things about my mom as we go along. I don't want to have to worry that everyone's hiding stuff from me. You know how that feels, Foster. You hate it as much as I do."

Sophie sighed. "Okay. From now on we'll share."

Keefe nodded, but he didn't look happy. And his frown deepened when Della pulled Fitz close for a good-night hug.

"Come on," Dex told Keefe. "We need to brainstorm ways to punish Wonderboy."

"That's right," Keefe said, perking up a bit. "We'll form our own Empath-Technopath Cognatedom. We can be Keefex!"

"Why not Deefe?" Dex asked.

"Because Deefe sounds lame."

"You guys *are* lame," Fitz said as he trailed behind them up the stairs.

"Are you sure it's smart to leave the boys alone?" Biana asked as she followed Sophie and Della to their tree house.

"'Smart' isn't the word I'd use," Della admitted. "But we'll sleep better than they will."

The gnomes had been busy while they were gone, hanging glass orbs filled with swirling flashes of color all over their tree house. The effect was breathtaking, even if it also made Sophie squirmy when she realized the dots of light were some sort of iridescent flying bug.

Della's bedroom had also been finished, and it looked like a presidential suite, complete with a private bathroom and a closet full of radiant gowns.

Sophie and Biana had new clothes too, and this time there were pants! Also: the world's weirdest pajamas. Sophie had no idea why the Black Swan would choose a purple furry onesie—with feet. It *was* quite comfy when she put it on, but she was glad her windows had thick drapes so no one could see her padding around her room.

Next she needed to find a place to hide Kenric's cache, but her options were limited. Her desk only had one drawer, and her canopied bed sat on an elevated platform with no space underneath. Her best choice was to tuck it into a hidden pocket in the strap of her purple backpack. The cache barely fit, but the lump wasn't noticeable, and she slipped the Imparter into another pocket and dumped out everything else.

Her eyes welled with tears when she found Grady and Edaline's note. They'd tied it to Ella, the bright blue stuffed elephant she couldn't sleep without:

*We will never be more than a few words away.*
*~Love, Mom & Dad*

Sophie wasn't sure what they meant, until she noticed the silver box they'd included. Inside was the teal memory log Alden had given her to record all of her dreams and triggered memories. And her *illegal, unregistered* Spyball from the Black Swan.

Her hands shook as she picked up the palm-size silver sphere and whispered, "Show me Grady and Edaline Ruewen."

The Spyball turned warm, and a bright flash filled the orb, painting the sphere with an image of her adoptive parents. They sat with Alden in his curved office with sleek glass walls. Half the room was made of windows overlooking the lake, and the other half was a vibrant aquarium. Sophie knew the room all too well. She'd been in it often—usually when Alden needed to have an unpleasant conversation.

But Grady and Edaline didn't look upset. In fact, all three of them were reading long yellowed scrolls. More scrolls were piled on the desk, the floor—every flat surface in the room. Sophie couldn't tell what they were working on, but it looked important.

"Stay safe," she whispered, tracing her fingers over their faces.

She watched for several minutes more, wishing one of them would look up. When they didn't, she let the image blink away. She realized then, with a twinge of guilt, that she hadn't checked on her human family in weeks—maybe even months. She'd been so distracted by all the huge problems she'd been facing, she'd . . . forgotten.

"Show me Connor, Kate, and Natalie Freeman," she told the Spyball, using the names she wasn't supposed to know. The elves had changed her family's identities after they'd erased Sophie from their lives, fearing she might try to contact them. Being erased had been Sophie's choice—her final gift to spare her family a lifetime of grieving a missing child. The only reason she knew who they were was because the Black Swan gave her the top-secret information.

The Spyball turned warm again, and when the image appeared it showed three different scenes. It must've been daytime where her family lived, because her dad was sitting at a desk in a windowed office, her mom was driving somewhere, and her sister was doodling on her notebook in a classroom. The normal, everyday moments looked so foreign compared to the things Sophie was now used to seeing.

"Is that your family?" a soft voice asked, and Sophie dropped the Spyball.

It rolled across the floor, stopping at Calla's feet.

"Sorry," the tiny gnome said, retrieving the Spyball and frowning at the images. "Everything looks so gray in their world."

"Humans don't have a lot of green in their cities," Sophie agreed.

"Such a pity." Calla handed back the gadget. "Plants are the best for soothing. In fact"—she hummed a song under her breath, and the vine growing over Sophie's canopied bed bloomed with deep purple flowers—"I know you struggle with nightmares," she told Sophie, "so I planted these reveriebells to give you sweet dreams. The secret is in their scent."

Sophie closed her eyes and inhaled. The smell reminded her of gardenias, with a hint of vanilla, and something spicier too. Maybe ginger?

She could feel it settle into her muscles, making her shoulders relax.

"Thank you," she said.

"It is my honor." Calla wove a loose strand of the vine carefully in with the others. "I must confess, it feels very strange to talk to you, after all these years."

"Years?" Sophie repeated.

Calla smiled her green-toothed smile. "I know this might be hard to believe, but I've been part of Project Moonlark since the beginning."

# TWELVE

**Y**OU WERE PART OF PROJECT Moonlark?" Sophie repeated, needing to hear it one more time.

Calla nodded. "I was the one who chose the project's name."

Moonlarks were incredibly rare because they didn't nest with their eggs like other birds. They laid them in the ocean and let them drift at sea, so that only the strongest made it to shore. Once they hatched, the babies had to survive alone. It was a fitting metaphor, though Sophie wished it didn't imply so much struggle.

"I know it must sound strange," Calla said, "a gnome helping with elvin genetics. But much of the project reminded me of cross-pollinating. Like these reveriebells. I blended dreamlillies, sweetshades, and aethrials, keeping the best traits of each."

"So . . . you helped tweak my genes," Sophie clarified, hoping Calla wasn't about to tell her she was part plant. It was hard enough knowing her genes had been modeled off alicorn DNA. She didn't need to be the horse girl *and* the tree girl.

"'Helped' is the wrong word. I was there to keep the Black Swan grounded, and ensure they never strayed from what was natural, or lost sight of the fact that they were sparking the life of an innocent girl."

"Does that mean you know what they're planning for me?" Sophie asked.

"'Plan' is *also* the wrong word. I know their hopes—mostly because I share them." She turned away, humming under her breath and making more reveriebells blossom. "Did you like the pin I gave you?"

It took Sophie a second to realize Calla meant her Prattles' pin.

She reached for her allergy remedy necklace, where the silver bird was still pinned through the cord. "How did you know the box would have the moonlark?"

"I have a friend who helps at the Prattles' bakery, and I'd heard that a baby moonlark hatched recently. I asked her to save me the box with the new pin. I wanted to show you that elves aren't the only ones who believe in you."

"Why?" Sophie had to ask. "I mean . . . I'm just one girl."

"All it takes is one to stand where others fall. Think of the way you defied the ogre king. No one on the Council was willing to take such a risk."

"But . . . wasn't that a bad thing?" Sophie needed a deep breath before she could mumble her next sentence. "It sounds like the attack at the Wildwood Colony happened right after I read King Dimitar's mind—"

"Are you blaming yourself for the plague?" Calla interrupted.

"It seems like they must be connected—assuming the ogres are responsible."

"Oh, they're responsible," Calla said darkly. "And someday we'll finally be able to prove it. But that doesn't mean you should put the blame on yourself." She took Sophie's hands, and her green thumbs felt warm and smooth, like stones heated by the sun. "You are a sprout, fighting to take root among the rocks of our world. It's going to cause a few cracks, but that is the only way for you to grow strong."

Sophie tried to feel the comfort Calla wanted her to feel. But all she found were more reasons to worry. "How bad is the plague?"

"I wish I knew. It's been very hard to get information."

"Mr. Forkle said the same thing. Why would the Council keep it secret?"

Calla released her hands, turning back to her blossoms. "I'm sure they're trying to spare us unnecessary panic. Hopefully Gora and Yuri will return with a happy report soon."

"They're the gnomes you mentioned earlier, who had family in the Wildwood Colony?"

Calla nodded. "Yuri's sister lived there, along with her husband and two daughters."

"Daughters," Sophie repeated. "So . . . they're kids?"

"Not as young as you," Calla said. "Though they are still far too young . . ."

. . . *to die,* Sophie's mind finished.

"The physicians should be able to find the cure, though, right?" she asked.

Calla smiled. "That is the plan."

Sophie tried to think of something else to say. All she could find was half a sentence.

"If there's anything I can do . . ."

"There may very well be," Calla said. "That's why you're the Moonlark."

She curtsied and turned to leave, then whipped back around. "Look at me, forgetting the reason I came here!"

She reached into her skirt pocket and pulled out a fist-size black cube. "This is the package you were promised, to swear fealty to the Black Swan. There's a sensor on the top that will respond to your DNA. Only when you truly mean your oath will the latch open."

"How can it tell?"

"That's one of the Black Swan's mysteries. But you are their heir. Your spot is reserved. All you have to do is accept it."

She curtsied again, leaving Sophie alone with the tiny black box that suddenly felt very heavy. In her mind she could hear hundreds of unanswered questions mixed with all her doubts and worries and insecurities.

She could also hear Mr. Forkle telling her she had a choice.

Hands trembling and stomach fluttering, she raised the box to her lips and gave the sensor the tiniest of licks.

As soon as her DNA registered, the cube flashed with white light. Words appeared through the glow, a single sentence written in frills and loops. The oath was far simpler than Sophie had imagined. But the words felt true. A promise she could stand behind. Believe in. Uphold.

*I will do everything in my power to help my world.*

Sophie closed her eyes, drawing the words from her heart as she whispered the oath.

The last word had barely left her lips when a latch on the box snapped open. Inside she found a pendant made of curved black metal, shaped like the sign of the swan. Set into the center was a magnifying glass.

Sophie assumed the tiny piece of paper enclosed with it would explain what the pendant meant. Instead it said—in Mr. Forkle's familiar writing:

*Glad you made the right choice.*

# THIRTEEN

OW MANY TIMES DID YOU HAVE
to say the oath before your cube opened?"
Biana asked, fiddling with her Black Swan
pendant as she followed Sophie and Della
down to breakfast.

"I think it was my fourth," Della said, lifting the hem of her
long black-and-white gown to descend the stairs.

Surprisingly, Biana had worn pants—though the tunic
she'd paired with them was embroidered with butterflies,
and she had jeweled butterflies pinned in her hair. Somehow Biana made it all seem effortless—even her matching
lip gloss. "I got it on my third try," she told Sophie. "What
about you?"

Sophie looked away. "My first."

"I guess I should've figured that," Biana said through a sigh. She held her pendant up like a monocle. "Do you have any idea what these do? All my note said was 'to show you the world in new ways.'"

"Mine said, 'For when you need to look closer,'" Della added. They glanced at Sophie.

"Mine said they were glad I made the right choice."

"Huh," Biana said. "It must be weird to be you."

Talk about an understatement.

All the things Calla had told Sophie were still buzzing around her mind—especially the part about Calla being involved with Project Moonlark.

For some reason she'd imagined the project only included Mr. Forkle, sitting alone in a lab with a microscope and some Petri dishes. But now she could picture a whole team—multiple people and species brainstorming and planning, resting their hopes on her to be their Moonlark. And what if—

All thoughts dropped away when they reached the gazebo.

"Your hair!" Della gasped, rushing to where Fitz sat at the table. His usual dark waves had been dyed green, and they stuck out in every direction.

"*Someone* slipped an elixir into my shampoo this morning," Fitz said, patting the spikes and eyeing Dex. "But it's cool. I kind of like it."

Dex snorted. "Keep telling yourself that."

"Actually, it's not that bad," Biana said.

"Yeah, Fitz can pull off anything." Sophie blushed as she considered the implication of her words.

Keefe groaned. "I knew we should've gone with the balding elixir. Next time!"

"Uh-uh," Della told him. "You need to fix this—now. Do you really want the Black Swan to see what you've done?"

Keefe shrugged and grabbed a pastry from one of the platters in the center of the table. "They're walking around crusted with ice and turning their bodies to stone. Cactus head is nothing."

"Okay, let's try this a different way," Della decided. "If you get to makeover my son, then I get to makeover both of you."

"Works for me," Keefe said. "I look awesome in everything."

"Tell that to your feet when they spend the rest of the week balancing in my tallest heels," Della told him.

"Okay . . . forget that." Dex reached into his pocket and pulled out a tiny brown vial. "This will get rid of the green."

"Thank you." Della rumpled Dex's hair as he gave the vial to Fitz.

Fitz downed it in one gulp, gagging at the taste.

"No more pranks," Della said, wagging a finger at all three boys.

"Or—what if Fitz *looks* normal, but doesn't smell very good?" Keefe asked.

Biana giggled.

Della sighed. "What am I going to do with you, Keefe?"

"I hear the Lord of the Universe title is up for grabs. Unless Foster's trying to snatch it."

"All yours." Sophie had enough responsibility already.

"So you guys didn't have any problems with the oath?" Biana asked.

"Nope! Got it on my third try," Dex said proudly.

"Me too!" Biana said.

"Ha—beat you both," Fitz told them. "Only took me *two*."

"Don't get so smug. I'm sure Foster nailed it the first try." Keefe laughed when she blushed. "I knew it."

"How many tries did it take you?" Biana asked him.

Keefe looked away.

"So what did everyone's notes say?" Sophie asked, saving him from having to answer.

"Mine said 'Because seeing is believing,'" Dex said.

"Huh, I didn't realize they were different." Fitz smoothed his back-to-normal hair. "Mine said 'The smallest things can be the most dangerous.'"

Everyone looked at Keefe.

"Do not lose your way."

Biana repeated the other notes and studied her pendant. "I still don't get what they do."

"Typical Black Swan," Fitz said.

"Seriously," Dex agreed. "Don't they realize riddles are a huge waste of time?"

"Are they?" Granite asked, crossing the bridge to reach the gazebo. His face looked like clay soil that had cracked in the sun. "And here I thought we were training your minds to think critically and solve problems."

"There are no easy answers in this world," Wraith added, his silver cloak appearing beside Granite.

Biana moved closer to study him. "How do you partially vanish like that?"

"Work hard enough and I'll teach you," he said. "But today we'll be perfecting the basics. Rescuing Prentice will require a level of precision you currently do not have, so prepare yourself for a long, exhausting day."

"Meanwhile, I'll be initiating your Cognate Training," Granite told Sophie and Fitz. "Today will be the test to see if Cognatedom is truly a possibility."

Sophie's stomach dropped into her toes, and she was very glad she hadn't eaten any of the pastries yet.

"What about us?" Keefe asked, pointing to himself and Dex.

"You both have study materials in your rooms," Granite said.

"You're seriously telling us to go read?" Keefe asked.

Sophie leaned close to whisper, "It's only one day."

"A lot can happen in a day, Foster. You know that better than anyone."

"It's cool," Dex jumped in. "I have a project we can both work on."

The way he said "project" made Sophie wonder what prank he was planning. She hoped it'd be worth it, since she was sure Della would make good on her threat of high heels. But she was glad to see Dex once again keeping Keefe from getting too frustrated.

Part of her wished she could go with them as they crossed the bridge and headed up the stairs. Instead, she followed Fitz and Granite down to the river, trying to convince herself Cognate training wouldn't be as scary as it sounded.

"Mr. Forkle and I spent last night preparing these," Granite said, handing Sophie and Fitz each a black notebook labeled *Cognate Lessons*. "But as we developed the exercises, we realized we were skipping a crucial step."

The three of them sat in the shade of a tree with purple leaves, watching the glassy river rush past. Across the water, Della and Biana were practicing with Wraith, pacing back and forth while vanishing. Biana could only walk half the distance of the others before she'd reappear.

"The Cognate relationship requires both trust and *balance*," Granite said, reminding Sophie she should be paying attention, "and it's impossible to work on the former without the latter. In your case, Fitz—while you're an incredibly talented Telepath—your skills simply do not match Sophie's."

Sophie cringed, wondering if the criticism would bother Fitz. But he grinned at her and said, "Yeah, she makes us all look bad."

"She does indeed," Granite agreed, his face cracking further as he smiled. "So if you're going to be her Cognate, we need to get you up to her speed."

"But aren't her abilities strong because of all the tweaks you did to her genes?" Fitz asked.

"Actually, much of Sophie's strength comes from practice. Her ability was triggered eight years ago, and Mr. Forkle trained her mind every night until last year."

"He did?" Sophie asked, shuddering at the mental image. "I thought I had to be conscious to learn telepathic skills. Wasn't that why he couldn't teach me to shield?"

"Certain skills, yes," Granite agreed. "But others can be absorbed. I'll show you how."

He instructed them to scoot closer, until their knees were touching. "It'll be easier if you hold hands."

Sophie tried to return Fitz's smile, but her palms were sweating—which was stupid. She'd held Fitz's hand every time they light leaped or teleported. It was no big deal.

"What now?" Fitz asked, twining their fingers together. Sophie hoped he couldn't feel her racing pulse.

"*Now* I want you to observe Sophie's mind in action. And

Sophie, I think it's best if you focus on the skill that seems to come to you the most effortlessly—transmitting long distances."

"Ohhh, I've always wondered how she does that," Fitz said.

"Who should I transmit to?" Sophie asked. "In my telepathy sessions I always practiced on Fitz. Or I call for Silveny, but I'm guessing that won't work, since she's not an elf."

"Actually, that could be interesting," Granite said. "It might open Fitz's mind to two skills—distance transmission *and* telepathy with animals. I'm not sure the latter skill can be taught, but it's worth the attempt."

"Does Silveny think in the Enlightened Language?" Fitz asked.

"Only the few words I've taught her," Sophie said. "Otherwise it's her language or images and memories."

"That may make it confusing," Granite warned, "but still a good test. In fact, this should be a definitive indicator of your Cognate success. If Fitz's mind can't learn from yours, it'll prove you're not compatible."

The last word dumped about a million pounds of pressure on everything.

*I won't care if this doesn't work, okay?* Fitz transmitted after she gave him permission to slip past her blocking.

But she could see the hope in his eyes—feel the excitement in his grip. And she definitely didn't want him thinking they weren't *compatible*.

"Okay," she said, stalling one second longer.

She closed her eyes and pictured the Sanctuary, with its rainbow sky and rolling pastures. The dwarves had built the lush animal preserve inside the Himalayan Mountains to keep it secret from humans. The rock walls also prevented the alicorns from teleporting away. Sophie wished Silveny could've kept her freedom, but the precious alicorn needed protection. The Neverseen had tried to capture Silveny *twice*. One time they'd even broken her wing.

*Silveny?* she transmitted, making Fitz jump.

"Sorry," she mumbled. "I should've warned you it'd be loud."

"But it's awesome," Fitz promised. "I need to learn how to project with that kind of power."

"Hopefully this process will teach you," Granite reminded him.

*Silveny,* Sophie said again, and this time Fitz barely flinched. He even held steady as she repeated the call a few more times. But he did jump when an exuberant shout filled her mind.

*FRIEND! SOPHIE! VISIT! FLY!*

"That is so crazy," Fitz said.

"Does that mean you can hear Silveny?" Granite asked.

Fitz laughed. "I'm surprised the whole universe can't. Every word she sends needs to end with an exclamation point."

"Tell me about it," Sophie said.

"Can you understand what she's saying?" Granite asked Fitz.

"So far. But I think she's speaking the Enlightened Language."

"She is." Sophie's mind filled with a new round of *VISIT! VISIT! VISIT!* plus several *KEEFE*s.

*Wow, she really loves Keefe, doesn't she?* Fitz transmitted.

*It's adorable and obnoxious, isn't it?* Sophie asked.

There were so many *KEEFE!* chants going, Sophie almost didn't notice when Silveny added a *GREYFELL!* to the mix.

*Is everything okay?* she asked.

Greyfell was the male alicorn who lived at the Sanctuary. He'd grown violent not long after Silveny arrived, but only because he was afraid of the ogre homing device hidden in Silveny's tail. Once the aromark had been removed, he'd calmed down. Still, Sophie remembered the ferocity in Greyfell's eyes and the darkness she'd seen in his memories. He'd lived a much harsher life than Silveny, and it had made him cold and wary.

And yet, the memories Silveny sent showed the two alicorns playfully dipping and diving through the hologram sky and chasing each other through the colorful meadows. If they hadn't been sparkly flying horses, Sophie would've teased them for flirting.

Plus, she honestly hoped that was what they were up to. Silveny and Greyfell were the last of their kind, and everyone was counting on them to repopulate the species. That was why the alicorns needed so much protection. The elves believed that letting any creature go extinct would cause the planet irreversible damage. So whoever controlled the alicorns controlled the Council.

*I'm glad you have a friend,* Sophie said, wishing she could reach across the world and stroke Silveny's shimmering nose. *You'll have to tell him "hi" for me.*

*MISS,* Silveny told her, making Sophie's eyes burn.

*I miss you too. But you're safe?*

*SAFE! SAFE! SAFE!* Silveny promised.

Which of course led her back to more pleas for Sophie to visit, and a host of additional *KEEFE*s.

Somewhere around the tenth chant a new voice joined the mix—one with a crisp accent.

*Hi.*

It was a small word, but its effect was huge.

Silveny pummeled Sophie with worries as Fitz shouted, "I DID IT!"

Sophie could hear Granite and Fitz celebrating, but first she had to calm Silveny down.

*That's Fitz,* she told the suspicious alicorn.

*FRIEND?* Silveny asked.

*Yes, a very good friend.* She sent her memories of the few times Fitz had been around Silveny to remind her who he was. When that didn't seem to be enough, she replayed the moment Fitz had saved her life, finding her when she was fading away after her kidnapping.

*LIKE,* Silveny decided.

*I like him too—as a friend,* she added quickly, in case Fitz was listening. But he and Granite were too involved in their deep discussion on Fitz's progress.

"It's only the first step," Granite told them. "But it's very encouraging. You two truly have the most unique connection I've encountered in all my years of telepathy."

Sophie's cheeks burned, and she was glad Fitz was too busy trying to transmit again. It took his mind two tries, but he managed another *Hi!*

*FITZ!* Silveny replied. *SOPHIE! FITZ! FRIEND!*

*FRIEND!* Fitz repeated, his voice louder. More confident.

They spent the rest of the day in a bizarre one-word-at-a-time conversation. Fitz couldn't understand Silveny unless she spoke the Enlightened Language, and no matter how hard Silveny tried, he couldn't pick up the emotions or images she sent. Still, Granite was very pleased with their progress.

"I have absolutely no doubt you two will be able to serve as Cognates," he announced when the lesson finished.

Fitz beamed at that, and Sophie smiled too, until she remembered that meant they'd have to get to work on the sharing-all-their-secrets thing. . . .

She told herself she'd find a way to get used to it, and she put on a brave face through dinner. But her mind was swimming, swimming, swimming, thinking of all the things she couldn't—shouldn't—share.

She figured she was in for a long, restless night, but Calla's reveriebells chased away her worries. She was dreaming of mallowmelt and custard bursts and cute boys flying on alicorns when a voice dragged her back to consciousness.

"Hey, Sophie—wake up. I think I found something."

# FOURTEEN

IT TOOK SOPHIE SEVERAL SECONDS TO realize Dex's voice wasn't part of a dream. A few more after that, she caught the silhouette of him sitting on the edge of her bed.

She gasped and pulled her covers around her neck, then remembered she was wearing her crazy pajamas. Dex looked just as furry, though his onesie was lime green.

"What are you doing here?" she whispered, turning toward her wall of windows. A triangle of gray-orange light leaked in where the curtains parted slightly, so she assumed that meant it was dawn.

"I had to show you this." Dex held up a gadget that looked like a gutted obscurer. The sphere had been sliced in half, and all kinds of springy coiled wires stuck out of the center. "I know it's ugly, but now it's a really powerful Evader. It let me break into the Council's archives and find records on Exillium—and I know what you're going to say," he added quickly. "I know the Black Swan told us to drop it. But I think Exillium's worth looking into. If we could find the Boy Who Disappeared, we might be able to find the Neverseen. Plus, I knew I could sneak in without getting caught. I'm sorry I didn't tell you first—I wasn't sure if we were being watched."

"You are."

They both yelped as Della blinked into sight near the curtains. "Don't tell me you thought I'd let you sneak into Sophie's room while she's sleeping and not see what you're up to."

"Good to know," Keefe said, striding into the room in a red furry onesie. "And don't think *I* was going to allow a Sophex meeting to happen. Hmm, maybe we should call it Deephie. Sophex sounds weird. Anyway, my point is, no secret meetings without me!"

"And me!" Fitz said, trailing behind in furry gray pj's.

"I'm here too!" Biana appeared in the corner wearing shaggy pink. "I followed my mom when she followed Dex."

"Wow, it's really crowded in here," Sophie mumbled. "And really . . . furry."

Even Della had a blue onesie that made her look like Cookie Monster.

"Cool, your window is right across from mine!" Keefe said, opening Sophie's curtains. "We could throw things at each other!"

"Or not." Della herded everyone to the bed. "Sit. We need to discuss the incredibly dangerous thing Dex has done."

"It wasn't dangerous," Dex argued. "I designed this Evader perfectly."

He held out the rickety gadget, and Della looked less than impressed.

"Did you find anything good?" Biana asked.

"Hopefully. I got all their prodigy records," Dex said. "Well, Exillium calls them Waywards, but it's the same thing. Every kid who's ever gone there has a file telling what year they started attending, who their family is, how old they are, what their talents are, what they did to get banished—all kinds of stuff. So now we just go through and search for anyone who looks suspicious."

"What counts as suspicious?" Della asked.

"Well, we sorta know his age, right?" Dex said. "At least a pretty good guess? And we know he was probably at Exillium about eight years ago. So we start with that."

"That's still going to leave you with hundreds of different boys," Della reminded him. "And even if you do find a good candidate, what then?"

"Then I break into the registry—"

"No you do *not*," Della interrupted.

"Don't worry, the registry is super easy to access, and I know how to make sure they don't catch me. Then I can cross check any suspicious names against pendant locations to find out where they are."

"You're assuming they'll be back in the Lost Cities," Della said. "I don't think you understand that Exillium is for the Unworthy. It removes those that do not belong in our world. Anyone sent in error can earn their way back. But very few do. Very few should."

Sophie wasn't sure she liked how casually Della talked about banishing, as if it were the perfect solution.

Then again, was locking them in Exile better?

"Well, I still think it's worth going through the records and seeing what we can learn," Dex said. "Even if we can't find the Boy Who Disappeared, we might find a Neverseen member hiding there now."

"Or it could be a waste of time," Della countered.

"But its *our* time to waste," Keefe said. "And it's better than reading boring books. Do you know what I learned yesterday? That when our minds break from extreme guilt, they can shatter different ways. Most people shut down and can't function anymore. But some turn erratic and reckless. Sometimes people even get violent."

"That's important!" Della told him.

Sophie had to agree. That explained why Alden went catatonic over his involvement with Prentice's memory break, while Brant turned into a deadly pyromaniac after he killed Jolie.

"Right, but how long did that take me to explain?" Keefe asked. "Ten seconds? Five? But it took me three hundred and twenty-nine pages to read! So yeah, I'll take searching through Exillium files any day."

Della started pacing. "What are the odds of you listening if I tell you not to pursue this?"

"Slim to none," Keefe said.

"That's what I thought. So fine—you already have the records. If you want to go through them, I won't stop you. But no breaking into the registry without consulting with me—clear?"

"Fine," Dex agreed. "I'll build something so you guys can see the files I copied. Maybe if I rewire an Imparter—I'd probably need gold instead of copper wire and—"

"Yeah, yeah, Technopath stuff we don't understand," Keefe jumped in. "What do *we* do while you do all of that?"

"How about we change out of these crazy outfits?" Biana said. "I mean really, *what* was the Black Swan thinking?"

"That if your pajamas were embarrassing enough, you kids would be discouraged from after-curfew meetings."

Everyone scrambled as Mr. Forkle stalked into the room, followed by Granite and Blur.

"Clearly our plan was not as successful as we'd hoped," Mr. Forkle said. "Dare we ask what made you willing to suffer the furry disgrace?"

"I think the better question is, what are you guys doing here so early?" Keefe countered.

"We promised we'd report to Calla as soon as we'd learned anything about Wildwood," Granite said.

"And?" Sophie asked.

"So far there's been no change—but that's good news in some ways," Blur said. "The gnomes' symptoms seem to be holding steady."

"But they still don't have a cure," Sophie clarified.

"No," Mr. Forkle admitted. "But they're working on it."

"They should have my dad try," Dex said. "He's the best alchemist out there."

"I'm sure he'll be their next call. Right now Lady Galvin is trying her hand," Granite said.

Even months later, Sophie still flinched at the name. Her old alchemy instructor had made her first year at Foxfire equal parts humiliating and stressful.

"So if all the best people are working on it," Sophie said, "why haven't they found the cure?"

"It comes down to isolating the pathogen," Mr. Forkle explained. "They haven't been able to find the source, and without that crucial information, they don't know what to target. The physicians suspect each gnome is plagued by only a single parasite, so finding it is a bit like that old human expression about needles in haystacks. But at least they're not pressed for time. The gnomes have responded well to the symptom treatments, so the need for the cure isn't as dire."

His eyes drifted to the Evader in Dex's hand, and his expression darkened. "Please tell me that's not what I think it is—or that you've at least had the common sense to not put it to use."

"Well . . . if you want me to lie . . . ," Dex mumbled.

Mr. Forkle's sigh sounded more like a growl. "This is about Exillium, right? I told you it wasn't worth the risk."

"But there was no risk," Dex said, pointing to a thinner wire on the Evader. "I call this a wiper. It erased every step I took, so there's no way the Council will know I was there."

Mr. Forkle took the gadget, examining it from all angles. "Well, I'm no Technopath—and this is one of the most bizarre executions I've seen—but I must say, it's rather . . . inspired."

Blur took the Evader and passed his smudged hand through. "It's a totally different approach than anything I've felt. But maybe that's what we need."

Dex looked ready to float away with the praise, and Sophie didn't blame him. After being underestimated his whole life, he deserved the recognition.

"Do not let our compliments overshadow our disappointment," Mr. Forkle said, bursting their brand-new bubble. "When we give orders, we expect them to be followed."

"Not if they're dumb," Keefe argued.

"I'm not going to debate this any further," Mr. Forkle said.

He turned to Dex. "I'd rather you focus your energy on a much more important assignment."

He paused to confer with Blur and Granite before he continued. "You have an incredibly unique approach to technopathy, Mr. Dizznee, and perhaps that fresh take can solve a problem we've been facing."

"For months we've been trying to gain access to a secret archive," Granite jumped in. "In fact, 'secret' isn't a strong enough word. It's an archive that should not exist. Our best Technopath discovered it, but hasn't been able to breach beyond that."

"What kind of archive?" Dex asked.

"We have no idea," Blur said. "All we know is it's hidden in Lumenaria."

Della's eyes widened.

"Yes," Mr. Forkle told her. "As I said, it should not exist. Lumenaria is where all the worlds gather for crucial negotiations," he added when he saw Sophie's confusion. "Any meetings there are not to be recorded, beyond the wording of the treaties. But it appears that someone has been transcribing the sessions."

"What kind of security are the files protected by?" Dex asked.

"That's the strangest part," Blur told him. "We'd assumed the archive was the Council's dirty little secret. But it's guarded by technologies from all of the intelligent species."

Dex whistled. "So I have to hack ogre technology?"

"And dwarven. And trollish. And goblin. And gnomish. And elvin as well," Mr. Forkle confirmed.

"I didn't even know the gnomes had technology," Biana said.

"Not all technology comes in the form of gadgets," Blur reminded her. "Which is why I think you'll be perfect for this, Dex. Only *you* would build a crazy Evader like that. So let's see what else you can do."

"And if you do manage to gain access," Granite added, "we'd like you to search for information on the Wildwood Colony. The Council's silence on the plague has made us want to further explore the Colony's history."

"I'll have supplies sent within a few hours," Mr. Forkle said. "And we need you to make this your number one focus. No more wasting time on *this*." He shoved the Evader into his pocket before turning to the rest of them. "You have assignments and training to work through as well. I suggest you get started."

"Anyone else getting tired of the Black Swan bossing us around?" Keefe asked after they'd de-furry-pajamaed and regrouped in the common room of the boys' tree house.

The room was decorated like a campsite, with indoor trees, a ceiling glinting with stars, and an enormous fire pit in the center. The flames burned in every color of the rainbow, and Sophie was sure the gnomes meant it to be just as stunning as the waterfall in the girls' house. But she would never see fire as anything but death and destruction.

"I think they just want to make sure everything goes right when we rescue Prentice," Biana said. She was working with Della by the window, learning to hold her invisibility in shifting light.

"It *is* annoying, though," Sophie mumbled, following Fitz to a clump of boulders that turned out to be beanbag chairs.

Dex had fortunately been smart enough to save a copy of the Exillium records he'd stolen, and he'd promised to make a gadget they could use to search through them. In the meantime, it was back to Cognate training, and it felt extra nerve wracking doing it in front of everyone. Dex had taken over most of the floor with tools and bits of gadget supplies. And Keefe had slumped into a chair in the darkest corner, pretending to read another empathy book. Every few minutes he'd mutter, "This is the stupidest thing *ever*."

"Should we start at the beginning?" Fitz asked, opening his Cognate training notebook.

Sophie nodded. Biana hadn't been exaggerating about Cognates having to share *everything*. Each exercise was designed to make them reveal more and more secrets.

The first assignment wasn't *that* bad. Just a list of questions they were supposed to ask while their minds were connected, so they could see each other's first thoughts.

"Is it okay if I enter your mind?" Fitz asked.

"Dude, do you realize how creepy that sounds?" Keefe interrupted.

"It's less creepy than reading her feelings all the time without telling her," Fitz argued.

"Hey, it's not like I *try* to do that! You're just mad that Foster can't hide things from me."

"Pretty soon, she won't be hiding anything from me, either."

"Yeah, and I can feel how *not* excited she is about that all the way over here."

Fitz turned to Sophie. "Is that true?"

"You make her super nervous," Keefe answered for her.

Sophie wished the Black Swan had given her laser eyes so she could skewer Keefe with her death glare.

"I take it that's a yes?" Fitz asked.

"Well . . . yeah. But, have you met *you*?" she asked. "You're, like, Captain Perfect! And I'm—"

"The most powerful elf our world has ever known?" Fitz finished.

"Grady's way more powerful than me."

"Grady *is* powerful," Della jumped in. "But not as powerful as you'd think."

"How can you say that?" Sophie asked. "Grady made all twelve Councillors smack themselves in the face!"

Della laughed. "Wish I'd been there to see *that*. But I've seen him test his power, and his limit was twenty-four people—and that left him drained and vulnerable. He can also only maintain his hold for so long. I assume that's why the Black Swan didn't make you a Mesmer. Mesmers have limits, and their power rarely triggers a permanent solution. Did the Council suddenly change their minds because of what Grady did?"

"They backed down a little." But Della had a point. In the end, Grady still had to let her be sentenced to the telepathy restrictor.

Sophie gave Fitz permission, but before he could pass her blocking, Keefe slammed down his book and shouted, "I refuse to read this!"

"The book can't be *that* bad," Della insisted.

"Yeah, it is. My dad wrote it."

"Your dad's a writer?" Sophie asked.

"More like a torturer of innocent readers." He held up the cover as proof. *The Heart of the Matter,* by Lord Cassius Sencen. "It's just a long ramble about how he's the only one smart enough to realize that emotions come from both the heart *and* the brain, and that Empaths can only read what's in the mind. Too bad he forgot to explain *why anyone cares!*"

Sophie hoped Keefe was far enough away that he couldn't tell she actually found the idea fascinating. Councillor Bronte had taught her that inflicting pulled emotions from her heart—and Fitz had seen an emotional center in her mind. So did that mean people could feel different things in different places?

*Okay, I'm in!* Fitz transmitted, making her jump. *Sorry, I thought you could feel me slip through.*

*Nope. I never know you're there until you say something. Is that how it is for you?* She stretched out her consciousness until she could hear his thoughts. *Did you feel that?*

*I wish. I always catch everyone else. My old Mentor said I should be a Keeper someday. And the fact that you can sneak by me means you would make an awesome Probe.*

*Huh. I always thought I was a Keeper, since, y'know, secret information planted in my brain and all.*

*Well, I'm pretty sure you could be either one. Way to make the rest of us look bad.*

Sophie smiled. *If we're going to be Cognates, do we each have to be a different thing?*

*I think that's usually how it works. I know that's how it was for my dad and Quinlin.*

*They're Cognates?*

*They were. Until they did the memory break on Prentice. Quinlin told my dad afterward that he hadn't wanted to do it, and it turned into this big fight.*

*Huh, when your dad brought me to see Quinlin in Atlantis, they acted like friends.*

*They got over it eventually. But they couldn't go back to being Cognates. The trust between them was breached, since Quinlin had proven he held things back.*

Sophie shifted in her seat.

*Wow, it really freaks you out having to share everything, doesn't it?*

*It doesn't scare you?*

*Not really. You already know about Mr. Snuggles.*

Sophie laughed. *Yeah, but Mr. Snuggles is the best.*

Fitz had confessed about the sparkly stuffed dragon he couldn't sleep without during one of their previous trust exercises. He'd even brought it over to her house to cheer her up.

*Did you bring him here?* she asked.

*Of course! We'll see how long it takes before Keefe catches me.*

*You don't care if he does?*

*I thought I would. I even spent forever finding a good hiding place for him. But now . . . I don't know. There are way bigger things to worry about than a little embarrassment, you know? I mean, we're getting ready to break into Exile.*

The words made her shiver.

*So what do you say?* he asked.

*What do you mean?*

*I mean, why not just blurt out whatever you're super embarrassed to tell me and get it over with. Wouldn't it be a relief?*

Or it could be the biggest disaster ever—it depended on how he felt.

*How I feel about what?* Fitz asked, reminding her he could hear what she was thinking.

*Come on,* he begged as she scrambled to get her thoughts under control. *I promise, whatever it is, it's not going to change anything.*

But it would.

It *had* to.

*Come on,* he urged. *All you have to do is trust me.*

Sophie looked away, her brain and heart beating so fast she was sure she would soon implode.

*How about you just blurt it out on three?* Fitz pressed. *You can do it. Here we go.*

*One . . .*

*Two . . .*

# FIFTEEN

**Y**OU GUYS OKAY OVER THERE?"
Keefe asked, right as Fitz transmitted, *three*.
"Foster's emotions are seriously wigging."

"Come on, man, we were *so* close!" Fitz said.

"Close to what?" Keefe and Dex asked at the same time.

"Nothing!" Sophie scooted her beanbag back, needing room
to breathe.

"You're blocking me," Fitz said, his tone more hurt than
accusatory.

"Am I? Sorry . . ." But it felt good to have her thoughts all to
herself again.

Had she actually been considering telling Fitz she *liked* him?

She shuddered just thinking about what would've happened.

"Seriously, you okay there, Foster?" Keefe asked.

"*You*," Fitz told Keefe, "have the worst timing *ever*."

Keefe smirked. "I try."

Fitz's eye roll was epic. "Sorry," he told Sophie. "I'm not mad at you. I just really thought we were making progress."

She looked away.

She knew she wouldn't die if Fitz didn't *like* her. But it would be crazy humiliating. And how would they ever be Cognates?

But . . . how would they be Cognates if she was hiding secrets from him?

She sighed.

Everything would be so much easier if she could just get over her silly crush. Would it be so bad to just be friends? It wasn't like she was ready for a boyfriend. She doubted she was even allowed to date, given the whole matchmaking thing. Not to mention all the problems it would cause with Dex—and maybe Biana.

She needed to let it go . . .

And yet, when she stole a glance at Fitz, her stubborn heart still fluttered. Especially when he flashed his movie-star smile.

"Whoa, now there's a whole lot of *staring into each other's eyes* going on," Keefe said.

"Let them work," Della told him. "And you should be working too—*really* working, not flipping pages and complaining. The Black Swan gave you that book for a reason."

"Right. Because they're more evil than we think," Keefe muttered under his breath.

"So . . . ," Fitz said through the silence that followed.

"Sorry I blocked you," Sophie mumbled.

"I'm getting used to it. But do I have permission to go back in?"

Keefe snickered. "Smooth, Dude."

They both ignored him.

Sophie gave Fitz permission, and within seconds she could hear him in her head. At least her subconscious still trusted him, even if her conscious wasn't quite as brave.

*Sorry again,* she thought.

*It wasn't all your fault.* He glared at Keefe, and Keefe blew them a kiss. *He's lucky I don't shove that book somewhere he really won't appreciate it. Especially since I'm guessing you're not going to tell me whatever it was you were about to say?*

*Maybe . . . another time, when we don't have Keefe paying such insanely close attention.*

*I guess that makes sense. Okay, we should get started on this exercise.*

They agreed to take turns, and Fitz went first.

*Favorite animal?* he asked.

Instantly Sophie pictured her pet imp, Iggy.

*Huh, I thought you would've said Silveny,* Fitz said.

*I know, me too.*

Leave it to her to pick the stinky imp over the majestic alicorn. Then again, she never thought of Silveny as an "animal." Plus, Iggy's breath might be toxic—and his farts could be weaponized—but he needed her as much as she needed him.

*Okay,* she said. *Favorite subject in school?*

*Telepathy.*

Her face flashed through his mind and Sophie had to force herself not to wonder what *that* meant.

*This one's harder,* he said, moving to the next question quickly. *Biggest regret?*

Sophie assumed it would be the moment she'd chosen to let Brant get away. But her mind filled with her friend Marella's face instead. Maybe it was because deep down she knew she'd *had* to let Brant go to save her friends. Or maybe it was because the last time she'd seen Marella, she'd let Marella's hurtful words get to her, even though she could tell there was something bigger going on. And now she'd run away and might never have a chance to make things right.

*Think we'll ever go back to Foxfire?* she asked Fitz.

*I have no idea.*

She could see how painful the thought was for him. He'd dreamed of being an elite level prodigy all his life, and now he might not even finish Level Five.

*Don't say you're sorry,* he told her. *This was my choice—and it was the right one. It's just hard not to want it all sometimes, you know?*

She did.

She checked her list again. *What are you most proud of?*

Her face popped into his mind again—but this time it was her terrifyingly transparent face from the day he'd rescued her.

*Where were we when you found us?* she asked, focusing on the strange tree in the background. She vaguely remembered describing it to Fitz in her desperate transmissions. It looked like four trees in one, each quarter representing a different season.

*That's the Four Seasons Tree, a gift the gnomes planted for us in Lumenaria.*

As soon as he said the words, the worries she'd been trying to set aside flooded back.

*Wow, I didn't realize you were blaming yourself for what's happening with the plague,* Fitz thought. *Why didn't you tell me?*

*Because I'm trying to believe that the physicians will have a cure soon.*

*I'm sure they will.*

She could see the doubts in his mind.

*I wonder why we ended up in there,* Sophie thought, trying to focus on less troubling things. *Do you think the tree is connected to the Neverseen, somehow?*

*My dad wondered the same thing, and he went back to investigate. But he didn't find anything important. And the pathfinder you took from the Neverseen was totally standard. So he's guessing it was just random.*

*Maybe . . .*

But the tree was so unique, it seemed to beg for attention. If she was ever allowed back in the Lost Cities she wanted to see it again.

*I'm forgetting whose turn it is,* Fitz said, reminding her that they should be training.

*Me too. So I'll go. If you could visit anywhere in the world, where would it be?*

A dark city flashed through Fitz's mind as he thought the word *Ravagog*.

Half of the city was above ground, carved into the side of a stark mountain. The other half was underground, in an enormous swampy cavern. A glowing green river separated the two halves, carving a deep canyon between them. A single bridge at the top provided the only connection. The dark metal structure was lined with arched towers glowing with green flames that blazed in hovering fireballs.

*It's like the ultimate Forbidden City,* Fitz said. *That doesn't make you curious?*

*No, I hope I never have to go there.*

But she had a horrible feeling that someday they would.

*Two questions left,* Fitz said. *Least favorite school subject?*

Her mind was a three-way-tie between her horrible alchemy sessions, her torturous inflicting sessions with Bronte, *and* her stressful linguistics sessions with Lady Cadence.

*Wow, I will never complain about my boring elvin history sessions again,* Fitz thought.

*Yeah, you haven't known fun until you've spent some time with Councillor Bronte, learning to inflict pain.*

And Bronte was one of her only supporters on the Council. No wonder she'd had to go into hiding.

*Person you look up to?* she asked him.

Alvar's face popped up in his mind.

*Huh, you'd think it'd be my dad,* Fitz thought.

*Well, Alvar's your big brother.*

*Yeah, but we've never been that close. He moved into the elite towers when I was still a kid, and never moved back after that. Plus, he's spent huge chunks of time with the ogres. I'm lucky if I see him more than twice a year. But maybe—*

Fitz's thought was cut short by Calla bursting into the room.

"Sorry for the interruption," she said, stooping to catch her breath. "I could not reach the Collective, and this cannot wait. Two of our guards just arrived with an emergency report."

"What guards?" Sophie asked.

"The gnomes that keep watch over one of the Neutral Territories. They saw members of the Neverseen."

# SIXTEEN

TWO GNOMES STOOD WAITING BY THE river, watching the colorful reeds sway in the rushing water. It should've been a peaceful moment, but their stance was too rigid. Their gray eyes were clouded with trouble when they turned to watch Sophie and Calla barrel down the winding stairs, with Fitz, Keefe, Dex, Della, and Biana behind them.

"This is Lur," Calla said, struggling to catch her breath as she pointed to a gnome in pants and a vest woven from leaves. "And his wife, Mitya."

"We asked for the Collective," Lur said in gnomish.

Calla used the same swishy language, sounding like rustling

leaves. "The Collective is in the Lost Cities, so I brought the Moonlark and her friends to help."

Lur and Mitya straightened at that, and their eyes stayed fixed on Sophie as Calla introduced the rest of the group.

"She looks younger than I imagined," Mitya whispered in gnomish. "Too young to bear this burden."

"She has borne far worse," Calla reminded them.

Sophie couldn't tell if Calla knew she could understand them, but she decided to clue them in. "Whatever it is, I can handle it," she said with a perfect accent.

Lur and Mitya lowered their heads and switched to the Enlightened Language.

"We meant no disrespect, Miss Foster," Lur said. "We did not realize how far your gifts stretched. And it is an honor to meet you in person."

"Lur and Mitya have served the Black Swan nearly as long as I have," Calla explained. "Usually from afar, keeping an ear to the ground, so to speak. They were actually the ones who found the hideout where the Neverseen held you captive."

"You did?" Dex asked. "I've always wondered how they found us."

"So have I," Sophie agreed.

"It really was not much," Mitya said. "The roots told us of the voices hiding deep in the earth. All we did was listen."

Sophie had no idea what that meant. But she knew enough to say, "Still. Thank you."

"Yeah," Dex mumbled. "I'd be dead right now if it weren't for you guys."

"Those were dark days," Calla agreed. "It was an All Call to action, everyone scrambling, using any resource they had to search the layers of our planet. We were beginning to lose hope when Lur and Mitya delivered their report."

"And what is the report you came to give today?" Della asked, reminding everyone why they were there.

Lur and Mitya shared a look, then focused on Sophie, switching back to gnomish.

"We will tell *you*," Lur said, "and let you decide if you'll share with the others."

"I would not recommend it," Mitya added, her focus drifting to Keefe.

Sophie's heart deflated, and she barely remembered to use gnomish when she said, "This is about his mother."

Lur nodded. "We spotted three of the Neverseen on our patrol today, on the far side of the Lake of Blood."

"The Lake of *Blood*," Sophie repeated, making sure she'd properly translated the words.

"That is what we call it," Mitya agreed. "The Starkrial Valley was once lush and hearty. But the ogres dammed the river and let everything wither on the southern end. The lake that remains is red and acidic. Many things that touch its surface do not survive."

"And the elves allowed that?" Sophie asked.

"The elves allow many things." An edge had crept into Lur's tone, turning the words to a windstorm.

"The Lake of Blood lies in the Neutral Territories," Mitya explained. "And many have long suspected the ogres ruined the valley to allow them to hide a stockade in the mountains."

"Uh, are you guys going to start using words us non-Polyglots can understand?" Keefe interrupted. "Because I think I speak for everyone when I say *we want to know what's going on!*"

"I will soon," Sophie promised. "I still need the rest of the story." She switched back to gnomish. "What was his mom doing?"

"Nothing," Lur said. "And that is the problem."

"She is in serious danger," Mitya added. "It's even possible she . . ."

"What?" Sophie asked when neither of them finished.

Lur heaved a sigh. "His mother was badly injured when we saw her."

"Injured how? From the battle?" The last time Sophie had seen Lady Gisela, she'd hurled herself off a cliff on Mount Everest, relying on a mysterious ogre skill called "phase shifting" to save her.

Mitya shook her head. "Her marks were the work of an ogre. They have a tool that leaves a very recognizable wound."

"Why would they . . . ," Sophie started, then answered her own question. "They tortured her?"

"Quite brutally." Lur shuddered.

Sophie sucked in air, trying to think through the explosion of emotions. "But the Neverseen are *partners* with the ogres."

"Yes, but the ogres do not tolerate failure," Lur explained. "Especially when it comes to the capture of prisoners. In the ogre code of warfare that is the worst possible offense."

*And Lady Gisela allowed Gethen to be taken.*

"So, you think the ogres tortured her and brought her to that stockade you mentioned?"

"It's possible," Lur said. "Or . . ."

Mitya took Sophie's hands. Her fingers were calloused, but still soft as they tightened around her own. "There are other rumors about the Lake of Blood—stories of a pyre, where the ogres burn the bodies of those they kill. It is possible that it's only a legend. But . . . the Neverseen dragged Lady Gisela into a cave. She was bleeding and wounded and screaming for mercy. After they were gone, all I found was blood."

"The cave could've been a secret entrance to the prison, though, right?" Sophie asked.

"Anything is possible," Lur agreed. "But that would not explain the smoke we saw drifting from the mountains."

Sophie swayed and Keefe grabbed her, holding her steady as

he whispered, "Please tell me what they're saying. You said you wouldn't hide things from me."

"I won't," Sophie told him, hoping she could keep her promise. She pulled slowly away from him, asking Lur and Mitya in gnomish, "Is that all you saw?"

"Yes," Lur said. "But we will continue investigating. We stopped only because we felt the Collective should know that the hierarchy of the Neverseen has shifted. Lady Gisela holds no authority. She is either a prisoner or a casualty."

"Can you understand what they're saying, Mom?" Biana asked.

"I'm only catching bits and pieces." But the hitch in Della's voice made it clear she'd understood enough.

"Please, Foster," Keefe begged. "I've heard them say my mom's name. I'm going crazy here."

"I need to verify first," she told him. "There could be a misunderstanding." It was a frayed strand of hope, but she was going to cling to it with everything she had.

"Can I have permission to search your memories?" she asked Mitya. "I need to see exactly what you saw."

"Reading our minds is not like reading that of your own kind," Mitya said. "It will be exhausting, and you already look weary."

"I can handle it," Sophie said, reaching for Mitya's temples. She rallied her full mental strength, slipped into Mitya's mind and . . .

. . . tangled in a web of memories.

No—not a web.

These were branches.

A mental forest, wild and unruly.

Each memory coiled like vines, wrapping so tightly there was no way to shove through. Even a brain push—a specialized telepathy trick—couldn't break past the gnarled chaos. And the trees seemed to grow and stretch until Sophie couldn't see how to escape the endless woods.

"You need help," Fitz said, sounding very far away. "I'm coming in."

Sophie was too lost to warn him.

*Wow, this is insane,* Fitz transmitted as his consciousness tangled near hers.

*We can't stay here,* Sophie said. *It's pulling us farther and farther away. But I'm not strong enough to break out.*

*Okay, so what if we pool our energy?* Fitz asked.

*Worth a try.*

She imagined her consciousness slithering across the vines like a snake. Fitz did the same, and when they finally reached each other . . .

*Whoa, is this what it's like to be Cognates?* she asked as a surge of warm energy worked like the sun, drawing the trees toward their light and leaving spaces for Sophie and Fitz to move.

*No idea,* Fitz admitted. *But it's awesome.*

It definitely was. The memory forest had divided into dozens of paths, and Sophie chose the darkest. Nightmares clawed with thorny stems, but with Fitz's help they pushed to the path's end. There they found a cold, stark tree, empty and quiet. But Sophie could see the truth hidden in the branches at the top.

Fitz's consciousness gave Sophie a boost and they climbed together, watching in wary silence as the memory unfolded. Two black-cloaked figures dragged a decloaked Lady Gisela past a red lake with dead carcasses scattered along the shore. Sophie could tell Keefe's mom had been wounded, but she couldn't see how bad the injuries were until Mitya snuck ahead of them and slipped into the bushes. The Neverseen passed by, mere feet from where Mitya hid, and Sophie felt her stomach heave when she saw the deep, curved puncture wounds on Lady Gisela's face. She had dozens of them, carved into her cheeks, her chin, her neck.

"Please," Lady Gisela begged as the figures dragged her toward the mountains.

Her captors ignored her cries, kicking her when she stumbled.

Her pleas grew more urgent as they headed for a rift, but the Neverseen did not slow. Mitya tried to follow, but by the time she found a way into the cave, the Neverseen had vanished, leaving nothing but red.

As she turned to head back, Mitya heard Lady Gisela scream, "Don't do this!" Then everything fell silent, and a raspy voice said, "It's done."

A million icicles stabbed Sophie's heart as she recognized the voice.

*Brant.*

Clearly he'd recovered from his wounds.

The memory shifted forward, to when Mitya rejoined Lur by the poisonous lake. He was studying the trail of red, which was darker than the deadly water. They both turned as the scent of smoke laced through the air. A single black plume rose into the sky, before the mountain winds whisked it away.

"That is all we know," Mitya said as Sophie removed her shaking hands from Mitya's temples.

"You'll share this with the Collective?" Lur asked.

"We will," Fitz answered when Sophie couldn't.

Mitya stepped closer, wiping the tears off Sophie's face. "I am sorry to burden you with this responsibility, Miss Foster. No one should face such horrors. Especially you."

"I'm not worried about *me*," Sophie told her, not feeling brave enough to look at Keefe.

"We must leave you now," Mitya said, dipping a slow bow. "But we promise to report anything new we discover."

"Be careful, my friends," Calla said, hugging them both. "Things are not as they seem."

"Indeed they are not," Lur told her, kissing Calla's cheeks.

They both took one last look at Sophie, their eyes focused on her moonlark pin. Then they disappeared into the trees.

"Okay," Keefe said, taking Sophie's hands again. "You have to tell me what my mom's done."

*Do you want me to talk to him?* Fitz transmitted.

Sophie shook her head. Keefe was asking *her*.

*I'll be right inside if you need me,* Fitz promised before he led the others away.

"Come on," Sophie whispered, pulling Keefe toward a tree that had fallen by the river. The bark felt rough and damp, but she knew this was the kind of conversation that needed to happen sitting down.

"If she killed someone, just tell me," Keefe whispered.

Sophie tangled their fingers together, squeezing so tight their knuckles faded to white. "It's not about what she's done, Keefe. It's about what might've happened to her."

Once she started, the story poured out, in every horrifying detail.

"But they haven't found a body," she finished. "So we don't know anything for sure."

Keefe stared blankly at the river.

"What are you thinking?" Sophie asked, when the silence turned suffocating.

"Strange question, coming from a Telepath."

"You know I would never invade your privacy like that."

Keefe sighed. "I'm thinking . . . she *deserves* to be dead."

His voice meant the words. But his eyes didn't.

"It's okay to be sad, Keefe."

"No it's not—not after what she's done."

"She's still your mom, no matter how angry you are."

"I'm more than angry, Sophie. I'm . . . I don't know what

the word is. But I don't care what happens to her."

"Then why are you crying?" She reached up to wipe his cheek and showed him the tear on her finger.

"I . . ." The rest of his words twisted into a sob.

Sophie held him tightly, letting him soak the shoulder of her tunic with tears. She wondered if Fitz had felt this helpless when she'd done the same thing to him. He'd seemed so strong and steady that day, when he'd taken her from her human family. She wished she could be the same for Keefe.

"We don't know anything for sure yet," she repeated.

"It doesn't matter. I don't even know what I'm rooting for."

"You don't have to *root* for anything. But as much as you hate her, part of you still loves her. So whatever happens, you're going to have to grieve."

"Not if I can help it." Keefe pulled away. His eyes were red and puffy, but they seemed dry now as he turned back to the river.

"Want me to leave you alone?" Sophie asked.

Keefe nodded. "Actually, no. It's not good for me to be alone right now. I'll do something stupid. I need . . . I don't know what I need. Just don't go."

Sophie stayed.

Keefe leaned his head against her shoulder and Sophie counted his breaths, considering what a strange thing grief turned out to be.

166

Grady and Edaline closed themselves off.

Fitz pushed everyone away.

She couldn't figure out how Keefe was handling it all yet. But she was glad he wanted her to stay.

Their houses were dark by the time Sophie and Keefe returned from the river, and Keefe clung to her hand until the last possible second. She tried to think of something to tell him, something that might help him sleep. The best she could come up with was, "If you need me, throw something at my window."

Keefe tried to smile, but it looked too painful. "See you tomorrow, Foster."

Then he was gone.

The girls' house was quiet when Sophie crept into the main room. She'd missed dinner and bedtime, but it didn't matter. Eating and sleeping were definitely out of the question.

"How's he doing?" Biana's voice asked as soon as Sophie set foot in her bedroom.

She bit back her scream as Biana appeared in the shadows.

"Sorry," Biana said. "I couldn't sleep."

She followed Sophie over to her bed and they both sat on the edge. Neither of them bothered to turn on the lights.

Sophie knew she should probably tell Biana everything was fine. But she went with the truth. "I think this is going to change him."

"Me too," Biana whispered. "So . . . what do we do?"

"I don't know," Sophie admitted. "Somehow we'll have to find out the truth. Keefe is going to need answers—or closure. In the meantime, we'll have to keep him together."

Seconds passed before Biana said, "I can't believe the Neverseen would do that."

Sophie couldn't either, which was the scariest part. She'd known their enemies were dangerous, but this was a whole other level of evil.

Lady Gisela was one of their leaders, and they'd tortured her and imprisoned her—maybe murdered her. So what would the ogres and Neverseen do to them, if they were ever captured?

"Is it okay if I sleep in here tonight?" Biana asked, the tremble in her voice hinting that she shared Sophie's worries.

"Sure," Sophie whispered.

She got up to change into her pajamas, and by the time she'd brushed her teeth, Biana had already crawled under the covers. The bed was so big she could barely tell anyone else was there. But the soft sound of Biana's breathing made the room feel warmer.

She'd thought Biana was asleep, until Biana asked, "We're going to stop them, right?"

Sophie stared at the wall, her mind flashing through all the losses they'd suffered.

Kenric. Jolie. Prentice. The dwarves on Mount Everest. Maybe Lady Gisela.

She had a horrible feeling there would be more casualties before this was over. But she was sure of one thing. "Yes, we're going to stop them."

# SEVENTEEN

MR. FORKLE SAT ALONE WITH Della when Biana and Sophie made their way down to breakfast. The tight line of his frown told them he'd already been given a thorough update.

"I've asked Sior to help Lur and Mitya," he said, handing them each a bowl of green porridge.

"That's one of the gnomes we met the first day, right?" Biana asked.

Mr. Forkle nodded. "This forest will miss him, but Calla feels confident she can cover his absence. And I think it's important we get answers quickly, don't you?"

"I do," Keefe said, striding across the bridge with Dex

and Fitz right behind him. "And I have a plan."

"Do you, now?" Mr. Forkle asked, studying Keefe closer.

The bruiselike dark circles under Keefe's eyes made it clear he hadn't slept. But Sophie was much more concerned about the state of his hair.

It hung flat against his head, completely unstyled.

Mr. Forkle handed Keefe a bowl of green sludge, but Keefe set it aside and plopped into a chair.

"I wish you would not punish the body over a troubled heart," Mr. Forkle told him.

"Fine. How about I eat if you promise to hear me out?" Keefe asked.

Mr. Forkle gave him a spoon.

Keefe devoured his porridge in three giant bites, then wiped his lips and said, "I want to speak to Gethen. I know he's *unresponsive* or whatever you called it. But his consciousness can't just disappear. I'm sure he can hear me. Or, more importantly, he can hear this."

He cleared his throat and his voice shifted several octaves higher as he said, "Gethen—it's time to go!"

Sophie cringed at how uncannily he sounded like his mother.

"Your mimicking is very impressive," Mr. Forkle told him.

Keefe sounded both bitter and sad as he said, "I was trained by the best. And now we can use what she taught me to fool Gethen. If we stage it right, I can make him think he's being rescued, which should draw his consciousness back. Then we can find out what he knows."

"You're assuming he knows something worth all of that risk," Mr. Forkle said.

"Why else would his capture get my mother . . ." He cleared his throat. "It has to be something important. And I can find out what it is. If he thinks he's being rescued, he'll come back. Then you can probe his memories."

Mr. Forkle stroked his double chin. "Your plan does have its merits, Mr. Sencen. But it's still far too dangerous. We have already determined what our priorities are at the moment—though we are amending them to include an investigation of Lur and Mitya's findings."

"That's not good enough!" Keefe snapped, pounding the table.

"Keefe," Della tried.

"No." He pulled his hand away from her before she could take it. "Aren't you guys sick of being treated like their little puppets? Go here. Read this. Wait for this. Eat this."

He whacked his bowl, knocking it off the table and sending it spinning across the floor, spraying the remaining bits of his green porridge.

"Keefe!" Della said again. "I know you're upset—"

"No, I'm just tired of being ignored," he interrupted. "This is a good plan—Dex and Fitz agreed."

Both boys shifted in their seats.

"It does seem like it might work," Fitz said after a second.

"I never said it wouldn't." Mr. Forkle rose and placed his hand on Keefe's shoulder. "But we've been over this with your schemes about Exillium. Just because a plan is feasible does not mean it's worth the risk. I understand your desire to bring something positive from everything that's happened. But one should never rely on their enemies to give them hope."

"I don't care about my mom—"

"Yes you do. As you should. And while I cannot base this on evidence, I wouldn't count your mother out yet."

Keefe snorted. "You say that like it's a good thing. Yay—she's alive so she can keep being evil!"

"Evil is better than dead, Mr. Sencen. Evil can change. Though neither is in your power."

"*Nothing's* in my power—that's the problem."

Mr. Forkle squeezed Keefe's shoulder tighter. "You are very important to our organization. You wouldn't be here if you weren't. I mean it"—he added when Keefe rolled his eyes—"You will play a crucial role when we rescue Prentice. And that is the mission that must remain our focus."

"Whatever." Keefe stood and stalked toward the boys' house.

Sophie rose to follow, but Mr. Forkle stopped her. "Best to give him space. He'll come back when he's ready."

Keefe didn't come down to dinner. At breakfast the next morning he picked at his food and didn't say much of anything. By the third day of one-word answers, Sophie was ready to stage an intervention.

But Fitz and Biana reminded her of how badly they'd handled themselves when Alden's mind had broken.

"We were awful," Biana mumbled. "Especially to you. And there was nothing anyone could say to make us act better. Alvar tried. Keefe even tried."

"I'm still figuring out how to make it up to you," Fitz added.

"No need," Sophie promised.

Her heart made an extra leap when Fitz smiled and said, "I'll keep trying anyway."

"Ugh, Keefe needs to get better," Dex mumbled. "I need someone to barf with me over Fitzphie."

"My *point*," Biana said as Dex made gagging sounds, "is that as long as Keefe knows we're here, that's really all we can do."

Sophie knew Biana was right. That didn't make waiting any easier. She found herself checking her window every night before bed, wishing she'd find Keefe standing at his.

On the fifth night, his curtains were at least open a crack, unleashing a shred of light. She decided to take the tiny opening.

She didn't have any rocks to throw, so she settled for her shoes, picking the wobbliest, most uncomfortable-looking heels.

Nothing happened from the first *THUNK!* But the second *THUNK!* did its job.

"Are you throwing shoes at me?" Keefe asked, sliding open the window.

"Seemed like a good idea. Now I don't have to wear them."

He gave her a half smile, but it faded as he waved the air away from his face. "Wow, that is a *lot* of worry you're hurling at me."

"You kind of deserve it."

Keefe mussed his still-unstyled hair.

"I'm guessing you don't want to talk about it?" she asked.

"Not really."

She dragged out her sigh. "Is there *anything* I can do?"

He started to shake his head, then stopped. "Actually . . . yeah."

"What?" Sophie asked, leaning out her window.

She didn't hear him the first time, and had to make him repeat.

"Promise me you won't hate me," he whispered.

"Why would I hate you?"

"I don't know. Maybe you'll decide I wasn't worth sacrificing your shoes."

"Now, *that's* never going to happen." She'd hoped that might earn her a smile, but Keefe wouldn't look at her. "I would never hate you, Keefe. Why would you even think that?"

"I don't know. I guess I just feel like I don't belong here anymore."

"You *do*. But . . . I know how it feels to be the outsider. The one with the *past*. The one with the shaky future. But you know what I've realized—or what I'm trying to realize, at least?"

"Is this the part where you give me some speech about how it's our choices that show us who we truly are?"

"Nah, that sounds like something an old guy would say."

Finally, he gave her a real smile!

"What I'm trying to realize is that it's okay to be different. If everyone were the same, we'd all make the same mistakes. Instead we all face our own things, and that's not so bad because we have people who care about us to help us through. You have that, Keefe. We're all here for you. No matter what. Okay?"

Several seconds crawled by before he nodded.

"You should go to bed," Keefe said as a gust of wind made Sophie shiver in her furry pajamas.

The suggestion was tempting—Alluveterre was so much colder than Havenfield. But she was afraid the glints of progress she'd made would be snuffed out when she left Keefe alone.

"I've got a better idea," she said, racing to her bed and grabbing Ella, her pillow, and the thickest quilt. She coiled the blanket around her and waddled back to the window like a fluffy burrito. "See? Window slumber party!"

Keefe laughed—*laughed*—and, after a slight hesitation, disappeared and returned with his own blanket and pillow.

The floor felt hard and cold. The problems ahead of them unimaginable.

But they weren't alone.

And that made all the difference.

# EIGHTEEN

SOPHIE WOKE WITH THE SUNRISE AND found Keefe still asleep by his window, his cheek smashed against the glass.

She smiled at how peaceful he looked—no signs of any nightmares.

She smiled even wider when she noticed the tiny trail of drool near his lip.

"You slept on the floor?" Calla asked from the doorway.

Sophie clutched her chest to calm her startled heart. "It was for a good cause."

She took one last look at sleeping Keefe before pulling her drapes closed. "How come you're up so early?"

"I'm always awake at this hour. I take my ten minutes at

midday, under the warmth of the high-noon sun."

Sophie couldn't imagine living on so little sleep, but she was more worried about the way Calla was nervously twiddling her green thumbs.

"Is everything okay?" she asked.

Calla's wide gray eyes met hers. "I . . . need help from the moonlark. There's something I need you to check for me—a whisper in the forest I do not understand."

The words felt colder than the floor as Sophie fumbled to change into pants and a tunic. She was still struggling into her boots as she followed Calla to the waterfall common room.

"We should leave a note for the others so they do not wonder where you are," Calla whispered, plucking a dry leaf from the carpet and carving a message with her thumbnail.

"Wait—are we leaving Alluveterre?" Sophie had assumed the forest Calla meant was the trees right outside.

Calla handed her the message she'd cut out in frilly lettering:

*With Calla in Brackendale. Be home soon.*
*~Sophie & Biana*

"Biana?" Sophie asked.

Calla pointed to the corner. "I assume you're planning to join us?"

"I am," Biana agreed, appearing in the shadows. "But how did you know I was there?"

"Gnomish eyes are not fooled by tricks of light," Calla told her.

"Seriously?" Biana asked. "How did I not know that?"

"It's not something we think to mention," Calla said. "Elves have no reason to hide from us. Are we ready? The journey ahead is long."

"Just let me grab my shoes," Biana said, and Sophie was relieved to see her return from her bedroom in a pair of sturdy walking boots.

Calla placed the leaf note on a table and led them down the winding stairs. Biana used the walk to play "how many invisible fingers am I holding up?" and Calla passed every test with flying colors.

"Wow, I can't believe you can see me," Biana said, blinking in and out of sight. "Can you teach me how you do it, so I can try to find a way around it?"

"I suppose we can give it a try." They'd reached the ground by then, and Calla dropped to her knees, pressing her palms against an exposed tree root.

She closed her eyes, singing a deep, slow song. The language sounded earthier than gnomish, and Calla seemed to sink straight into the soil. The roots started twisting and twirling and sweeping aside the soil, creating a narrow tunnel that stretched underground.

Biana looked at Sophie, her eyes pleading *you first* as Calla motioned for them to follow her into the earth.

Sophie had to duck her head as she plodded into the dark tunnel, her eyes barely registering Calla's silhouette up ahead. Biana stayed close, keeping one hand on Sophie's shoulder. After several minutes of stumbling in the dark, Calla told them to hold still.

"You need to be secured," Calla said, coiling roots around their feet and waists. "The trees will carry us to Brackendale. All you must do is trust—and try not to scream."

The *not screaming* part definitely wasn't reassuring. Neither was the way Calla hummed to make the roots squeeze even tighter.

Sweat trickled down Sophie's spine and she reached for Biana's hand, glad Biana's palm felt as clammy as hers.

"Where is Brackendale?" Biana whispered.

"The one place I should not take you. But I must. It's in the Neutral Territories."

Sophie couldn't decide which was scarier: knowing she was heading somewhere Councillor Oralie had specifically warned her to stay away from, or riding Nature's Most Terrifying Tree Root Roller Coaster.

Calla sang as they traveled, and the lyrics seemed to spur the roots faster until they were tearing through the earth so fast Sophie could feel her cheeks ballooning out like a cartoon character. She did *not* want to know what things were getting stuck in her teeth. She also had no idea where they were going.

The tunnel was pitch black, and every few minutes they would stop and Calla would tangle new roots around them to change direction.

"Can you travel anywhere like this?" Sophie asked.

"Within limits. Deeper parts of the earth can only be reached by ancient root systems. And the ogres uprooted all the pathways into Ravagog—unless you believe the legends."

Sophie wanted to ask what legends Calla meant, but she could feel the roots pulling them toward the surface.

"What are we supposed to do when we get to Brackendale?" she asked.

"You will be serving as my eyes and ears. A friend of mine used to live here, but I received word that she had fled. She said the forest felt too anxious, and I need you to find out what that means."

"How can a forest be anxious?" Sophie asked—but Biana had a much better question.

"Does that mean you're not coming with us?"

"I do not think it would be wise. The whispers in the roots feel like a warning. They sing of weakness, and darkness, and some sort of unnatural tampering."

The lump in Sophie's throat made it hard to whisper, "The plague."

"It's possible," Calla agreed. "That's why I need you. The plague only harms plant life, and plant-related things. You and Biana will be able to search the forest safely."

Assuming there were no ogres running around infecting the trees. . . .

Biana must've shared Sophie's worry because she leaned closer and whispered, "I'm guessing you aren't carrying a melder?"

"I wish. But I have my Sucker Punch. And Dex's panic switch. And I can inflict. And you can turn invisible."

"I also brought you these." Calla pressed a cool, smooth crystal into each of their palms. "They'll leap you to a forest in the Forbidden Cities, should you need to make a quick getaway. I will find you there and return you to Alluveterre."

Sophie squeezed the crystal, trying to convince herself it would be enough. All they'd need is a few seconds and a beam of light and they'd be far away from any danger—they could do this!

The pep talk didn't ease her nerves nearly as much as she wanted. Especially when the roots screeched to a stop.

Calla hummed a new song and the soil parted above them, letting light stream into the tunnel, burning their eyes like laser beams.

"The roots say to follow the sun," Calla whispered.

"And you don't have any idea what we're looking for?" Biana asked.

Calla shook her head. "But I suspect you'll know it when you see it. I'll leave the tunnel open so it's easier to find when you return."

Sophie nodded, tucking her crystal into her easiest to reach pocket. Biana did the same and latched onto Sophie's hand with a death grip as they climbed the slippery soil wall and emerged into the forest.

The scene looked normal enough—mossy trees, overgrown paths, an abundance of green and brown. But something felt *wrong*.

Sophie tried to tell herself it was only her paranoia, but she still scooted closer to Biana as they shoved through the ferns and bushes.

"Bet you're wishing you hadn't gotten up to spy on me, huh?" Sophie whispered.

"Actually, I was already awake." Biana twisted her hair into a fancy knot to keep it from blowing in the damp wind. "It's hard sleeping in a strange bed."

An earth-shaking *ROAR!* drowned out Sophie's reply.

"What was that?" Sophie glanced over her shoulder, sure she'd spot some sort of hungry beast come to devour them.

Biana pointed to a high branch, where a black parrot-size bird watched over them with glittering dark eyes. "Don't worry, it's just a boobrie."

"That's seriously its name?"

"Yup. You should hear the jokes Fitz and Keefe make."

The bird's head was crowned with a yellow feather Mohawk, but its most distinct feature was its long, curled eyelashes. It looked like it should be doing a mascara commercial as it batted its eyes and let out another *ROAR!*

That was when Sophie realized what was wrong with the forest.

It didn't rustle.

Or crackle.

Or make any of the sounds trees normally made.

Other than the roaring boobrie, the whole place seemed to be holding its breath.

"Come on," Sophie said, checking the sky to make sure they were heading in the right direction. "We shouldn't spend too much time here."

They doubled their pace, chasing the sun as it curved across the horizon. Sophie tried to make a mental note of each place they rerouted around rocks or streams or overgrown patches, but she wished she had something to mark their trail.

"How much farther do you think we should walk?" Biana whispered when they stopped to catch their breath.

"How about we count to one thousand, and if we still haven't found anything, we double back on a different path?"

They counted every footfall, and at step seven hundred and ten, they curved around another rocky outcropping and froze.

"What is that?" Sophie breathed, pointing ahead to a small thicket, where one of the trees was shrouded under a dome of pure white light.

"It looks like some sort of force field," Biana whispered.

Sophie grabbed a small stone and flung it at the tree. As

soon as it touched the force field, white lightning flashed, and the stone ricocheted toward her head at ten times the speed. She barely managed to duck before it streaked past, embedding in a nearby trunk.

"I don't get it," Biana whispered, pulling Sophie behind the rocks to hide. "Why would anyone shield a tree?"

Sophie had a theory—and it wasn't good news. "I need to get a closer look."

Biana grabbed her wrist to stop her. "Do you think it's safe?"

"If someone's around, don't you think they would've checked after all that lightning?"

"True." Biana reluctantly followed Sophie to the tree, glancing over her shoulder the whole way. "I don't like this," she mumbled. "Something feels wrong."

Indeed it did—but not for the reason Biana probably meant.

Sophie had expected the shielded tree to show some sign of the plague. But it looked perfectly healthy. In fact, its leaves were a brighter green than the other trees around it, and the bark almost had a sheen.

She squatted and grabbed a handful of fallen sticks, holding them up to see if the dried leaves matched.

"What are you doing?" Biana asked.

"Trying to see if any of these are from the same tree—though it might be better to dig up a root. That way we can bring a sample back to Alluveterre and test if this tree is infected."

"But if the tree *is* infected, you'd be exposing Calla and Sior and Amisi to the plague."

Sophie dropped the stick—but she'd already touched it.

Were her hands contaminated?

"Maybe I should leap away and you can tell Calla to send someone else to get me—someone with a lot of disinfectant."

"I don't know if it's a good idea to split up," Biana said.

"Isn't that better than putting Calla at risk?"

"Of course," Biana said—though she didn't look happy about it. "But . . . we could still walk back at least part of the way together."

"I shouldn't go more than halfway, though, just to be safe."

They'd only taken a few steps when a flash of light drew their attention. A black-cloaked figure appeared a few feet away, his sleeve bearing the unmistakable white eye symbol of the Neverseen.

# NINETEEN

THE MEMBER OF THE NEVERSEEN seemed as surprised as they were, but Sophie recovered quicker. Her instincts took over, red fury rimming her vision as she pooled her anger, preparing to inflict.

"That's enough of that," the Neverseen member said, raising his hands and triggering a flash of blinding light.

Sophie charged forward, hoping to grab him before he could leap away, but Biana blocked her, shouting, "He's a Psionipath!"

The warning rang in Sophie's ears as the light solidified, encasing the cloaked figure under a glowing dome.

"He makes force fields?" Sophie asked.

"You sound impressed." He smoothed the sleeves of his black cloak and gave a bow.

Sophie knew it wouldn't work, but she grabbed a rock anyway, launching it at his head with all the strength she had.

Biana yanked them out of the way as the rock ricocheted, knocking a football-size crater in the tree they'd been standing in front of.

"You have to stop doing that," Biana said.

"I agree," the Neverseen member told them. "Those energy blasts are such a waste. And I believe this is what we call a stalemate. You can't get to me—and if I leave this shield, you'll unleash your Inflictor rage. So I'm going to stay right here, where it's nice and cozy."

Sophie turned to Biana, keeping one eye on the Psionipath. "How long before the force field wears off?"

"Long enough for someone to come to check on me," he told her.

"And there's no way to break through the force field?" Sophie whispered.

Biana shook her head. "Psionipaths created the shields that keep Atlantis livable underwater."

"Like I said"—he traced his fingers along the glowing field of white energy—"we have a stalemate. So what are you going to do?"

"More of them could show up any second," Biana whispered.

"But one of the Neverseen is *right there*—how can we just leave?" Sophie asked.

They hadn't learned what he was doing to the tree—and what if he knew what happened to Keefe's mom?

"Your Telepath tricks won't work," he said, somehow guessing what Sophie was planning.

Sophie ignored him, hoping her tweaked abilities would come through as she gathered her mental strength and reached for his mind. As soon as her consciousness hit the force field, it split into a thousand directions, like shoving her thoughts in a blender without the lid on.

The Psionipath laughed as she clutched her temples, struggling to fight through the headache. "Clearly the Black Swan forgot to give you any common sense."

Fury and frustration clouded Sophie's vision, and she fought them back, knowing she had nowhere useful to inflict them.

"Don't think I haven't realized you're not here alone," he added. "You couldn't have leaped here—our sensors would've detected it. So that leaves dwarves and gnomes, and I'm betting on a gnome. Where's your little friend hiding? Probably not close, otherwise they would've tried to help you."

"You seem to know a lot about us," Sophie said, hoping she sounded calmer than she felt.

Maybe if she egged him on, he'd slip and tell her something useful.

"How could I not?" he asked. "I've been hearing about Project Moonlark for years. How does it feel to know the sum total of your existence is to be someone else's puppet?"

"She's not a puppet," Biana spit through gritted teeth.

"No, perhaps you're right," he agreed. "I've always suspected her role would be far more sinister."

"You want to talk about sinister?" Sophie asked. "I know what you're doing here. This has to do with the plague, right?"

He snorted so loud, snot probably crusted the inside of his hood. "Is that my cue to outline our entire plan for you? Would you like names and dates, too, or just the general gist? I could also use hand puppets if you'd like, to make it more entertaining."

Okay, so maybe egging him on wasn't going to work.

But Sophie had realized something much more troubling.

He could've leaped away when they first startled him. But he *chose* to stay.

Why would he do that—unless he had a plan? And why did she have a feeling they were playing right into it?

Her feet itched to run, but if they turned their back on him, he could drop his force field and attack. And if they leaped away he could go after Calla.

"Ah, you're turning pale," he said. "I'm guessing that means you've finally realized the gravity of your situation. So what's it going to be? Run and hide? Don't think I won't find you. I know this place better than anyone. I came here all the time when I was a kid."

"Why would you be in the Neutral Territories?" Biana asked. "The only people who . . . ohhhhhhhhhhh."

"What?" Sophie asked as Biana shielded her eyes to squint through the force field.

"He went to Exillium," Biana whispered.

Sophie covered her mouth.

That would mean . . .

"Whatever you think you've figured out—you're wrong," he insisted.

But Sophie could tell by his rigid shoulders that he was lying.

"Okay, I'm done with this game," he said. "Surrender now, and save yourselves the pain I'll put you through otherwise."

"Or, we could do this," Biana said, ripping off her Black Swan pendant and flinging it toward the force field.

Sophie braced for the ricochet to blast them with a swan-shaped meteor. But when the glass of the monocle hit the force field, it refracted the light a hundred different directions, unraveling the energy shield in a burst of white flames.

The Psionipath screamed as fire licked up his cloak, and he leaped away before Sophie could charge him.

"Come on," Biana said, dragging Sophie back the way they came. "We have to get to Calla before he returns with reinforcements.

They channeled all their energy to their legs, letting it fuel their sprint. Their feet barely skimmed the ground as they raced through the forest.

Somehow Biana knew exactly where they were going, and within minutes they'd made it back to Calla.

"No time to explain," Biana shouted as they tumbled underground. "Just get us out of here."

Calla belted out a song, collapsing the tunnel's entrance as she coiled roots around them and the trees whisked them to safety.

"WHAT WERE YOU THINKING?" Mr. Forkle shouted the second they resurfaced in Alluveterre. The other four members of the Collective stood beside him, along with Fitz, Keefe, Dex, and Della.

Sophie stepped forward, ready to plead her defense—but Mr. Forkle wasn't focused on her.

"I did not give you permission to put these children in danger!" he growled at Calla.

Calla didn't blink. "I thought the only permission I needed was their own."

"Yeah, we chose to go with Calla," Biana agreed.

"And we're fine," Sophie added.

"Plus, we found something big," Biana said, giving a quick recap of their encounter.

Only then did Sophie realize the dangerous detail she'd forgotten. She backed away from Calla. "I touched those sticks—and then I let you tie the roots around me—what if I just gave you the plague?"

"Relax, Miss Foster," Mr. Forkle said. "The plague has shown no signs of being transmitted by touch. And anything outside the force field likely wouldn't have been contaminated—assuming anything was."

Calla nodded her agreement. "Do not worry over me. Our real concern is the Neverseen."

"Yeah," Keefe jumped in. "We're going after them, right?"

"*You* are not going anywhere," Mr. Forkle told him.

"But this is our chance to finally catch these jerks!" Keefe said.

"We might not get another opportunity like this," Blur agreed.

"You aren't actually considering staging an ambush?" Granite said when Mr. Forkle stroked his chin.

"There's no time to prepare," Squall added.

"Why are we arguing about this?" Keefe asked. "It's a no-brainer. They're going to come back to that tree at some point, and when they do, we blast them with everything we have."

"There will be no blasting!" Mr. Forkle told him. "And again, there is no 'we.' You kids are not a part of this. Go upstairs to your rooms. And *you*"—he wheeled on Calla—"need to explain yourself when we return."

"I can explain on the way," Calla said. "You'll need me to bring you to Brackendale."

"You can't leap," Sophie agreed. "He said something about sensors."

Mr. Forkle sighed. "Then Amisi can—"

"She doesn't know her way around as well as I do," Calla interrupted. "And she doesn't know where we were today. So you can take my help now and be angry with me later."

"All of us should be going," Keefe said.

"For the last time, Mr. Sencen, you are staying here!" Mr. Forkle snapped. "And I do not want to hear another word about it!"

"We're wasting time fighting," Sophie said, stepping between Mr. Forkle and Keefe. "Every second we delay gives the Neverseen time to prepare."

"You will not change my mind," Mr. Forkle added. "We're going. You're staying."

"What if something happens to you?" Della asked the Collective.

"If we're not back by sunrise, have Amisi alert our Proxies," Granite told her.

Sophie waited for Mr. Forkle to assure her they didn't need to worry.

Instead he said, "Upstairs. All of you!"

"Come on," she told her friends, who looked just as nervous as she felt. "There's something else we need to work on."

"It better involve studying your lessons," Mr. Forkle warned.

Sophie didn't bother replying as she dragged Keefe toward

the stairs. He fought her for a second, but eventually gave in.

No one looked at each other or spoke as they climbed to the tree houses. The only sound was the slow melody of Calla opening a new tunnel into the earth to bring the Collective to confront the Neverseen.

# TWENTY

KEEFE GLOWERED AT THE CAMP-
fire in the boys' common room, keeping his
back turned to all of his friends. "I can't believe
you went to face the Neverseen without me!"

"And me," Fitz added.

"And me," Dex said.

Both boys had very noticeably chosen beanbag chairs as far
from Sophie and Biana as the room allowed.

"We didn't know that's what we were doing," Sophie said,
holding out her arm so Della could smear ointment on a deep
scratch. "Calla only told us there were weird whispers in the
forest—and she needed us to leave right away."

"If it makes you feel any better," Biana added, uncoiling the knot in her hair and looking way too good for someone who'd just survived a showdown with their enemy. "I'm pretty sure Calla only brought me because I happened to be there."

"It's a good thing you were," Sophie told her. "You stopped me from making a ton of dangerous mistakes. And I never would've thought to throw my pendant at the force field."

Warm spots colored Biana's cheeks. "I just remembered what Fitz's note had said about the smallest things being the most dangerous and I thought . . . why not?"

"Well, it was brilliant," Sophie said. "You saved us."

Biana smiled. "Anytime."

Keefe ruined the moment by grumbling, "But you didn't learn anything! You had the Neverseen right in front of you—you *talked* to him!"

"I know," Sophie mumbled. "I tried to trick him into telling me something, but he was too smart. And when I tried to probe his mind, I couldn't push through the force field."

"I bet we could've done it together," Fitz said.

"Maybe," Sophie admitted. "I wish you could've been there."

"Me too. Don't run off like that again, okay?" he asked.

"I'll try not to." Sophie hoped his small smile meant she'd been forgiven.

"And we did learn something super important," Biana added. "The Neverseen guy we met today went to Exillium."

"Does that mean he's the Boy Who Disappeared?" Fitz asked.

"It seems like it," Sophie said. "And even if he isn't, now we might have a way to find out who he is."

"Already on it," Dex said, running toward his bedroom. He raced back a minute later holding a Dexified Imparter, with wires jutting out the corners of the small silver square.

"I put all the stolen Exillium records on here," he said, twisting the wires and tapping the screen. "We're looking for Psionipaths, right?"

Sophie nodded. "There can't be many of those, can there?"

"You'd be surprised," Della said, treating a thin scratch on Biana's cheek. "The talent can be unstable, like pyrokinesis. Not quite as dangerous, but it's one of the most common abilities among the banished."

"Well, we still know his age range *and* his special ability," Sophie said. "That will have to narrow things down. And once we figure out who he is, we'll work on finding him—assuming the Black Swan hasn't caught him already."

Dex frowned. "Looks like there's eight guys with that ability who were at Exillium at the right time. And none of them ever made it back to the Lost Cities."

"Great—so it's another dead end," Keefe said, looking like he wanted to punch something.

Sophie heard him mumble under his breath, "*He was right in front of them.*"

She wished she could make him understand how much she'd wanted to learn something about his mom. Instead, she joined Fitz and Biana, who had gathered around Dex, studying the list of eight Exillium Psionipaths. None of the names looked familiar, and they were all banished for some variation of the same reason: *proven unstable and unfit for society.* But surely there had to be something that would clue them in to which one was him.

"That does not look like an approved assignment," Mr. Forkle said, stomping into the room.

Sophie was too happy he was still alive—and safe—to care about his grumbling.

The rest of the Collective filed in behind him, all equally unharmed.

Her joy evaporated when Mr. Forkle said, "All of Brackendale is an inferno of Everblaze. The Neverseen must've torched the area after you left."

"Do you think the tree will survive in its force field?" Sophie asked.

"I suspect it was already gone," Calla said. "I searched underground most carefully and couldn't find a single root."

"So that's it?" Fitz asked.

"For the moment," Mr. Forkle said, collapsing into one of the empty beanbag boulders. "We'll find a way to alert the Council so they can extinguish the Everblaze."

A loud *THUMP!* turned everyone's heads, and they spotted Keefe shaking his fist.

"We echo your frustrations, Mr. Sencen," Mr. Forkle said.

"But punching walls is not the answer. Remember, Miss Foster has a photographic memory." He turned to Sophie. "I'm going to need to see all of your memories of the tree."

Sophie nodded, proud of herself for not fidgeting as he poked around her mind. She tried to feel his presence, but his telepathy was completely undetectable.

"The tree was healthy?" he asked after several seconds.

"I thought that was strange too," Sophie said. "I'd figured it was incubating the plague under the force field, but if that were true, the branches or leaves would've looked sickly, right?"

"One would assume," Mr. Forkle said.

"So maybe they were incubating something else." Granite glanced at the other members of the Collective before adding, "It's possible the Neverseen could be working on a cure."

"That almost makes sense," Mr. Forkle admitted. "If they develop a cure before the Council, they could use it as leverage, much the same as if they'd managed to capture the alicorns in their previous attempts."

"But how can a tree be the cure?" Dex asked.

"It could be a test subject," Blur suggested.

"Or it could be a Panakes," Calla breathed.

For a second Sophie thought Calla had said "Pancakes" and found herself picturing a tree made of fluffy griddle cakes drizzled with syrup and butter.

"What's a Panakes?" she asked.

"Nothing more than legend," Squall said.

"That is what many believe," Calla agreed. "But I've never been convinced either way. There are so many songs, all telling the same story of the Brave Ones—the Trees of Healing that grew along the shores of the Eventide River during our years in Serenvale. Some say the trees were lost when the river ran dry and we were forced to flee our homeland. Others claim they never existed beyond the stories. And still others claim the Panakes thrive today, imprisoned behind the gates of Ravagog."

"The last myth has never been confirmed by any who've visited the city," Mr. Forkle reminded her.

"Yes, but hasn't their access been severely limited?" Calla asked. "I'm not a fool. I know the possibilities are slim. But until I have proof either way, I will not completely abandon my hope."

"Do you know what the Panakes look like?" Sophie asked.

"Only my imaginings," Calla said.

"Well," Mr. Forkle said, shattering the silence that followed. "These are all certainly things we must investigate. But first, we have bigger issues."

He rose from his beanbag—which required quite a lot of thrashing and flailing—and moved to stand over Calla. "You acted without orders."

"I did," Calla agreed. "But I will not apologize."

Sophie wasn't sure if she wanted to give Calla a high five or hide her from the furious Collective.

Calla, meanwhile, remained remarkably calm. "Have you ever wondered why moonlarks do not bring their hatchlings back to their nests?"

"What does that have to do with anything?" Wraith asked.

Calla ignored his question. "They leave their hatchlings alone because they know their young need to be strong. Moonlarks face more predators than most other creatures. So even though the parents follow their eggs across the ocean and are never far away from the babies, they do not make contact, and they do not bring them to the nest. Their instincts know that if they did, they would shelter the younglings and weaken their ability to survive."

"So if I'm understanding you correctly," Granite said, "you're implying we're overprotecting our moonlark?"

"Have you put her—or her friends—to use since bringing her here?"

"It's only been a few days," Squall argued.

"And we're giving them in-depth training," Granite added.

"Plus, we'll be putting them in *major* danger when we rescue Prentice," Blur finished.

Sophie wasn't sure she loved that emphasis on "major danger." But she also knew Calla was right.

"The mission we went on today," she said, "was no different than any of the other places you've sent me with your notes and clues. How many times have I almost died?"

"All the more reason why we're taking only calculated risks," Mr. Forkle said.

"Which is what this was," Calla insisted. "You've known me for centuries. You know that endangering Sophie—or any of these children—is the last thing I would ever do. But you also must accept the reality that sometimes we're going to need their help."

Mr. Forkle walked to the fire and stared at the flames so long Sophie felt twitchy.

"Perhaps you're right," he finally said. "We have not been utilizing their talents to the full. And in light of today's developments, it's crucial we attempt to discern what the Neverseen are planning. So I think it's time we attempt Mr. Sencen's plan."

"*My* plan?" Keefe asked, looking as confused as Sophie.

Surely the Black Swan weren't implying they were going to go barreling into Ravagog.

But then she remembered that Keefe had suggested another plan—one Mr. Forkle had even said had its merits.

Mr. Forkle confirmed her suspicions when he said, "Tomorrow the three of us will pay a visit to Gethen."

# TWENTY-ONE

**W**HAT DO YOU MEAN BY 'three'?" Fitz asked the Collective. "There are five of us—six if you include my mom."

"I'm aware," Mr. Forkle said. "But I only need Miss Foster and Mr. Sencen for this."

"But I'm Sophie's Cognate!" Fitz argued.

"Cognate-in-*training*," Mr. Forkle corrected. "Besides, Miss Foster will only use her abilities *if* I decide it's safe. And Mr. Sencen is only going to be the ruse." He turned to Keefe. "You're confident you can mimic your mother's voice?"

"You have no idea how many detentions I've talked my way out of."

Mr. Forkle didn't find that as reassuring as Keefe intended. But all he said was, "Be ready at sunrise."

He met them in the bridge's gazebo the next morning, wearing a long black cloak with the Neverseen's symbol on the sleeve. To say the costume triggered panic was an understatement.

When everyone was done screaming and bracing for attack, Mr. Forkle tossed back his hood and gave Sophie and Keefe matching cloaks. Sophie's hands shook as she slipped on her costume, and she couldn't take her eyes off the sleeve, remembering all the times the same white eye had taunted her dreams.

Keefe looked just as pale, but his jaw was set with determination.

"Be safe," Della whispered, pulling them both close for a hug.

"You're sure you don't want me to come?" Fitz tried one more time.

"Yes, Mr. Vacker. But don't worry, you'll have plenty of opportunities to risk your life in the future."

The sad part was, Mr. Forkle wasn't *really* joking.

"Remember your panic switch if you need me," Dex told Sophie.

"That is very generous, Mr. Dizznee. But we're going somewhere you'll be unable to follow unless you have one of these."

Mr. Forkle pulled a grayish vial out of his cloak pocket,

and Sophie groaned when she recognized the weak glow of Candesia—one of the five unmapped stars. Sophie had endured a leap with its light once before, during an exhausting test the Black Swan put her and Keefe through to try and figure out how the Neverseen kept following them.

"It is not my first choice either, Miss Foster. But there was only one place we could think to move Gethen that the Neverseen could not easily burn."

Sophie sighed. "Underwater."

The leap felt every bit as endless as Sophie remembered, as if time had screeched to a halt, trapping them forever in the empty gray nothing. And yet, somehow it still seemed too soon when they collapsed in the soggy circle of sand. An invisible force field created a dome of air around them.

"Was this made by a Psionipath?" Sophie asked, holding up her balefire pendant to inspect the edges of the force field.

"One of the best," Mr. Forkle agreed.

"Where's our kraken buddy this time?" Keefe asked, squinting at the empty ocean.

"The water is too warm here. Last time I sent you to our northern retreat. This is our eastern hold."

Sophie shouldn't have been surprised that the Black Swan had more than one underwater hideout—or a Psionipath on their team. But it was hard to process how truly huge their organization was turning out to be.

"Am I the only one who doesn't see a prison?" Keefe asked, pacing the length of the bubble.

Mr. Forkle stomped his feet. "The prison is beneath us."

He removed a parcel from his cloak pocket, releasing a plume of stink as he unwrapped a blob of solidified black slime.

"What's that?" Sophie asked, plugging her nose to block the sour-cheese smell.

"Congealed selkie skin," Mr. Forkle said. "I've just signaled the dwarves below to take out the slice I sent them. A tredgeon will soon find the smell irresistible and create our tunnel."

Sophie had no idea what a tredgeon was, but she had a feeling it was better not to ask. Instead she said, "Does that mean the dwarves are working with us again?"

"A handful of them, yes. And they are incredibly generous to do so considering Yegor passed away yesterday."

Sophie's heart felt like it had been dunked in ice water. "He was the dwarf injured on Everest, wasn't he?"

Mr. Forkle nodded.

The fury made Sophie shake—or she thought that was the reason, until she realized the ground was shaking as well. Seconds later she noticed a giant bump racing toward them, but when she flinched back, Mr. Forkle told her, "Remain still. And make no sound."

He tossed the selkie skin to the center of their small space, just as a huge iridescent claw popped out of the sand. A second claw followed, along with way too many squirming legs and antennae and some sort of giant glowing opalescent shell.

The tredgeon gobbled up the selkie skin and burrowed back into the sand, leaving a gaping tunnel.

"Our path awaits," Mr. Forkle said.

"Isn't that thing still down there?" Sophie whispered.

"Probably. But it's perfectly harmless."

"It didn't look harmless." In fact, Sophie was pretty sure those claws would feature prominently in her nightmares.

Still, she followed Mr. Forkle into the tunnel. Every shift of the sand made her jump, anticipating a tredgeon attack.

"Easy, Foster," Keefe told her, offering her his hand.

She took it. "You're shaking. . . ."

"Uh, yeah. Giant claws could come popping out of the sand any second!"

"Honestly, have you two never seen a sand crab before?" Mr. Forkle asked.

"Teeny tiny ones I caught in the waves when my parents took me to the beach," Sophie said. "Is that what those things look like when they're bigger?"

She scratched her arms, feeling like the time she'd seen a butterfly under a microscope and deeply regretted ever letting them land on her fingers.

"Actually, tredgeons are much prettier," Mr. Forkle promised. "The dwarves esteem tredgeon carapace above any gem. King Enki's crown is carved from a single piece."

"That's . . . super gross," Keefe said.

Mr. Forkle ignored him and they moved in silence, until the tunnel brightened with flickering blue light.

"Is everyone ready?" Mr. Forkle asked.

Keefe flipped up his hood. "Bring it on."

Their plan was simple: pretend to break into the chamber, and hope Gethen believed he was being rescued. Mr. Forkle had already alerted the guards so they'd know to play along.

"There it is," Mr. Forkle whispered as a round door came into view. It looked like a giant abalone shell with swirling blotches of blue, green, and silver.

Keefe moved to the lead.

"Remember, if at any point you need to abort, cry swan song and our guards will get us out," Mr. Forkle told him.

"I can handle it," Keefe promised.

Sophie hoped that was true. The warning Mr. Forkle had given Keefe a few days earlier kept echoing through her head.

*One should never rely on their enemies to give them hope.*

"Here goes nothing," Keefe whispered, then shouted "NOW!" and rammed his shoulder against the abalone shell, slamming the door open.

The next few minutes were filled with more screams and bangs and crashes than a summer blockbuster movie. The dwarven guards made an excellent show of resisting before collapsing to the ground with defeated groans. Keefe shouted orders in his mother's voice and threw open another abalone door, revealing a thick net of dried kelp.

Sophie backed away as Mr. Forkle shattered his balefire crystal against the crackly leaves. Blue sparks showered the kindling, filling the cavern with thick, salty smoke. The fire burned hot and fast, and then it was gone. As the smoke cleared, Sophie got her first glimpse of Gethen hunched against the wall, bound, gagged, and blindfolded. His black Neverseen cloak was gone, revealing a wrinkled shirt and military-style vest. Yet he still bore the Neverseen symbol on a wide black band tied around his bicep.

"Gethen, wake up!" Keefe-as-Lady-Gisela shouted. "Time to go—someone untie him."

This was the trickiest part—the moment where everything could unravel.

Gethen had likely been trained to wait for some sort of code word in case of traps like this. And they were hoping all the excitement would have him thinking about the word. Sophie and Keefe needed to amp up the charade while Mr. Forkle plucked the code word from his mind.

Keefe shouted more commands in his mother's voice, and Sophie set to work removing Gethen's gag. The fabric was soaked with drool, and Sophie felt her stomach lurch as the slimy moisture coated her fingers. She wiped them on his wrist bonds as she removed those next, her eyes fixating on the crescent-shaped scar on Gethen's hand. The mark had been a present from the dog Gethen used the first time he tried to kidnap her, and it had faded since the last time Sophie saw it.

Why did he get to heal, when the hurt he'd caused would never go away?

She was so focused on the scar, she hadn't noticed that Keefe had come up beside her. So she jumped when he shouted, in Lady Gisela's voice, "Polaris!"

Mr. Forkle nodded at Sophie, confirming that was a word he'd found in Gethen's mind.

"Polaris," Keefe repeated. When Gethen didn't stir, he slapped Gethen's face. "Didn't you hear me? I said Polaris!"

Keefe went to hit Gethen again, but Sophie grabbed his wrist and pointed to Gethen's hand, where two fingers had begun to twitch.

"That's right," Keefe said in his mother's voice. "Wake up, we have to get out of here."

Gethen moaned and thrashed, knocking off his blindfold.

Sophie had about three seconds to celebrate their victory. Then Gethen's lips cracked with a smile as his eyes settled on her. "Sophie Foster. Just who I wanted to see."

# TWENTY-TWO

**Y**OU DIDN'T HONESTLY THINK YOU could fool me, did you?" Gethen asked, laughing as Mr. Forkle scrambled to pull Sophie away from him. "Apparently you did. That's hilarious."

He tossed his blond hair out of his face, revealing a black eye from where Sophie had Sucker Punched him during his capture. His nose also looked swollen and crooked. Sophie hoped it was broken.

Her fingers curled into a fist—ready to pummel him again—when he told her, "Thank you for untying my hands. I probably should've waited until you'd untied my feet, too."

"There's no way you can escape," Mr. Forkle said, motioning

to the fire-scarred doorway. Half a dozen dwarves stood in a tight line with melders trained on Gethen's head.

"Do I look like I'm trying to leave?" Gethen asked. "I honestly haven't minded my visit here. I do my best thinking when I can tuck my consciousness away. I only came back because I couldn't pass up a chance to chat with Miss Foster. Plus, I couldn't take another second of your charade." He turned to Keefe. "Your mother will laugh when she hears about your performance just now—though clearly some of her preparation has taken hold."

"Preparation for what?" Sophie demanded.

Gethen's smile dripped with ice. "Can't ruin the surprise. He'll find out soon enough."

"Yeah, I don't think I will, seeing as how my mom is dead."

Sophie was stunned at how calmly Keefe delivered the news—almost as stunned as Gethen was to hear it.

"Another part of the trick?" Gethen asked.

Keefe leaned closer. "You tell me. Some gnomes saw her all cut up and bleeding and being dragged into the mountains near the Lake of Blood. We're assuming the ogres had her killed because she let you get captured."

"That does sound like something King Dimitar would do," Gethen said quietly.

"You really think Lady Gisela is . . . ?" Sophie couldn't say the last word.

Gethen stared at the ceiling. "How would I know? I've spent

213

the last days locked away in my own mind. I told you I'd been trained for this." He turned to Mr. Forkle. "I feel you poking around, by the way. Your telepathy isn't nearly as clever as you think. Hers is, of course." He winked his unbruised eye at Sophie. "Too bad she doesn't know how to use it."

"I know plenty," Sophie snapped.

"STOP!" Mr. Forkle grabbed Sophie by her shoulders. "Do not—under *any* circumstances—attempt to read his mind. Do you understand me?"

"Forkle's right. I can feel too much hope coming off him." Keefe slammed Gethen into the wall and pinned him by his neck. "What were you planning to do to her?"

Gethen wheezed for breath.

"Let him go," Mr. Forkle ordered.

Keefe hesitated before he dropped him. Gethen doubled over, clutching his throat as he hacked and coughed.

"You'd make this a lot easier on yourself if you'd just answer our questions," Sophie told him. "Tell us what the Neverseen were doing in Brackendale."

"Brackendale?" Gethen asked.

"Don't play dumb. We found your stupid force field around the tree," Keefe snapped.

Gethen's brows shot up. "That is . . . unexpected."

"We also met one of your buddies," Sophie added. "He thought he was so special with his Psionipath tricks."

"He *is* special," Gethen said. "I recruited him myself."

"But he's not supposed to be taking action yet," Mr. Forkle said. "Is he?"

Gethen's eyes narrowed. "Very good. Your pathetic telepathy scraped out one secret—a worthless one you already know most of. Yes, we have many timelines. And yes, it looks like one has changed. All that means is everyone's roles will soon be much clearer."

"Why are you looking at me?" Keefe asked, backing up a step.

"Why do you sound so afraid?" Gethen countered. "Wouldn't it be nice to finally feel useful—not that you haven't had your moments. But someday you'll be more than just the wannabe rebel. Once you stop trying to impress the Black Swan's little doll."

"SHUT UP!" Keefe shouted.

"Oh, come on. Haven't you always wanted to hear that someone believes in you?" Gethen asked. "*We* do. Or rather, your mother convinced us that we should."

"Maybe we should go," Sophie said when she noticed how hard Keefe was shaking.

"Yes, I think that's a good idea," Mr. Forkle agreed.

"Not yet," Keefe said, stalking closer to Gethen. "How long have you known my mother?"

"She joined us not long after she got pregnant with you. Puts things in perspective, doesn't it? All the lies you believed. All the clues you missed. And now she could very well be gone and you'll never get to know why. Unless *I* tell you."

"You're a monster," Sophie growled.

"Said the living lab experiment. Tell me, did he spark your life and then freeze you and keep tweaking?"

"Of course not!" Mr. Forkle turned to Sophie. "Any tweaks I made to your DNA were done before your inception. I implanted your embryo *immediately*."

"Okay," Sophie said, not sure why he seemed so upset by the idea. Humans froze embryos all the time. And either way, she was still an *experiment*.

But for the first time, she didn't care.

She stalked closer. "If whatever they did to me makes it so I can stop you, it's worth it."

"You may inconvenience us occasionally," he sneered. "But you will never stop us."

"We'll see about that," Mr. Forkle told him. "She's done an excellent job keeping you distracted. And now I've found the information we came for. Looks like the next stage of your timeline will be in Merrowmarsh."

Gethen's jaw dropped.

"I can divide my consciousness," Mr. Forkle said with a smile. "One part of my mind was being rather obvious while the other slipped past and dug out what I needed. Clever enough for you?"

"It'd be more clever if you had any chance of stopping what's happening."

"There's always a way," Mr. Forkle said, dusting off his hands.

"Oh, and we'll also be removing that bludgeblot from your nails so we won't have to worry about your friends tracking you."

Gethen snorted. "There's no way to remove bludgeblot— that's why the ogres use it. Burned like the sun when they painted it on."

"Well then. I guess we'll just have to remove your nails entirely. Our Froster will be by soon to freeze them off. So I'd recommend you go back to that place you've been hiding and hope your pain receptors stop working."

Gethen shouted threats as they left, but the warnings were as empty as his sandy cell.

His final words to Keefe were the only ones with any impact.

"You're choosing the wrong side, boy. You'll regret it when you see your mother's vision realized. But then it'll be too late."

# TWENTY-THREE

"YOU GUYS DON'T LOOK SO GOOD,"
Dex said as Sophie and Keefe stumbled back
to the girls' main room. "What happened?"

Sophie didn't know where to begin as she
collapsed into the nearest chair. Keefe flopped onto the otto-
man next to her and stared at the ceiling.

They'd had to use light from Marquiseire to leap home, and
the unmapped star's glow felt like getting sliced and diced by
a shattered disco ball. But Sophie's unease had much more
to do with the fact that Calla and Blur were on their way to
Merrowmarsh—another Neutral Territory—to investigate,
while Mr. Forkle had left to get Squall so she could freeze off
Gethen's fingernails.

The latter task haunted Sophie more than the first, making the black swan pendant around her neck grow a million pounds heavier. She knew they had to stop the Neverseen from finding Gethen, but . . . wasn't what they were doing to him *torture*?

Della crouched in front of Sophie and turned Sophie's face from side to side, then squeezed Sophie's cheeks, giving her a fish face.

"What are you doing?" Sophie asked—though it came out more like "Wharyoooing?"

"Attempting to fill in for Elwin. He gave me a Sophie Survival Kit, as well as a separate list called Crazy Messes That Sophie Will Find A Way To Get Herself Into."

Sophie sighed as Della fished a huge collection of crumpled papers from her pocket, each covered in Elwin's messy writing.

"Here it is," she said after flipping through several. "Light poisoning. Symptoms include fatigue, severe dehydration, bluish tint to the gums, and glints of sparkle in the irises."

"Poisoning?" Sophie repeated. "And wait—what about my irises?"

"It means your body re-formed with light particles still in it. Not surprising considering you were leaping with the unmapped stars." Della handed Sophie a mirror. "See what I mean?"

"Great. My eyes look like alicorn poop."

Della laughed. "It is a strange effect, I'll admit. Even stranger how it makes Keefe look like a Vacker."

Della was right. The shimmer in Keefe's eyes made them look teal for some reason.

"Always wanted to be part of the family," Keefe mumbled. The sadness in his voice broke Sophie's heart.

"Are you okay?" she whispered.

Keefe shrugged and scooted away from her.

"You'll both feel better once you take Elwin's remedy." Della opened a huge medicine cabinet—which Sophie had thought was just a big shrubbery—and studied the shelves of small glass vials. There were elixirs, balms, and poultices in every color. Della handed them each a tarlike vial and one that looked a lot like snot.

Sophie uncorked the black one and took a whiff. "Ugh, this smells like Iggy burp."

"Here," Della said, giving them each a bottle of Youth. "Wash it down with this. You need it for the dehydration, anyway."

The slightly sweet water helped a little. But Sophie could still taste the burpy medicine even after she'd swallowed. And the snotty elixir tasted like a bug smoothie.

"So are you guys ever going to tell us what happened?" Biana asked. "Because I think Dex is going to explode if you don't."

"Hey, don't put it all on me," Dex argued. "If Biana twists her hands any tighter, she's going to pull off one of her fingers."

Biana blushed. "I guess we're all a little worried."

Sophie turned to Keefe. "Do you want to tell them?"

He shook his head. "You'll do a better job."

Sophie doubted that, but she did her best to sum up every-thing Gethen had said. Every word seemed to make Keefe slouch smaller.

"You know he was just saying that stuff to get in your head, right?" Fitz asked him.

"Well, mission accomplished." Keefe rubbed his temples so hard, he left red marks on his forehead. "I mean . . . according to him, she was in the Neverseen my *entire* life. That means every memory I have of her is a lie. Every. Single. One!"

Della wrapped an arm around him. "I know it's hard, Keefe—"

"Do you? Because I can't imagine any of the perfect Vackers being longtime traitors."

The silence felt painful.

"Sorry," Keefe mumbled. "It's not your fault she's evil. And don't try to defend her—there's no debating it anymore. I mean, don't you realize what this means?" His eyes darted to Sophie. "My mom was probably part of everything that went down with Jolie."

The words were a punch to the gut, and Sophie knew Keefe could tell. Jolie's journal had mentioned a woman communi-cating with her when the Neverseen tried to recruit her. She'd also mentioned a woman being there the night the Neverseen tried to force her to set fire to a human nuclear power plant. Either could've been Lady Gisela—or both.

"Do you have any theories for the 'vision' your mom had for

the future?" Sophie asked. "Or what this timeline is with the Neutral Territories?"

"Not yet. But I *will* figure it out. Do you have any fathomlethes in there?" he asked Della.

"I don't know if that's a good idea," she said.

"Why, what are fathomlethes?" Sophie asked.

"Tiny pearls we sometimes find in rare river oysters," Dex told her. "They give you *crazy* dreams, but they can also help you access your long-term memories—"

"Which is exactly what I need," Keefe jumped in. "Please?" he asked Della. "He said she's been *preparing* me. That means there have to be clues I didn't pick up on. Now that I know what to look for, I can find them."

Della sighed and took out a bottle filled with what looked like blue-green caviar. "You can have *one*," she said, removing it with tiny tongs. "And this is a one-time-only thing."

Keefe popped it into his mouth and swallowed. "How long do I have before it hits me?"

"Probably about fifteen minutes," Dex said.

"I guess that's my cue, then." Keefe waved good night and left for the boys' tree house. "Time to get some answers."

# TWENTY-FOUR

CALLA AND MR. FORKLE STILL HADN'T returned by bedtime, and even the reveriebells couldn't calm Sophie's tangled dreams. Lady Gisela's wounded face kept morphing into Gethen's as he sat chained in his cell. Squall loomed over him, and he screamed in Keefe's mom's voice. Then his fingernails turned to ice and everything splattered red.

She dragged herself out of bed at sunrise, hoping a walk by the river would clear her head. A soft song rustling through the forest caught her attention.

She raced into the trees, chasing the sound to a small clearing where she found Calla singing with her palms pressed against one of the trunks.

"You're back!" she said, startling Calla so much the poor gnome nearly fell over. "Sorry. I'm just glad you're okay. I was worried when you weren't home last night."

"We only returned an hour ago, wanting to make sure we hadn't missed anything."

"And?" Sophie pressed.

Calla slumped against the tree. "*And . . .* we found nothing. No shielded trees. No whispers of warnings in the roots. The Black Swan is moving one of Gethen's dwarven guards to keep an eye on the area, but it's possible that will only make the Neverseen change their plan."

"Do you have any idea what they're up to?"

"I don't. And *that's* what terrifies me. In all my four thousand, three hundred and twenty-nine years on this planet—"

"Four *thousand*," Sophie interrupted. "You're *four thousand, three hundred and twenty-nine* years old?" She knew the elves had indefinite lifespans, so it wasn't *that* big of a stretch to know that gnomes did too. But the number was too huge to fit in her brain.

"I believe that's the right age," Calla agreed. "Though there have been stretches where I lost count. But in all that time, I've never felt anything like the worry I felt coming from Brackendale. That's why I took such a risk to bring you and Biana to investigate. Whatever we're facing is unlike anything I've experienced. The melodies reminded me of our ancient warnings."

"Warnings?" Sophie repeated.

"Songs so old we don't even know who first sang them. They warn of a great Withering before an endless Fall. But our history holds no record of any such occurrence."

Sophie wasn't a fan of the word "endless." "But you believe there's a cure?"

Calla pressed her ear against the tree. "I believe nature always finds a way. But it also does so on its own timeline. We must hope that timeline is faster than the Neverseen, or whoever is behind this plague."

Sophie wanted to do more than hope—she wanted to act. They had to be missing something, some deeper meaning behind what Gethen had said, or some detail in the Exillium records they'd overlooked to help them find the Psionipath.

She returned to her tree house prepared to gather her friends and come up with a plan. But they'd already gathered—all except Keefe—and were waiting around the waterfall.

Dex held up a gadget that looked even crazier than his Evader. "I figured out how to break into the Lumenaria database!"

It looked like he'd wired pieces of Imparters together and shaped them into a pyramid, with six long antennas sticking out of the top point. Five were made of different metals—gold, silver, bronze, copper, and iron. And the sixth looked like a twig.

"I know the stick part is weird," Dex said, "but I needed

this thing to broadcast in all six technologies. The elves, ogres, trolls, goblins, and dwarves were easy to figure out, but I had no idea what to do for the gnomes. I tried solar-powered stuff, but it still seemed too techie. Then I saw some branches on the ground and thought, why not?"

Only Dex would decide to jab a gadget with a stick.

"You should've heard him squeal when it worked," Fitz said. "I thought a banshee had snuck into the room."

"Ignore my son," Della told Dex. "You deserve to be excited."

"Yeah, I can't believe you figured it out so fast," Biana told him.

Sophie smiled. "Dex is a genius."

Dex's grin turned supernova.

He pressed the base of the gadget, making the pyramid glow green. He had to wave it around a few times, like when humans try to search for a stronger cell phone signal, but eventually a crackly hum filled the room and a fuzzy hologram appeared.

Sophie squinted at the image. "Is that a scroll?"

"A super old one. The database is filled with them. I've just started going through. I was looking for stuff about the Wildwood Colony, but this one caught my eye because of all the smudges." He pointed to black smears covering whole paragraphs. "These runes have been blacked out, which means someone is trying to keep something secret. But they must've run low on ink because at the end it's thin enough for a few words to peek through—and if I'm reading them right, it proves the ogres have something that gives them leverage with the Council."

It took a moment for the gravity of the revelation to hit.

"So . . . you're saying the ogres have a way to control the Councillors?" Sophie asked.

"It kinda makes sense," Fitz said quietly. "Alvar's always talking about the crazy restrictions the ogres put on him when he visits Ravagog, and how none of the other creatures would get away with them."

"Right," Dex agreed. "And the really weird part is, you can see it right in the treaty—I checked. The treaties for the other species basically say, 'We will allow you to remain free because you will do whatever we tell you.' But the ogre treaty is like, 'We promise we won't use our abilities on you, or visit your cities, or ask too many questions about anything you're doing, and you're allowed to continue building weapons as long as you promise not to use them, and you can do all kinds of other dangerous things too and we won't stop you, and if we do, you have the right to declare war.' Why would the Council agree to any of that? It doesn't make sense. Until you look at this."

He twisted the gadget again, and the hologram zoomed in to part of the scroll where the ink had run thin.

Sophie squinted at the runes peeking through the faded ink. "What does it say?"

"You can't read it?" Biana asked her.

"Only if it's written in the Black Swan's code."

Mr. Forkle had taught her mind to translate their special cipher runes, which came in handy—until she needed to read anything in normal runes. Great plan, guys!

"It's hard to tell without most of the context," Dex said, "but this sentence is talking about how the ogres will retain possession of something that's clearly super important, and the word they tried to black out is 'drakostomes.'"

Sophie frowned. "That sounds like some sort of fungus."

"So it doesn't trigger any memories?" Dex asked.

His shoulders slumped when she shook her head. "I was hoping I'd say the word and the memory would click and you'd have all the answers."

Sophie sighed. "Welcome to working with the Black Swan. It's full of disappointments!"

"Or maybe the Black Swan doesn't know either," Fitz reminded them.

"Well, whatever they are, they seem to be something the Council really wants," Dex said. "And I'm guessing the Neverseen allied with the ogres because of them, probably after they realized they'd never get their hands on Silveny and Greyfell. Wouldn't that explain why the Council's gotten so weird lately? Haven't their craziest decisions happened since the ogres got involved? Then suddenly Sophie was the number one enemy and they were vowing to hunt down the Black Swan instead of the Neverseen?"

"It does explain a lot," Della agreed. "Alden and I have had *many* conversations about how the ogres have slaughtered hundreds of goblins without punishment. They also stole the gnomes' homeland—dammed up the river and starved the gnomes out. And even after the gnomes came to us for aid, the ancient Council let the ogres keep Serenvale as part of the treaty."

"I thought that was because the ogres refused to leave," Fitz said. "So the only way to force them out would've been war."

"That's true," Della agreed. "And they offered the gnomes protection in the Lost Cities—and not because they suspected how useful the gnomes would become. I've heard stories from the ancient Vackers about how stunned they were the first time the gnomes shared their harvest, and it was the gnomes who volunteered to help with other tasks. Still, the Council made the trolls return the dwarven mines they'd stolen—but in that case, the trolls needed our medicine."

"Exactly," Dex said. "And these drakostomes seem to work the opposite way. Something the Council wants—or maybe something they're afraid of—that gives the ogres the upper hand."

"But what are they?" Biana asked. "What would make the Council grant the ogres' demands?"

A question formed in Sophie's mind—one she didn't

want to ask, even after all the times the Council had sided against her.

"Do you think they have something to do with the plague?" she whispered.

"I thought of that," Dex said, "but . . . this scroll is *ollllllllld*. So if the ogres have had the drakostomes all this time, why would they suddenly be like, 'Let's use it on Wildwood!'"

Sophie didn't have an answer.

Could trying to read King Dimitar's mind have been *that* big of a deal?

"And that's all you've found about the drakostomes?" she asked.

"So far. But there's a lot to sort through." Dex tapped his gadget, shutting down the hologram. "I'll search as fast as I can. But right now I have to check each scroll one by one. I'm hoping I can make some tweaks to search by keyword or something."

"Please be careful," Della said. "It's amazing that you've been able to gain access this quickly, but doesn't that worry you? I don't mean this as an insult—you're clearly a brilliant Technopath—but doesn't it almost seem *too* easy?"

Dex flipped over the gadget to show her a tightly coiled wire. "Don't worry. This emits a signal that erases any trace of where I've been. No one will have any idea I was there."

"Assuming you haven't missed a security protocol," Della reminded him. "Let's all try not to underestimate the Council.

If these drakostomes are a crucial secret, they'll have gone to great lengths to protect it."

"She's right," Sophie said. "And we should be really careful who we tell about this—especially Calla."

If the drakostomes were related to the plague, they wouldn't just have proof that the ogres were behind it.

They'd have proof the Council knew this could happen and never warned the gnomes.

# TWENTY-FIVE

THE NEXT FEW DAYS WERE QUIET—too quiet for Sophie's liking.

The dwarf stationed in Merrowmarsh kept reporting "no change," as did Sior when he'd check in with the Collective to update them on his search for Keefe's mom with Lur and Mitya. Keefe hid in his room, searching his memories, and so far he hadn't found anything worth sharing. Even Dex didn't make any progress with his new gadget. He'd named it the Twiggler, because it seemed to grow more powerful with every stick he added. But he still couldn't make it search the scrolls any faster.

Mr. Forkle must've sensed everyone's angst, because he kept reminding them to focus on their training. The

Collective was still moving forward with their plan for rescuing Prentice.

She kept busy by working through trust exercises with Fitz, which did at least seem to be helping. By the end of the week Fitz could transmit to Sophie even when Calla had led her deep into the forest. And Sophie could feel herself needing way less concentration, even when she worked alone. She barely had to strain when she called Silveny to check on her, and the alicorn's memories were so sharp Sophie often had to remind herself she was still in her tree house.

Biana made progress as well. She could hold her vanish for so long, Sophie would forget she was in the room. But Biana couldn't figure out how to hide from Calla, and neither could Della. Calla kept explaining that she saw "glints of life"— which sounded a bit like pollen—gathering on their skin and giving them away. But they couldn't sense those glints, so they didn't know how to block them. Biana was determined to figure it out, though, and tried all kinds of crazy methods, most of which did nothing more than give her a headache.

When they weren't improving their abilities, Della insisted they learn basic fighting skills, since self-defense was a type of violence the elvin mind could tolerate. The moves weren't all that different from human martial arts. And of course Sophie's clumsy limbs refused to cooperate, while Fitz, Biana, and Dex excelled.

Sophie quickly grew tired of feeling sore and pathetic—and

even more tired of only seeing Keefe when he sulked out of his room for meals—so when Fitz, Dex, and Biana were practicing some sort of scissor-kick that would surely tear every muscle in her body, she slipped away and pounded on Keefe's bedroom door.

"I'm not leaving until you talk to me," she told him.

When Keefe finally relented, she ducked under his arm and snuck into his room.

"Um . . . wow," she whispered, stepping back to take in the full effect.

Three of his four walls had been covered floor to ceiling in scribbled-on pieces of paper, like something a serial killer would do. More notes were scattered on the floor, his desk, the bed.

"So . . . you've been busy," Sophie said carefully. "Did the fathomlethe make you remember all this?"

Keefe kicked a crumpled note under the bed. "It gave me a surge. But the rest is just me."

Sophie crossed to the most cluttered wall and squinted at his messy writing.

First day of Foxfire—where was she?
Level Four midterm gift—reason?
Why did she make them test me twice to see if
I'd manifested as a Conjurer?

Keefe kicked another crumpled note that said something about the Celestial Festival. "It's a lot to search through, y'know? Photographic memory."

Sophie nodded. She turned to the wall that sat catty-corner, where the notes seemed to be focused on his more recent memories.

> Dad's missing blue pathfinder—was it her? Where did she go?
>
> When did she rig my Sencen Crest?
>
> Was she one of Sophie and Dex's kidnappers? Did she hurt them?
>
> What is she "preparing" me for?

Sophie traced her fingers over the last note. "Can I help?"

"I don't see how. It's all about what's in *my* memories, and lucky for you, you didn't grow up in that house."

"I'm a Telepath," she reminded him. "I can search your memories and project them in a memory log. Wouldn't it be nice to have the whole picture, instead of just scraps of paper?"

Keefe ran his hands through his hair. "I don't know."

Sophie picked up a note that said: Did she ever love me?

"Please let me help," she begged.

Keefe sank onto his bed. Scraps of paper fluttered to the floor and Sophie checked the messages:

*Door on level thirty-three—where does it go?*

*Why so many books in her office—she never reads!*

*Did she ever wear the necklace I gave her?*

"Please," she whispered. "Working alone is so much harder—it's what I used to do, remember? Until *someone* forced me to include them."

One side of his mouth twitched with the hint of a smile. "Sounds like that person is a genius. Probably shockingly good-looking, too."

"Eh." She laughed when he actually looked wounded. "Oh please, you *know* you're a heartbreaker. You don't need me to tell you that."

"Hey, I have never broken any hearts."

"Maybe not intentionally. But come on. When you or Fitz start dating, there will be crying in the Foxfire halls. I bet there are girls crying now, wishing you guys hadn't left."

"Not if they've heard how awesome my mom is."

"There are still just as many Keefe fangirls, trust me. Everyone loves the bad boys."

She expected some epic Keefe teasing about her use of the word "everyone." Instead, his shoulders dropped and he asked, "So . . . you think I'm bad?"

She grabbed a note that said "The Great Gulon Incident" and handed it to him.

236

His half smile returned. "Point taken."

She brushed more notes off the bed and sat next to him. "You haven't answered my question, by the way. Will you let me help?"

Keefe stared at his ceiling. "I don't know if it's a good idea."

"Why not?"

"Let's just say my head is not an awesome place right now."

"So? I've been in Prentice's head, remember? And Fintan's. And Brant's!"

"Great. So you think I'm the same as a bunch of psychos."

"I never said that. And Prentice isn't psycho."

"Close enough. For right now."

Sophie hated that he was right. "All I meant was that nothing could shock me."

"I *seriously* doubt that."

"I don't. I've also been in Alden's mind after it shattered, remember? Shoot, I've been in an ogre's mind—though that was surprisingly soft and calm. But still. An ogre brain! And I've been in Lady Galvin's head too, when I stole the Alchemy midterm questions."

"I forgot about that. Who knew you were such a rebel?"

"I have my moments."

He almost looked proud. "But . . . now you're used to spending your days trading secrets with Captain Perfect. And I guarantee you, my mind is nothing like his."

"Who said it should be? And Fitz isn't perfect, by the way."

"He's close enough." He moved to the one wall in his room not covered in paper scraps. "I hate watching it," he whispered. "Them and Della. It's all so happy and easy."

Sophie moved to his side.

He didn't look at her as he added, "I used to wish I was a Vacker. I'd be over at their house, dreading the moment I had to go home. But nope. I'm a Sencen. And it just keeps getting worse and worse."

No words existed to make anything better. So she reached for his hand.

On the wall in front of them was a particularly small note with only three words:

Who am I?

"Easy question," she said, taking it down. "You're Keefe Sencen. Master mischief-maker. Tormenter of principals. Frequenter of Detention. And one of the best guys I know."

He raised one eyebrow as he turned to study her. "I'm not *the* best?"

"It's a three-way tie. And you're also always there when your friends need you. So how about you let one of us be there for you for a change?"

He looked away again. "You really think you can handle it?"

"Psh, I can handle anything." She usually didn't feel comfortable making such bold, confident statements. But for once it actually felt right. "Please? Don't keep doing this alone."

Keefe sighed. "Okay . . . but remember—you promised you wouldn't hate me."

"I did. And that's one promise I'll have no problem keeping."

"We'll see . . ." He looked like he wanted to say something else. Instead he turned away.

"So do you want to get started now?" she asked.

"Not really." He rubbed his eyes, and the dark circles seemed to sink deeper into his skin. "I've been up all night the last few days. And the one time I did sleep was with the fathomlethe. Dex was right about the dreams." He tangled his arms around himself and shuddered. "But I don't know if I can fall asleep."

"Well, you're never going to relax in this hive-of-crazy!"

She grabbed a handful of notes and pulled them off the nearest wall.

"Don't—"

"I'm just getting them out of sight so we can organize them. This was you working alone. Now you have me."

"I do."

Sophie couldn't tell if that was a statement or a question.

"Try to rest," she told him. "I'll be out of here as soon as I'm done cleaning up."

Keefe opened his mouth to argue but the words were swallowed by a yawn. He crawled into bed and buried his face in his pillow. Sophie resisted the urge to tease him about drooling.

It took her longer than she'd expected to de-serial-killer

his room. But by the time she'd pulled down the last note, Keefe's breathing had slowed. She listened to the rhythmic sound as she stacked the tattered pages together, wishing she could clear away his worries as easily as she could clear away the scraps.

"Sweet dreams," she whispered as she turned to leave. "You deserve them."

Keefe didn't move, and his breathing stayed steady. But when she turned off the lights, she could've sworn his lips were smiling.

"How troubled is he?" Mr. Forkle asked, giving Sophie a minor heart attack as she entered the boys' main room. He stood by the fire pit, his eyes reflecting the flickering flames.

"Mr. Sencen," he clarified. "How concerned should we be?"

"What do you mean by 'concerned'?" Sophie asked.

"You did see the state of his room just now, yes?"

Sophie looked away. "I took down all the notes, so hopefully that'll let him sleep. And he agreed to let me search his memories and record them."

Mr. Forkle traced his fingers along his chin.

"Do you think we're going to find a clue about the Neverseen in his memories?" she asked, the words so quiet she could barely hear them.

"It seems likely. No one keeps up a pretense perfectly. In fact, I've made several slips I'm stunned you didn't catch."

"Like what?" Sophie asked.

A smile was all he gave her.

"I'm also inclined to believe Gethen wasn't exaggerating about the Neverseen having plans for Mr. Sencen. He's a very talented boy. But as for whether we'll find clues . . . well . . . searching an entire lifetime is a daunting task. Either way, I'm counting on you to keep me informed of anything concerning—and by 'concerning,' I mean anything relating to our fatal flaw. You've likely heard of the concept in your human studies. Elves all bear the same one."

"Arrogance?" Sophie guessed.

"I'll pretend you didn't look at me as you said that. And that is a vice. Our fatal flaw is *guilt*. We all react to it in different ways. In Mr. Sencen's case, it appears to have set him on a quest for understanding. Such quests often end at a crossroads, and should that be the case I cannot say which path Mr. Sencen will choose."

"You realize that makes *zero* sense, right?"

He shrugged. "Let us hope it remains that way. But keep your eyes open to warning signs. And be sure to get some rest. Tomorrow will be very . . . complicated."

# TWENTY-SIX

**D**ON'T SCREAM," A DEEP VOICE told Sophie as she passed through the breakfast area on her way for another early morning river walk.

Of course she screamed—but who wouldn't scream if they found a strange figure lurking in the shadows? Especially if that figure happened to look like a giant two-legged poodle?

Curly white fur covered his body, leaving only his dark blue
s and pink lips exposed.

"W-who are you?" she whispered.

The poodle figure rubbed his furry arms. "Apparently my code name is Coiffe."

"I hope that means you're part of the Black Swan," Sophie said.

"Would I be here if I weren't?" He stepped closer and she backed up. "If I meant to harm you, Sophie, I would've grabbed you when you entered the gazebo. I had plenty of time, and I'm much stronger than you."

"Is that supposed to reassure me?"

"Yes." He scratched his shoulder, then his chest, then his arms and legs. "Argh—I swear I've picked up ichrites in this infernal fur."

"Ichrites?" Sophie asked.

"A type of insect that feeds on unicorn blood." He leaned against the post of the gazebo, rubbing his back like a bear scratching on a tree. "My involvement with the Black Swan is usually more hands off. But today I must play babysitter, so I get to be *this*." He waved his hands at his fur before going back to scratching, and Sophie got a feeling she wasn't going to be a fan of Coiffe.

"Sophie?" Dex shouted, racing down the stairs two at a time. "Are you okay? I heard you scream."

Fitz and Biana were right behind him, with Keefe a few steps farther back. They froze when they spotted Coiffe.

"Is this guy bothering you?" Fitz asked.

"*Is* that a guy?" Dex added.

"He says he's with the Black Swan," Sophie told them.

"Couldn't anyone say that?" Fitz asked.

Coiffe rolled his eyes and pulled a monocle pendant like theirs out of the curls of his fur. "Happy now?"

"Just when I thought this place couldn't get any weirder," Biana mumbled.

Dex moved closer to Coiffe and squinted at his fur. "What'd you do, mix a bunch of Curly-dew with Macho-Macho and a couple drops of Body Warmer?"

"I don't know. But I wouldn't be surprised if your father's ridiculous store was involved," Coiffe muttered. "Only Kesler Dizznee would waste time figuring out how to give someone a fur coat."

Yeah . . . Sophie definitely wasn't going to be a fan of Coiffe.

"My father is one of the most talented alchemists in our world," Dex snapped.

"He is," Coiffe agreed. "But even you must admit he gravitates toward the absurd."

"That's intentional," Sophie told him.

Kesler kept Slurps and Burps strange to make the stuck-up nobility uncomfortable.

"So wait," Keefe jumped in. "Are you naked right now? Because I think I speak for everyone when I say: Yuck."

Sophie smiled, relieved to see Keefe acting more like his old self. Shadows still darkened his eyes, but his smirk had returned with full force.

"If you must know," Coiffe snapped, "I'm wearing a bathing suit under all of this. You try wearing ten pounds of fur and see if you feel like putting a cloak on top of it—especially with the way it *tugs*. And shouldn't there be one more of you? I was told there would be six."

"There are." Della appeared next to him.

He scrambled back, tripping over the black bags piled at his feet. "Ms. Vacker. How ironic to see you among our ranks, considering the task we are about to perform."

"And what task would that be?" Della asked, not bothering to correct her name.

"Isn't it obvious?" He tossed them each one of the black bundles. "Get dressed. It's time to see if you're talented enough to break into Exile."

"This isn't the desert," Sophie said as they reappeared in a forest high in the mountains.

"How astute of you," Coiffe told her, leading them up a narrow path. A thin layer of snow had turned the mountain gray and crunchy, and Sophie snuggled deeper into her dark cloak, glad the heavy fabric was extra warm.

"Question," Keefe said after they'd climbed for several minutes. "Why do all the trees look like they want to eat us?"

He wasn't wrong. The gnarled, bulbous trunks reached for them with clawed, branchy hands, and the knots in the wood looked like eyes.

Sophie checked each one, squinting as far into the distance as she could, wondering if she'd find any with a force field.

"You okay?" Dex asked as Sophie tripped over the edge of her heavy cloak.

"Yeah. I just wish this thing fit better."

"Tell me about it." His sleeves completely covered his hands.

"Are you sure this is the right way?" she asked Coiffe as the forest thinned around them. "Last time we entered Exile through a sand pit."

"And last time you had permission to be there," Coiffe reminded her. "Do you really think you can walk in the main entrance?"

"No. But it's hard to know what's going on when no one's told us the plan," she snapped.

"That was not my decision."

They passed several more trees before Coiffe doubled back. "Finally," he said, tracing his furry fingers down a sun-bleached trunk. "It takes a keen eye to find the trail."

"Yeah, well, did those keen eyes of yours also see you just stepped in a big pile of sasquatch poop?" Keefe asked.

Coiffe muttered something about the Black Swan testing his patience as he attempted to scrape his furry foot clean. Then he led them west, counting eight trees before turning north and counting four more. They repeated the process through several more twists and turns, until they reached a tree on the edge of a slope.

It wasn't the biggest tree they'd seen, but Sophie could tell it was ancient. Its curled branches stretched toward the clouds, daring a storm to take it down.

Coiffe knocked on the lumpy trunk, making five quick thumps, two soft pats, and seven slaps in a strange rhythm.

"And now," he said, "I'm free of further responsibility."

"You're leaving?" Fitz asked as Coiffe pulled a crystal pendant from his tangled fur.

Coiffe laughed. "Surely the Champions of the Everest Ambush have no reason to fear an empty forest—though it doesn't *feel* empty, does it? Better hope whatever's nearby isn't hungry."

"He's kidding, right?" Biana asked as Coiffe glittered away.

"I'm sure he is," Della said. But she scanned the forest carefully.

"The Black Swan needs a better screening process for their helpers," Dex decided.

Sophie tucked her hands into her cloak pockets to keep them warm, and her fingers grazed the edge of Kenric's cache. She'd figured that breaking into the world's most secure prison was the kind of place where it might be smart to have a powerful bargaining chip.

"Anyone have any theories on where we are?" Fitz asked. "I'm guessing somewhere human, since I don't see any Pures."

The Pures were palmlike trees with fan-shaped leaves that filtered any pollutants out of the air. Every elvin city and manor had at least one.

Sophie hoped they were in a Neutral Territory and continued scanning the forest for any trace of the Psionipath. But something about the tree Coiffe had chosen felt familiar, and after a moment she remembered where she'd seen it.

"I think we're in California," she said, "and one of these trees—maybe even this one—is the Methuselah. Humans think it's the oldest living thing on the planet. But clearly they've never met Bronte."

"Ha! Good one, Foster," Keefe told her. "How old is the Miss-use-a-what-a tree?"

"Methuselah," Sophie corrected. "And something like forty-seven hundred years."

Fitz whistled. "That *might* be older than Bronte. But not older than Fallon Vacker, our great-great-great-great-great-great-great-great-great-great-great-great-great-great-great-great-great-great-great-grandfather. He's one of the three founding members of the Council, and served for about a thousand years, before he fell in love with my great-great-great-great—"

"Yeah yeah, your really old grandma," Dex interrupted. "We get it. You guys have lots of super-old, super-important relatives. Whoop-de-do."

"Uh, the Vacker legacy is one of a kind," Fitz snapped back.

"Why is that?" Sophie asked, making Dex grin. "I mean, I know the Vackers are legendary—but what I don't get is . . . if all elves have an indefinite lifespan, doesn't everyone have a bunch of super-old, super-important, pointy-eared relatives?"

"Ancient, yes," Della agreed. "But as Fitz said, the original Council was only three members. And they added Emissaries much later. So for a long time only a handful of elves were classified as nobility. Hence the Vacker legacy. It can be quite intimidating, actually. That's why I initially rejected your father's advances. I wasn't sure I wanted that kind of scrutiny."

"Ugh, can we please not talk about you and dad and *advances*?" Fitz asked.

"Seriously," Biana agreed.

"You mean you don't want me to tell you about the first time your father kissed me?" Della teased, laughing as she pulled her children into a squirmy hug.

Keefe looked away.

"So," Sophie said, changing the subject for him, "do you think the tree is supposed to *do* something? We've been standing here for a pretty long time and nothing's happened."

"That's because you haven't been paying attention," Calla said, leaping from the top branches and landing gracefully on her toes.

"Looks like those old bones still have some spring in them," another gnome said, emerging from among the tree's roots. It took Sophie a second to recognize her as Amisi, the other gnome who lived at Alluveterre.

"Sorry we couldn't bring you here ourselves," Calla told them. "It took longer than expected to gather the others."

"Others?" Sophie asked.

Four gnomes Sophie didn't recognize appeared among the branches.

"What are we all doing here?" Della asked as the newest gnomes leaped to the ground.

"Waiting for us."

They spun around to find Mr. Forkle and Squall marching up behind them. Wraith appeared soon after, followed by Blur.

Granite arrived a few moments after. "Sorry I'm late. King Enki was still perfecting the carvings." He held up six sleek black pendants cut with jagged facets.

*Magsidian.*

Only dwarves could mine the rare mineral, and the dwarven guards in Exile could sense its presence—or lack thereof—and determine if someone had permission to be there. The stone also changed its power depending on how it had been cut. Sophie had seen it draw water from the air, affect the pull of a compass, and create special beams of light. But she'd never seen Magsidian cut so sharply.

Granite passed the pendants to Sophie, Fitz, Dex, Keefe, Biana, and Della.

"You guys don't need them?" Sophie asked, noting that the Collective members also weren't wearing heavy cloaks.

"We have other protections," Mr. Forkle said. "Has everyone been introduced?"

"Sorry, I got distracted," Calla said. "This is Brier, Kloris, Nesrin, and Vered."

"I thought we needed nine," Granite said.

Calla twiddled her thumbs. "This was the best I could gather. After what happened in the Strixian Plains—"

"What happened in the Strixian Plains?" Sophie interrupted.

"That's another Neutral Territory, isn't it?" Della added.

"Yes," Mr. Forkle said, through a sigh that made his shoulders slump. "It's where a family of gnomes recently contracted the plague."

"We thought it would be best to inform you after today's mission," Granite said when they all shouted "WHAT?"

"We needed to make sure your minds were focused," Wraith added.

"So you've been lying to us?" Dex asked.

"Not *lying*. Withholding," Mr. Forkle corrected. "And you're overestimating the gravity of this news. Only one more family of gnomes has been added to the quarantine in Lumenaria."

"Yeah, but it means the plague is spreading," Sophie argued. "That's how it turns into a full-fledged outbreak."

"That's what many of the gnomes I spoke to today feared as well," Calla whispered.

Mr. Forkle rubbed his temples. "I do not have to check your thoughts to know you're angry with me, Miss Foster. And I understand everyone's worries. But chasing clues about this plague is like chasing the wind. The only way to gain control is to get ahead of it—which is something we *are* working on. In the meantime, we can't ignore other important matters, like what we're here to achieve. We know Prentice is hiding something. Perhaps it relates to some of these problems. But even if it doesn't, we are freeing him *today*. All our surveillance indicates that this is our best chance. A group of additional dwarven guards arrives tomorrow. So please set your emotions aside and prepare yourselves for the mission." He turned to Calla. "The six of you can hold the tunnel?"

"Our voices are strong," she agreed.

The gnomes spread out, forming a circle around the old tree as they sang a slow song. The tree swayed as the roots twisted and tightened. Dirt, rocks, and debris were swept aside until a burrowlike opening appeared.

"Vered will keep the exit open," Calla told them as all but one gnome scurried into the dark tunnel.

The Collective followed the gnomes.

Sophie glanced at her friends, wondering how they felt about risking their lives when the Collective had just admitted to lying to them.

"Come on," Fitz said. "Let's go get Prentice."

# TWENTY-SEVEN

**A**NYONE ELSE THINK IT WOULD be easier to just carry Foster?" Keefe asked as Fitz caught Sophie from falling for what had to be the two-billionth time.

In her defense, it was dark, and the roots under their feet kept shifting—but still. Couldn't the Black Swan have given her a *little* more coordination when they tweaked her genes?

"Any reason we're not letting the roots drag us along this time?" Sophie asked.

"Roots this ancient do not hold the same strength," Calla explained. "We're saving their energy for our escape."

The tunnel narrowed as they sank further into the earth, forcing them to walk single file.

"Couldn't we at least have more than one balefire pendant lighting up this place?" Dex called from the back.

"This tree has been generous enough to lend us its strength," Mr. Forkle told them. "The least we can do is try not to bother it."

"You also don't want to see what's crawling around us," Blur said.

Something rustled near Sophie and she decided to take his word for it.

She counted her steps, and each time she reached about ten thousand, one of the gnomes stayed behind to ensure the song kept the tunnel open.

"It won't be long now," Mr. Forkle said when Calla was the only gnome left journeying with them. "And once we're inside, a small team of us will go after Prentice. The rest of you will be in charge of causing as much chaos as you can generate. Squall, Blur, and Mr. Sencen will head to the most unruly residents. Between your various abilities, you should be able to get them sufficiently riled up. Just be sure to stay on the move so the dwarves don't catch you."

"Meanwhile, I'll take Della and Biana," Wraith said, "and we'll head for the main entrance. We want to look like we're fleeing, so they divert other patrols to prevent our escape."

"Does that mean we shouldn't vanish as we run?" Biana asked.

"Only intermittently," Wraith said. "We need to ensure they

follow us—but also not give away that it's our intention. And once we reach the Room Where Chances Are Lost, we'll vanish completely and hold for Mr. Forkle's signal."

"For the record," Keefe told Biana, "my job sounds way better."

"But they are both equally important," Mr. Forkle said. "Our hope is that all of your efforts will create enough of a distraction for Sophie to lead the rest of us to Prentice. Mr. Dizznee will then be in charge of opening his cell, and Granite and I will tend to Prentice and signal when we're ready to leave."

"What about me?" Fitz asked. "It doesn't sound like I'm doing anything."

Dex laughed at that, but fell silent when Granite said, "You're here for Sophie. She will need someone to lean on, to keep her calm and boost her strength while she tackles our most difficult task."

"And what is that?" Sophie asked.

Mr. Forkle cleared his throat. "Prentice has been moved to one of the adjuncts, and we've been unable to determine precisely which one. Imagine the main prison as a spiral, with smaller spirals branching off the outermost edge. The adjuncts have been added over the centuries to house the special cases."

"He means the most dangerous cases," Granite clarified. "Another reason we will not want to choose the wrong one."

"How many adjuncts are there?" Fitz asked.

"We have no idea," Squall admitted. "There are no blueprints for Exile."

"So how do I . . . ," Sophie started to ask. But then she knew.

"Whoa, let's not add projectile vomiting to the list of Awesome Things We Get To Do Today," Keefe said, clutching his stomach.

"Sorry," she whispered, but she couldn't fight back the nausea.

"What are you guys forcing her to do?" Dex asked.

"We're not *forcing* her to do anything," Mr. Forkle said. "But we are *asking* her to track Prentice's thoughts."

"You mean like what she does when we play base quest?" Biana asked.

Sophie nodded. She had the rare ability to follow someone's thoughts to their source. It was how she'd found Silveny, and why her team always won in their games.

"Why is that so bad?" Biana asked.

"It's not," Sophie tried to tell herself. "It's just going to be . . . intense."

"You have to open your mind to *all* the thoughts," Fitz guessed.

"Yeah, until I can lock in on his."

"And how many prisoners are in Exile?" Fitz asked the Collective.

"Last reported count showed five hundred and eleven," Mr. Forkle said quietly.

"Dude," Keefe breathed. "And these are all psychopathic murderers and stuff? Yeah, never mind, that is definitely vomit worthy, Foster. Panic away."

"Is there any way I can help?" Fitz asked.

"Too many broken minds," Sophie reminded him. "I'm the only one who won't get dragged under."

"She's right," Granite agreed. "But we'll still support her any way we can."

The promise sounded as empty as the tunnel ahead.

"Is everyone clear on what they need to do?" Granite asked.

"Uh, did I miss the part where you told us how we're getting out of here?" Keefe asked.

"We leave the same way we came in," Blur said. "Unless the worst should happen. Then you use those pendants we gave you to create a unique path of light and leap away."

"Why don't we just do that in the first place?" Keefe asked. "That sounds way more awesome than carrying Prentice through a tunnel with angry dwarves chasing us."

"I can assure you, it isn't," Mr. Forkle told him. "The Council has added a new force field around Exile, designed to pulverize anyone trying to leap through. The cloaks you're wearing will dissolve into a protective coating, but the leap will still take a large toll. So only use your pendants if we're captured."

"Then why aren't you wearing them too?" Biana asked.

Several seconds passed before Mr. Forkle said, "We will

foolishly be viewed as the more important targets. Our surrender would give you a chance to leap away."

"WHAT?" Sophie and her friends shouted together.

"Don't look so afraid," Granite said. "This is only a last
resort. But *if* it comes to that . . ."

"This is crazy," Della said after a stunned silence. "You
should've sent lower members of the order to help us."

"And make the Council's mistake?" Mr. Forkle asked.
"No, I think not. The centuries they've spent delegating
responsibilities to their Emissaries have made them lose touch
with the realities of our world."

"Leaders must *lead*," Granite agreed.

"But aren't you worried about what secrets they'll learn if
you're captured?" Fitz asked.

"We're prepared," Mr. Forkle said.

All five of the Collective held up their hands, revealing
identical black-banded rings.

"They have poison in them," Sophie guessed.

Mr. Forkle nodded. "But it only erases our memories."

"Duuuuuude. You guys need some better planning skills,"
Keefe said. "How about—"

"There will be no amending the plan," Mr. Forkle interrupted. "But we do need all of you to promise that you will
respect our wishes."

"You seriously expect us to just leave you?" Sophie asked.

Mr. Forkle's voice filled her mind. *You think the Black Swan*

*cannot function without us—but you're wrong. Our Proxies would*
*handle things until you five are ready.*

It was the second time he'd mentioned Proxies, and she
wasn't entirely sure she knew what he meant, but she was
more nervous about the last part of the statement.

*Yes,* he told her as an impossible thought started to form.
*That is our eventual hope.*

*Are you reading my mind?!*

*These are not normal circumstances.*

He was right about that.

Five members of the Collective.

Five of her and her friends.

*But . . . we're just kids,* she thought.

*For the moment, yes. But we are talking about the future.*

*You really think we'll still need a Black Swan that many years*
*from now?*

*Yes. I believe we will always need a Black Swan. The world has*
*gotten too complicated to leave any one group solely in charge. There*
*needs to be a system of checks and balances. We do hope to someday*
*work hand in hand with the Council. But even if that never hap-*
*pens, we should be there to keep them honest.*

"So, are we all in agreement?" he asked out loud.

No one said yes, but no one argued.

They marched in silence the rest of the way, until they
reached a web of roots. Calla pulled a specific thread and the
whole web unraveled, revealing a wooden door.

"It begins now," Mr. Forkle said as Calla removed a pouch from her pocket. Sophie smelled anise, saffron, and something smokier as Calla sprinkled them each with dried leaves.

"These herbs are the gnomes' version of magsidian," Granite explained. "Hopefully the dwarves will scent them and assume we're here for a food delivery. It will not buy us long, but it should give us a few precious minutes."

"From this moment on the mission begins," Mr. Forkle said. "Trust yourselves. Let your talents aid you. And above all, remember your promises."

Sophie remembered her promise all right—but she'd silently made a new one.

She was getting everyone safely out of Exile, no matter what.

# TWENTY-EIGHT

SOPHIE HAD FORGOTTEN THE SHARP, bitter smell of Exile. But this time there was an underlying sourness, masked by something artificially sterile—as if the whole place were a carelessly bandaged wound, oozing beneath the surface.

The hallway they'd entered was plain, cold metal. No windows, no doors, and thankfully no blaring alarms or guards. Mr. Forkle closed the door behind them and it vanished seamlessly.

"That was supposed to happen, right?" Keefe asked. "Because it feels like we just got locked in."

His voice was barely a whisper, but the sound felt like a T. rex roaring. Sophie remembered Exile being filled with muffled moans. But she heard nothing except the rush of their hurried breathing.

"We must not linger in the somnatorium," Granite warned. "These prisoners are the irredeemable cases, brought here for permanent sleep."

"So . . . basically they're dead," Sophie said.

"If you want to see it that way," Blur told her. "But they're also very much alive, which is what keeps the guilt from shattering the Councillors' minds. It's also why we need to move quickly. We shouldn't test the thoroughness of the sedatives."

Sophie wasn't sure the whole sedate-the-evil-people plan sounded all that solid—but what did she want the Council to do? Kill them?

"That light up ahead is the main corridor of Exile," Mr. Forkle told them. "That's where we must separate. I'd also advise you to keep your eyes on the floor from here on out."

Sophie had used that trick last time, avoiding any glimpse through the porthole windows into the cells. But she was determined to face whatever waited for her.

"What's so scary about—" Keefe started to ask. Then a face slammed against the glass.

The ogre's lumpy skin was so swollen that it could barely open its eyes—and yet, the glare it fixed on them burned with rage as it licked its bloody teeth.

"Oooooooooooooookay, looking down now," Keefe whispered,

pressing his chin into his neck. "So . . . are we going to be messing with creepy dudes like that?"

"Worse," Blur said, clapping Keefe on the back. "Welcome to the land of monsters."

*And Prentice,* Sophie thought.

One weak star, tucked among the suffocating darkness. She wondered if any other innocents were trapped in these metal cages.

"Your group goes that way," Mr. Forkle told Blur, pointing to the left as the hall forked.

"Come on," Blur told Keefe and Squall. "Time to see who can cause the most chaos."

"Well . . . when you put it *that* way!" Keefe rubbed his hands together.

"Please be careful," Sophie begged.

"There you go caring about me again, Foster. Your fan club is going to get jealous."

He zipped away with the others before anyone could respond.

Granite pointed down the opposite path. "The Room Where Chances Are Lost is that way. Avoid the adjuncts and the hall will dead-end there."

Wraith and Biana turned to leave, but Della hesitated.

"I'll be fine, Mom," Fitz promised. "Just take care of yourself—and Biana."

Della strangled him with a hug and pulled Sophie and Dex in. "Take care of each other."

"We will," they promised.

Della held them a second longer, then took Biana's hand and they ran after Wraith, vanishing down the hall.

"I guess that means I'm up," Sophie whispered.

She leaned against the wall to hold herself steady, then gasped as a shock of cold stabbed through her cloak.

"A Froster froze the walls," Mr. Forkle explained. "After Fintan, the Council is not taking any chances with excess heat."

"Is there a Pyrokinetic here?" Sophie asked.

"Two," Granite said.

Sophie hoped her path to Prentice kept her far away.

"Here," Fitz said as she tried to lean against the freezing wall again. "Lean on me—that's what I'm here for."

Sophie doubted the Black Swan had meant it quite so literally. But he was much warmer than the wall. Fitz wrapped his arms around her shoulders, and Sophie was grateful Keefe wasn't there to feel her mood shift—though she was proud that her heart kept an even tempo, even when Fitz leaned closer and whispered, "You can do this."

She pinned the words in her mind, saving them in case she needed them later.

*Three . . .*

*Two . . .*

*One.*

She spread out her consciousness, and hundreds of voices rampaged into her brain.

*Just take it one mind at a time*, she told herself as their thoughts scraped and clawed at her defenses like wild animals. She concentrated on the nearest memory.

*A starved, rabid troll chased two teenagers through a lonely forest. The teens were fast, and for a second it looked like they might get away. Then the troll was on top of them, raising its clawed hands over their stomachs and—*

Sophie shoved the memory away.

She'd thought she understood what evil looked like—but clearly she'd only experienced the PG version. The uncensored director's cut was a thousand times worse.

Every memory she searched was madness and mayhem, blood and gore, death and destruction. It didn't matter what species they were—though the ogres' minds were surprisingly the most bearable, their hidden thoughts like sticky spiderwebs.

"You okay, Sophie?" Fitz asked.

"They're so awful," she whispered. "I can't . . ."

"Yes you can," he told her. "You're stronger than them."

Maybe she was. But she needed something *good* to cling to.

"I need a happy story," she said. "Something that always makes you feel confident."

"Okay. Um . . . Gah—I'm drawing a blank."

"I'll do it," Dex offered.

"No wait—I've got it! When I was five, my dad brought me

with him to pick Alvar up after he'd been descryed. I'd been so jealous, since Councillor Terik was making a huge exception to his no-descrying policy just for my brother. But when we got to Councillor Terik's castle he offered to descry me, too. It was the best surprise ever. And then he told me I'd grow up to become an even more powerful Telepath than my dad, and . . . that was the first time I ever thought I could be special. It made me feel unstoppable. And you're a thousand times more talented than I am, Sophie. I *know* you can do this."

Sophie stacked his words into a wall, and the violent noise seemed to dim, clearing her head enough to think.

The last time she'd been in Prentice's mind, he'd responded when she'd transmitted her name. She tried that again, powering the words with the last of her mental strength.

Agonizing seconds slipped past, but eventually she caught a faint whisper through the darkness.

*Swan song.*

"I found him!" She pointed the way Della, Biana, and Wraith had gone.

"You're sure?" Mr. Forkle asked. "It's strange that they would place him near the exit."

Sophie checked again, and the sound was definitely coming from that direction. But Prentice's voice was slipping away.

She took off running.

Dex caught up with her first, "You okay?"

"I've been better," she said as the path forked, and she

turned down the narrower hall. No one questioned her, even as the hall shrank with each curve of the spiral.

The third turn led them to another fork.

"An adjunct within an adjunct?" Granite asked. "How is that even possible?"

"One path goes up to higher ground." Mr. Forkle turned to Sophie. "Which way?"

Sophie listened for Prentice, but his ghostly voice had gone silent. She transmitted her name again, and when he didn't respond, she tried *Black Swan! Follow the pretty bird across the sky! Wylie!*

The last word brought him back.

"Left," Sophie said, taking the path that went up.

"Why would they want him closer to the surface?" Mr. Forkle asked Granite as they followed. "That seems illogical."

"Perhaps there was no more room for additions. Or—"

A groaning alarm drowned out the rest of Granite's sentence.

Sirens rumbled and croaked, reminding Sophie of a didgeridoo.

"Sounds like they know we're here!" Mr. Forkle shouted.

Their run turned to a sprint, leaving them breathless as the hallway widened again. Sophie could feel Prentice ahead, each step turning his presence warmer.

Warmer.

WARMER.

"There," she said, dashing up a flight of stairs.

They dead-ended in an unmarked silver door and Dex set to work on the enormous padlock.

"This is different than the one you gave me to practice on," he grumbled.

"But you can open it?" Granite asked.

"I hope so."

"How are you feeling?" Fitz asked Sophie as she shivered against the frozen wall. "Have you blocked out the voices?"

She rubbed her throbbing head. "Some are a little too strong right now."

"Then let me give your mind a boost." Fitz reached for her temples, and as soon as his fingers touched her skin, a burst of energy rushed into her consciousness. It felt like her brain had guzzled about fifty of Elwin's healing elixirs and then got showered with caffeine.

"Is that better?" he asked, his hands shaking as he lowered them.

Sophie nodded. "What did you just do?"

"He shared his mental energy," Mr. Forkle said. "Impressive, Mr. Vacker."

Fitz blushed. "I've been practicing."

"Got it!" Dex shouted, and they all spun toward the door.

Something passed between Granite and Mr. Forkle then, a look equal parts fear and hope as they pulled open Prentice's cell.

The room was massive—easily as big as Sophie's bedroom

at Havenfield, which took up the entire third floor of the house. And it was empty, save for a large bubble of glass in the center, lit by silvery spotlights. Curled on the floor inside, lying on a thin blanket, was Prentice. His dark skin glistened with sweat and his hair was a tangled, matted mess. Drool streamed from his lips as he whispered words they couldn't hear.

"Is there a way in?" Sophie asked as Dex placed his palms against the bubble.

"I don't know. This glass feels solid. But there has to be a door."

"Perhaps underneath?" Mr. Forkle suggested.

Dex dropped to his knees and put his ear against the floor.

The room made Sophie's nerves prickle. Why waste all this space if they were going to keep Prentice locked in a bubble? And why was the ceiling a web of roots and wires and metal rods? Everything else in Exile was solid metal, to prevent anyone from tunneling in.

And now that she was thinking about it, hadn't the Collective said that today was some sort of special day, before extra security arrived?

"I can't figure out how this stupid cage works!" Dex shouted over the still blaring alarm. "It's like they designed it specifically to resist Technopaths. But don't worry, I came prepared." He pulled open the left side of his cloak to reveal a half-dozen small metal cubes strapped to his chest. "I wasn't sure what we'd need, so each of these does something different. And at least two of them should be able to shatter the glass."

"Wouldn't Prentice get speared by the raining shards?" Fitz asked.

"Perhaps we could shield him using telekinesis," Granite said to Mr. Forkle.

"I do not like leaving so much to chance," Mr. Forkle said.

Sophie shook her head, no longer able to ignore the prickles. "This is wrong. It has to be a trick."

"Finally, someone who sees wisdom," a voice said behind them.

The alarm went silent as they turned to face all twelve Councillors, blocking their only escape.

# TWENTY-NINE

**S**URRENDER IS YOUR ONLY OPTION," Councillor Emery told them, his eyes looking as dark as his skin and hair.

Once upon a time, Sophie had counted the spokesman for the Council among her advocates. But she heard no trace of compassion in his velvet voice.

"We designed this trap most carefully," he said. "Nothing was missed—including your inflicting ability, Miss Foster."

Sophie unclenched her fists, but held fast to the frenzy she'd been brewing. "How are you going to stop me?"

"Councillor Bronte will. Should you attempt to inflict, he will be *obligated* to respond. And we are confident his power will overshadow yours."

Several Councillors nodded, though a few looked apologetic. Surprisingly, Bronte fell into the latter category.

For months the sharp-featured, pointy-eared Councillor had fought to make Sophie's life miserable. But something had changed between them, and now she believed Bronte when he traced a hand across his cropped hair and said, "I am bound by my oath. If forced, I must protect the Council, regardless of how distasteful it may be."

"*Distasteful,*" Councillor Alina scoffed. "Look around you, Bronte. These children were attempting to steal a prisoner from *Exile!*"

"A prisoner you should've pardoned weeks ago," Fitz argued.

Councillor Alina sighed as she tucked her wavy, caramel-colored hair behind her ear. "Clearly this is your mother's influence, Mr. Vacker. She's hiding here somewhere, isn't she? Don't worry. We'll find her."

It was no secret that Councillor Alina had tried to stop Alden and Della's wedding, begging Alden to marry her instead. Alden had dodged a bullet there—though she hadn't been as bad when she was principal of Foxfire. The power of being a Councillor had gone to her head.

"I feel you trying to invade my mind, Emery," Mr. Forkle said. "Having any luck?"

"Enjoy your last moments of anonymity," Councillor Emery told him. "They will soon end rather dramatically."

"Perhaps." Mr. Forkle twirled the ring on his finger, and terror boiled through Sophie.

*Not yet,* he transmitted. *All is not lost yet.*

He must've sent Dex and Fitz the same message, because they both straightened, neither looking particularly reassured.

"We knew you would use Miss Foster to rescue your associate," Councillor Emery told them, "and we knew we could leak enough information to draw them here today. But I must say, we never imagined you'd be foolish enough to come along."

"I could say the same for you," Granite told him. "All twelve Councillors out on a mission—and without their goblins?"

"Our bodyguards exist to make our opponents underestimate us. But you do not look properly intimidated." Councillor Emery glanced over his shoulder. "Would you mind, Clarette?"

A bronze-skinned Councillor stepped forward, her silky black hair swaying with each swish of her hips. She reminded Sophie of a volcano goddess, and the comparison made Sophie brace for some sort of earthquake. But all Clarette did was part her lips.

The sound that came out wasn't elvin or human. Sophie wasn't entirely sure it was earthly. The clicks and chatters and flutters sounded like a dolphin crying as a million dragonflies attacked.

"That's it?" Dex asked. "That's . . ."

His voice trailed off as the ceiling rumbled.

Mr. Forkle pulled Sophie to his side while Granite grabbed Dex and Fitz. The five of them barely got out of the way before a dozen massive boulders crashed into the room.

No—not boulders.

Boulders couldn't uncoil, or stretch eight feet tall, towering over them with hundreds of writhing legs.

"Arthropleura," Councillor Emery said. "Remarkable, aren't they?"

Sophie remembered learning about the giant, supposedly extinct arthropods in her human science classes. "I think they're plant eaters," she told her friends.

"True," Councillor Emery agreed. "But that doesn't mean they're defenseless."

He pointed to the long antennae jutting off the creatures' heads. The ends had forked points, glistening with some sort of clear slime.

Councillor Clarette clicked again, making all the arthropleura drop to a ready-to-pounce position.

"Polyglots," Mr. Forkle grumbled.

Sophie met his eyes.

*No, you cannot control these creatures,* he transmitted. *Clarette is arguably the most powerful Polyglot our world has known—and has hundreds of years of practice.*

"And this is merely one of our defenses," Councillor Emery warned.

Sophie studied each of the Councillors, realizing how little she knew about many of them. She didn't even know most of their names, much less their special abilities. But it seemed safe to assume they were all absurdly powerful.

*It's time for you to use your emergency pendant,* Mr. Forkle told her.

*I'm not going to abandon you—*

*Yes, you are! I have no intention of surrendering, but I can't have you here for the fight. I'm ordering Dex and Fitz to do the same.*

*What about Keefe, Biana, and Della?* she asked.

Almost on cue, Councillor Emery turned toward the doorway. "It looks like the rest of your group has arrived."

The line of Councillors parted to allow Squall, Blur, Wraith, Della, Biana, and Keefe to march into the room, followed by a group of dwarves. Keefe's eyes went right to Sophie, and she could see the panic he was trying to hide. Even more troubling was the state of his cloak. Huge chunks of fabric were missing, along with one of the sleeves. Sophie doubted there was enough left to protect him in a leap. Worse still: Della and Biana no longer had their escape pendants.

*I'll find a way to spare them,* Mr. Forkle transmitted. *You must leave—now!*

*I'm not leaving my friends!*

Biana screamed as one of the arthropleura hissed at her.

Keefe pulled Biana behind him. "Yo guys, I hate to break it to you, but giant bugs are so last year. All the cool villains are threatening with ogres now."

"*We* are not the villains," Emery snapped.

"Are you sure?" Granite asked. "Threatening children seems rather villainous to me. As does leaving a damaged prisoner in a cell without so much as a bed."

"Brave words coming from a talking rock," Councillor Alina said. "Do you honestly expect us to take you seriously in those disguises?"

"We do indeed," Squall said, tilting her frozen head.

All twelve Councillors' circlets crusted with hoarfrost.

"We can do tricks too," a female Councillor said, holding out her hands. Electricity sparked from the edges of her fingertips, tiny lightning bolts filling the air with static.

"You're not honestly going to electrocute us, are you, Zarina?" Mr. Forkle asked.

"There are different levels of shock." She made the air crackle until their hair stood on end.

*LEAP AWAY NOW!* Mr. Forkle screamed in Sophie's mind.

But Sophie wasn't going anywhere.

She let the fury in her heart swell and surge, filling her with a rush of churning energy. She didn't care if Bronte would inflict on her, she could handle the pain. She could—

"RUN!" Dex shouted, flinging a copper cube into the line of Councillors.

The gadget exploded in a mist of green, putrid smoke that burned like rotten jalapeños. The Councillors hacked and wheezed, and the arthropleura scattered as Dex charged into

276

the fray, hurling a second gadget that filled the room with loud squawking.

Dex yelled something to Sophie, but she couldn't make out all the words as he placed a third cube in the center of the room and scrambled toward her. Blinking lights in the corners flashed like a countdown, but before it reached its end, Councillor Zarina zapped it with her lightning.

She probably meant to fry the circuits and shut the device down, but the gadget absorbed the power instead. The metal turned red-hot and the lights on the gadget started flashing and beeping a whole lot crazier as smoke curled out of the top.

"EVERYBODY GET DOWN!" Dex screamed.

The room was too loud to hear him—too many other things happening. The only person who noticed was Fitz.

He lunged for the cube, grabbing it with a yelp of pain as he raced for the door and flung it away. The gadget launched into the hall—but even with the distance, the explosion flung Fitz backward. He flew several feet before crashing down, right on the antenna of a charging arthropleura.

Sophie screamed as the barb pierced Fitz's chest and snapped off clean. He crumpled to the floor in a convulsing heap.

# THIRTY

S TOP!" SOPHIE YELLED, BARELY REC-
ognizing her voice.

The room fell silent—even Dex's gadget stopped
wailing—as those who hadn't seen Fitz's fall took
in the carnage.

Sophie hurdled the wounded arthropleura and dropped
to her knees at Fitz's side. Dex had beaten her there, and his
hands were pressed on Fitz's chest trying to stop the bleeding.

"What happened?" Della asked, fighting her way to her son.
Her skin turned ghostly pale when she saw how painfully still
Fitz was.

"It was an accident," Councillor Zarina said. "He—I—"

"It was my fault," Dex mumbled.

Della removed her cloak and draped it around Fitz. "He needs a physician!"

"Exile has medical facilities," Councillor Emery said, shouting orders at two dwarves.

"He needs elvin medicine, not dwarven," Mr. Forkle insisted.

Sophie agreed. She'd seen how the dwarves had treated Alden's head wound when he'd collapsed in Exile. Fitz needed much more than a plasterlike patch.

His blood was thickening like applesauce from the venom, and his breathing sounded shallow and ragged.

"Mr. Forkle says to leap Fitz out of here," Dex whispered.

Sophie could hear the same instructions filling her head, along with details for how to contact the Black Swan's physician. She wanted to grab Fitz and leap away, but she couldn't leave the rest of her friends trapped in Exile.

Dex must've decided the same thing, because he held up his leaping crystal. "I'll take care of him," he promised as he grabbed Fitz and leaped the two of them away.

Outrage erupted, the Councillors ordering the dwarves to restrain the rest of their group.

"You're seriously going to arrest us?" Biana shouted. "After what you just did to my brother?"

"It was an accident!" Councillor Zarina insisted.

It was—but it shouldn't have happened.

A glance at Oralie told Sophie the pretty Councillor knew what she was planning—and a nod told her Oralie agreed.

Before Sophie could change her mind, she reached into her pocket and stepped to the center of the crowd. "You're going to let us go now—or I'm going to use this."

She held out Kenric's cache, eliciting a round of gasps, even from the Collective.

Councillor Emery reeled on Oralie. "Is this your doing?"

"It is," she said. "I honored Kenric's last request. He feared Sophie would need protection—and he was right."

"Treason!" Councillor Alina shouted, and several other Councillors agreed. Bronte and Terik tried to calm them, but it turned into a screaming match.

The only Councillor not arguing was Clarette, who sat hunched over the wounded arthropleura, whispering promises that its antenna would regrow.

Sophie was glad to hear it, but she hated that she couldn't say the same for Fitz. A wound like his might not—

She shut the thought down before it could finish.

But what if Dex hadn't been able to reach the physician?

Or what if something happened during the leap?

Mr. Forkle had warned them that leaping through the force field was dangerous—what if the two cloaks Fitz had been wrapped in weren't enough?

"We don't have time for this!" she shouted, grabbing her pendant and holding the crystal to the dim light. "So here's how this is going to work. You let us go right now, or I will leap out of here and you'll never see this cache again."

*This is too dangerous of a game,* Mr. Forkle warned.

*I don't care,* she transmitted back. She would find a way to make it work.

"Too hasty, Miss Foster," Councillor Alina told her. "Caches can only be accessed by the person who created them."

"Do you really think Kenric would've given it to her if he hadn't made a way for her to gain access?" Oralie asked.

"Even if that's true," Councillor Emery said, "are you going to betray your world and hand it over to our enemies, Miss Foster? Do so, and you will prove that you're every bit as evil as we've expected."

The word "evil" hit hard, but not as hard as the question.

What *would* she do with the cache?

"You're right," Sophie said after a moment. "The cache can never go to the ogres or the Neverseen. But I could give it to Sandor. Or maybe King Enki would want it."

Sophie had no idea if the cache held any secrets related to the goblins or dwarves, but it was the only card she could think to play.

Another nod from Oralie told her she'd played it well.

Councillor Emery closed his eyes to moderate the thoughts of the other Councillors, and Sophie bit her lip so hard she tasted blood.

"What are your demands?" Councillor Emery finally asked.

"Let us go!" Sophie said.

"Yes, we figured that. What else?"

"Full pardons for all of us, including Prentice!"

Emery gritted his teeth. "*That* is not an option."

Sophie leaned toward the jagged beam of light.

"Stop!" Bronte shouted. "Grant them the pardons! That cache must not fall into anyone else's hands."

"So they break our laws with no consequences?" Emery asked.

"Expel them from Foxfire," Bronte suggested.

Councillor Alina snorted. "*That* goes without saying! They need a *proper* punishment, not a slap on the wrist."

"Then send us to Exillium," Sophie said, hardly believing the words as they came out of her mouth.

Mr. Forkle couldn't believe it either, and filled her mind with a plethora of objections. Oralie was shaking her head as well.

But it would give them a chance to find out more about the Psionipaths who'd gone there.

It was also too late. Councillor Emery accepted the deal.

"What of their leaders?" Alina asked. "Surely we're not letting them go."

*Do not worry about us,* Mr. Forkle transmitted to Sophie.

But she wasn't leaving anyone behind.

"They're coming with us," she said, moving her foot closer to the light.

Councillor Emery sighed. "Fine, we'll grant a *temporary* reprieve—and resume our hunt tomorrow."

"And Prentice?" Granite asked. "He does *not* belong here."

Emery frowned at the bubble cage. "Rumor has it you've captured one of the Neverseen. We'd be willing to make an exchange."

"Deal," Mr. Forkle jumped in. When he saw Sophie's surprise, he transmitted, *Prentice is more important than Gethen.*

"Very well," Councillor Emery told them. "Bring your prisoner to Lumenaria at sunrise tomorrow for the trade. Are you done?"

"What about Oralie?" Sophie asked.

"I can handle myself," Oralie promised.

"She can," Bronte agreed. "So hand over that cache, Miss Foster, and you may leave."

"The cache isn't part of the deal," Sophie said. "Otherwise how do I know you won't betray us tomorrow?"

When they started to argue she moved toward the light. "Does that mean you'd rather I take this to the goblins? Or maybe the gnomes?"

The last word triggered the strongest reaction yet and left Councillor Emery waving his arms for silence.

"If you leave here with that cache, Miss Foster," he warned, "you will be accountable for its protection. And should you fail, the consequences will be *far* worse than Exillium."

"I can handle it," Sophie said.

Emery glared at Oralie. "So be it. And you can find your own way out of Exile," he told Mr. Forkle. "We'll give you ten minutes, then the guards will restrain anyone in the halls."

"We'll be gone in five," Granite promised as the Councillors raised red crystals up to the light.

Before they glittered away, Councillor Alina's eyes met Sophie's.

"You're forgetting that Exillium is for the Unworthy," she said. "You've just banished yourself and your friends from the Lost Cities—permanently."

# THIRTY-ONE

PHYSIC IS TREATING FITZ RIGHT NOW," Dex told everyone as they rushed into the boys' tree house. He sat on the floor, his legs curled into his chest, staring at the flickering fire pit.

"Can we see him?" Sophie asked.

Dex shook his head. "She said I should stay out here because it was going to get messy."

"I'm his mother," Della said. "I can handle messy."

"I can as well," Mr. Forkle said, following Della down the hall.

"Will you be okay?" Granite asked Sophie, Biana, and Keefe. "The rest of us should get back to the Lost Cities to avoid suspicion."

Sophie nodded, wishing she could leap away with them—but she was *banished*.

She could never go home.

Never see her family or friends again . . .

She wanted to curl up in a ball on the floor—or at least pace anxiously back and forth like Keefe and Biana. But Dex's eyes were rimmed with red, and tears stained his cheeks.

"Hey," she said, sitting beside him. "You okay?"

Dex wiped his runny nose. "My invention caused all of this."

"No, that was the Council," Sophie corrected. "They set the trap. And Fitz's injury really was an accident."

"Still, if I hadn't rushed to attack—"

"You were trying to help," Sophie told him. "No one blames you for that."

"I know my brother won't," Biana promised as she sat on Dex's other side.

Dex didn't look convinced.

"So what's Physic like?" Keefe asked, sitting next to Sophie. "Did it seem like she knew what she was doing?"

"I don't know," Dex mumbled. "Normally I'd think someone wearing a sparkly mask and calling themselves Physic was crazy. But it's the Black Swan, so . . ."

Sophie sighed. "She better be as good as Elwin."

"If she's not, we'll sneak into the Lost Cities and kidnap him," Keefe promised. When she didn't smile, he nudged her with his elbow. "Aw, don't worry too much, Foster. Fitz didn't look half as bad as you did during your last few brushes with death, and you're still with us—though maybe you two could cool it with the almost dying thing, okay?"

"I agree," Mr. Forkle said, striding into the room. "Physic has things stabilized if you would like to see Mr. Vacker."

Sophie's knees shook so hard Keefe had to steady her on her way to Fitz's room.

"Relax," Keefe told her. "You'll be back to Sophitz in no time. I bet . . ."

His joke died on his tongue when they slipped through the doorway and caught their first glimpse of Fitz. He was shirt-less and unconscious, his chest covered in a black spiderweb of veins. Della sat beside him, holding a silver compress against his forehead.

"I killed Wonderboy," Dex whispered, *not* helping things.

Keefe tightened his hold on Sophie's shoulders.

"It looks worse than it is," Physic promised, adjusting her mask, which looked Mardi-Gras style, with black swans painted around the eyes and purple jewels rimming the edges. The same purple jewels had been woven into her long, thin braids, and dotted along her dark skin. "I've already sealed the wound," she added. "And I have the damaged tis-sue repairing. Now we just need to get the venom out of his system."

She fished through a golden trunk, pulling out handfuls of tiny bottles. "This will make for a pretty awful day," she warned as she emptied a vial of dried leaves into her palm. "But I'm guessing that's probably true already. Now, which one of you can help me?"

"Foster volunteers!" Keefe said, then whispered in her ear, "You'll feel better if you help."

"Ah, it's the moonlark," Physic said as Sophie stumbled forward. "Glad we get to meet—though I wish I weren't stuck behind this mask. I'd tell you my real name, but then I'd face the wrath of that one." She tilted her head toward Mr. Forkle, who did not look pleased. "See those serums I took out?" she asked, pointing to a cluster of vials on the bed. "Pop the lid on the purple one and hand it to me. Then uncap the green and blue and wait until I'm ready."

Sophie did as she instructed, and Physic smashed the herbs in her other hand until the leaves formed a pulp. "Okay, on three I need you to pour those on his chest at the same time I pour this one. Got it?"

Sophie nodded.

On "one" Physic sprinkled the leaf-mush all over the veiny spiderweb.

On "two" she massaged the pulp into Fitz's pale skin.

On "three" they both drizzled the syrupy elixirs all over the leaves until every single bit of the spiderweb was covered.

"That will draw the venom out of his skin," she explained as she wrapped Fitz's chest with a roll of silver silk. "And *this*"—she dusted off her hands and poured a vial of thick yellow sludge under Fitz's tongue—"will get it out of his system. It will make him vomit. *A lot.*"

"Don't we need to get him a bowl or something, then?" Della asked.

"Way ahead of you." Physic pulled out what looked like a shiny silver handkerchief and shook it a few times, turning it into a bag big enough to hold a bowling ball. "Keep this sealed tight when he's done. I need an uncontaminated sample."

"You want a bag of Fitz's barf?" Keefe asked, snapping out of his daze. "Wow, that's even too gross for me."

Physic shrugged. "It's not even in the top ten grossest things I've done."

"What's in the top ten?" Keefe asked.

"I'll tell you another time."

"Wait, are you leaving?" Biana asked as Physic closed her trunk.

"Only briefly. I need to run to the apothecary to pick up one more supply to make sure none of this leaves a scar."

"Are you going to Slurps and Burps?" Dex asked. "My dad will get us anything you need. I could even go with you to make sure."

"You're sweet to offer," Physic told him, "but that would ruin my incognito thing." She adjusted the tilt of her mask and glanced at Mr. Forkle. "You know it's only a matter of time before I slip and use my real name, right? But today I'll play along. And I actually need to go to a gnomish apothecary," she told Dex. "They have a much better selection of feces."

"Is that in the top ten?" Keefe asked.

"Not even close. And speaking of gross things, someone needs to stay here with Fitz and make sure he doesn't choke on his vomit."

"Fun as *that* sounds," Keefe jumped in, "I have a project to work on."

"And what project would that be?" Mr. Forkle asked.

Keefe's eyes darted to Sophie before he said, "I . . . might have remembered something."

He slipped out the door before Mr. Forkle could ask more questions.

Physic left too, but not before she warned them that Fitz looked ready for "Retching round number one."

"So we'll take turns?" Sophie asked, feeling less than excited.

"Actually, why don't you let Della go first," Mr. Forkle said. "You and I need to talk. *Now.*"

The sound of Fitz's violent vomiting felt oddly appropriate as Sophie and Mr. Forkle paced in front of the common room campfire.

"You've been lying to me," he said. "You should've told me about Kenric's cache. And you definitely should've consulted with me before you volunteered for Exillium."

"I didn't lie, I *withheld*," Sophie said, using his earlier excuse against him. "And it's not like you tell *me* anything—or involve any of us in your decisions."

Mr. Forkle rubbed his temples. "I gave one of your memories back."

"And *I* swore fealty. But that doesn't make us equals, does it? All you guys do is boss us around."

"And all you kids do is push."

"Because we have to!"

Mr. Forkle's sigh ran so long, Sophie was sure he'd pass out from lack of breath. "What would earn me more trust?" he eventually asked.

"A name would be nice. Physic is willing to give us hers and she just met us."

"Have you considered that it's easier for her *because* she's just met you?" Mr. Forkle asked. "She's never had to lie straight to your face."

"And continuing to lie makes it better?" Sophie countered.

The most endless silence in the history of endless silences followed.

"Fine," he whispered. "Have it your way. You want my name?"

It took Sophie several seconds to remember to nod.

"Very well, then." Mr. Forkle paced the room twice more.

When he finally spoke, his voice had turned soft and whispery, a ghost in the shadows. "You also know me as Sir Astin."

# THIRTY-TWO

"SIR ASTIN," SOPHIE REPEATED. "AS IN . . .
my Level Two Universe Mentor."

"That would be me, yes."

She tried to picture Mr. Forkle looking young and
pale with long blond hair, but her brain refused to cooperate.

His new whispery voice did sound awfully familiar, though . . .

"How else do you think you got assigned the list of stars to
find Elementine?" he asked.

The room tilted sideways—or maybe that was Sophie.

She needed to sit.

That Universe assignment had changed *everything*. She
went from being the slightly weird "human girl" to Project
Moonlark. She'd also had to face a Tribunal, and the Council

had ordered her to keep a memory log, and she'd had to be descryed by Councillor Terik and . . .

"Wait—Sir Astin testified at the Tribunal that the lists for that assignment were given at random," she argued.

"Of course I did! I couldn't exactly say, 'I'm with the Black Swan and this was part of our plan!' This is what I mean, Miss Foster. Disguises require lies. I had to be so careful of every word I spoke to you, every gesture I made, to be sure I didn't remind you of this." He waved his arms around his Mr. Forkle-shaped self. "You'd just spent so many years seeing me every day, I knew the slightest cue might trigger a connection. And up until that Universe assignment your mind had been so sweetly unsuspicious. I was there simply to build your confidence as you struggled to adjust to life at Foxfire. Wasn't my session one of the few you didn't worry over?"

It definitely had been.

"But . . . Sir Astin was *surprised* when I showed him the bottle of Quintessence."

"Well, yes, because *I never thought you'd bring it to Foxfire!* Or carry it around in your satchel, letting it get shaken and jostled all day! It's amazing you didn't blow the school to pieces. That was when I learned to never make assumptions about what you'll do. I'd foolishly figured you'd run straight to Alden. Just like I'd figured Mr. Dizznee would have you two wearing protective gloves—proper starlight bottling procedure. Instead you burned your hands and called for Elwin, and then you showed up to your session and plopped the bottle on the table. Of course I panicked! I knew I'd have to make a report to Dame Alina, and you'd face a Tribunal, and all kinds of other consequences we could've avoided if you'd gone to Alden."

"Oh." Sophie stared at her hands, remembering the burns. "So . . . you really were Sir Astin?"

"I still *am* Sir Astin. Mind you, he's taking some time away from Foxfire now that you're a Level Three. But as far as our world is concerned, Sir Astin is off mapping stars."

Sophie wasn't sure if she wanted to cry or laugh. All the time she'd spent wondering about him, and he'd been right there, teaching her for two hours a week.

"So . . . should I call you Sir Astin now?" she asked.

"I'd prefer you didn't. It's easier to compartmentalize my life. When I'm here, I'm Mr. Forkle. Though you are welcome to tell the others."

"Oh, I will." Even if part of her still struggled to believe it.

She kept replaying her Universe sessions, searching for any clue that might have given him away. But there were none. He'd played his role perfectly.

"Are you satisfied now?" Mr. Forkle asked.

"Satisfied" wasn't the right word.

It all felt a little anticlimactic. She'd asked. He'd answered. He hadn't even taken one of those callowberries and morphed into Sir Astin. And she couldn't think of any of the "slips" he'd mentioned earlier.

"Is that your only identity?" she asked. "Or are there others?"

"Sir Astin is the only one I'm willing to share."

"How many are there?"

He sighed. "One for my actual life. Another for a role I've taken on. Another for the fertility doctor I played to your human parents. I couldn't be their doctor *and* their next-door neighbor, after all—but I'm assuming you already guessed that."

She nodded, even though she hadn't really thought about it. Yet another layer of weirdness to her life.

"And that's all I'll say for now," Mr. Forkle said firmly. "Can you accept that?"

Sophie studied his eyes, still not seeing Sir Astin staring back at her. "You're not Alden, right?"

Mr. Forkle laughed. "Even with every elixir ever made, I could never be that handsome."

He had a point.

"What about Tiergan?" Her telepathy mentor had always been a mystery. And he'd been close with Prentice.

"You can stop guessing. Even if you get it right, I'm not going to tell you."

"So that's a yes, then?" she pressed, not sure what she'd do if it were true.

"I'm not Tiergan. And *that* is the last thing I'm going to tell you."

"No, you have to at least tell me if I've met the other yous."

"I most certainly do not. We've talked enough about me. It's time for you to share. Can I see Kenric's cache?"

Sophie's palms turned sweaty as she handed him the marble.

"I can't believe you're carrying it in your pocket," he said.

"What am I supposed to do with it?"

"That's what we must figure out." He held it up to the light. "Oralie was very brave to give this to you."

Sophie swallowed a lump of guilt. "What do you think her punishment is going to be?"

"It's impossible to know. She's crossed a line that has never been crossed. But she knew that when she gave this to you, so I'm sure she's prepared. Oralie is far cleverer than you know. It's easy to underestimate the quiet beauties."

"Ain't that the truth," Keefe said, striding into the room.

"You are many things, Mr. Sencen, but *quiet* is not one of them."

"So you're saying I'm a beauty?"

Mr. Forkle scowled. "We're trying to have a private conversation."

"Then you shouldn't have it in a common room." Keefe plopped into one of the boulder-beanbag chairs, propping up his feet. "And by the way, *Sir Astin*? How'd you pull off being a Mentor while you were living next to Sophie in human land?"

"*That* is a secret I'm not willing to share."

Keefe got up and circled Mr. Forkle. "I bet if I really think about it I can guess the other yous."

"I thought you had a project to work on," Mr. Forkle reminded him. "Something to do with a memory?"

"Yeah . . . it wasn't what I thought it was." He tried to shrug it off, but his fists were clenched. "Besides, I thought I should be a good friend and check on Fitz. Do *not* go in there. It's pretty much the Great Vacker Hurlfest. Every time Fitz spews up black gunk, it makes Biana barf, and then Della loses it— and repeat!"

"Does that mean he's getting worse?" Sophie asked.

"Actually, he looks pretty good—y'know, when he's not gagging up bug venom. He's awake now, and he's got some color back in his cheeks. But I couldn't stick around. I don't know how Dex is doing it."

"It's remarkable what one can withstand when one feels they must punish oneself." Mr. Forkle rolled the cache around his palm before handing it back to Sophie. "Protecting this is your responsibility now. And you must take it as seriously as the Councillors do. They swear on their lives to never let it out of their possession."

"But I thought you didn't want me carrying it around."

"I don't. You haven't tried to access the secrets within the cache, have you?"

Sophie shook her head.

"Good. Do not attempt it. I couldn't tell if Oralie was bluffing when she suggested that Kenric made a way for you to open it, but her reasoning makes sense—and trust me when I say you don't want that responsibility. There are reasons the Councillors erase these secrets from their minds."

"Are the secrets the same in every cache?" Sophie asked, wondering if any involved the drakostomes. That would explain their reaction when she'd mentioned giving it to the gnomes.

"The Council divides the secrets up to ensure each of them is only responsible for protecting a portion. This cache contains seven."

"Okay, but here's what I don't get," Keefe jumped in. "How does it help to forget about something? It's not like that makes it go away."

Sophie had been wondering the same thing. It was like an ostrich hiding its head in the sand.

"Some of the secrets are removed for the Councillors' self-preservation," Mr. Forkle explained. "Ruling the world is full of impossible choices. Sometimes they must act in ways that would shatter them from guilt. So they erase it from their minds to spare themselves the agony. But there are also secrets that would send the planet spiraling into chaos if they ever came out. The safest option is to ensure no one knows about them." He stared longingly at the cache. "Never let me have this. The temptation is too great."

"So what do I do with it?" Sophie asked.

"I'll have to enlist the aid of a trusted Conjurer. In the meantime, that cache must not leave your possession—and you will not leave this hideout. Is that clear?"

"But I have to go to Exillium."

"No you don't. You're in hiding," he reminded her. "The Council can hardly force you."

"But I *want* to go," Sophie argued.

"So do I," Keefe jumped in. "I'm tired of being cooped up in this hideout all day."

"You mean you're tired of being *safe*?" Mr. Forkle asked. "Tired of training and improving your abilities?"

"Pretty much," Keefe said.

"Most of our training was to prepare us to rescue Prentice," Sophie added, "and now we've done that. Well, we've almost done that. He'll be rescued tomorrow morning. Meanwhile, we still don't know what the Neverseen is doing with those trees. And we're about to hand Gethen over—"

"*Not* a good trade, by the way," Keefe interrupted.

"It was, actually," Mr. Forkle told him. "We've learned all we can from Gethen. Plus, the Council is not without their talents. Why not let them try their hand? Anything they learn we'll be able to recover."

"Okay, but my point," Sophie said, getting back to her argument, "is that with Gethen gone, Exillium is our best chance of discovering more about the Psionipath. *Someone* has to remember something about him. Or if nothing else, we'll learn about the Neutral Territories."

Mr. Forkle rubbed his head, leaving red marks from pressing so hard. "All I can promise is that I will discuss the matter with the Collective."

"That usually means 'yes,'" Physic said, making everyone jump as she swished back into the room. "He knows the Collective never rejects his ideas. Why else do you think we have these stupid code names?"

"Well, now we know one of his identities," Keefe said.

"He told you he's—"

"Sir Astin," Mr. Forkle jumped in. "And nice try, Mr. Sencen. No one will be revealing any of my other identities, accidentally or otherwise. Physic will also not be revealing hers. Did you get the ingredient for Mr. Vacker?" he asked her.

Physic held up a palm-size white jar. "It wasn't easy. My usual apothecary was closed, so I had to go to the Hekses' unicorn preserve. Why didn't you tell me the plague had spread to the Starkrial Valley?"

Mr. Forkle looked pale as he mumbled, "I wasn't aware that it had."

"Wait, isn't that where the Lake of Blood is?" Sophie asked.

"It is," Mr. Forkle said. "But it's a large valley, and the Lake of Blood is on the other side. Still, I'd better check on Sior, Lur, and Mitya."

He pulled his crystal from his cloak and turned to Physic. "You can handle things without me?"

"Don't I always?" She offered Sophie her hand as Mr. Forkle leaped away. "Come on, let's go finish healing your friend."

# THIRTY-THREE

PHYSIC'S GOOPY, POOPY SALVE—OR AS Keefe called it, the pooplosion!—did its job, erasing the last remains of the black spiderweb veins on Fitz's chest. After that it only took another hour of dry heaving and fifteen other medicines before Physic pronounced Fitz "cured."

"You're not *healed*," she warned Fitz. "You're going to need another week of recovery for that. And you'll need to drink a vile tea every morning."

"Did you say 'vile'?" Della asked.

"Oh yeah—it's nasty stuff. But so is getting impaled by a giant bug." She set a jar on the table filled with seven spiky red flowers. "Steep one hollowthistle into a cup of boiling water and make him down the whole thing in one gulp. *Try* not to throw it up," she told Fitz. "And no getting out of this bed except for essential things."

"So, like, a few rounds of tackle bramble?" Keefe asked.

"Very funny," Physic said. "But seriously—no. Fitz will look worse before he gets better. Just know that's part of the process. I promise he'll be his old self by the seventh cup."

"Can't I just down all seven cups right now?" Fitz asked.

"Not unless you want your insides to liquefy."

"Am I the only one who thinks that would be kind of cool?" Keefe asked, earning another laugh from Physic.

"I like your style, kid," she told him. "Though I have a feeling I'm going to need to keep an eye on you."

"You can try," Keefe told her. "And dude, now that you're done with the Great Vacker Hurlfest, we can tell you that Foster found out one of Forkle's identities. Sir Astin."

Della's eyes widened the most. "He was my Mentor when I was a Level Three."

"He was?" Sophie asked. "Do you think he was in the Black Swan back then?"

"I don't know, it was a long time ago." Della stared out the window, her mind in the past.

Fitz, Dex, and Biana meanwhile didn't seem *that* impressed. They were surprised, of course. But crazy as the revelation was, it still felt like Mr. Forkle's other identities had to be an even bigger mind blow.

Sophie jolted back to the present when Fitz yelped.

"Sorry," he mumbled, "I was just trying to sit up."

"Vertical is not your friend yet," Physic told him. "Make horizontal your buddy for the next seven days."

Fitz sighed, and winced from the sigh. "Can I at least practice Telepathy?"

"You might be up to it in a few days," she told him. "But I doubt it. You *need* to rest. You came pretty close to dying."

"I knew it," Dex mumbled from the corner. Sophie hadn't seen him this miserable since the Council had forced him to adjust her ability-restricting circlet. "Can I . . . um . . . talk to you for a sec?" he asked Fitz. "Alone?"

"Uh . . . sure," Fitz said slowly.

"Come on," Della said, herding everyone out. "Physic should check us, too."

"Indeed I should," Physic agreed.

"But we're going to stand close enough so we can eavesdrop, right?" Keefe asked.

Fitz flung a pillow and smacked Keefe in the head—then yelped, clutching his shoulder.

"Don't make me restrain you!" Physic warned him. "And don't you dare fling that pillow back!" she told Keefe as he lined up his aim.

Sophie was the last to leave the room, trying to guess why Dex wouldn't look at her. Her theories evaporated when she entered the main room and found Mr. Forkle and Calla whispering.

"What's going on?" she asked.

"Probably nothing," Calla said, but the strain in her voice was too noticeable.

Mr. Forkle cleared his throat. "I was unable to find Lur, Mitya, or Sior. I'm sending Calla to make a more thorough search."

"Won't she be exposed to the plague?" Sophie asked.

"I won't surface unless the roots assure me it is safe," Calla promised.

Keefe's eyes darkened. "If anything happened to them because they were searching for my mother—"

"The two would have nothing to do with each other," Calla promised.

When Keefe started to argue, Calla made her way to his side. Sophie couldn't hear what Calla whispered to him, but his whole expression softened.

"I'll be home soon," Calla said, nodding to Sophie. "Try not to worry."

"Here," Physic said when Calla was gone. She handed Sophie a small green vial. "This will help you destress."

Sophie sniffed the elixir. "This doesn't have limbium in it, right?"

"Nope—I learned my lesson last time."

"Last time?"

Physic adjusted her mask. "Oh, you know. The time we healed your abilities. I was consulted on the cure. Looks like we missed a spot with that scar on your hand."

The story made sense, and Sophie would've accepted it—if Physic weren't studiously avoiding her eyes.

Did that mean Physic was there for her *other* allergic reaction? The one the Black Swan had erased from her memory?

*I know what you're thinking,* Mr. Forkle transmitted. *And not because I'm invading your privacy. So in the interests of our new-found honesty . . . yes. Your theory is correct. And that is all I will say.*

*Thank you,* Sophie transmitted back. He wasn't giving her all the answers she wanted. But she could live with this compromise.

Further discussion was interrupted by Dex shuffling past. He headed straight for his room, but Sophie wouldn't let him escape that easily. She caught him before he closed his door.

The floor of his room was strewn with gadgets and tools and things that could only be described as "doodads." Dex kicked some aside to clear a path, mumbling, "You don't have to check on me."

"I know I don't *have* to. I *want* to. Besides, how many times have you checked on me?"

"Yeah, but this is different." He picked up what looked like a dismantled melder and started tweaking the wires.

"So what did you and Fitz talk about?" she asked.

Dex added a new gear to his contraption. "I told him I'm sorry."

"What happened today wasn't your fault, Dex."

"It kinda was. But that isn't why I'm sorry." He added another wire to the gadget and it whirred to life, playing a tinkling musical sound. He let the notes play until the song came to an end. "I told him I'm sorry for hating him so much."

"Oh," Sophie said. "That must've been awkward."

"Yeah."

"So . . . what did he say?"

"He wanted to know *why*."

"Why *do* you hate him?"

"You can't guess?"

She had one theory—but it would start a conversation she didn't know how to finish. Plus, Dex had made it clear he was not a member of the Vacker fan club from her very first day at Foxfire, when Fitz didn't remember Dex's name.

"I know he wasn't always nice to you," she tried.

"He used to ignore me. And he's just so *perfect*." Dex sighed, pulling apart his new gadget and dropping the bits to the floor. "But . . . he's not a bad guy. And he saved us today."

It was the nicest thing Dex had ever said about Fitz, and Sophie could tell part of him only begrudgingly admitted it.

"So what did Fitz say?" she asked.

"He said we should be friends. And I said I'd *try*. And then he looked like he wanted to hug it out, so I bolted out of there."

Sophie laughed. "Wow, you and Fitz—BFFs! That'll be new."

"He's *not* my best friend. That spot's already taken."

"It is?" Sophie asked.

"Duh. Did you really think it changed?"

"I don't know. So many things are changing."

"I know," he agreed quietly. "But that one won't. Ever."

She felt her lips stretch into the biggest smile she'd had in a long time. "Same. You know that, right? Best friends no matter what."

"Does that mean we're supposed to hug it out?" he asked.

"I . . . guess we could." After the day they'd had, a hug sounded pretty good.

Dex looked a little nervous as he curled his arms around her shoulders. But it didn't feel awkward. It felt like coming home.

"I'm always here," he whispered.

"Me too." She knew she should probably let go, but she stayed a little longer.

They pulled apart when Keefe shouted, "YOU GUYS HAVE TO SEE THIS!"

They ran to the main room and found Keefe standing under the skylight, holding up Mr. Snuggles like it was a baby lion about to be made king. The sparkly red dragon twinkled almost as much as Keefe's eyes as he said, "I went in to check on our boy and found him cuddling with *this*!"

"Isn't that the same dragon Fitz brought to your house that one time?" Dex asked Sophie.

"WHAT?" Keefe shouted. "YOU KNEW AND YOU DIDN'T TELL ME?!"

"Mr. Snuggles wasn't my secret to share," Sophie said.

"IT'S NAME IS MR. SNUGGLES?! That is . . . . I can't even . . ." Keefe ran back to Fitz's room shouting, "ARE YOU MISSING YOUR SNUGGLE BUDDY?!"

"Fitz is going to die of embarrassment, you know that, right?" Biana asked.

"I didn't know he had a stuffed dragon," Della said. "I wonder where he got it."

"Elwin gave it to him when Alden was sick," Sophie explained. "And Elwin named him."

"Wow, you really know my brother super well, don't you?" Biana asked.

Sophie's cheeks flushed. "Well . . . we have to do a lot of trust exercises."

Dex sighed.

Down the hall, Sophie could hear Keefe laughing hysterically.

"I better make sure Fitz is still talking to me," she said.

"You should be worried about *me*," Keefe told her, stalking back into the room. "You deprived me of the Snuggles—that cannot be forgiven! Actually it can, but you have to convince Fitz to call himself Lord of the Snuggles from now on."

Sophie laughed. "I'll see what I can do."

Fitz's door was closed, so she knocked before going in.

"I told you, Mr. Snuggles's visiting hours are over," he called through the door.

"What about *your* visiting hours?" she asked.

"Oh! I thought you were Keefe."

Sophie pushed open the door. "I get that a lot."

"YOU SHOULD BE SO LUCKY!" Keefe shouted from the main room.

Fitz had Mr. Snuggles perched on his lap, and the sparkly dragon looked almost defiant. Like, *Yeah, I'm cute and glittery—what's it to you?*

"So . . . I guess the secret's out," she said.

"Looks like it. You'd think almost dying would earn me a little slack."

"NOT WHEN YOU'RE CUDDLING WITH A GLITTERY DRAGON, DUDE!" Keefe shouted.

Fitz smiled.

"So you're not mad?" Sophie asked.

"Nah. It's good to see Keefe acting normal again."

"It is," Sophie agreed, hoping it would last. "But what about you? How are you feeling?"

Fitz shrugged, then winced again, which made it a little hard to believe his "Fine."

"I'm mostly embarrassed," he promised. "I mean, who gets impaled by a giant bug? And I'm feeling guilty for all the times I've teased you about almost dying. It's not a lot of fun."

"It really isn't." Sophie sat on the edge of his bed. "Don't do it again, okay?"

"I won't if you won't."

Sophie sighed, knowing it was a deal neither of them could honestly make.

He yawned, and she patted Mr. Snuggles on the head as she stood to leave.

Fitz mumbled something, the words too sleepy to be coherent. But Sophie could've sworn he'd said, "Miss you."

"How is he?" Mr. Forkle asked as she entered the hallway.

She shrugged. "Resting."

"You should do the same. We have an early morning tomorrow. You're coming with us to make the exchange for Prentice. And then we'll start the process of learning what he's hiding."

# THIRTY-FOUR

THE LAST TIME SOPHIE HAD STOOD outside the glowing castle in Lumenaria, she'd been with Fitz, learning that the world was not at all what she'd thought it was.

Somehow, it didn't feel any less surreal to be standing in the cold ocean breeze again, waiting for the Council to deliver Prentice.

All five members of the Collective waited at her side, along with four dwarven guards, each holding one corner of the cot Gethen had been bound to. He seemed as lifeless as before, and Sophie wondered if he realized he was being moved, or if he'd retreated so far into his mind he'd lost connection with his body.

Squall checked the sun, which had risen well beyond the horizon. "The Council's late. I don't like leaving Gethen in the open."

"I thought the Neverseen can't track him now," Sophie said, looking anywhere but at Gethen's hands.

"It bothers you that we removed his nails," Mr. Forkle said.

"Well, you did torture him," she mumbled.

"Is *that* what you think?" Granite asked.

"The process was painless," Squall promised.

"I only said otherwise to frighten him," Mr. Forkle added. "It does raise an interesting question, though, doesn't it? How far are we willing to go in this fight? For instance, would you have been willing to hand your cache over to the dwarves or goblins if the Council had called your bluff?"

"I don't know," Sophie said—but that was a lie.

*You would've done it,* Mr. Forkle transmitted.

*Is that bad?*

*Quite the opposite. It's a sign that you're close to being ready.*

Sophie knew better than to ask, *Ready for what?*

"Where are the gnomes under quarantine?" she asked instead.

She'd hoped to catch a glimpse of the treatment area, but all she could see was the solid stone and metal of the castle's walls and gates.

"There's a small grove behind the inner tower," Mr. Forkle said. "I hear they're being contained there."

"You haven't seen them?" Sophie asked.

"Only physicians are allowed to enter, and they haven't been allowed to share any details."

The castle bell ended their conversation, followed by the echo of heavy footsteps. When the gates creaked open, ten goblins stood arm in arm to block them from entering.

Sophie searched for Sandor among them, knowing it was a vain hope. She found only strangers, and none who looked friendly enough to ask if they'd heard any news about her recovering bodyguard.

Behind them, the Four Seasons Tree stood proudly on a small patch of grass. As Sophie studied its colorful branches, Bronte and Emery leaped into the courtyard.

"Where's Prentice?" Mr. Forkle demanded.

"On his way," Councillor Emery promised. "He didn't respond to the sedatives Terik gave him for transport, so we sent Alina to calm him."

"Alina is a Beguiler," Granite explained to Sophie. "Her voice can be irresistibly soothing."

"Then why is she always so awful?" Sophie had to ask.

Bronte's lips twitched with a smile, and even Emery sounded mildly amused as he told her, "Much like Telepaths, Beguilers have restrictions for when they can use their power."

"Without those restrictions, Alina would surely be a Vacker," Granite added.

Sophie felt her jaw drop. "She's that powerful?"

"It's why we elected her to our ranks," Emery agreed. "In these troubling times we may very well need the power of persuasion."

His tone wasn't threatening—but the words still felt that way.

"I take it this is our prisoner?" Bronte asked. "I see he had no issue with the drugs."

"You will find him much the same when the sedatives wear off," Mr. Forkle told him. "He's using some sort of telepathy trick to keep his consciousness hidden."

"I've never heard of such a skill," Emery said.

"Neither had we," Granite agreed. "But we're growing used to finding ourselves in unfamiliar territory." He motioned to the goblins standing at the ready. "You honestly thought this was necessary?"

"You *are* fugitives," Emery said. "And this area is under quarantine."

"It is indeed," Mr. Forkle agreed. "Any progress on the cure?"

"All work is progress," Emery said.

"Which is political-speak for 'no'?" Granite pressed.

Bronte cleared his throat. "Unfortunately, it means we have little news to report."

Sophie wished she could ask about the drakostomes, but it would be too risky. The Council had gone to great lengths to keep their existence hidden, and she couldn't risk hindering the exchange for Prentice.

"Are you monitoring the Neutral Territories?" she asked.

"We're watching everywhere the plague has spread," Emery agreed.

"And have you found any trees with force fields around them?" she asked.

Bronte frowned. "What do you mean?"

"The Neverseen have a Psionipath working with them," Mr. Forkle explained. "We've been trying to ascertain his purpose."

"Then why have we heard nothing of this?" Emery snapped.

"Well, I suppose that's the problem with treating us as fugitives," Mr. Forkle said. "It makes it rather hard to work together."

Emery and Bronte shared a look, but Emery shook his head.

"What about the Vacker boy?" Emery asked. "How is he faring?"

"He's expected to make a full recovery," Mr. Forkle said.

Both Councillors looked noticeably relieved.

"What about Oralie?" Sophie asked. "What did you decide for her punishment?"

"She should have been removed from the Council," Emery said. "But our world does not need the uncertainty of another election, so she has been put under surveillance and relegated to menial assignments until she earns back our trust."

"At the moment, she's enduring our most odious task," Bronte said. "Monitoring Lord Cassius's investigation."

"What is Keefe's father investigating?" Sophie asked.

"His own memories. He's working with Telepaths, hoping to uncover any clues his wife might've given. Oralie's there to read his emotions and ensure he's honest about what he finds."

"Has he found anything?" Blur asked.

"Nothing of note. Lady Gisela was very careful."

Before anyone could respond, a light flashed next to Bronte, and Councillor Alina appeared in all her jeweled finery.

"Where's Terik?" Bronte asked her.

"He should be here right . . . now." Alina waved her arms like a spokesmodel and Councillor Terik appeared beside her. Something dark was slung over his shoulder, and Sophie realized it was Prentice.

"The sedatives kicked in once Alina calmed him down," Terik explained through huffing breaths. "I'd given him some pretty strong stuff, so he'll probably be out for hours."

Granite moved forward to help, but the goblins raised their swords.

"First, our prisoner," Emery told him.

"You think we're going to betray you?" Mr. Forkle snapped.

Councillor Alina adjusted her peridot circlet. "I wouldn't put it past you."

"Fine." Mr. Forkle turned to their dwarves. "Make the exchange."

The dwarves passed Gethen's cot to two of the goblins, and Terik handed Prentice to Granite.

"What did you give him?" Granite asked, cradling Prentice like a baby. Prentice's head lolled to the side, his body limp and pale.

"You can blame his condition on Alden Vacker," Alina told him. "And yourselves, for violating our laws."

Sophie was tempted to grab a handful of dirt and throw it in Alina's face, but somehow she found the willpower to refrain.

"He should be fine once the drugs wear off," Terik promised, wiping sweat off his forehead. "Well . . . as fine as he ever is."

Granite held Prentice tighter, whispering, "It's going to be okay."

Sophie wanted to believe him, but she could see the clammy sheen on Prentice's skin.

"Thus ends our truce," Councillor Alina said, raising a hand to order the remaining goblins back into position.

"Your real enemy is tied to that cot," Mr. Forkle warned the Councillors.

"Said the elf hiding behind a disguise," Alina argued.

Sophie didn't understand why the Council refused to see that the Black Swan wasn't evil. But then she remembered the doubt she'd felt because of Gethen's fingernails.

It was far too easy to misunderstand a single action.

Prentice was living proof of the pain such mistakes could cause. And now she had a chance to set things right.

They brought Prentice to a stone cottage, surrounded by crumbling paths and mossy walls. It sat nestled in a verdant valley, blanketed with grassy fields and rolling hills, under a gray sky swirling with mist.

"Are we in England?" Sophie asked, feeling like she'd fallen into a period movie. The only thing missing were horse-drawn carriages.

"It's possible," Mr. Forkle said, licking one of the stones to open the door to the house. "We rarely consider human land claims when we choose our hideouts."

He led everyone inside, and the house's interior reminded Sophie of the Healing Center at Foxfire. The floor was sleek silver, and along one wall was a neatly blanketed cot, as well as a table covered in bottles of Youth and vials of medicine. Two of the other walls were floor-to-ceiling apothecary shelves—hundreds of tiny square drawers Sophie was sure were filled with all manner of elixirs. The last wall had a window overlooking the lush valley, along with a counter, a sink, and a full set of alchemy equipment.

"How long have you had this place?" she asked.

"Since Prentice's memory break," Mr. Forkle said. "We knew we had years to wait for your abilities to develop—but we wanted to be ready just in case."

"I'll take the first shift," Blur said, heading down a flight of stairs in the corner. Another flight went up to some sort of loft.

"Private quarters," Mr. Forkle explained. "So that those staying here to care for Prentice have somewhere to rest."

Granite set Prentice on the bed as Squall grabbed a crystal basin from the counter and filled it with water. They toweled off Prentice's face and hands and tied back his dreadlocked hair. Blur returned with a clean robe, and Sophie turned away as they changed him. She helped Wraith and Mr. Forkle sort through the drawers, pulling out various ointments and unguents. By the time everyone was finished, Prentice's skin looked clean and smooth—all cuts and scratches healed.

If he hadn't been so unnaturally still, he might've looked normal.

"It's strange for the sedatives to take such a strong effect, isn't it?" Granite asked.

"Indeed it is," Mr. Forkle said. "And to last this long."

Sophie thought back to the dark days after Alden's mind had broken, when Elwin was attempting to treat him. The sedatives had worn off so fast, Elwin couldn't keep up with them.

"Do you think there's something wrong?" she whispered.

"I don't know what to think," Mr. Forkle admitted. "Not until I have more information."

She realized that everyone was looking at her. "You want me to heal him right now?"

"Not *heal*," Granite said.

"Unless you feel like you're capable," Mr. Forkle jumped in. "But what we truly need is a better sense of his mental state. None of us can enter a broken mind except you."

Sophie's mouth went dry, but she took a deep breath and stepped closer, trying not to think about the last time she'd been in Prentice's mind. She focused on Alden—and the joy she'd felt bringing him back—as she reached for Prentice's temples and pushed her consciousness into his.

His mind was dark—but not like any darkness she'd experienced before. She was used to blackness that had a shape. A space. An end.

This was absolute *nothingness*.

No light. No sound.

Not a whisper. A breath. A flutter.

She tried to call Prentice's name, but the transmissions vanished. It felt like trying to light a match in a room with no oxygen.

Heaviness settled over her, burying her in the emptiness, until all she had left was a single, solitary thought—a truth so inescapable, it turned solid in her mind, creating a lifeline to climb up and out of the black.

Sophie stumbled back from Prentice, the world crashing around her in a tornado of senses. But even the chaos of reality couldn't change the heartbreaking truth she'd discovered.

She gave herself several long breaths before she turned to face the Collective.

Their hopeful expressions crumbled as she whispered, "Prentice is gone."

# THIRTY-FIVE

I S HE USING THE SAME TRICK AS GETHEN?"
Biana asked when Sophie had finished her update.

After hours and hours of trying, Mr. Forkle had brought her back to the tree house to rest.

Sophie sighed. "I don't know."

She wandered to her window, staring at the dark forest. She had no idea what time it was. It didn't matter.

It was too late.

"Mr. Forkle and Granite tried to check," she whispered. "Since they'd both been in Gethen's mind and knew how it felt. But neither of them could last longer than a few seconds. They said Prentice's head felt like being thrown into a pit of boiling tar."

"I've never heard of anything like that before," Della said, appearing in the doorway.

"Neither have I." And it made Sophie want to kick things.

She knew so little about her purpose—but one fact had been made perfectly clear: the Black Swan *designed* her to heal minds.

And yet, the one person who'd counted on that ability more than anyone else was lying on a cot in a small stone house, and she couldn't do a single thing to help him.

"Prentice's mind felt like the darkness had somehow taken over," she whispered. "And what I don't understand is, what changed? The last time I read his mind it was a cage of nightmares—but he was *there*. He gave me a vision of Jolie, and told me how to escape."

"But you said he was drugged today, right?" Biana asked. "Maybe he was still sedated?"

"Drugs rarely have any effect on a broken mind," Della said. The sadness in her voice made it clear she was reliving the days she'd spent holding down Alden's thrashing body while Elwin struggled to keep him sedated.

"Unless . . ."

"Unless what?" Della and Biana both asked, making Sophie realize she'd spoken aloud.

"What if . . . Dame Alina did something?" she whispered. "We all saw him yesterday, and he wasn't catatonic like this. Terik even called for backup because he needed someone to calm Prentice for transport."

"But what could she have done?" Biana asked.

"I don't know," Sophie admitted. "I know nothing about Beguilers."

"Neither do I," Biana said.

The bigger question Sophie had was: *Why?*

Why would Dame Alina risk harming her own sanity by hurting Prentice?

"What's wrong?" Biana asked her mom.

Della shook her head and wiped her eyes. "I'm just . . . glad Alden isn't here to hear this."

Biana covered her mouth. "You don't think he's going to . . ."

"No," Della said, rushing over to hug her daughter. "Your father is strong, he won't let this break him again."

Biana's eyes welled with tears anyway.

Sophie's eyes burned as well. "If it helps," she said, trying to convince them as much as herself, "the Collective thinks we just need to give Prentice time. He's been surrounded by so much misery in Exile, he might've retreated to protect himself. So now that he's free, we can surround him with happier things to draw him back out. Plus, Fitz and I haven't tried working together as Cognates yet."

"That's true," Della said, clearing thickness from her throat. "We all have to remember, Prentice has only been free for a few hours. We need to be patient."

"I'm tired of being patient," Biana said.

Sophie was too.

Della hugged them both. "It's late," she said. "We should all get some sleep so we're ready for whatever the Black Swan needs tomorrow."

Sophie tried to take Della's advice. But her head was too full of questions. She stayed up reading, scouring the telepathy books the Black Swan had given her, hoping to find some clue that might explain what was happening.

"I feared I might find you like this," Mr. Forkle said from her doorway.

Sophie jumped so hard she knocked the books off her lap.

"Any news?" she asked, sitting on her hands to stop from reaching for her eyelashes.

"No change—but we're counting that as a good thing. At least he is not getting worse."

He crossed her room and pulled open her drapes, staring out the window. It was brighter outside than Sophie had expected it to be.

"Caring for Prentice is going to be far more time consuming than we'd originally planned," he said. "Especially since Calla and the other gnomes have yet to return. Do not let that trouble you," he added quickly. "Calla warned us it would take several days for her search. But . . . the fact that the plague keeps spreading proves we should be doing more to investigate. We've been pinning so many hopes on Prentice that it's made us shortsighted. So I brought your request to the Collective, and we've reached a decision." He turned back to face her, and she could see the worry in his eyes as he said, "We've agreed that the five of you should attend Exillium."

Sophie nodded, her voice momentarily abandoning her.

"You're right to be nervous," he told her. "Exillium is on the front lines of this plague. And their program is far more rigorous than anything you've experienced. But we have no doubt that you and your friends can handle it. You've proven time and again that you are both resourceful and brave. Still, you will need to prepare. And we'll have to wait until Mr. Vacker is fully recovered. You also must secure your cache in the void."

"The void?" Sophie asked.

"It's a confusing process," Mr. Forkle admitted. "But I've brought a Conjurer to guide you through. She's waiting for you in the main room."

Sophie dressed quickly, expecting to find another elf in a crazy disguise.

Instead she found an achingly familiar figure in a simple blue gown waiting for her by the waterfall.

"Edaline?"

# THIRTY-SIX

**T**EARS STREAMED DOWN SOPHIE'S cheeks as she tackled her mom with a hug. "I can't believe you're here!"

"I'm having a hard time believing it myself," Edaline whispered. She glanced around the room, smiling at Della and Biana. "This definitely wasn't what I'd been imagining for your hideout. It feels almost . . . homey."

"It's not as good as home," Sophie promised.

Edaline traced her hands across Sophie's back, and for a second it felt like they were back at Havenfield, everyone safe, nobody hurt or banished.

"I love you, Mom," Sophie whispered, taking her chance to say it.

"I love you too."

Sophie leaned back, trying to read the shadows on Edaline's face. Rings under her eyes hinted that she wasn't sleeping, and a crease between her brows gave away her stress. But otherwise she looked pretty normal.

A sniffle from the doorway made them turn to where Dex stood.

"Sorry," he mumbled, wiping his eyes. "Just . . . you know."

Dex's mom and Edaline were sisters, and they looked a lot alike—same wide turquoise eyes and soft, amber-colored hair.

"Come here, Dex," Edaline said, stepping aside to include him in the hug. "Your family is going to be so jealous when I tell them I got to see you."

"They don't know you're here?" Sophie asked.

"No, even Grady doesn't. He's off with Alden. I was out working in the sasquatch pasture when Mr. Forkle appeared."

"Sorry to catch you by surprise," Mr. Forkle said. "The Council is monitoring Havenfield extremely closely."

"Are they doing the same to my family?" Dex asked.

"Of course," Edaline said. "But your dad's enjoying it. He's been rigging traps all over Slurps and Burps to catch anyone snooping. *Several* Emissaries have left covered in pink slime."

Dex grinned. "Wish I could be there."

"He wishes you could too. But he's so proud of you. Your whole family is— Oh! I can't believe I forgot!"

She reached into her pocket and pulled out a wriggling bundle of orange fur.

"IGGY!" Sophie and Dex shouted at the same time.

The tiny imp squeaked and flapped his batlike wings, fluttering over to Sophie's waiting hands. She kissed his furry cheeks, gagging from the Iggy breath.

Dex coughed. "Whoa, I think he's gotten stinkier."

"He has," Edaline agreed. "He's been refusing to clean himself. And if I leave him in his cage, he flings his poop. So I've been carrying him in my pocket and bribing him with treats."

Sophie poked Iggy's belly, which felt chubbier—though it was hard to tell under the orange dreadlocks. His natural fur was gray, but Dex had a habit of slipping Iggy elixirs.

"Next time you're getting shorter fur," Dex told Iggy. "So it won't hold the stink in."

"You should make him blue," Biana said. "With sparkles!"

Iggy responded with an extraordinarily loud fart.

"Fine, no sparkles," Sophie said, rubbing his fuzzy chin and filling the room with his squeaky purr. "I didn't realize how much I missed him. I wish Grady . . ."

"I know," Edaline said.

"What is he doing with Alden?" Della asked.

"Does it have to do with the scrolls I saw you reading through my Spyball," Sophie asked.

Edaline smiled. "I've wondered if you were watching."

"What's in the scrolls?" Mr. Forkle asked.

"We're honestly not sure. The Council had ordered them destroyed, so Alden snuck them home to figure out why. So far they've all been about testing trees for something called drakostomes."

Sophie, Dex, and Biana shared a look.

"Why do I feel like there's something you haven't told me?" Mr. Forkle asked them.

Dex explained what he'd found in the archive, and how the drakostomes seemed like something the ogres held as leverage against the Council.

Mr. Forkle rubbed his temples. "*That's* the kind of information I expect you to tell me."

"We meant to," Dex said. "But things have been crazy."

"Yes, I suppose they have," Mr. Forkle agreed. "But if the Council wants those scrolls destroyed, they're clearly trying to cover their tracks."

"So you think the ogres are behind the plague?" Sophie asked. "And that the Council knew it could happen?"

Mr. Forkle sighed. "It's looking more and more possible."

"Then why hasn't the Council sent the goblins into Ravagog to shut the ogres down?" Dex asked.

"Because war with the ogres will kill *thousands*," Mr. Forkle reminded him. "And presently the plague hasn't killed a single gnome."

"It could," Sophie pressed. "Any day we might get the bad

news. How could the Council not warn the gnomes that this could happen?"

Mr. Forkle glanced over his shoulder, lowering his voice before he said, "You must be very careful with these accusations, Miss Foster. That is the kind of revelation that would shake the very foundation of our world. Let's also not forget that the only gnomes currently affected are those who chose to live beyond the protection of the Lost Cities—and that we don't even know what these drakostomes are. Can I borrow those scrolls when I bring you back to Havenfield?" he asked Edaline.

Sophie grabbed Edaline's hand. "You're not leaving already, are you?"

"No, but I'll need to bring her home soon," Mr. Forkle said. "So we should focus on hiding the cache."

Edaline flinched at the word. "I can't believe you're responsible for guarding one, Sophie."

"It'll be much safer once the cache is tucked into the void," Mr. Forkle promised.

"Do you mean the same void I go to when I teleport?" Sophie asked. "How do you hide something there?"

"Everything in the universe is connected," Edaline said. "Tied together with thin threads of energy. The void is where all those threads converge. Conjurers can pull at the threads in small ways, snapping things back and forth." She snapped her fingers and a plate of custard bursts appeared in her hands. When everyone had taken one of the crunchy-gooey treats, she snapped her fingers again and the plate disappeared. "I can also leave something tangled in the web, if I choose."

"Does that mean I won't be able to reach the cache without your help?" Sophie asked.

"Not if I do my job right. I can tie a new thread between your mind and the cache, which you'll be able to pull on. I'll also add an emergency command, to be safe."

That sounded a bit wibbly-wobbly for Sophie, but she took Edaline's word for it. Plus, it explained how Oralie had made Kenric's cache appear.

"Do you have the cache with you?" Edaline asked.

Sophie removed the tiny marble from her pocket. As soon as the light hit the glass, Iggy zipped off her shoulder and snatched the cache in his tiny paws.

"Give that back!" Sophie shouted as he flitted to the top of the waterfall.

Iggy's eyes narrowed and he dragged his teeth along the cache with a cringe-worthy *scraaaaaaaaaaaaaaaaaaaaape*.

Edaline snapped her fingers and the cache popped back into Sophie's palm. When Iggy dove to steal it back, Edaline snapped again, bringing his cage from Havenfield and dropping it right in his flight path. The startled imp crashed inside, and Edaline slammed the cage shut behind him.

*"Well,"* Mr. Forkle said, clutching his chest. "Perhaps we should send that infernal creature home, before it does any permanent damage."

"Aw, we can't send him away," Biana said. "He looks so sad. Can't he stay here?"

"You want to keep him?" Dex asked. "You don't think he's gross and stinky?"

"Uh, I grew up with two older brothers—and Keefe. I'm an expert on gross and stinky—and troublemakers," Biana reminded him. "Plus, he's so cuddly, and my room feels so empty at night and—"

"You want to keep him in your room?" Sophie interrupted.

Biana's cheeks flushed. "I know he's your pet. I just thought it might help me sleep."

"He snores like a growling bear," Sophie warned. "But if you want to brave it, I can tell Iggy likes you."

"I like him, too." Biana slipped her fingers through the bars of the cage and Iggy snuggled against them.

"Fine," Mr. Forkle grumbled. "But I will hold you responsible if he causes any more trouble, Miss Vacker."

"He wouldn't do that, now would he?" Biana said, proving how little she knew about imps. "Come on, let's get you all set up in my room—and then we'll see what we can do about this stinky fur."

"I can brew up a new elixir," Dex offered, following Biana. "You really want him blue?"

"I'd better make sure things don't get out of control in there," Della said, leaving Sophie alone with Mr. Forkle and Edaline.

Edaline motioned for Sophie to sit in one of the shrubbery chairs. "We should get to work. So I need you to study the cache like it's the only thing in the universe."

Sophie leaned closer, focusing on the cache's minute details. She'd never noticed the hairline fissures peppered through the glass, or how each jewel was wrapped with a single threadlike ring. Some of the rings were silver. One was gold. The others were black. She was trying to guess the significance when she felt a soft *Pop!*, like what her ears did every time the altitude changed.

A blue thread glinted off the cache like a laser, shooting straight into Sophie's forehead.

"That's supposed to happen, right?" Sophie asked, resisting the urge to flail.

"That's the thread I tied between you and the cache," Edaline explained. "It won't always glow. Now we just have to move the cache to the void."

Edaline snapped her fingers and the cache disappeared. The glowing blue thread also blinked away. But when Sophie concentrated, she could still feel a soft tug, as if her mind were clinging to the string of a kite drifting high on the breeze.

"Perfect," Edaline said. "Now you can drag the cache wherever you want in the web. It works best if you find something identifiable to leave it near."

Sophie closed her eyes and tried to focus as everything turned swishy and swoopy. She noticed a patch of warmth, and it led her to what felt like a pool of bubbling energy. She was about to leave the cache there when she realized everyone probably chose the comfortable paths. She turned her mind toward the coldest corner of the void.

Her teeth chattered as she left the cache surrounded by frosty waves. "Now what?"

Edaline snapped her fingers, and it felt like someone shoved Sophie back into her body and dumped a bucket of water on her brain.

"You okay?" Edaline asked.

Sophie rubbed her forehead. "That was really weird."

"Conjuring is a strange ability," Edaline agreed. "But now your cache is safe. And to retrieve it, all you have to do is find the pressure in your mind, wrap your consciousness around it, and focus."

Sophie did as Edaline said and . . . *SNAP!*

"Okay, before we put it back," Edaline said, "you need to think of a word or phrase—one you won't forget, but also would never accidentally say."

Every word that ever existed vanished from Sophie's mind.

"Take your time," Mr. Forkle told her. "This will be your failsafe if something makes you lose your hold. It will only work once, and it will sever all other connections."

Sophie's brain darted to silly things like, *Accio cache! Allons-y! Use the force! Bibbidy-Bobbidy-Boo! My precioussssssssssssssssssssss.* But then she remembered how when she was little and had moved to the "older kids' school," her parents gave her a code phrase to say if she ever wanted to be picked up and didn't want anyone to know she'd called her parents. Her dad was a huge Sherlock Holmes fan, so he'd chosen "221B Baker Street." She remembered complaining that no one could work those words into normal conversation, and her dad had just said, "But you'll never forget them."

"I think I've got it," she said.

"Okay, keep those words as the only thing in your mind, and when I tell you to, say them to the cache."

Edaline's brows scrunched so tightly they nearly touched, and the cache glowed warm in Sophie's hand.

"Now," Edaline said.

The cache disappeared as soon as Sophie said the phrase.

Edaline leaned wearily back in her chair. "That should do it. If you say those words and snap your fingers, the cache will find you."

"Does that mean you guys can call for it?" Sophie asked. "Since you know the words?"

"It has to be your voice," Mr. Forkle said.

"And remember, it will only work once," Edaline added. "So keep it for a last resort."

"I assume this means we're done," Mr. Forkle said, pulling out his leaping crystal.

Sophie threw her arms around Edaline, wishing she could beg her mom to stay.

"At least this time I'm saying a proper goodbye," Edaline whispered. "I'm sorry we didn't before."

"You don't have to be sorry," Sophie said, wiping her eyes. "It made it easier, actually. Made it feel more temporary."

"This *is* temporary." Edaline tightened her hold. "I won't let the Council keep us apart forever—that's a *promise*. And now I need you to promise something to me. Don't worry, I won't tell you not to take risks, or not to worry about us, or any other impossible things. I just need you to promise that you'll never give up. No matter how hard it gets. Or how hopeless it feels. Never, *ever* give up."

"I won't if you won't," Sophie whispered.

"Never," Edaline promised.

"And tell Grady I love him."

"I will," Edaline said, kissing both of her cheeks.

She swiped a strand of hair off Sophie's forehead. Then she took Mr. Forkle's hand and the two adults leaped away, leaving Sophie alone.

# THIRTY-SEVEN

FITZ'S RECOVERY MOVED SLOWLY, JUST like Physic had warned—and yet Sophie kept worrying it was *too* slow. He got dizzy every time he stood, and felt a stabbing pain in his chest if he took a deep breath. And the elixirs Physic gave him during her check-ins seemed to be making him worse.

Sophie was starting to put serious thought into Keefe's "kidnap Elwin" plan. But she knew she should at least wait until Fitz was done with the vile tea. If he wasn't better after the last sip, she was running a heist in the Lost Cities.

It didn't help her mood that Calla still wasn't back. The Collective also wouldn't bring her to see Prentice. She'd offered *many* times, and they told her she needed to save her mental energy. But when Della asked to go, they agreed—which Sophie tried not to find insulting.

Meanwhile Dex spent all his time wrestling with the Twiggler, and Biana was obsessed with Iggy. Dex had given the tiny imp a coat of silky blue fur, and Biana spent every free second trying to train Iggy to eat vegetarian.

Which left Sophie on her own, with a notebook full of Cognate exercises and a bedridden telepathy partner. The only useful thing she could do was help Keefe search his memories. Part of her was desperate for them to find a clue about the Neverseen's plan. The other part of her was terrified of how Keefe would handle that.

"You never told me about the memory you thought was going to be useful," she said as she paced around his room, noticing he'd added new notes to the walls.

"That's because it was stupid." He grabbed a crumpled piece of paper off the floor. "I was trying to figure out how she stayed in touch with the Neverseen, and I remembered she had this bracelet my dad hated, so I knew he didn't give it to her. I thought maybe it was a communicator, but I don't see how."

He uncrinkled the paper and showed Sophie a sketch he'd done of a bracelet made of round sparkly beads.

"Wow, I didn't realize you could draw."

"It's no good." Keefe snatched it away and crumpled it again.

He was wrong—his drawing looked like a photograph. But he was also right—Sophie didn't see how the bracelet could be a clue.

"Well," she said, "that's why I'm here. It's easier to see what's important when you can look at the memory on paper."

She held up her memory log and flipped to a blank page.

"We'll start with something easy," she promised when Keefe turned almost as green as Fitz had during the Great Vacker Hurlfest. "I was thinking it'd be smart to record your memories of the Neverseen's attacks. You might spot something you didn't notice before, and you'll get a feel for how this is going to work. And it shouldn't be too weird for you, since I was there."

Keefe's shoulders relaxed. "Yeah, I guess that could work. So how do we do this?"

"Well, first you need to think about those memories so they're in the front of your mind. And then you need to give me permission to enter your consciousness—and yes, I know, you think that sounds creepy."

Keefe smiled half a smile. "It sounds less creepy from you."

She reached for his temples.

He flinched. "Sorry. Wasn't expecting that. You don't do that with Fitz."

"I'm so used to his mind I don't need to make contact anymore. Just relax—this isn't going to be a big deal."

Keefe nodded and held still, sucking in a slight breath as her fingers settled against his skin. That was when she realized how close they were standing.

"You okay there, Foster?" he asked, the other half of his

smile curling his lips. "Seems like your mood just shifted."

"Just bracing to relive those attacks. You ready?"

He swallowed hard before he nodded.

Sophie did the same, adding a couple of deep breaths before opening her mind to his.

She still wasn't prepared for how vividly Keefe remembered everything. Fitz didn't have a photographic memory, so his memories were always slightly faded. But Keefe's mind was in high definition—and the soundtrack could've been THX certified.

Her hands trembled as she watched herself leave the Black Swan's ocean cave with Keefe. Silveny had barely lifted off the ground when five black-cloaked figures knocked them out of the sky. For Sophie, the fight had happened through a haze of pain and exhaustion after nearly dying. But Keefe had lived the full-color reality. His rage made her stomach heave—especially when one of the cloaked figures flung a rock at his head. They knew now that the figure was his mom, but as the fight replayed, Sophie saw nothing to clue them in. Lady Gisela never used her real voice—even when Keefe sliced her arm with a goblin throwing star. And she fought without remorse, even when challenging her son.

*Good old Mom,* Keefe thought. *Doesn't it give you warm, fuzzy feels?*

His memories shifted, bringing them to Mount Everest, during the part of the battle Sophie had missed. An ogre had dragged her through the cave's ceiling, and she'd never realized how hard her friends fought to get to her. No one fought harder than Keefe. His aim with the throwing stars was flawless, nailing one dwarf in the hand right before it threw a rock at Fitz, clipping another dwarf in the leg so it couldn't chase them. He waded through snowdrifts, trudged through the freezing winds, refusing to stop until he caught up with the Neverseen. And then . . . panic slowed his hand when he pointed his weapon at the figure he thought was his father.

More dwarves burst out of the snow, and Keefe chased down his dad, his only thought, *I need to end this*. When he'd caught up, he'd been ready to do what was necessary. But then the wind threw back his father's hood and Keefe saw who it really was . . .

"Oh," Sophie said as Keefe's emotions exploded.

*Shock.*

*Anger.*

*Betrayal.*

*Hate.*

But the strongest emotion was *grief*.

As the sadness swelled in Keefe's mind, so did a cyclone of older memories. Keefe tried to push them back, but they were too strong.

Sophie saw a young Keefe—he couldn't have been older than three or four—curled up on the floor of his room, crying. His mom came in to tell him to be quiet and realized he'd wet the bed. "Dad's going to be so mad," he whispered. His mom agreed and started to walk away, then sighed and called for the gnomes. She asked them to change out the bedding and have the room looking normal by morning. "Your father doesn't have to know everything," she told Keefe. "But don't let this happen again."

In another memory Keefe was six or seven, waiting by a fountain in Atlantis.

And waiting.

And waiting some more.

Crowds came and went. The balefire streetlights dimmed. And still, Keefe sat all alone. Finally his parents rolled up in a eurypterid carriage, along with another dark-haired elf that Keefe didn't recognize. Keefe's father was so deep in conversation with his friend that he didn't even look at his son. Keefe's mom said, "Sorry, we forgot you."

The memory shifted again, to Keefe wearing an amber-brown Level Three Foxfire uniform. He'd just gotten home from school and found his parents waiting in his room. Keefe's father demanded Keefe show him his notebooks, and when Keefe handed them over, his dad freaked. The pages were covered in sketches, each more intricate and amazing than the last. But his father tore out each drawing, crumpling them beyond ruin as he shouted about Keefe needing to pay attention during his sessions. Keefe argued that he could draw and learn at the same time, and his father stormed off, calling Keefe a disappointment. Keefe's mom said nothing as she followed her husband out. But she did retrieve one of the drawings from the floor—a sketch of her—and tucked it into her pocket.

The theme of each memory became achingly clear.

*Two awful parents.*

*But one was better—or that was what Keefe had believed.*

Keefe stepped back, severing Sophie's connection. "So . . . *that* just happened."

"It's okay," she whispered.

He shook his head. "I never wanted anyone to see that."

"I know. But . . . I'm glad I did. You shouldn't have to carry all of that alone."

"And you shouldn't have to know I used to wet the bed."

"Lots of kids wet the bed."

"Not according to my father."

He kicked the wall so hard it had to be painful.

Sophie inched closer, hesitating before resting a hand on his shoulder. "You know what I think when I see things like that?"

"'I never should've agreed to help such a loser—even if he has awesome hair?'"

"Not even close. Okay, fine, the hair part is kinda true. But other than that, all I think is, 'Keefe's even braver than I thought.' And I already thought you were incredibly brave. Between the way you held your cool in those battles, and the way you've stayed my friend despite all the rumors and gossip about me. You're just . . . I don't even know how to say it. But you're so much more than what your family made you believe. And by the way, I want to see more of your drawings."

"I don't have any," he told the floor. "I stopped drawing years ago."

"You have that one you just drew of your mom's bracelet."

"That one was stupid."

"I'd still like to keep it—can I?" she bent and picked it up, tucking it into her memory log.

"Anyway," she said after an endless stretch of silence, "I guess I should record those attacks with the Neverseen."

She projected the battle scenes on the pages using a telepathy trick. Keefe watched over her shoulder and took the book from her when she got to the moment he'd learned the cloaked figure was his mom.

"You made her look afraid," he said.

"That's how she looked. Photographic memory, remember?"

Keefe frowned. "I remember her looking angry."

"She did look angry. But first she looked scared—like she didn't want you to see her."

Keefe stared at the projection for a painfully long time, then shut the book and handed it back. "You're not going to record the other memories, right?"

"No. I think we should keep those between us."

He nodded.

"Is this going to be too hard for you?" she whispered.

"Is it going to be too hard for *you*?"

Sophie chewed her lip. "I *hate* seeing them hurt you. If I ever face your father again . . . well, he better hope I'm not wearing my Sucker Punch, because I'd knock him to Timbuktu."

"I would pay so much money to see that."

She smiled sadly. "I don't want you dealing with all of this alone, Keefe. You've spent long enough hiding the bruises and scars behind jokes and pranks—"

"He never hit me," Keefe interrupted.

"I know. But words cut deeper than goblin throwing stars. So I hope you'll keep letting me help."

He raised his eyes to the window, looking as scared as his mom. Sophie could definitely see the family resemblance between them. But Keefe was missing her hard edges.

"Just promise me that if this gets to be too much for you, you'll run away," he whispered.

"It won't be too much."

"It might be. I have a major dark side, Sophie."

"So does everyone."

He raised one eyebrow. "Even the Mysterious Miss F.?"

"Uh, yeah, I'm an Inflictor, remember?"

Keefe turned away again. "I wanted to manifest that ability so bad. I begged my ability detecting Mentor to try to trigger it. But no, I got my *dad's* ability."

"Hey, being an Empath is a *way* better talent. I've wondered sometimes why the Black Swan didn't give it to me."

"Maybe you'll trigger it eventually. Along with another fourteen or fifteen talents."

"Man, I hope not. Four is enough."

"Psh, you should at least go for five. But don't waste your last slot on empathy. Go for something cool, like Hydrokinetic."

"Okay seriously—how many abilities are there?"

"A *lot*. That's why they make such a big deal when someone doesn't get one. There are *so* many chances to have a talent."

"I still don't think it's right to treat them like a secondary citizen because of it," Sophie mumbled. "Even if they have the same money or whatever, it's still not fair."

"I bet that's why you scare the Council so much," Keefe said after a second. "I never thought about things like that until I met you."

"That's why she's the moonlark," Calla said from the doorway.

Sophie smiled as she turned to greet her friend, but it vanished when she saw the tears staining Calla's cheeks.

"What happened?" Sophie asked, hoping she hadn't already guessed the answer. But it was everything she'd feared, and so much more.

"I found Lur and Mitya—and Sior," Calla whispered. "They're in Lumenaria. Under quarantine. All three of them are infected with the plague."

# THIRTY-EIGHT

THE WORDS BOUNCED AROUND SOPHIE'S head, making her ears ring.

Lur and Mitya and Sior had the plague.

They could be dying.

No—not "could be."

They *were* dying, if someone didn't find a cure.

"How long can someone have the plague before . . . ?" She couldn't finish the question.

"We still do not know—but that's good news, in a way," Calla said. "All the Wildwood colonists are still alive and fighting."

The answer helped a little—but it didn't change the fact that the infected gnomes were running out of time. Maybe they had months. Maybe weeks. Maybe days. Whatever it was, they deserved more.

"But you're safe?" she asked Calla. "You haven't been exposed?"

"I was very careful," Calla promised, drying her eyes with her long braid. "I would not have come back if I wasn't certain. I would never risk Amisi's safety."

"So what happens now?" Keefe asked.

Calla let out a slow, heavy breath. "I don't know. This . . . there was no plan for this." Her eyes welled up again.

"Does the Collective know yet?" Sophie asked.

"I couldn't find them."

"They're taking care of Prentice," Sophie said.

"Does that mean he hasn't been healed?" Calla asked.

"I tried—"

"It's okay," Calla interrupted. "I have no doubt you'll do everything you can. Do you know if they're at the Stone House?"

"Is that a cottage in the middle of the Moors?" Sophie asked.

Calla nodded and turned to leave. "I need to speak with them before I tell Amisi. They might know something that could bring her better comfort. She and Sior are courting."

"I'm going with you," Sophie said, following Calla down the hall.

Keefe rushed after them. "Me too."

"I don't know where you're going," Dex said as they entered

the boys' main room, where he sat on the floor, surrounded by Twiggler supplies. "But you're not going without me."

"I suppose that means you're coming too?" Calla said, glancing toward an empty corner.

"Ugh, I really thought I'd figured out how to hide that time!" Biana said as she appeared. "But yep, I'm in. Where are we going?"

Sophie did her best to catch them up.

Dex looked like someone had crushed all his gadgets to dust. "We have to help them," he whispered. "They saved us, Sophie. Lur and Mitya."

"I know," Sophie said.

Biana rushed to give Calla a hug. "Are you sure it's safe for you to leave Alluveterre? The plague seems to be popping up everywhere."

"We'll travel deeper than normal, and I'll steer clear of the Neutral Territories," Calla promised, heading outside and down the winding stairs. When they reached ground level, she sang a deep, earthy song to create a tunnel and tangled the roots around them. The journey was faster than ever—so fast Sophie was sure she lost her stomach several times. But it was worth the nausea when they arrived at the Stone House after only a few minutes of journeying.

Sophie had assumed it would still be sunny, but when they climbed out of the tunnel the sky was bruised by twilight, the only light coming from the early stars and the hideout's windows.

"Should we knock?" Biana asked as they crept toward the cottage's door.

"No need," Blur said, phasing through the wall and making them all scream. "But you do need to explain what on earth you're doing here. How . . ."

His voice trailed off when he noticed Calla. "Better come in."

They squeezed into the room, trying to find places to stand in the small, crowded space. Sophie's heart twisted when she saw that Prentice hadn't changed at all since the last time she'd seen him.

He also had guests.

Della stood with three figures that Sophie recognized right away, even though her brain kept telling her they couldn't possibly be there.

"Magnate Leto?" Keefe asked, sounding equally confused to see Foxfire's principal in a Black Swan hideout.

Next to him stood Tiergan, Sophie and Fitz's Telepathy mentor. And on his other side was his adopted son, Wylie.

Prentice's son.

Sophie had only talked to Wylie twice, and both times had been a disaster. She'd never forget their fight at his mother's grave, when he'd told her, "You were supposed to make it right." That was when she'd realized she'd been designed for healing minds, and that something must be wrong with her if she couldn't. She'd gone to the Black Swan and risked her life to reset her abilities. And yet, there Prentice rested, farther from being healed than ever.

Wylie resembled his father even more than Sophie had realized. His skin was a slightly lighter shade of black, and his features a bit sharper. But he had his father's hair and lips and eyes.

"I'm guessing you weren't expecting to find us here," Magnate Leto said.

"It's weird," Biana admitted. "Are you part of the Black Swan?"

"That would be rather impossible." Magnate Leto smoothed his black hair, even though it was coated with so much gel it couldn't possibly move. "I'm here to cover for these two."

Sophie shouldn't have been surprised that Magnate Leto would help—he'd protected her when he'd discovered the ability-restricting circlet didn't completely stop her telepathy.

"The Council is watching us," Tiergan said, tugging on the sleeves of his simple gray tunic. His usually deep olive skin looked almost as pale as his blond hair as he added, "The Collective hopes that if Prentice hears our voices, it might reach him."

"So they pretend to be meeting with me in my office every evening," Magnate Leto added. "And instead we come here."

"Our pendants have to stay near each other or the Council won't believe we've been together," Tiergan explained.

"I might be able to fix that," Dex offered.

"Maybe another time," Blur said. "Right now you need to tell us why you're here."

"Should we wait for the rest of the Collective?" Sophie asked.

"They can't get away from their other identities right now," Blur said.

Calla asked everyone to head downstairs, not wanting to reveal the bad news in front of Prentice. The round bedroom below was simple but cozy—a bit too cozy once they'd all squeezed in. Sophie was surprised Blur let Tiergan, Magnate Leto, and Wylie join them.

She spent most of Calla's update staring at her feet so she wouldn't risk meeting Wylie's eyes. Every time he looked at her, she could see such heartbreaking sadness and disappointment. She was trying to think of something to say to him when she realized the room had gone quiet.

"Calla was wondering if you could transmit to Lur, Mitya, and Sior," Keefe whispered to catch her up.

"I can try," Sophie said, hoping her voice sounded less shaky than she felt. "What do you want me to say?"

Calla cleared the thickness from her throat. "Tell them we're not giving up, so they must not give up on themselves. And remind them that the good in nature is always stronger than the bad. Ask them if there's anything they can share that might help us find the cure. And . . . tell them we love them."

Sophie translated the message to gnomish and transmitted it in every direction. Her brain hurt from the strain, but she kept repeating the call, stretching out her consciousness and listening for any trace of a response.

For several endless minutes all she found was a headache. Then a voice that sounded like Mitya's filled her mind.

"They say the plague works in stages, and that they're only stage one," Sophie whispered.

"How many stages are there?" Magnate Leto asked.

Sophie transmitted the question and the room seemed to hold its breath.

"They don't know," Sophie said. "So far the healers have counted six. But they won't know the final count until someone dies."

The word struck a blow, and Sophie was glad Biana could take Calla's hand—especially since she had an even more upsetting message to deliver.

"They say there are two hundred and thirty-seven gnomes in quarantine."

The number was too big to fit in such a small room.

Two hundred and thirty-seven gnomes, all sick and slowly dying.

*We're going to find the cure,* Sophie transmitted. *We'll do whatever it takes.*

Calla was crying by then, and Sophie nudged through the crowd, hugging her tight and repeating the promises she'd given Lur, Mitya, and Sior.

Calla swallowed hard and reached for the chain of Sophie's

allergy remedy, which still held the moonlark pin.

"If anyone can do it, it's you," Calla whispered, then pulled away. "I need some air."

She disappeared upstairs, and others started to follow.

"Can I . . . talk to you for a second?" Wylie mumbled as Sophie passed him.

"Uh, sure," Sophie said, even though her stomach felt like a nest of fire ants had taken over. She wasn't sure she could handle another fight.

"Let's give them some space," Tiergan said, herding Dex, Keefe, and Biana away.

Once they were alone, Sophie studied the patchwork quilt and the crystal lamp—anything to spare her from having to look at Wylie.

He cleared his throat. "You know I blame you for what happened to my dad—and I can't promise I'm ever going to stop. But . . . I think I finally get why he sacrificed himself for you. What you just did there—sending that message around the world. And the way everyone was looking to you . . . they all believe in you."

"Thank you?" Sophie said, not sure if it was the right reaction.

He nodded, and she thought maybe the awkwardness was over. But he stepped closer, his voice deep and intense.

"Just make it worth it, okay? Everything he did. Make. It. Worth. It."

Sophie wanted to tell him she would. But she didn't want to lie. "I promise I'll try as hard as I can."

Wylie nodded.

He turned to leave, but before he disappeared up the stairs she told him, "Don't give up on your dad yet, Wylie."

He reached up, wiping tears from his cheeks. "I won't if you won't."

She held his gaze. "I *won't*."

# THIRTY-NINE

THE NEXT MORNING FITZ DRANK the last cup of vile tea and was instantly back to normal, just as Physic had promised.

He spent the day working through Cognate exercises with Sophie, but their progress didn't feel like enough. Neither did Dex's attempts to improve the Twiggler. And Biana and Keefe found nothing new in the Exillium records Dex had stolen.

"We need a plan," Sophie said, pacing around the girls' common room. Della was visiting Prentice again, so they had time to scheme. "Exillium is our chance to finally get some answers. We need to find out who the Psionipath is and figure out how to find him, and what he was doing with that tree. We'll also be in the Neutral Territories, so we need to learn anything we can about the plague. We need proof that the ogres are behind this—*if* they're behind it—and we need to figure out if the drakostomes are involved."

"That is quite a large to-do list," Mr. Forkle said.

He stood in the doorway, holding a large gray trunk. Granite lurked behind him, carrying the same.

"Lur and Mitya saved my life," Dex said as the two members of the Collective shuffled into the room and set their trunks in the center of the floor. "Now they need our help."

"I understand the stakes," Mr. Forkle told him. "But that doesn't mean you can put aside caution. One of the hardest parts of our role is not letting things become personal."

"But it *is* personal," Keefe argued.

"It is and it isn't," Mr. Forkle said. "The problems our world is facing go beyond protecting the people we know and care about. Believe me—I understand the struggle. Do you think we were never tempted to break Prentice out of Exile before now? We knew where he was. We knew the nightmare he was trapped in. But we couldn't risk that kind of exposure until Sophie was ready. And now"—his voice cracked—"it's possible we were too late. But that doesn't mean we were wrong to focus on Sophie's safety."

"We're not saying you can't investigate," Granite added quickly. "We're saying to manage your risks wisely. Enduring Exillium will be your greatest challenge yet, in many ways. Do not let your goals distract you from surviving."

"*Surviving?*" Sophie repeated. "Enduring" didn't sound very awesome either.

"Exillium is not so much a school as it is an institution," Mr. Forkle warned. "It exists for the Unworthy—the hopeless cases that must be kept in line. Expect rules—*lots* of rules— which absolutely must be followed, regardless of how unfair or bizarre they may seem. Names are forbidden. Friendship is forbidden. Talking or interaction of any kind is forbidden. Refusing an order or an assignment is—"

"Let me guess," Keefe jumped in. "Forbidden?"

"Yes, Mr. Sencen," Mr. Forkle said. "And as our resident rule breaker I cannot emphasize enough how important it will be for you to submit to authority this time. Exillium is beyond the protection of the Lost Cities, which means there are no restrictions for how the Coaches punish disobedience. Also, the less you draw attention to yourselves, the safer you'll be. You need to blend in at Exillium. Embrace your anonymity."

"Will we really be wearing masks?" Biana asked.

"You will." Granite opened the chests, which Sophie noticed had been painted with a black *X* across the top and the letter *E* embossed where the lines intersected. "Your uniforms are the same for boys and girls, and they are designed to hide your identities."

He handed them each a thick stack of gray and black clothes, along with a pair of heavy black boots, and a silver-studded black half mask.

"I'll try it on," Biana said, heading toward her bedroom.

She clomped back a few minutes later in the steel-toed boots, which laced up over the fitted black pants. The long-sleeved shirt was also black, and worn tucked under a gray vest with silver buckles and chains across the front. The back half of the vest draped low and flared like a trench coat. Sewn under the collar of the vest was a hood with a deep cowl that cast Biana's face in deep shadow. Paired with the mask, it was impossible to tell what Biana looked like, and the full effect was incredibly intimidating.

"I never thought I'd say this," Sophie mumbled, "but I miss the dorky Foxfire capes."

"I dunno," Fitz said. "I think it's kinda cool."

"See, and I'm not on board with the hood," Keefe said. "It totally kills the Hair."

"The mask smells funny," Biana added. "And this heavy fabric is making me sweaty."

"Is the campus somewhere cold?" Dex asked.

"It changes every day, as part of their security," Mr. Forkle said. "But it's always in the Neutral Territories. You'll find the campus tomorrow at dawn using these." He reached into one of the trunks and pulled out a small black pouch, which contained five long black cords strung with a single bead.

The bead was blue and dotted with a flake of crystal no bigger than a speck of glitter.

"The crystal only works for a single leap," Granite explained. "After that, you'll have until sunset to prove that you deserve another bead to return the next day."

"What happens if we don't get one?" Dex asked.

"Do not find out," Mr. Forkle warned. "I have no doubt that all of you are capable of handling their curriculum. Exillium focuses on skills, not abilities. Tasks like night vision, slowing your breath, regulating body temperature, suppressing hunger, levitating, blinking in and out of perception, telekinesis, on and on. It will be exhausting, and physically demanding, but could prove useful in the future. We know you'll also be trying to gather information—and we'll be grateful for anything you learn. But do not do so at the expense of your safety."

Keefe fiddled with his necklace, coiling the cord so tightly around his finger it turned his fingertip red.

"You okay?" Sophie asked him.

He shrugged. "You know what gets me? My dad always said I'd end up in Exillium."

"Well, if it makes you feel any better, Biana and I will be the first Vackers ever sent there," Fitz said. "Pretty sure that means we're officially the disgrace of our family."

"No, you're not," Della said, appearing in the doorway. Her eyes looked shadowed as she studied the uniform Biana was modeling. "You're sure sending them to Exillium is a good idea?"

"We're going," Biana said before Mr. Forkle could answer. "And we'll be fine."

She adjusted the collar of her vest and her fingers grazed a button-style pin. It had a cloudy sky as the background with a black outline of half of a standing figure. Squiggly lines in all the colors of the spectrum had replaced the other half of the figure.

"Is this because I'm a Vanisher?" she asked.

Granite nodded. "You each have pins to reflect your abilities."

"So Sophie's going to have four?" Fitz asked. "Won't that kind of ruin her anonymity?"

"We raised that question with the Magistrate," Mr. Forkle said, "and were told the ability pins are mandatory."

"But I thought Exillium was about skills over abilities," Sophie argued.

"It is," Granite agreed. "And that's why you have to wear them. The Coaches need to see what you're naturally able to do, in order to ensure you're not using your abilities to cheat."

"It's also a safety measure," Mr. Forkle added. "To warn what strengths the other Waywards have. The Coaches keep careful records of what everyone can do."

"Speaking of which," Granite said, reaching into one of the trunks and pulling out a stack of thick gray envelopes with the same X symbol. "We need you to verify that we filled out these forms correctly so we can return them to the Magistrate."

"Should we really give them this much personal information?" Della asked, reading over Biana's shoulder.

"We have to," Mr. Forkle said. "The records must exist in case you are ever granted a return to Foxfire."

Sophie snorted. "Like that's ever going to happen."

"You never know," Granite told her. "Timkin Heks managed it, and he'd been caught up in *quite* the scandal."

Sophie frowned, remembering some gossip she'd once heard. "I didn't know he went back to Foxfire after he was expelled."

"Only for his final weeks, so he could graduate with his class," Granite said. "It was a rather strange case. Perhaps someday Timkin will share the story with you."

"Yeah, I'm sure he'll have me over for lushberry juice and mallowmelt," Sophie mumbled. "Right after he tells me to call him Uncle Timkin."

The Heks family included most of Sophie's least favorite people in the Lost Cities. Their daughter Stina was one of the biggest brats at Foxfire, and both her parents had spread more slander about Sophie than anyone.

"You might be surprised," Granite insisted. "Timkin has a challenging personality, no doubt about that. But you both see problems with the Council's current methods. And perhaps you may understand him further after your time in Exillium."

Sophie seriously doubted that.

She also didn't want to think about what the Hekses must be saying about her. Stina had predicted she'd end up in Exillium, and now here she was, with "Sophie Elizabeth Foster" printed across an Exillium registration form, along with her height, weight, hair color, eye color, and all kinds of other personal information.

"Why does it say my address is the Crooked Forest?" Keefe asked.

"They all say that," Mr. Forkle explained. "They needed to know where you'd be going after you left campus. We could hardly mention Alluveterre, so Calla will meet you in the Crooked Forest every day and escort you home."

"That's not in the Neutral Territories, right?" Sophie asked, worried about the plague.

"No, it's actually in the Forbidden Cities," Mr. Forkle said. "It's one of those 'unsolved mysteries' humans are always spinning out wild theories for. Calla requested it specifically."

He passed them each a leaping pendant with an oval crystal cut with only a single facet. Sophie tied it around her neck along with her Exillium bead. She was getting quite the necklace collection.

"How come Foster's form says 'et cetera' on the line for special abilities?" Keefe asked, making Sophie wonder when he'd grabbed her pages. "On mine it says 'Empath.' But on hers it lists the four and then has an 'et cetera.' That means she has more hidden abilities, doesn't it?"

"You cannot read too much into a simple 'etcetera.'" Mr. Forkle told him.

"Psh, with you guys we can," Keefe insisted as Sophie snatched her forms back. "And please tell me she's not a Beguiler—that would get way too complicated."

Keefe kept listing talents he hoped Sophie did or didn't have and Sophie knew she should probably be listening. But her eyes had found a much more life-changing line on her form.

Written in clear block letters, on the line designated for the names of her family.

MR. ERROL L. FORKLE.

# FORTY

SOPHIE SCOOTED BACK HER CHAIR, needing room to breathe.

There'd been a time when she'd wondered if Mr. Forkle could be her real father, but somewhere along the way she'd shoved the thought out of her mind. She couldn't imagine her real father would experiment on her, or abandon her as many times as he had—not to mention looking her in the eye every time he saw her and never saying anything.

"You?" she asked Mr. Forkle. "All this time it was you?"

A pucker pressed between his brows. Then understanding dawned. "I'm not who you think I am."

"Who does she think he is?" Biana asked as Fitz snatched Sophie's forms.

His jaw fell. "He's . . . her father."

"No, I'm not."

"Then why would you list yourself as *family*?" Fitz asked.

"Because I *am* family. My name is the one on her Inception Certificate. Someone had to vouch for her existence. And since her genetic parents couldn't reveal themselves, I took the responsibility. Though of course I had to use an assumed identity. But Mr. Forkle is still me."

"Why the secrecy?" Della asked. "Can't she know her family?"

Granite and Mr. Forkle shared a look.

"Someday you may understand," Mr. Forkle told Sophie. "But for now I can at least assure you—as I did with your concerns about Jolie—that *I* am not your genetic father."

Keefe grabbed Mr. Forkle's wrist. "He's telling the truth. And . . . he actually feels kinda bad about it."

"Of course I do! Project Moonlark may have been *unconventional*. But I *am* your family. And you are mine."

His voice cracked as he said the last sentence, and he turned away, wiping his eyes.

Was he . . . crying?

*I'm aware of the offenses you hold against me,* he transmitted. *And I won't claim I don't deserve them. But I need you to know that I do care about you, Sophie—as much as I can allow myself to. And you may not want to believe this, but your genetic parents care too. They have incredibly important reasons for remaining anonymous—but that does not mean they don't wish they could be a part of your life.*

*Have I ever met them?* Sophie transmitted back.

*I can't tell you that—and I'm begging you to stop guessing. Should you finally settle on the correct answer, you will trigger a chain reaction that could topple our world.*

*How would me knowing who they are "topple" anything? Unless . . .*

A new idea emerged—one far more heartbreaking than any of her other theories.

Mr. Forkle sighed. *I can tell you're still pondering possibilities. So I will add that your genetic parents had no connection to each other. There was no unrequited love. They weren't even friends. I did that purposely, because I couldn't allow them to know who each other were.*

*But they do know I'm their daughter?* Sophie asked.

*Yes. And that truly is the last I can say.*

His voice went silent in her mind, but her head was still reeling with her new theory. What he'd told her ruled out half of it—but not the most heartbreaking part.

Her father still could be . . .

She couldn't bear to think the name.

But he was a Telepath. And he'd always been incredibly kind to her. And it would explain why he'd given her his cache . . .

"Okay, you guys are doing that *staring into each other's eyes* thing," Keefe said, "and it's a lot creepier when it's Sophorkle."

Mr. Forkle looked away, drying his eyes. "So . . . are we good?"

Sophie nodded. "I guess everyone has a few crazy family members they'd don't know what to do with. You'll be mine."

Granite cracked up at that.

Fitz handed her back her Exillium papers, and Sophie studied Mr. Forkle's name.

"Errol?" she asked.

"It's a good strong name," he agreed.

"You do realize your initials spell ELF, right?" Keefe asked.

"Of course. I couldn't resist, once I knew my surname would start with an *F*."

"How did you choose 'Forkle'?" Della asked.

"Somewhat randomly. I was looking for a word that was memorable, but not too complicated, and I wanted the meaning to bear some sort of logic. Forkle is close to the word for 'disguise' in Norwegian, a part of the human world I've always been partial to, so it seemed the best fit—though strangely, I believe it also means 'apron.' Ah, the quirks of human languages."

"What does the *L* stand for?" Dex asked.

Mr. Forkle looked slightly flushed as he mumbled, "Loki."

"Loki," Sophie repeated, tempted to roll her eyes. "You named yourself after the Nordic trickster god?"

"Actually, *he* was inspired by *me*. Do not credit me for the insane stories humans made up—especially that one about the

370

stallion. But as I said, I've always been partial to that part of the world, and in my younger days I may have had a bit too much fun there. It was so easy to take on disguises and cause a little chaos. And over time my escapades morphed into the stories of a shape-shifting trickster god. So I thought it only fitting, as I assumed yet another disguise, that I accept the title officially as part of my new identity."

"Guys, I think the Forkster just became my hero," Keefe said. "And is anyone else wondering about the stallion?"

"Trust me, you don't want to know," Granite promised. "And getting back to relevant things, have you all ensured that your forms are accurate?"

"Mine is," Biana said, handing hers back.

Sophie was about to do the same when she noticed a field her eyes had glossed over the first time. "What does ID mean?"

"That's your inception date," Mr. Forkle said. "The moment your life began."

"But the date you put is months before my birthday."

"Of course. Birth comes after inception."

"Wait—I remember seeing something about this in one of those human movies my dad has," Dex said. "Humans celebrate birthdays, right?"

"Most of them, yeah," Sophie said, wishing her brain could work faster. She could tell there was something important she was missing, but she couldn't seem to catch up to it.

And then it clicked.

"Wait—do elves count age from this ID thing?" she asked.

"Of course," Mr. Forkle said. "The day you were born is simply the day you took your first breath—no more significant of a milestone than when you spoke your first word or took your first step. And don't worry, despite your unusual beginning, I was *very* careful to ensure your inception wasn't affected. There were only seconds between the moment I sparked your life and the moment I had you safely implanted in your mother. Her belly button even turned pink and popped out like it would've if she were an elf—I still can't understand why it did."

The important thought Sophie had caught nearly slipped away in the deluge of *super-weird information*.

"Okay," she said, counting the months on her fingers to double check. "My ID and my birthday are nine months apart."

"Technically, they're thirty-nine weeks apart," Mr. Forkle corrected. "It should've been forty, but your mother delivered a week early. I'd worried that meant something had gone wrong, but it was a flawless delivery, even if watching her fight through the labor pains made for one of the longest nights of my life. Honestly, it's incredible human women ever choose to have children. The agony they go through is unimaginable."

"It doesn't hurt for elves?" Sophie asked.

"Not at all," Della said. "It's exhausting, of course, and there are a few moments where it's difficult to find a comfortable position. But then they hand you your beautiful baby, and the baby gazes up at you and says hello, and your heart just melts."

"*It talks?*" Sophie asked, then remembered Alden telling her months earlier that elvin babies spoke from birth. It sounded even stranger now that she could picture it.

"Your speaking caused quite the uproar," Mr. Forkle told her. "Though luckily no one could understand the Enlightened Language, so they thought you were babbling. I spent the majority of your infancy inventing excuses for the elvin things you did."

"Okay," Sophie said, wishing he'd stop with the *weird-info overload*. "But what I mean is . . . I've been counting my age from my birthday."

Mr. Forkle didn't look surprised.

"Why didn't you tell me?" she asked.

"How could I? Humans built everything around their birthdays. As long as you were living with them I had to let you do the same. And since you've been in the Lost Cities, we've had so little contact. I assumed someone would notice, since your proper ID is on your Foxfire record—and in the registry. But I don't think anyone realized you were counting differently."

"Alden wouldn't have thought to check," Della agreed. "Neither of us knew humans didn't count inception."

"So wait," Biana jumped in, "does that mean that by our rules Sophie is—"

"Thirty-nine weeks older than she's been saying," Mr. Forkle finished for her.

Fitz cocked his head as he stared at Sophie, like everything had turned sideways. "So then you're not thirteen . . ."

"Not according to the way we count," Mr. Forkle agreed. "Going by Sophie's ID, she's fourteen and a little more than five months old."

Keefe laughed. "Only Foster would find a way to age nine months in a day. Also, welcome to the cool fourteen-year-olds club!"

He held out his hand for a high five.

Sophie was too stunned to return it.

"Please try not to stress, Miss Foster. Nothing has actually changed. You're the exact same girl you were a few minutes ago. You're simply learning the proper way of counting."

She knew he was right—but it felt *so much* huger than that.

Especially when Biana said, "Huh, so you're older than me."

Based on their IDs, Biana was a little more than thirteen-and-a-half. Dex was also thirteen, but he would be fourteen in a few weeks. Keefe was less than a month away from turning fifteen, and Fitz was about two months away from turning sixteen.

"So, you're kind of in the middle," Dex said. "But you and I are still the closest in age."

He was right—though now she was six months older than him. And the gap between her and Keefe and Fitz had narrowed *significantly*.

"Wait—was I in the wrong level in Foxfire?" Sophie asked.

"Your age falls in the middle of the grade level brackets," Mr. Forkle said. So you could've started as a Level Two just as easily as a Level Three. And given how behind you were from your human education, you needed the time to catch up."

"I guess," Sophie said, still fighting to squish all this huge information into her already full brain.

So . . . she was fourteen—as far as elves were concerned. Almost halfway to fifteen.

"Why do humans count age differently?" Biana asked.

"I suspect it's partly because their bodies do not have such a clear indication of the moment of inception the way ours do," Mr. Forkle said. "And partly because their pregnancies are much more uncertain. Humans miscarry all the time, at any stage of the pregnancy."

Della clutched her stomach, like the very idea pained her.

"I know," Mr. Forkle told her. "Sophie's mother lost five babies before she sought my help. And while I was working at the clinic I met hundreds of women like her. The most heartbreaking part was that I could've fixed them all with a few elixirs—much like I did with your mother. She had no trouble having your sister after you, right?"

Sophie nodded. "So why didn't you help them?"

"Because humans lost the right to our assistance when they violated our treaty and prepared for war. We even tried to help them secretly afterward. But they took the gifts we gave them and twisted them into weapons, or bargaining chips for their political agendas, or soggy, chemical-filled Twinkies. So I understand why we had to stop. But it was hard to watch."

"I bet," Della said, still holding her middle. "Humans are such temporary creatures."

"They are indeed," Granite said. "I've often pondered what it would be like to live each day knowing you only have seventy or eighty years on this planet. I wonder if that's the real reason they wait those nine months and begin their timeline at birth. Once their clock starts ticking, there's no turning it back."

"That was one of the most striking things I noticed during my years living among them," Mr. Forkle agreed. "Each generation dumps their problems on the next because they simply do not have enough time to deal with them. I suspect that if they could see a bigger picture, they would not destroy themselves and their planet the same way."

Sophie nodded, remembering some of the thoughts she'd heard growing up. Death truly was humans' constant companion. Maybe if it wasn't, they'd care more about others and take the time to do things the right way.

And yet, later that night, as she tossed and turned in bed, nervous for what the first day at Exillium would bring, Sophie couldn't help wondering if the elves' indefinite lifespan hindered them just as much as the humans' fleeting lives.

Would the Council—and even the Black Swan—be so willing to sit back and ignore problems if they couldn't rest so comfortably in the knowledge that they still had centuries and centuries ahead of them?

The more she thought about it, the more she realized both sides had lost an important alternate perspective. And maybe *that* was what she'd been created for.

A girl from both worlds, who'd seen the follies and triumphs of each side.

And her job was to shake things up and do something new.

# FORTY-ONE

**B**IANA WAS RIGHT—THESE MASKS smell funky," Keefe said as the five friends leaped to Exillium.

The fleck of crystal on their beads dissolved as soon as they arrived on the slope of a misty mountain. Sharp winds stung their cheeks while they climbed the rocky path ahead, and the slender trees around them looked normal and healthy.

"No sign of the plague here," Sophie said, not sure if she was relieved or disappointed. No plague meant no chance of finding any clues, either.

"So, um . . . where's the school?" Biana asked. "Do you think we leaped to the wrong place?"

"How?" Dex asked. "We used their beads."

"True." But Sophie had yet to see another person, or even a sign that anyone had ever been there. No footprints marred the path, no voices buzzed in the distance. "If we're lost . . ."

"Then we all jump off these cliffs," Fitz said, "and teleport as close as we can get to Alluveterre."

"*Or* she could take us to Foxfire," Keefe jumped in, "and we could run through the halls screaming, 'YOU CAN'T GET RID OF US THAT EASILY!'"

"I like that plan," Dex said.

"Me too," Biana agreed.

"Of course you do. It's brilliant."

Their path curved, leading to a rocky clearing so thick with mist, they couldn't see the ground. An enormous arch made of jagged black metal loomed over the entrance, woven from iron thistles.

"This place is freaky," Dex whispered. "Do you think this is it?"

Sophie pointed to the center of the arch, where the same *X* symbol they'd seen before seemed to taunt them.

"Okay," she whispered. "From this point on we keep a low profile, and if we find something we—"

The rest of her instruction disappeared in a scream.

A thick rope had tightened around her ankle, yanking her off the ground and leaving her dangling upside down from the arch. Her friends hung beside her, flailing and thrashing, the ground very far below.

"Welcome to your Dividing!" a raspy female voice shouted from somewhere in the fog.

The mist parted and a figure in a red hooded cloak stepped forward, followed by a figure in a blue cloak and another in royal purple.

"You must find your way to freedom," the purple figure told them. Her voice sounded stiffer than the other figure. More reserved.

"There's no right answer to the problem," the blue figure added, his voice high and nasal. "But light leaping doesn't count. You must untie or sever the cord. And choose wisely. This will determine which one of us will be coaching you."

Sophie's brain throbbed from the head rush, and her snared foot went numb as she tried to curl her body up to reach the knot. She couldn't even make it halfway before her abs gave up.

Why had that always looked so much easier in movies?

"Anyone having any luck?" Fitz asked, clearly not experiencing the same ab challenges as Sophie. He pried at the rope with shaking hands. "This knot is impossible."

"Almost out," Keefe said.

Sophie tried to catch sight of him, but Dex was in the way.

Keefe mumbled "ow" several times before shouting, "YOU THINK YOU CAN HOLD M—"

A loud *RIIIIIIIIIIIIIIIIIIIIIIIIIIIIIIIIIIIIIIIIP* cut him off, and he shouted a bunch of words that would earn him a month of detention before a *CRUNCH!* left him silent.

"Are you okay?" Sophie called.

"I've been better," Keefe groaned. "Guess I forgot to brace for the fall."

"He also forgot his pants," the blue-cloaked figure noted.

A wave of snickers followed, and Sophie realized the whole school was hiding in the mist, watching them dangle like sides of beef at the butcher shop. Keefe's boot dangled with them, along with a shredded pair of black pants.

"Oy, his boxers are covered in little banshees!" a kid shouted.

"Bet he peed himself too," another said.

"SILENCE!" the blue Coach snapped. "Those of you still trapped should not concern yourselves with those who are free. He's passed the test. Can you say the same?"

"I can in a second!" Dex shouted back.

Sophie spun around and found Dex curled up like a monkey, sawing at his rope with something silver. The cord snapped a second later, leaving him hovering there.

*Levitating.*

"Should've thought of that," Keefe grumbled as Dex floated to the ground and tossed his silver blade—fashioned out of his vest's buckles—at the purple figure's feet.

"Impressive," the purple Coach said. "Too bad you won't be in my hemisphere."

"And then there were three," the red Coach called to Sophie, Fitz, and Biana.

"Try *two*!"Biana shouted, pumping her arms to swing back

and forth. Her rope frayed against the metal thistles of the arch, and she stopped her fall with shaky levitating. She got most of the way down before her concentration gave out, but she was able to tuck and roll when she hit the ground.

Sophie tried Biana's method, but her rope refused to fray. And there was *no* way she was dropping down pantless, like Keefe—not that she really understood how he'd managed that. She also had no idea how to turn her vest into a blade. But there had to be something else she could use. She checked all of her pockets.

"GOT IT!" Fitz shouted, doing a gold medal–worthy flip to stand on top of the arch. He unknotted his rope easily, then climbed over to Sophie.

"NO ASSISTANCE ALLOWED!" all three Coaches hollered at him.

"I'm not going to leave her up here!" Fitz shouted back.

"It's okay," Sophie told him. "I have a plan."

She doubted it was a *good* plan—but he didn't need to know that. She refused to be the only one who couldn't get out on her own.

Fitz reluctantly floated to the ground, and Sophie reached under her vest and dug out her Black Swan pendant, remembering how it had worked with the force field. She held it by the swan-shaped handle and tipped the glass into the orangey rays of sunrise. As soon as the light hit the lens, a blue beam flashed like a laser. She aimed it for her rope and it erupted with white-hot flames, spreading down her boot and igniting the metal arch in a shower of sparks.

She thrashed and broke free, but the fire kept burning her leg, the pain making it impossible to levitate as she fell. She curled into a ball, bracing for a brutal landing and . . .

A powerful stream of cold water knocked her back.

She sank into the wet, glad to feel the flames vanish on her leg. Then the wave rolled forward, tossing her gently to the dirt like the ocean crashing onto the shore. She gasped for breath and tried to pull herself to her feet, but the searing pain of her burns was too unbearable.

The last thing she saw was a giant wave crashing against the burning arch. Then everything faded to black.

# FORTY-TWO

L EAVE IT TO YOU TO TRY TO BURN down Exillium on the first day," Keefe said as Sophie's eyes fluttered open, revealing that she'd been moved to a dimly lit tent. Her narrow mattress rested on the floor, and her ankle felt tender, but the rest of her seemed okay—until she realized her boots were missing. And her pants . . .

She scrambled for a blanket and discovered she'd been dressed in a faded gray robe. She decided not to ask when and where the change had happened.

She rolled to her side, and the bed made an embarrassing squeaking sound.

"That was the mattress," she said.

Keefe giggled. "Everybody farts, Foster. It's cool. I still think you're cute."

Sophie became very interested in studying the tent. The canvas had been decorated with bold swirls of color. It might have once been pretty, but there were too many patches and tears, and the whole thing looked like it could use a thorough wash.

"How's your ankle?" she asked Keefe as he stretched and winced. He wore a robe just like hers and had a black bandage wrapped around his foot.

Keefe hiccupped. "The boobrie dude said it's not broken. And he gave me this to help with the pain." He held up an empty vial and hiccupped again.

"Boobrie dude?" Sophie asked.

"He wouldn't tell me his name. And he has this crazy bird mask." He giggled again.

"Where did he go?" Sophie asked.

"Hopefully to get me more of this." Keefe tried to take another drink from the empty vial, then settled for licking the rim.

Must've been a *powerful* elixir.

"What's in it?" she asked.

"No idea. All I know is it tasted like kissing a muskog."

"And you have a lot of experience with that?"

"Hey, I never say no to a dare!"

"Wait—you seriously kissed a muskog?" Sophie asked, remembering the burpy froglike thing Stina had put in Dex's locker once.

Keefe hiccupped again. "I've kissed *lots* of things! Just ask Biana."

"You kissed *Biana*?"

"A couple years ago, yeah," he mumbled. "Mostly on the cheek."

"What do you mean by 'mostly'?"

"You want a demonstration?"

"Um . . . I think I'll pass." She was sure her face was redder than Mr. Snuggles.

"It wasn't a big deal," he told her. "It was just a dare."

"Okay," she said, not sure why she was clenching her fists so hard.

Keefe narrowed his eyes. "You're a hard one to read, Miss F., you know that? Sometimes I think you—ohhhh, the boobrie dude gave you some of the awesomesauce!" He pointed to a vial on the floor next to her mattress, filled with swirly purple syrup. "You should take it. Or if you don't want it, you should give it to me!"

Sophie snatched the vial out of his reach. "I think you've had enough."

"Boo—you're worse than my mom! Actually, no you're not. No one is. Was. What's the right verb? It needs to be past tense, right?"

The thought seemed to sober him up and he rolled onto his side, curling his legs into his chest. He tapped his empty vial with his fingernails.

*Tap. Tap. Tap.*

Sophie studied his expression, wondering if this was the *real* Keefe. Without the jokes to hide behind, he looked angry. And *really* scared.

"Right now it's in the 'we don't know' tense, Keefe," she said gently.

"Yeah." *Tap. Tap. Tap. Tap. Tap.* "I made her a necklace one time. Did I tell you that? I made it out of beads to match her favorite bracelet. I painted a different flower on every one. And do you know how many times she wore it?"

Sophie was pretty sure she could guess.

He held up both of his fists with no fingers raised. "That many. I really thought she would. She even defended it. My dad said I'd wasted an afternoon when I could've been preparing for my Foxfire entrance exams, and she told him she thought it was pretty. I'd painted the flowers from memory *after* studying for the agriculture exam—not that my dad cared. So I thought she'd wear it. But nope. She always wore the ugly ruby necklace *he* bought her."

He tapped the bottle so hard it slipped out of his hand and bounced to the edge of the tent.

Sophie got up to grab it, sucking in a breath as she put weight on her burned leg.

"That's what you get for climbing out of bed before I tell you," a sharp voice scolded.

"Hey—it's the boobrie dude!" Keefe said as a green-cloaked

figure slipped into the tent. "Got any more of the good stuff?"

The boobrie dude frowned, which looked especially strange now that Sophie understood what Keefe meant about his mask. The black metal had been decorated with yellow feathers that stuck through the fabric of his hood.

"I don't think you should give him any more," Sophie told him.

"No, I don't think so either," the boobrie dude agreed. "Don't worry, his head will clear soon. What about you?" he asked Sophie. "You're not having the same side effect?"

Sophie held up her still-full vial. "Didn't seem like a good idea. Plus, I had to make sure there's no limbium in it."

"Ah, so you're the one with the allergy—I wasn't sure if it was you or the other girl. I was careful just in case. Now let's see that burn."

Sophie stretched out her leg, cringing when she saw the blisters coating the top of her foot and running all the way to the middle of her calf.

He pulled out a nearly empty tube and squeezed the last of its contents onto the burn. The cream was gray and chalky and felt scratchy on her blisters.

"We're out of numbing ointment," he explained. "We're out of most everything, but this should be enough. I make what I can with any herbs I stumble across, but what I wouldn't give for one measly supply shipment."

"The Council doesn't send any?"

He snorted. "All they ever send is more Waywards—though never five in a single day before. How'd you manage that?"

Sophie shrugged. "The Council doesn't like us."

"Well, it's good you're used to that, since the Coaches don't like you either. You ruined the Arch of Dividing."

"They were the ones who left us dangling like piñatas."

"Piñatas?" he asked.

"They're a human thing."

"Well, I'm assuming comments like that are what got you here. Probably those eyes, too."

"Hey, I like Foster's eyes," Keefe told him. "Brown is so much warmer than blue."

"You two should be careful," the boobrie dude said as Sophie blushed. "Names are not welcome here."

"Does that mean I can keep calling you boobrie dude?" Keefe asked.

"If you must. But I'm serious about my warning. Keep to yourself. Focus on the skills. And wipe off that leg."

It took Sophie a second to realize he wanted her to use the towel he was offering, which didn't necessarily look clean. But there weren't any other towels, so Sophie wiped the gray gunk off her skin, relieved to see no trace of the blisters.

The boobrie dude nodded. "You're lucky she put out the fire so quickly."

"She?" Sophie asked.

"Our Hydrokinetic. She called the wave that caught you—

which should've gotten her ejected, by the way. But she also put out the rest of the fire, so the Coaches let it slide."

"Why would helping me get her ejected?" Sophie asked, hoping it meant "expelled" and not actually being launched out of the campus.

"Because here it's about everyone for themselves. And since you seem like the type, you should know it would be a terrible idea to thank her. Communication will get you both in trouble—and then you'll have to deal with the Shade."

The way he said the word gave Sophie chills. "Who's the Shade?"

"The worst Wayward here. And he's incredibly protective of the Hydrokinetic. If you want to survive here, you'll keep your distance from both of them."

He turned his attention to Keefe, unwrapping the bandage and rubbing a green gel on Keefe's ankle.

"How long have you worked here?" Sophie asked, hoping he'd say a long time. If she could learn something about the Psionipath, it would make the whole physician-visit-on-the-first-day thing less embarrassing.

"Honestly, I've lost count," he said. "I think it's been ten years, but it all blurs together."

Ten years was a good answer. "Did you ever treat a Psionipath—or remember meeting one—over the years?"

"I've met several," he said, turning back to face her. "Why?"

Sophie shrugged, hoping she looked casual. "I ran into one

a few weeks ago and he said he used to go to Exillium."

He shook his head. "If this is a crush thing, you can do better."

"It's not a crush thing," Sophie said, ignoring Keefe's snickers. She realized it was going to take a little more "truth" to coax out the right answer, so she added, "I think he might be part of some sort of rebellion."

The boobrie dude flinched, and she knew she was onto something. Especially when he said, "Stay away from him."

"So you know who I'm talking about?"

"I'm pretty sure I do, though I couldn't tell you his name. And he's even worse than the Shade. Anger at the Council is pretty standard around here, but I remember thinking, 'This guy could spark a revolution.' And given the strangeness I've seen in the Territories . . ."

"What strangeness?" Sophie asked, her heart officially in thunder mode.

"These are dangerous questions," he said. "The kind that could get you ejected—or worse."

"It's wrong to want to know what's happening in our world?" Sophie asked.

"You don't have a world anymore. You're banished."

"She's just trying to settle a bet," Keefe jumped in before Sophie could argue any further. "I bet her that the guy was lying about being at Exillium to sound tough, so she's trying to prove me wrong. And my leg feels all better now. Thanks."

The boobrie dude didn't look convinced by Keefe's excuse. But all he said was, "Both of you need to get dressed." He pointed to new pants and boots at the foot of their beds and lowered a curtain between their beds to give them privacy. "The Coaches are ready to mark you."

"*Mark* us?" Sophie asked, trying not to picture a dog marking its territory.

"Yes. It's time for you to learn your place in Exillium."

# FORTY-THREE

THE BOOBRIE DUDE ESCORTED THEM from the Healing Tent to a stage under a golden canopy, where the three Coaches stood in their colored robes in the center of the platform. The rest of the Waywards were lined up in front, in neat rows with their arms at their sides, like soldiers.

Sophie searched the crowd for the rest of her friends, but the hoods and masks made it impossible to recognize anyone. The only distinguishing marks were colored handprints on their sleeves—either a red handprint on their left arm, a blue handprint on their right arm, or a purple handprint on both arms. The colors corresponded to the Coaches' robes, and also to the three tents set up in the remaining corners of the campus. The canopies reminded Sophie of the pictures she'd seen of celebrity weddings, with raised peaks in the middle and silky panels of fabric flapping in the strong mountain winds. The tent on the right was deep blue, the left tent was ruby red, and the center tent was royal purple. The Coaches stood in the same order, each holding a bowl of matching paint.

"Since these two have taken it upon themselves to delay today's lesson with their *accidents*," the red Coach said in her raspy voice, "we will be skipping lunch and switching today's skill to appetite suppression."

Every Wayward groaned, and Sophie was pretty sure she was officially the most hated girl in school. Fortunately, that was familiar territory.

"And now, for your marking," the red Coach said.

The blue Coach stepped forward and faced Keefe. "Your immediate, impulsive action—despite being foolish—made it clear that you belong in the Right Hemisphere."

He dipped his hand in the paint and smacked Keefe's right arm, leaving a blue handprint on his sleeve.

"You enjoyed that, didn't you?" Keefe asked.

"Very much," the blue Coach said.

He moved back to the other Coaches, and the purple Coach stepped forward, handing Sophie the bowl of purple paint.

"Your indecision to act, as well as your unconventional solution, made it clear you are neither right nor left, but Ambi."

She dipped both of her hands in the purple paint and marked each of Sophie's sleeves.

Sophie stared at the purple handprints, wishing she wasn't being separated from Keefe. The Coaches dismissed the crowd, and she hoped she'd find at least one of her friends at the purple Ambi tent. But there were definitely no friendly faces. A few Waywards even tried to trip her as she walked past.

The tent had no chairs. Only mats on the floor, and the fabric had seen better days. Everything was frayed, with patches and stains. She chose a spot in the back to hide. No one sat near her—though no one sat next to anyone, except for one boy and a girl who sat as close as they could sit without technically touching. Sophie sucked in a breath when she noticed the girl's pin: swirling waves and drops of rain. She had to be the Hydrokinetic.

The girl sat hunched, like she was trying to shrink away. The boy was her opposite. Everything about him felt *defiant*. His uniform sleeves were rolled up, and he angled his body toward the girl, making it clear he would not be kept away from her. His ability pin was silver, with a black hand reaching from the center like it was trying to claw free. Sophie assumed that meant he was the Shade.

She was still studying the boy, trying to decide if she believed the boobrie dude's warnings about him, when the purple Coach shouted for everyone to get into position. Sophie copied the others as they folded their legs crisscross-applesauce and kept their backs rigid.

"Our bodies need food," her Coach said, "but they do not need to be *hungry*. Hunger is a choice—a warning system that can be switched off by those strong enough to defy it. Take control. Concentrate. And put your head between your knees if you feel faint."

The first hour passed easily, though Sophie had to keep tilting her legs so her butt wouldn't go numb. But as the second hour stretched into the third, she could feel the sloshy sourness in her belly growing. She hadn't had breakfast—choosing to nab an extra fifteen minutes of sleep. She regretted that decision when her stomach started growling.

"Stop giving in to your weakness," her Coach told her.

*GROOOOOOOWWWWWWWLLLLLLLLLLLL!* her stomach protested.

She tried to take her mind off it by repeating what little she'd learned. Clearly the physician knew something about the plague, but he wasn't telling. She wondered if asking adults was the wrong way to go. Maybe she'd have better luck if she found a way to talk to one of the Waywards—but who? Without seeing their faces she couldn't tell if any of them looked friendly. All she had to go by were their ability pins.

She knew the Telepath pin was blue, with a silhouette of a face and a lightning bolt zapping across the brain—way prettier than her Inflictor pin, which was black with a silver hand radiating jagged silver lines. Her Polyglot pin had a purple background with pink lips and a white speech bubble, and her Teleporter pin was her favorite—a starry sky with a flying alicorn. She also knew from Dex that the Technopath pin was dark green with a silver handprint covered in black lines like circuits and wires, and Keefe's Empath pin was red with an open book and a silver heart painted across the pages.

But the rest she had to guess. Could the yellow pin with two hands holding the sun mean a Flasher? Was the tree with wind-whipped branches a Guster? And what did it matter anyway? Were certain abilities friendlier?

Her eyes traveled back to the Shade and she sucked in a breath when she realized his head was tilted toward her.

*Sophie?* Fitz transmitted, nearly making her scream. *Sorry for slipping past your blocking without permission,* he said. *I kept trying to get your attention, but you never looked over, and I realized you didn't know Biana and I both ended up in Left Hemisphere. I'll cough so you can see where we are.*

Soft hacking drew her gaze to two cloaked figures somewhat close together on the far side of the red tent.

*Where's Dex?*

*He's with Keefe in the Right Hemisphere. You okay over there all alone?*

*Of course.* But her mind wandered to the Shade.

*Why's he staring at you?* Fitz asked, reminding her he could see what she was thinking.

*I don't know. But the physician said he's the worst Wayward here.*

*I wouldn't be surprised. Shades control darkness with a force they call shadowvapor. I don't really understand it. But you should never trust a Shade—especially one who ends up here.*

And yet, when the Hydrokinetic girl started swaying from hunger, the Shade scooted closer, helping her put her head between her knees until she caught her breath.

*That's the girl who saved you,* Fitz transmitted. *You should've seen how crazy her power is. She waved her arms and this huge wave curled out of the fog, and I swear it looked like she grabbed you with a giant water hand. Then she set you down and the hand reached up and smacked the arch until all the flames had been stamped out. I'm pretty sure everyone thinks you're a Pyrokinetic now, by the way. Even I wondered for a second—especially when I saw how fast the flames moved. And they were white, like those fires Brant set before.*

*I know—I don't understand,* Sophie said. *Why would the Black Swan give us something to make fire like Pyrokinetics?*

*Maybe they wanted to even our chances against Brant.*

*Maybe.* Not that she loved the idea.

Her stomach growled again and she clamped her hands around her middle.

*Wow, I heard that all the way over here. You need to think about food. It tricks your stomach. What would you eat right now if you could?*

Sophie's mouth watered as she thought of Calla's stark-flower stew. But the happy memory quickly drifted to how she imagined the gnomes in quarantine must look—which did at least kill her appetite.

*How long do you think we have before someone dies?* she asked Fitz.

*Hopefully long enough.*

*And hopefully tomorrow they move the campus to somewhere we actually learn something—assuming I get a bead. My fire incident was a pretty epic disaster.*

*Try not to worry—I think you'll be fine.*

But really, were any of them "fine"?

She thought about Keefe in the physician's tent, in that brief glimpse of the fear and anger he was hiding.

*Do you think Keefe is really okay?*

*I . . . don't see how he could be.*

It was an honest answer—and totally terrifying. Neither of them seemed to know what to say. So they sat in silence, connected but separate as the sun slowly sank toward the horizon.

A gong finally dismissed them, and Sophie followed the Waywards to the golden pavilion, where the blue Coach held a jar of green beads. The purple Coach clapped her hands, making the beads float until each Wayward had a bead hovering over their head, even Sophie.

"To our new Waywards, who do not understand our traditions," the red Coach said. "We offer beads only to those we deem deserving. But it's always your choice to refuse or accept."

"Accepting comes with sacrifice," the blue Coach warned. "The cost of continuing your fight for redemption. Refusing has no consequence, but it is also irreversible."

"We won't tell you how to decide," the purple Coach finished. "You choose your path."

Sophie reached for her bead and a jolt of electricity stung her hand. She hadn't realized the sacrifice would be such a literal consequence. But she was glad to know she could survive it.

She tied the bead onto her black cord, and it looked so small next to the blue one. Especially considering how many beads the Waywards around her had.

"If you're thinking it'll get easier, it won't," a deep voice whispered in her ear.

She turned to find the Shade with his head tilted toward her. But he was too far away to be the whisperer.

She opened her mouth to reply and he nudged her attention to where the purple Coach stood watching.

"You should be careful," his whispery voice said, despite the distance between them. "The Coaches are *very* interested in you."

She couldn't figure out how he was doing it, until she glanced down and noticed his shadow crossing hers.

*Wait,* Sophie transmitted, as he turned to walk away.

She hadn't forgotten the physician's warnings—or Fitz's—but she couldn't pass up a chance to make a connection.

She didn't trust him, though, so she went with something safe.

*Can you tell your Hydrokinetic friend "thank-you" for saving me?*

His shadow slipped over hers again, and she could almost feel his eyes studying her. "You're different," his voice whispered. "I can't decide if that's a good thing."

*It is,* she transmitted, surprised at how much she wanted him to believe her.

He walked away without another word.

# FORTY-FOUR

THE FIVE FRIENDS HELD HANDS AS they leaped away from Exillium, and all the Coaches and Waywards stared.

"I don't think we're doing so great at the whole 'blending in' thing," Keefe said as they reappeared in a gray-skied forest. "Which is why you guys are my favorite."

"What happened here?" Biana whispered as she turned toward the trees. Their trunks were unnaturally bent and crooked. "It's not the plague, is it?"

"No, the forest has been like this for decades," Sophie said. "I remember seeing pictures of this place on the Internet."

"The *Internet*," Dex snorted. "Humans and their technology."

"It looks like somebody bent them intentionally," Fitz said, tracing his hand down one of the C-shaped trunks.

"I did." Calla dropped into the clearing from the top of one of the trees. "I sang to them, and they followed my voice."

"Why only these trees?" Sophie asked. There were hundreds with the same distinct shape, but the forest beyond was straight and normal.

Calla placed her palm against the sharpest part of the curve, where the tree stood only inches above the ground. "These trees were dying. My friends told me I should uproot them to spare the rest of the forest. But I could feel too much life in their trunks to pluck them from the ground."

"How did you save them?" Biana asked.

"I *listened*. And I realized their voices had been silenced. So I gave them mine. I sang of sunlight and rain and rich soil. And hope. Always hope." She moved to another tree, one that had the widest curve of them all, and lay in the slope of its trunk. "For a week I stayed right here. I didn't stop, even to rest my throat. I could barely rasp by the end, but I could feel their strength returning. They'll forever bear the mark of their trials, but they are *survivors*. Proof that anything can be overcome."

Keefe sat on one of the curved trunks, and Sophie waited for him to make a joke. But he just slid his fingers over the rough bark.

"I thought we could all use the reminder that nature tells us what it needs," Calla whispered. "That's why I chose this as our meeting place."

She closed her eyes, singing a slow melody. It was the sweetest song Sophie had ever heard, and the forest shimmered in response. The crooked trees rustled as if they were joining in the chorus, and the wind whistled through their leaves.

"It's beautiful," Biana whispered, waving her fingers in front of her face. "I think I finally see the glints of life you told me about, Calla."

"If that's true, then you now know how I see you." Calla smiled when Biana's eyes lit up.

Calla repeated the song again, and the sparkles intensified, until the whole forest looked painted with glitter. It faded when she kneeled at the foot of the tree. Her song turned softer, and the roots twisted and twirled until they'd swept aside the soil and formed a tunnel.

Calla motioned for everyone to follow her underground, and as Sophie stepped into the earth she swore she heard a new song take over—a hushed whisper circling around her, prickling her consciousness.

Her eyes found Calla's in the dim light, wondering if Calla could hear it too.

"I don't know where it's coming from," Calla said. "It's as if the earth itself has joined the call, trying to tell us what it needs."

Goose bumps peppered Sophie's skin as her mind translated the lyric. A single word, sung over and over and over.

*Panakes.*

"What if we're focusing on the wrong thing?" Sophie asked when they'd regrouped in the girls' common room, after they'd eaten and changed out of their uniforms. "Maybe we should be searching for the Panakes instead of the drakostomes."

"If you're saying we should sneak into ogreville instead of sitting here watching Dex poke a gadget with sticks, I'm *in*," Keefe said.

"Easy there," Sophie told him as Keefe tried to drag her toward the door. "That's *not* what I'm saying—not yet at least. I meant we should be searching for *information* about the Panakes."

Keefe flopped back into his chair with a sigh so dramatic it had to have hurt his throat.

"And excuse me," Dex said, "this happens to be an incredibly technical process." He held up the Twiggler, which now looked like some sort of twig-and-wire spider. "You try merging six different technologies into one gadget."

"I'm not saying it's not important," Keefe said. "But the rest of us are just sitting here wasting time."

"Speak for yourself," Biana said, appearing by the waterfall. "I think I figured out how to hide from Calla. I just need to make sure I can hold it."

"Yeah, and Sophie and I are about to do some Cognate training," Fitz added.

"But what do you mean by focusing on the Panakes?" Dex asked Sophie.

"I meant we should be trying to find information about the *cure*, not the *cause* of the plague. Calla said nature tells us what it needs, and nature was singing about the Panakes. We need to figure out what they are and how to find them."

"Assuming they're real," Fitz reminded her.

"If the earth is singing about them, wouldn't they have to be?" Sophie asked. "And if there's any record of them, I'm betting it's in there." She pointed to the Twiggler, wishing it didn't look so ready to fall apart. "Are you getting any closer to making it search by keyword?"

"I'm trying," Dex said. "But the different technologies are super specific. They'll each only serve a single function. The elvin tech provides all the power I need, and the dwarven stuff works like a backup. The goblin tech is my security, the trollish tech is what breaks through the barriers and whatnot, the ogre tech is the really sneaky stuff that gets me past the subtle defenses. And the gnomish tech seems to smooth out all the connections between everything. That's why I keep adding more sticks, hoping it'll make the parts cooperate better. But none of that helps with searching. It almost feels like that comes from a totally different technology. But I already have all the intelligent species represented, so I don't know what that means."

"What about humans?" Sophie asked. "I know they're not part of the treaties anymore—but they *were*."

"The archive is super old, right?" Fitz added. "So it could've been built before the humans betrayed everyone, and that would mean it includes their technology."

Dex scratched the top of his head. "I guess. But I have no idea what I'm supposed to use for human technology."

"There's my iPod," Sophie offered, even though she *really* didn't want it destroyed. The small human gadget had been her constant companion growing up, her only way to drown out the bombarding human thoughts before she knew how to shield. Plus, it was one of the few human things she had left from her old life—and Dex had made all kinds of cool tweaks.

"Nah," Dex said. "Anything modern would be too advanced. I don't even know if humans knew electricity existed back when this archive was made."

They didn't, Sophie realized. "Okay . . . so we have to figure out what they *did* have."

Chariots? Plows? Bows and arrows? Were any of those thousands of years old?

"I remember learning in school about an Iron Age, a Bronze Age, and a Stone Age," she told them. "Where humans made tools from those different materials."

"Hmm. I'm already using bronze and iron for some of the other creatures," Dex said. "But I guess I could try stone—though I have no idea how stone counts as 'technology.'"

"It makes a pretty decent weapon," Keefe mumbled. "Just ask my mom."

He rubbed his head where she'd given him a gash during her attempt to steal Silveny.

No one seemed to know what to say to that.

"I think that's my cue," Keefe said, heading for the door. "Call me if you decide on an ogre invasion."

Dex stood too, stuffing the Twiggler into his satchel. "Guess I need to go rock hunting. Wanna come with me?" he asked Sophie.

"We really need to work through some Cognate exercises," Fitz reminded her. "We lost a whole week when I was sick."

The old Dex would've glowered and muttered something about Telepaths. But the new Dex just nodded and said, "Yeah, that makes sense."

"Can I go with you?" Biana asked him. "If I don't let Iggy get some exercise, he's going to shred another one of my favorite shoes."

Biana must really love the little imp if she was willing to forgive footwear destruction.

"At least he's doing well on his diet," she told Sophie. "I think he's finally getting a taste for vegetables!"

It turned out Iggy had most definitely *not* gotten a taste for vegetables, and Biana stomped back an hour later, muttering about "stubborn imps." Sophie assumed it had something to do with the giant moth wing Iggy was crunching on.

Della returned not long after, looking uncommonly frazzled. Her hair was tied back in a sloppy bun, and her gown was stained and wrinkled.

"Everything okay?" Sophie asked.

Della shook her head. "Physic had done some research on human comas, and she'd come up with a treatment plan for Prentice, with cold and hot compresses and balms and elixirs. We tried it today, but somewhere in the process he stopped breathing and everything unraveled. We got him breathing again—don't worry. But . . ." Della stared at the ceiling. "I think we're officially out of ideas. Nothing seems to matter."

If words could cast a shadow, they would've darkened the whole house.

"I'm sorry," Della said, heading toward her room. "I don't mean to despair. I'm just tired of sitting at Prentice's bedside telling happy stories and trying to pretend I'm not partially there for completely selfish reasons. I want him to get better, but . . ."

Sophie knew what she meant.

Della was still worried about how Prentice's condition would affect Alden.

"Anyway, good night." Della kissed her son on the top of the head, then did the same to Sophie before she headed for her room. "Don't stay up too late working. You'll need plenty of rest before another day at Exillium.

Sophie knew Della was right, and went to bed an hour early.

She also ate a double portion of breakfast the next morning in case they were in for another round of appetite suppression. She was prepared for anything Exillium could throw at her—until they leaped to campus and arrived in the heart of a plague zone.

# FORTY-FIVE

NOW SOPHIE KNEW WHAT THE ANCIENT gnomish songs had meant by their warnings of a great Withering and an endless Fall.

The Exillium tents had been set up along the edge of a sheer cliff, overlooking a blackened, shriveled woodland. The tree trunks were twisted and cracked, their branches sagging and drooping, and their speckled leaves blanketed the ground in heaps of mold green and sallow yellow.

"Where are we?" Sophie whispered.

"It doesn't matter," her purple Coach said behind her.

The five friends turned to find all three Coaches looming

over them. Waywards milled nearby, pretending they weren't eavesdropping.

"How can you say that?" Biana asked the Coaches. "Don't you know what's happening down there?"

"We don't," the red Coach said, "and we aren't supposed to."

"That's not *our* world," the blue Coach added. "It's simply scenery."

"So you don't care that—" Sophie started.

"We don't," the blue Coach interrupted.

"We *can't*," the purple Coach clarified. "We know our place, and the role we're expected to play. The five of you need to learn yours."

"You're no longer part of a community," the red Coach added. "You're fighting for survival and redemption."

"But how is it redeeming to only care about ourselves?" Sophie asked.

The silence that followed felt like it was breathing down their necks, probably because the whole school was watching.

The Coaches' eventual reply was to order everyone to their Hemispheres.

Sophie kept her head down as she ran to her purple Ambi tent and sat near one of the tent poles. A shadow passed over her, and she looked up to find the Shade and the Hydrokinetic standing beside her.

The Shade's whispery voice filled her head. "You'll get in

huge trouble if you keep talking to the Coaches like that."

*Probably,* Sophie transmitted. *But someone needs to tell them they're wrong.*

The way he tilted his head made her wonder if he was smiling. It was impossible to tell between the mask and the hood.

"This place is called Bosk Gorge," he whispered, "and it's not the worst we've seen of the desolation."

*Where was the worst?*

"Wildwood. There's pretty much nothing left."

Before Sophie could reply, the purple Coach stormed into the tent and clapped her hands.

"Everyone rise!" she ordered.

Sophie moved to stand, then realized the Coach meant a different kind of "rise."

The rest of the Waywards floated off the ground as the Coach announced they'd be practicing levitation-in-motion.

"Choose any movement you'd like," the Coach said. "But you must keep moving. Every time you fall, you prove yourself Unworthy."

Sophie could've sworn the Coach looked at her as she said the last part, and it made her determined to stay airborne. She closed her eyes, pushed against gravity, and floated her body off the ground. But she couldn't figure out how to move like the other Waywards. Motion required resistance—something to bounce off and create thrust. So when she tried to "walk," her legs only flailed, and the longer she hovered there, the heavier her body felt.

*How you holding up?* Fitz transmitted as she collapsed for a break.

*I don't understand how they're all doing this,* she grumbled.

*Neither do I. I've dropped twice already, and Biana's hit the ground three times. My Coach says we're not motivated enough.*

*You're lucky you guys are together. I'm the only one struggling in my group.*

She forced herself to levitate again, and tried flapping her arms, which mostly made her look like a giant chicken. She felt even more ridiculous when she stole another look at the plague-infested forest.

*I can't believe we're wasting time on this when we could be down there investigating.*

*Maybe it's better,* Fitz said. *We wouldn't want to accidentally infect Calla.*

Sophie definitely didn't want that—but it still felt like they were missing an opportunity. They could be learning things that might help the gnomes, and instead she was trying to air-swim.

"You're focusing your efforts too narrowly," her Coach said as Sophie dropped on her belly so hard it knocked the wind out of her. "Gravity isn't the only force you have to work with."

A gong announced their break before Sophie figured out what that meant.

She stumbled to the eating area, where all the Waywards

414

were lining up for lunch. The food itself was simple—baskets of whole fruit for them to choose from—and Sophie noticed everyone only took *one* piece. They also sat separately, on threadbare blankets the same color as their Hemisphere. The only sounds were the wind and the awkward crunch of chewing.

She'd chosen a pear-shaped fruit with a smooth teal skin. It looked too pretty to eat, and Sophie wished she'd gone with that instinct. It tasted like juicy cheese, and each bite felt greasier than the last. The Shade and the Hydrokinetic sat across from her, sharing a purple spiky fruit between them. Sophie wondered if that meant they were boyfriend and girlfriend.

"You should be more careful about your telepathic conversations," the Shade's voice whispered inside her head.

*One of these times you're going to give me a heart attack,* Sophie transmitted. *How do you talk like that?*

His shadow stretched farther over hers. "It's called shadowwhispering. My shadow is carrying my consciousness, so no one can hear me except you—but I still only do it when no one's looking. You need to take the same precaution. If the Coach catches you, they'll punish everyone. They want us to hate each other. It's how they keep control. They know there are only three of them and hundreds of us. If we unite, we could take them out easily."

*Or they could try getting us to like them,* Sophie suggested. *Fear isn't the only way to control people.*

"No, but it's the quickest. I would know."

The darkness in his tone was almost as unsettling as watching his shadow crawl back to its proper angle. Sophie could definitely see why Fitz would find Shades creepy. But she couldn't shake the feeling that this one was worth knowing.

The gong rang again, ordering them back to their tents, and the stronger afternoon gales made the exercise even more challenging. Waywards were tossed around the tents, crashing into the poles and each other. Sophie tried to use the wind's momentum to finally get herself moving, but the wind seemed to be a force she couldn't manipulate.

She stretched out her mind, feeling for other forces to play with, and instead picked up a faint sound. It came from the withered woods, and after a minute of concentrating she realized it was a voice.

A word.

The same word over and over, growing more chilling every time.

*Help.*

# FORTY-SIX

SOPHIE RACED TOWARD THE CLIFF and jumped, planning to teleport into the woods to find whoever needed help.

But as the forces whipped around her, she realized that levitating would be easier. She could feel a strange rush of resistance in the air now that she felt the thrill of falling. And when she focused on that energy, she finally had the thrust she needed to propel herself forward. A little additional concentration and she was sprinting so fast it made her eyes water.

"Where are you going?" Fitz asked, racing up beside her—and triggering a panicked plummet.

"Sorry," he said as she fought to regain her concentration.

"Didn't mean to scare you. When I saw you jump, I jumped. Biana tried to come too, but our Coach grabbed her. What's wrong?"

"Someone needs help. I can hear them calling me, but I don't know where they are. I'm trying to track them now."

She closed her eyes, but all she could hear were the angry voices shouting from the cliff above. Sophie was pretty sure they were setting a record for Exillium disobedience.

Fitz grabbed her hand so they could keep pace together. "How can I help?"

"Can you boost my concentration? It might clear my head."

"Done," he said as warmth trickled into her mind.

The extra energy snapped everything into focus. "He's that way," she said, pivoting in midair and running toward the densest part of the woods.

They sank lower as they moved, until their feet were skirting the tops of the withered trees.

"Down there," she whispered, pointing to a small clearing.

The speckled leaves made a sickening squish as they touched down.

"He's here somewhere—I can feel it," she said as they combed the ground, kicking up the fallen leaves.

Several agonizing minutes passed before Fitz shouted, "I found him!"

Sophie raced to his side, feeling her stomach lurch when

she saw the body lying in the shadow of the tallest, most shriveled tree.

The frail gnome's eyes stared blankly ahead, and his skin was covered head to toe in the same speckles as the leaves.

"What do we do?" Fitz asked, shaking the gnome gently by the shoulders. "He's breathing—but only barely."

Sophie's brain felt like it was trying to run in sixteen directions at once.

She took a breath. "Okay, we need to get him to the physician. Maybe he has some medicine that would make the gnome stronger. And then we'll have to figure out how to get him to the quarantine in Lumenaria."

"So back up the cliff?" Fitz asked.

"Yeah, is your levitating strong enough for that?"

"No idea." Fitz scooped up the unconscious gnome. "When I jumped I just focused on your mind and followed your lead, like our Cognate training."

"Well . . . I guess we should do the same thing again, then."

Her panic fueled her push as she shoved against the forces in the air and launched straight up, with Fitz keeping pace beside her. The shouting grew to a deafening roar as they landed on the cliff's ledge and faced the gathered crowd.

"We need the physician," Sophie said, running toward the small tent.

The purple Coach blocked her. "You're exposing us all."

"The plague only affects gnomes and plants," Sophie said, but she noticed the other Waywards were still scrambling away from her. "Please, this gnome needs help—it's not going to hurt anyone."

"Stay right there," the physician called, shoving his way through the cluster of onlookers with the help of the red Coach. He helped Fitz set the gnome on the ground and checked the gnome's pulse. "I'm not familiar with gnomish medicine. Even if I had a full apothecary, I wouldn't know where to begin."

"Then we need to get him to Lumenaria—quickly," Sophie told Fitz.

"That's impossible," the red Coach called from the front line of Waywards. "All of us are banished from the Lost Cities."

"Who cares?" Sophie asked.

"Yeah, do you seriously think the Council will arrest us for delivering a sick gnome?" Fitz added.

Councillor Alina probably would, but Sophie decided not to mention that.

"Even if the Council would spare you," the blue Coach said. "You're forgetting that none of us have crystals to leap you there."

"We don't need a crystal," Sophie told him.

And she was tired of wasting time.

She turned to Fitz, glad to see he was already ahead of her.

He lifted the gnome over his shoulder and carried him to the cliff's edge.

"Lumenaria's on the other side of the world," the purple Coach told them. "You can't levitate there."

"No," Sophie said, reaching for Fitz's hand. "But we can teleport."

They jumped without another word, holding tight to each other as thunder crashed and they slipped into the void.

Sophie started to envision Lumenaria, but all she could picture was the burly goblin guards, blocking the city's gates with their deadly swords.

"Do you think the Council will have us arrested?" Sophie whispered.

"I don't know," Fitz admitted. "I want to say no—especially since we still have the cache. But last time we were around them it didn't go so well."

His hand moved to his chest, rubbing where the arthropleura barb had pierced him.

Sophie decided it wasn't worth the risk.

She'd also realized there was a safer place they could take the gnome, where he could get medical treatment, and they could count on a few allies.

"Change of plans," she said, then pictured their destination so vividly that white light cracked the darkness.

They launched out of the void and Sophie focused on the

force of their fall, using her newfound levitating skills to make her first gentle landing.

Their feet touched down on the soft purple grass outside the glass pyramid in the center of the Foxfire campus.

# FORTY-SEVEN

**S**OPHIE HAD NEVER THOUGHT SHE could feel more conspicuous than she had on her first day at Foxfire, when Dame Alina had literally shined a spotlight on her to introduce her to the other prodigies.

But as she and Fitz clomped through the glittering main building in their crazy Exillium uniforms, she felt like they might as well be carrying a sign that said WE DON'T BELONG HERE!

Instead, they were carrying a very sick gnome, so she was glad it seemed to be the middle of session. The colorful halls were vacant, and Sophie was *very* familiar with the path to the Healing Center. They rushed through the doors in record time.

Sophie called for Elwin as she surveyed the three rooms—a treatment area, a working laboratory, and the physician's office.

All three were empty.

"Now what?" Fitz asked, setting the gnome on one of the beds in the treatment area.

"I don't know," Sophie admitted. She'd never considered that Elwin might not be there. "I guess we could leave him here and go find Magnate Leto."

But then she imagined the gnome waking up all alone, not knowing where he was or what had happened to him.

"Should one of us stay here?" she asked.

The slamming of the Healing Center's doors saved them from making a decision.

"This is why you're not supposed to catch more than one lightning bolt at a time," Elwin said, leading a familiar round-faced boy into the treatment area.

"I thought I'd found a way to do it," Jensi said, patting the ends of his brown hair, which was sticking out in every direction.

Both Jensi and Elwin froze when they spotted Fitz and Sophie—and the panic in their eyes reminded Sophie they still had their masks on.

"It's okay," she said, tossing back her hood and shoving her mask up on her forehead.

Fitz did the same, and Jensi and Elwin each did a double take.

Then Elwin laughed. "Should've known you'd find a way to end up here," he said, wrapping them up in a group hug.

Sophie hugged him back, remembering how once upon a time she'd been afraid of Elwin. It hadn't been Elwin's fault—she'd been afraid of *all* doctors after growing up with needles and hospitals and scary human medicine. But now she knew that Elwin was a giant teddy bear, with dark, messy hair, and smiling dragons all over his tunic.

"Yeah—they told us you were banished," Jensi said in his trademark rapid-fire manner. "But I knew they couldn't keep you away—and cool—you have to tell me about Exillium—are those the uniforms—they're awesome—but what are the masks for?"

The happy reunion lasted about ten seconds, until Elwin noticed their patient.

"What happened?" he asked, scrambling for his crazy iridescent spectacles and flashing a blue orb of light around the gnome. "Where did you find him?"

"We were in Bosk Gorge today," Sophie said.

Elwin frowned. "Bosk Gorge?"

"It's in the Neutral Territories," Fitz explained.

"I know. But that doesn't make any sense. I heard the goblins reporting in when I was working in Lumenaria a few days back, and Bosk Gorge was still on their safe list."

"Well, the plague must've spread," Sophie said, "because the whole place was overrun with it."

"That doesn't make sense either. All our reports say the plague moves slowly. Wildwood took weeks to get overwhelmed." Elwin switched to a red orb of light. "And he has injuries that aren't plague related. Like these here?" He held up the gnome's limp hand, pointing to the blisters on the palms. "These are burns."

"Maybe he lit a fire to keep the plague away," Fitz suggested.

Elwin scratched his chin and flashed a few more colored orbs. "Well, I can treat the burns and get some fluids in him. But all the remedies are in Lumenaria."

"Remedies?" Sophie asked.

"Not a cure," he said. "But they slow the symptoms, and make it a bit more bearable. It's a good thing you guys found him—he's progressing faster than I'm used to seeing."

Sophie sank onto the edge of one of the beds, more exhausted than ever. Maybe it was the adrenaline fading, but she had a feeling it had more to do with how much she'd been hoping Elwin could fix everything.

"Hey now," Elwin said. "Don't go looking so defeated. Bullhorn's staying quiet—see?"

He pointed to the bed in the corner, where the beady-eyed banshee was resting. Banshees could sense when someone was dying, and squawked their heads off around anyone in mortal danger. So if Bullhorn wasn't bothering to get up, the gnome still had some time left. But how much time?

"I'd better hail Magnate Leto and let him know what's going on," Elwin said. "You're both going to need to shower and change uniforms—and you're both getting a full checkup."

"What about me?" Jensi asked. "I need a new uniform too."

"And a checkup," Elwin agreed. "But first I need to take care of the fugitives."

Elwin said it with a smile, but the word still turned Sophie's stomach.

Jensi tugged on his cape, showing Sophie the blackened edges. "This reminds me of the first time we met—remember? I walked you to your elementalism session—and I warned you not to get zapped?"

Sophie smiled. "I remember."

Jensi was one of the first kids who reached out to her at Foxfire.

"So how's it been around here?" she asked.

Jensi looked away, his words slower than normal as he said. "Not the same."

Magnate Leto arrived then and put the Healing Center on lockdown. After that, there was a lot of showering and changing, and drinking ten billion elixirs. Sophie was stunned that Elwin could find signs of everything she'd been through, from the healed burns of her Dividing to the light poisoning Della had treated after they'd gone to see Gethen. But the weirdest part was putting on a Foxfire uniform again. Magnate Leto had brought her a green Level Four uniform, and Sophie kept staring at her reflection, wondering if she'd ever make it back to Foxfire to wear one for real. She suspected Fitz was thinking the same thing as he fidgeted with the cape of his white Level Six uniform.

"Are you going to tell the Council we brought the gnome here today?" Fitz asked.

"Of course," Magnate Leto said. "They should know who the true heroes were."

Fitz smiled at that—and Sophie tried to do the same. But it was hard to feel heroic every time she looked at the gnome. Elwin had moved him to a clear quarantine bubble, and his skin looked less pale—and his sleep looked more restful—but he was clearly very, very sick.

"You kids should head back," Magnate Leto said. "Assuming Elwin's given the all clear, of course."

"Yep, they're totally clean," Elwin said. "Though I hate to see them go."

"Me too," Jensi agreed. "Will you tell Biana I said hi—and Dex and Keefe?"

Sophie nodded, her voice too thick to work.

"Don't worry," Magnate Leto said. "I suspect this won't be the last time we see you standing among these halls."

Sophie stared out the window at the expansive Foxfire grounds and let herself hope he was right. But as she took Fitz's hand and prepared to leap to the Crooked Forest, she realized getting back into Foxfire wasn't their biggest problem.

After everything they'd done, and all the rules they'd broken, there was a very good chance they'd gotten themselves expelled from Exillium.

# FORTY-EIGHT

SOPHIE HADN'T KNOWN WHAT TO expect when she and Fitz arrived in the Crooked Forest, but she'd assumed lecturing and freaking out would play a major role.

Instead, her friends greeted them with the tacklehug to end all tacklehugs, and when they finally let them breathe—and were done pestering them for every detail about their time at Foxfire—she noticed Calla watching from her perch on one of the curved trunks.

"We're safe," Sophie promised. "Elwin quarantined us before we left."

"I can tell," Calla said. "I just . . . don't know how to thank you. The risk you both took . . ."

She looked away, trailing her green thumb along the straightened edge, where the tree had morphed into a survivor.

"I wish we could've done more," Sophie said, swallowing back the knot of all her frustrations. "How bad was it at Exillium after we left?" she asked her friends.

"Well, let's see," Keefe said. "The purple Coach fainted when you guys teleported, and I'm pretty sure the other two peed their pants. Then everyone started screaming and freaking out about the plague, and it took a couple of hours for the Coaches to calm them down. That's when a group of Waywards started demanding to know if you guys were going to be ejected or expelled or whatever they call it—"

"Are we?" Fitz interrupted.

Dex, Keefe, and Biana shared a look.

"They wouldn't give me any extra beads when I asked for them," Dex said, "which turned into another whole-school shouting match. But the Coaches said their decision was final."

"So I guess that's that," Sophie mumbled.

"Not necessarily," Biana said. "Before we left, the Shade came up to me and did this freaky whisper-in-my-head thing." She shuddered. "And he said to tell you 'If you really want to prove the Coaches wrong, you should return with your friends and make a stand.' So I'm guessing he wants you to leap with us in the morning—but I don't know if it's a good idea."

"Me either," Dex said. "Who knows what the Coaches will do?"

"I don't think the Shade would've suggested it if he thought we'd be punished," Sophie said. "He told me when they punish someone, they punish *everyone*."

"Maybe he thinks we're all going to be punished anyway, so he wants you to suffer with us," Dex said.

Sophie shook her head. "That doesn't sound like him."

"But you barely know him," Fitz reminded her.

"Yeah, and isn't this the guy I heard the boobrie dude warn you about?" Keefe asked.

"It is," Sophie agreed. "But I think the real reason the Coaches don't like him is because he disagrees with their rules and finds ways around them—sound familiar?"

"Right," Keefe said. "But I'm not a Shade."

"You're seriously going to judge him because of his ability?" Sophie asked.

"We do it with Pyrokinetics," Dex jumped in.

"And I don't know if that's right either," Sophie admitted. "Think of how much the ban on pyrokinesis has made them what they are. That's why Fintan rebelled. And why Brant joined the Neverseen. If being Talentless hadn't made him a bad match for Jolie, their story might have had a very different ending."

"Maybe," Keefe agreed. "But Shades will always be *shady*. It's in the name! And they control shadowvapor, and call it 'the darkness within us all.'"

"Does that mean they can control *us*, like Mesmers?" Sophie asked.

"It's more about being able to *read* people," Fitz said. "It's kind of like what Councillor Terik does when he descrys someone—only Shades are looking at your potential for darkness."

"Tell me that's not creepy!" Keefe said.

"Uh, I can inflict *pain* on people," Sophie reminded him. "Besides, how is judging him for his ability any better than judging people for being Talentless?"

"So you're saying you want to trust him?" Fitz asked.

"I don't know. Maybe we should see what the Collective thinks. They may not want any of us going to Exillium anymore, so we can focus on what's happening with the plague."

She was honestly hoping for the latter, so they could go back to Bosk Gorge and figure out why the plague seemed to be spreading faster there, and make sure no other gnomes were stranded in the area.

But when they returned to Alluveterre, Mr. Forkle was waiting for them in the bridge's gazebo—and he'd brought Sophie and Fitz new Exillium uniforms.

"I take it this means we'll be going to school tomorrow," Fitz said.

"You did the right thing, helping that gnome," Mr. Forkle told them. "The Coaches should see that."

"And if they don't?" Dex asked.

"Then it's your job to convince them. We need to get them on our side—they know more about what's happening in the Neutral Territories than anyone."

"But they don't seem to care," Sophie mumbled.

"Then *make* them care. That's one of your greatest gifts, Miss Foster—one we had nothing to do with. You're a natural force for change. And here's a chance to make a true difference."

Her friends looked as nervous as Sophie felt, but they didn't argue as they headed for their rooms.

*Actually,* Mr. Forkle transmitted to Sophie. *If you could stay behind, there's something I need to discuss with you . . . privately.*

Sophie figured it had to do with the sick gnome or her visit to Foxfire. So she definitely wasn't prepared when he told her, "I have news for Mr. Sencen."

"Is it about his mom?" she asked, sinking into one of the chairs. She had a feeling this was the kind of conversation she wanted to be sitting down for.

"It is—but not in the manner you're thinking. The news is about her past, not her present, and that's why I'm sharing it with *you.* You seem to have a better sense of how Mr. Sencen is handling things, so I trust you to decide how we proceed from here. As you know, Councillor Oralie has been working with Lord Cassius, searching for clues to his wife's Neverseen activities. And word has reached me that a few days ago they discovered a trunk hidden in Candleshade. I'm sure you can imagine how easy it would've been for the family to overlook it all these years."

Sophie nodded. Keefe's house had at least two hundred

stories—but Sophie didn't care about that. "What was in the trunk?"

"*Lots* of maps. The Council's still working to determine their purpose. And a kit for making temporary leaping crystals, like the ones you use at Exillium. We're assuming that's one of the ways she slipped away to the Neverseen's hideouts without anyone noticing."

"And?" Sophie pressed, since none of that merited a private conversation.

"*And* . . . there was also a note. Lord Cassius wanted it returned to his son, so it found its way to me."

He reached into his cape pocket and handed her a plain piece of paper that seemed too large for the tiny message scrawled at the top in loopy writing.

*Dear Keefe,*
*I'm doing this for you.*
*Love, Mom*

"So what are we going to do?" Mr. Forkle asked. "Tell Mr. Sencen? Or spare him?"

Sophie stared at the page, trying to decide what bothered her more: the word "love," or all the blank space.

And she kept picturing the Keefe she'd seen in the physician's tent, the angry scared Keefe lurking just under the surface.

But she'd promised Keefe she wouldn't hide things from him, and this was a *Very. Big. Thing.*

"It's not easy, is it?" Mr. Forkle asked. "Deciding how to protect someone you care about? I'm sorry to add this burden to you—especially after the day you've had. But I know you're the one who will choose what's best for him."

Sophie sighed. "Can I think about it?"

"Take all the time you need. All I ask is that you warn me before you share it with him—*if* you decide to share it with him. Otherwise I'll assume you've kept this to yourself."

Sophie nodded and stumbled back to her room. She was up most of the night going back and forth, making up her mind and changing it the next instant.

Eventually, she tucked the note into her purple backpack in the cache's old hiding place.

# FORTY-NINE

**A**RRIVING AT EXILLIUM THE NEXT morning felt like a scene in a movie where the soundtrack scratched to silence and everyone turned to stare.

Fitz's hand turned clammy in Sophie's as the two of them stood together, with Keefe, Dex, and Biana flanking them on all sides.

They'd leaped to the middle of a sweltering desert, with the school's tents scattered across the rolling dunes. Sophie saw no sign of the plague, but there was no life for it to contaminate. Not even a cactus or a scrubby bit of brush. Just endless dry sand, rippled by the wind and bleached white by the sun.

From the corner of her eye Sophie could see the Shade nod

his approval, but she was too focused on the three Coaches stalking toward them, kicking up clouds of dust.

"So you've chosen the path of defiance," the blue Coach said, his tone as heated as the air.

"We mean no disrespect," Sophie told him. "Just like we meant none yesterday."

"We were just trying to do the right thing," Fitz added.

"And yet your 'right thing' disregarded our authority," the red Coach said. "You understand the position this puts us in, don't you?"

Sophie had a whole speech prepared, ready to shame the Coaches for their selfish lack of consideration. But as she studied the three figures in front of her—and the hoard of anxious Waywards gathered behind them—she realized the Coaches weren't trying to be cruel. They were fighting an impossible battle, placed in charge of a group that even the highest authorities in the Lost Cities couldn't control—without proper resources or backup to support their efforts.

They were simply struggling to keep their fragile hold.

"Sometimes the greatest power comes from showing mercy," she told them quietly. "Especially to those who may not deserve it."

The Coaches looked at each other, something silent passing between them.

"Aren't we all hoping for a second chance?" Sophie added.

Several agonizingly long seconds crawled by before the

red Coach nodded—only once, but the small movement was enough.

"Don't make us regret this," the blue Coach said.

"We won't," Fitz promised as the red Coach ordered everyone to disperse to their tents.

Sophie plodded through the sand, nearly losing her balance when her purple Coach came up beside her.

"The gnome we saw yesterday," her Coach whispered. "Is he . . . ?"

"He's in quarantine with the others," Sophie told her. "Still waiting for someone to discover the cure. So if you've seen anything in the Neutral Territories that might be helpful . . ."

"I haven't," the Coach said. She started to walk away, then slowed her pace long enough to add, "But I will keep my eyes open."

"Thank you," Sophie said.

They'd reached the tent by then, and her Coach ordered everyone to grab their mats and drag them into the sweltering sun. The rest of the day was very long and hot and sweaty as they practiced body temperature regulation. Around the third blistering hour, Sophie learned to shift her concentration to her cells and turned her skin hyperaware to any traces of coolness. Then the tiniest breeze felt like a blast of arctic wind and the slightest trickle of sweat felt like a bucket of ice water.

When the sun sank low enough to stretch the shadows into angled smudges, the Shade's whispered voice filled her mind.

"How were you not arrested yesterday?" he asked.

*I still have a few friends in the Lost Cities.* She debated a second before adding, *I hope I have a couple here, too.*

"You already have the four you came with," he reminded her. "Do you really have room for more?"

*Can you have too many friends?* she asked.

He was silent for a long time. Then he whispered, "I wouldn't know."

The next day Exillium brought them to the side of a rocky mountain, where a gaping hole granted entrance into a dark cavern. The Coaches led them inside, and they walked farther and farther until the damp, black air blotted out the light.

"Today you'll be improving your night vision," the Coaches said in unison, their voices echoing off the cavern walls. "Let your eyes adjust and your mind will do the rest."

It sounded far simpler than it turned out to be.

Sophie tried everything she could think of, but all she ever saw was inky darkness. And the longer it surrounded her, the heavier it felt, until she had to remind herself that she could still breathe and the air wasn't running out.

"Are you afraid of the dark?" the Shade whispered in her head.

*I'm afraid of things that use darkness to hide,* she told him.

"Creepy crawly things?" he asked.

*Those aren't my favorite,* she admitted.

"But clearly not what's making you shiver," he said. "Monsters, then?"

His whispered voice was teasing, but Sophie couldn't smile.

She'd been kidnapped from a cave—which probably wasn't the best memory to relive at the moment.

*Monsters come in all shapes and sizes.*

"Like the ones behind the plague?"

*What do you mean?* she asked. *Did you see something?*

"I've seen a lot of things."

*Like what?*

Her eyes were finally adjusting—or maybe her mind was—because blurry forms were taking shape around her. The closest silhouette was the Shade.

*Like what?* she transmitted again, leaning closer.

He backed a step away. "Not now."

*When?* she pressed.

"When I know whether or not I can trust you."

He vanished into the shadows, taking his whispers with him.

By the time they'd reached the end of the week, Sophie had never been so tired, between the long Exillium days and the late nights of Cognate training. But she was more tired of the lack of progress. Her friends had been trying to learn about the Psionipath, but their Coaches were too guarded to answer their questions. And the campus had moved to yet another location without the slightest trace of plague.

They'd leaped to a glassy lake at the base of a snowcapped mountain to practice holding their breath, and two small tents had been added so they could change into wetsuits. Swim caps covered their hair and enormous goggles covered their faces, and they waded into the chilly water to float facedown and try to stay there.

It was the most brutal skill yet, and Sophie's lungs were constantly screaming, BREATHE NOW OR YOU WILL DIE! Even the Hydrokinetic struggled with the assignment—in fact, she seemed to have it harder than anyone. As soon as she'd put her face in the water she'd thrash and flail, and when the Shade tried to calm her she kept mumbling, "I can't, I can't, I can't."

By the second hour, the girl was in tears, and Sophie realized she might be able to help.

*I can keep you calm,* she transmitted to the girl. *But I wanted to ask before I tried it. If you don't want me to, make a sound so I know.*

The girl stayed silent.

*Okay, here goes.*

Inflictors were only supposed to be able to inflict negative emotions, but thanks to Sophie's alicorn-inspired DNA, she could trigger positive emotions as well. She closed her eyes and replayed a bunch of memories that made her feel happy and calm, letting the feelings gather in her heart until it felt like her chest would burst. Then she shoved the heat away, sending it shooting across the water. She couldn't tell if it was working, but the Hydrokinetic stayed quiet, so she kept sending additional waves.

She was so focused on her inflicting that she forgot about everything else. It wasn't until two hands pulled her out of the lake that she realized she hadn't been breathing.

"It appears we have a new record!" her purple Coach announced. "Forty-six minutes."

"Forty-six?" Sophie gasped for breath, wincing at the burn in her lungs.

Her Coach helped her wade back to shore and gave her a fraying gray towel to dry off. "Take one hundred deep breaths and your head will clear."

Around breath seventy-three, a shadow slid across hers and the Shade's voice filled her mind. "You want to know what we know?"

*Of course,* she transmitted.

"Okay." She waited for him to say something, but he turned and walked away.

After they'd gotten their beads and changed into their regular uniforms, though, he slunk up beside her and whispered, "Now or never."

The Hydrokinetic girl held a scratched yellow crystal up to the sunlight, and Sophie tried to think through the risks as she reached for the Shade's offered hand.

*I'll be back soon,* she transmitted to Fitz.

The light pulled her away before he could respond.

# FIFTY

THE LEAP FELT SHAKIER THAN NORMAL, or maybe that was Sophie. She couldn't believe she'd left Exillium with two strangers—without even asking where she was going.

They'd leaped to a place that had probably once been a beautiful garden. But now the cascading vines and enormous trees looked withered and crunchy and speckled with plague.

"Where are we?" Sophie asked.

"Introductions first," the Shade said, throwing back his hood and tearing off his mask.

The Hydrokinetic girl did the same, and Sophie was stunned by the similarities between them. They both had the same pink lips and creamy complexion. But the biggest similarity was their eyes—the palest of pale blue, with flecks of silver glinting in the sunlight. Touches of silver in their hair enhanced the effect. The girl's waist-length jet-black hair looked like the ends had been dipped in platinum, and the tips of the boy's jagged bangs glinted every time he tossed them out of his eyes.

Together they looked like K-pop idols, or like they'd stepped straight out of anime. But Sophie realized the more logical option was, "You're brother and sister."

"Twins," the Shade corrected. "Is that going to be a problem?"

"Why would it . . . ," Sophie started to ask, then remembered how rare multiple births were in the Lost Cities—and how judgmental most elves were when it happened. "Of course not," she promised. "I know what it's like to be different."

She threw back her hood and pulled off her mask, not missing the way they gawked at her eyes.

The Shade glanced at his sister before he said, "I'm Tam, and this is Linh."

Sophie smiled. "I'm Sophie."

"That's a human name," Tam said.

"It is." Sophie realized then that Tam and Linh wouldn't have heard any of the gossip about her. Judging by the length of their necklaces—long enough to wrap around their necks four times—they'd been at Exillium way before her arrival to the Lost Cities. In fact, she doubted they knew about anything that had happened over the last year, except whatever they'd seen in the Neutral Territories.

"So where are we?" she asked again.

"Home sweet home." Tam kicked a piece of rotted, speckled fruit.

"It used to be beautiful," Linh said. "We used to feel so lucky to have found it. But that was before the gnomes fell ill."

"Wait," Sophie said, climbing on a fallen trunk to get a better view. Farther down the weed-lined path she spotted a grove of black, collapsing trees with colored pieces of wood in their trunks, like doors. "Was this the Wildwood Colony?"

Linh nodded. "They used to bring us dinner every night, and I loved falling asleep to their songs." She brushed aside a blackened vine as she whispered, "Do you know what's happened to them?"

"Only that they're in quarantine—and that they're all still alive," Sophie added to reassure her. "But wait . . . you're the teenagers who made the footprints they found?"

"Who are *they*?" Tam demanded.

Sophie stumbled back a step as she told him, "The Council investigated after the colonists arrived at Lumenaria."

The twins might look similar, but their personalities were opposites. Linh was a baby bird. Tam was a stalking tiger.

"I wouldn't call it an *investigation*." Tam snorted. "They didn't seem to care. They were here for five whole minutes, scraped some bark and gathered a few leaves. They didn't even ask us about the lights." He pointed to the speckled forest in the distance. "We'd been seeing white flashes for weeks before the plague hit. We tried to find what was causing them, but it was coming from somewhere across the ogres' borders."

"You've seen ogres?" Sophie asked.

"Not recently." He turned toward the dark mountains to the east. "But Ravagog is through that pass."

The name slipped icy pins into Sophie's spine. "Do you think the lights were connected to the plague?"

She wondered how brightly a force-fielded tree could glow—enough to be seen from that far away?

"You ask a lot of questions," Tam said, making a slow circle around her.

"I thought you brought me here to tell me everything you know," she countered.

"I don't remember promising *everything*," he said.

"She's trying to help the gnomes," Linh reminded him. "Just like she helped me today. You must think me so foolish, by the way—a Hydrokinetic afraid of drowning."

"Hey, having an ability doesn't mean everything's suddenly easy," Sophie told her.

"Said the girl with *four* abilities." Tam leaned closer, squinting at her Teleporter pin. "So the big question is—what did you do to get banished?"

"Most of the Councillors wanted me gone the moment they

knew I existed," Sophie admitted. "I just finally gave them a good enough reason. What about you guys?"

Tam started to shake his head, but Linh put her hand on his shoulder.

"She can know the truth, Tam. It was my fault." She raised her hands and mist swarmed around them, glinting with a million rainbows. "Water pleads for my attention. But too often it's a trick."

As she spoke, the mist thickened into a storm that soaked them with a heavy downpour.

"I became the Girl Of Many Floods," she whispered. "And after too many mistakes, my parents had no choice but to let them banish me."

"They had a choice," Tam spat.

"You'll have to excuse my brother. He carries more bitterness than I do. But he doesn't have to be here—"

"Yes," Tam interrupted, "I do."

His voice had softened. So had the angles of his face.

"No one sentenced my brother to Exillium," Linh explained. "He chose to stay with me."

"I didn't want her to face this alone," he mumbled. "And I wouldn't stay with my family anyway. They'd always wished they didn't have the shame of *twins*. I wasn't going to let them pass me off as an only child."

Linh flinched, and Sophie wished she could hug both siblings. The elves were supposed to be this superior, enlightened species—but they sure had some terrible parents in the mix.

"How long ago was that?" she asked.

Linh's hand moved to her Exillium necklace. "Twelve hundred and fourteen days."

A little more than three years, Sophie realized. "That's a long time to be banished."

Linh nodded, pulling the water from their clothes and hair with a sweep of her arm. "We should get out of sight. There have been many visitors to the Colony since the gnomes left."

Sophie froze. "Were any of them wearing black cloaks?"

"Three were, yes," Linh said. "They came a week ago and checked the roots."

Sophie ran to the abandoned grove and dropped to her knees in front of the largest tree. Curled red roots jutted out of the ground all around her.

"Did you hear the Neverseen say anything?" she asked.

"The Neverseen?" Tam repeated.

"Remember when you asked me about monsters? They're who I was imagining. If you ever see them again—*hide*. They're involved with this plague somehow. The ogres are too. We just haven't been able to prove it."

She reached to take a sample of the roots, then realized it could infect Calla.

"Who's 'we'?" Tam asked.

"Me. My friends. And . . . others." Sophie wasn't sure how much to tell them about the Black Swan. "Let's just say I know people who are good at uncovering secrets. And when you're facing a group like the Neverseen, you need lots of backup."

Branches crunched behind them, making the three of them jump. But it was only the wind creaking through the sickly trees.

"This way," Linh said, leading them up the crest of a hill, where they could see the span of the narrow valley.

A river cut down the center before it disappeared into the jagged gray mountains, and an enormous iron gate barred the pass beyond the foothills.

"Ravagog," Sophie whispered, her feet itching to run toward the city—and far, far away.

"Sometimes, at night, we can hear them marching," Linh said.

"Are you sure it's safe to stay here?" Sophie asked.

"We're banished," Tam reminded her. "Nowhere is *safe*."

They'd reached the river by then, and Linh raised her hand, flicking her wrist and making the water lift out of the riverbed. The river made an arch over their heads, leaving dry ground for them to cross underneath. As soon as they reached the other side of the shore, the water crashed down and surged away.

"Wow," Sophie breathed.

Linh blushed.

Tam headed for a thicket of gnarled trees, which didn't look particularly inviting, but at least the grove hadn't been infected yet. He waved a clump of shadows away, revealing a gap hidden in the branches. Sophie followed Linh through, finding herself in a nook of green grass with two weathered tents. The threadbare quilt Linh spread out for them to sit on had been patched together from the craziest bits of fabric—old human T-shirts, lace doilies, the butt pockets of a pair of jeans.

"This is really where you guys live?" she had to ask.

"We don't need much," Linh said.

Maybe not, but the twins didn't seem to have *anything*.

An idea formed then—one Sophie knew would be gloriously complicated. But it could give Tam and Linh a better life, and make use of their incredible talents.

"How long are you going to wait before you tell her the rest?" Linh asked her brother, reminding Sophie she should be paying attention.

"Tell me the rest of what?" Sophie asked.

Tam shook his head. "We still don't know her well enough."

"Okay, so what do you need to know?" Sophie said. "Ask and I'll answer."

Tam smoothed his bangs over of his eyes and gave her his most defiant stare. "Answers can be lies. If you really want me to trust you, I need to read your shadowvapor."

"It doesn't hurt," Linh promised. "He just has to let his shadow pass through your mind."

"That . . . might be a problem," Sophie said. "It's hard to explain without getting into a bunch of crazy stuff about my genetics. But my mind is impenetrable. Even Councillor Terik couldn't descry me."

"Shadowvapor is simpler to sense than potential," Linh said.

"Since when are you the expert on my ability?" Tam asked her.

"Same reason I know you're stalling," Linh told him. "I've lived with you for almost fifteen years. And this is why we brought her here. Do the reading and we'll tell her—assuming you don't mind," she added, turning to Sophie.

Sophie wasn't *thrilled* with the idea, but she knew she needed their information. "You can try the reading," she told Tam. "But you have to promise you'll tell me even if you can't understand what you see in my head."

"Deal," Linh said, earning a glare from her brother. But he moved toward Sophie without further argument.

"Hold still," he said as Sophie flinched away from his shifting shadow. "Linh's right—it won't hurt. But it will give you chills."

*Chills* was an understatement. It felt like a blizzard blasting through her head. But once his shadow retreated, the freezing thawed immediately.

"I can see why Terik struggled with his descrying," Tam said, rubbing the spot between his brows. "You have a *lot* of shadowvapor. But you also have a lot of illumination, and they cancel each other out."

"Is that a good thing?" Sophie asked.

"Balance is good," Linh agreed.

"But it can be hard to hold on to," Tam countered.

"Which only matters for her future," Linh pressed.

The words felt like a warning, and Sophie wanted to pick them apart. But Linh was urging her brother to share his secret, and it looked like Tam was finally ready.

He moved across the clearing, staring at Wildwood through a small gap in the trees. "Before I tell you, you should know that what I'm going to say technically counts as treason. And you told me you still have a few friends in the Lost Cities, so you're probably hoping to go back someday."

"I still want to know," Sophie said.

Tam nodded and turned to face her. "When the Council was here gathering samples, they didn't think I could hear them. But I used my shadow to carry my consciousness to where they were working. I couldn't tell which Councillors it was—only that it was a male and a female. And the female Councillor said, 'We should've warned them this could happen.' Then the guy said, 'No one can know.'"

# FIFTY-ONE

"OH GOOD, SHE'S BACK," KEEFE SAID as Sophie arrived in the Crooked Forest. "Now we can clobber her."

Fitz stalked forward. "We're supposed to be a team! That means you take us with you when you run away with strangers, not give me four lousy words and disappear!"

"I'm sorry," Sophie said, her brain still reeling from the afternoon's revelations. To know the Council could've prevented everything that was happening was too terrible of a thought to settle.

But she couldn't tell her friends with Calla nearby. So she focused on safer explanations. "Tam only gave me a second to decide and—"

"Tam?" Dex interrupted.

"Yeah. That's the Shade's name. And his sister is Linh."

"They're brother and sister?" Biana asked.

"Twins," Sophie agreed. "They're also the teenagers who left the footprints near Wildwood."

"You were at Wildwood?" Calla called from the treetops.

"Are you worried I'm contaminated?" Sophie asked. "I tried to be careful. The only time I got close was to check the roots. Linh said she'd seen the Neverseen inspect them, so I almost took a sample, but then I—"

"Describe them to me," Calla interrupted, jumping to the ground.

By the time Sophie had finished, Calla looked as green as her thumbs.

"The roots were red?" she whispered.

"What does that mean?" Biana asked, draping an arm around Calla's shoulders to hold her steady.

"It means their time is almost up," Calla said. "Red roots are the end. Always. Every time."

"How long does that mean the colonists have?" Sophie whispered, clutching her stomach, trying to fight down the nausea.

"It's hard to say," Calla murmured. "Trees have simpler systems than us. But the path is the same. Once those infected see red, they will only have days."

• • •

"Lur and Mitya said none of the colonists are showing any red," Sophie told Mr. Forkle as his pacing wore a groove in the rugs of the girls' common room.

"Yet," he added.

Calla had asked Sophie to transmit to Lumenaria as soon as they'd returned to Alluveterre, to find out if any of the gnomes had reached the final stage. None had, and Sophie had been careful not to tell Mitya what the red meant. But everyone could guess. And the gnome she'd found in Bosk Gorge was still progressing through the stages at a much faster rate. Sophie asked if he remembered what happened to him, or anything that might be useful. But he only remembered blacking out, and then the pain of the plague.

Sophie glanced over her shoulder to make sure Calla was gone before she said, "Now we have proof that the Council knew about the plague."

"Do we?" Mr. Forkle asked. "I thought we had the word of two banished teenagers—one of whom is a Shade and known for insubordination."

"You think Tam and Linh are lying?" she asked.

"Of course not. But their word doesn't hold the weight you think it does. Especially when you consider how vague the conversation was. All they heard was 'this *could* happen,' and the Council will claim they didn't mean the plague."

"They did also say, 'No one can know,' didn't they?" Dex asked.

"Which applies to everything the Council does," Mr. Forkle said. "The majority of their investigations are classified."

"And that's their problem," Sophie mumbled. "Too many secrets."

She thought about Kenric's cache, wondering what horrors it contained. How many tragedies could that knowledge prevent?

"I'm often the last to defend the Council, Miss Foster," Mr. Forkle said, pausing to stare at the waterfall. "But if they've chosen to keep this secret, they must've had their reasons. Over the centuries the Councillors have shown deep affection for the gnomes. I can't believe they would intentionally endanger them. Which is why we should focus on the larger discoveries you gained today, and keep our other suspicions to ourselves until we have actual, concrete proof. The lights in the forest could've been many things, but I suspect the Psionipath is involved—which would mean the tree you saw before likely has more to do with the plague than a cure. We need to figure out how. And why the tree within had appeared greener and healthier."

"Okay, so how do we do that?" Sophie asked.

"I say we storm Ravagog," Keefe said. "Who's in?"

Mr. Forkle ignored him. "Honestly, Exillium is still the best answer. Look at how much we've learned from your attendance there."

Keefe sigh-growled. "So we're wasting the whole weekend?"

"We never *waste* anything," Mr. Forkle told him. "You all have very important things you should be studying and learning. But first, we must address Miss Foster's plan."

"My plan?" Sophie asked, feeling just as confused as her friends.

"You were going to suggest having the twins join our order, were you not?"

Sophie's jaw dropped. "Were you reading my mind?"

"I could have," Mr. Forkle told her. "Your reckless actions today more than called for it. But no. I simply know you too well. I was there when you found the starving kitten in the bushes and begged your parents to let you keep him. What did you name him?"

"Marty." Sophie was surprised at the way her voice caught. He used to sleep on her pillow every night, even though his big fluffy body stole most of the space for her head.

"Tam and Linh aren't a cat," Sophie said. "And I don't want to *keep* them. I just thought . . . we have these huge houses, and plenty of food, and they're really talented, and—"

"*And* it's a phenomenally bad idea," Mr. Forkle finished. "They know nothing of our organization, or the sacrifice it requires. We need members who are committed and understand the heavy responsibility, not who are looking for a good meal and warm bed."

"But—"

He held up his hand, silencing her next argument and

making her realize how very quiet her friends were being.

None of them had said a single word in Tam and Linh's defense. In fact, they all seemed to be avoiding her eyes.

"I'm not saying we won't help them," Mr. Forkle added. "I'll make arrangements to ensure they have food and safe shelter. But it won't have anything to do with the Black Swan. Nor should you tell them anything about us."

Awkward silence followed, and haunted Sophie the rest of the night. Even after she went to bed, the quiet of her room made her twitchy.

So she nearly jumped out of her skin when Silveny transmitted, *FRIEND?*

*Is everything okay?* Sophie asked. This was the first time Silveny had been the one to reach out to her.

*OKAY!* Silveny promised. *SOPHIE OKAY?*

Sophie tried to convince her she was fine, but Silveny could feel her mood, and after some coaxing, Sophie found herself telling Silveny everything. She knew it was silly—she doubted the alicorn could translate half the words she was saying. And yet, Silveny understood enough to transmit, *SOPHIE. GOOD. FRIEND.*

*Maybe,* Sophie thought. Though she wasn't so sure. She kept thinking about how ready she'd been to endanger Tam and Linh's lives by bringing them into the Black Swan. She'd already separated her friends from their families and gotten them banished. When would she stop putting people at risk? Even Silveny had endured major changes as a result of their friendship. Before they met, the alicorn had been free to explore the world. Now she was stuck in the Sanctuary, unable to teleport through the mountain walls.

*NO,* Silveny insisted. *HAPPY! HAPPY! HAPPY!*

She filled Sophie's mind with memories of Sophie petting her. Caring for her. Protecting her. Flying with her.

*AND KEEFE!* Silveny added. *AND GREYFELL!*

More memories flooded Sophie's head of Silveny's life at the Sanctuary—everything clean and comfortable and cared for.

Plenty of food.

Plenty to do.

Flying with Greyfell. Chasing Greyfell. Playing with Greyfell.

Wait—that wasn't playing. . . .

"Gah!" Sophie said, shoving the last images out of her mind. *TMI, Silveny. Too. Much. Information!*

She knew it was supposed to be a natural, beautiful thing. But *ewwwwwwwwwwwwwwww.*

*TRUST,* Silveny told her. *FRIEND. SHARE.*

*That's okay—you don't have to share anymore, I'm good!*

But Silveny had something she needed to tell Sophie. A new word she'd learned, even though Sophie had never taught it to her.

*BABY.*

# FIFTY-TWO

**S**ILVENY'S PREGNANT," SOPHIE TOLD
her friends when she joined them for breakfast.

Fitz dropped his fork. "Are you sure?"

"Oh yeah," Sophie mumbled, sinking into the
chair next to him. "She *showed* me. . . ."

"GAH!" everyone said.

Keefe pushed his plate away. "I'm done with food forever."

"Me too," Dex agreed.

"Me three," Biana said.

"Seriously, that is one batch of memories you do *not* have to
share with me," Fitz told Sophie. "I don't care if it's part of our
Cognate training."

"But it's still *huge*," Biana added. "Do you know how far along she is?"

"I'm guessing it's new, since the last few times I transmitted to her she didn't mention anything about—"

"STOP!" Keefe held up his hands. "Ground rules for this conversation: All talk of alicorn baby-making is off the table— got it? Otherwise I'll have to rip my ears off. And for the record, I do *not* want to be there when Baby Glitterbutt arrives."

"Me either," Fitz said. "My dad made me go to the Hekses' unicorn preserve for a delivery one time." He shuddered. "Who knew they came out so *slimy*?"

"Ew, dude," Keefe said. "I did not need to know that. Can we talk about something else? *Anything* else?"

"Does anyone know how long alicorns stay pregnant for?" Sophie asked.

Biana shook her head. "We've never had a baby alicorn before. But I'm pretty sure unicorns are pregnant for eleven months. So maybe it's the same?"

"Do you think Silveny knows?" Fitz asked. "If her instincts are telling her she's pregnant, maybe they'll also tell her how it's going to work."

"I guess I can ask. It was hard to get information out of her. All she wanted to tell me about was—"

"STOP!" Keefe said.

"I wasn't going to say *that*. She was telling me that she's *really* hungry. I'm not sure if it's a pregnancy craving or an excuse to get more treats, but she went on and on and *on* about how she needs more swizzlespice. We'll have to find a way to let Jurek know."

"Do you think he already knows?" Fitz asked. "He's the equestrian caretaker at the Sanctuary. Maybe he . . . saw stuff."

"WHAT DID I SAY ABOUT THE GROUND RULES?" Keefe shouted, covering his ears. "That's it, this conversation is officially over. Next person who says 'alicorn' is getting pelted with fruit."

"What's wrong with the alicorns?" Granite asked behind them.

He'd arrived with Mr. Forkle, each of them carrying stacks of scrolls.

"Silveny's pregnant," Sophie said, and all the scrolls went *THUNK!*

"Are you certain?" Granite whispered, bending to gather the uncurling paper.

Sophie nodded, and Mr. Forkle rushed to her side. "Tell me *everything.*"

"And I'm out!" Keefe said, covering his ears and singing, "LALALALALA! I CAN'T HEAR YOU!" as he raced up the stairs to the boys' tree house. Fitz, Dex, and Biana followed— but not before Granite gave them scrolls and asked them to put them somewhere safe.

It was a good thing they left, because Mr. Forkle wanted *all* the details. When Sophie finished, both he and Granite stared at each other so long she was sure they were having a tele-pathic conversation.

"Is something wrong?" she asked. "I thought this was what everyone's been waiting for."

"It is," Granite said. "But it also complicates things."

"The Council had plans to move the alicorns," Mr. Forkle explained. "So that will obviously have to be canceled."

"Why were they going to move them?" Sophie asked.

"Secrecy is better than security," Granite said. "No one can steal something they can't find."

"A few days ago the Neverseen attempted to breach the Sanctuary," Mr. Forkle added.

"WHAT?" Sophie asked, knocking over her chair as she stood. "Why didn't you tell me?"

"The Council is getting better at protecting their informa-tion," Mr. Forkle said. "I only learned of it yesterday—and then we were sidetracked by your *expedition*. But that's what we came to tell you. Both members of the Neverseen managed to escape—and both were male. There were also no reports of force fields, so we have no news on the Psionipath or Lady Gisela."

Sophie sank back in her chair, feeling her brain reach Maximum Worrying Capacity.

Wasn't it enough that they had the plague, and Prentice, and Keefe's mom, and the ogres, and the Council, and Exillium to wrestle with—did they *have* to worry about the alicorns, too?

"They're never going to stop trying to capture them, are they?" she asked.

"Unfortunately," Granite said, "the alicorns are too important. It's strange, all the years we only had one alicorn, no one cared. I guess the situation felt too hopeless. But now that we actually have a chance to reset the Timeline to Extinction—"

"Are you guys even sure that's a real thing?" Sophie interrupted. "For all you know, the planet could be fine if something goes extinct."

"Is there any creature that you could imagine the world without?" Mr. Forkle asked.

"I doubt I'd miss spiders," she mumbled. "Or mosquitos."

Granite's cracked lips twitched. "I'll admit, those aren't my favorite either. But nature is an intricate jigsaw puzzle, and every piece matters. Unfortunately, that means that certain species—like the alicorns—leave us vulnerable. But that may change with the baby. And thankfully the Sanctuary has extensive security measures."

"Then how did the Neverseen almost get in?" she asked.

"Through an old air shaft the dwarves used when they were hollowing out the mountains," Mr. Forkle said. "We're assuming the Neverseen thought we didn't know about it—and in truth, we didn't. If Lord Cassius hadn't found those maps in Lady Gisela's trunk, we might be reporting different news. The Council added guards to the area only days ago. That's why we brought those scrolls today. They're copies of everything

Lord Cassius found. The map of Ravagog seems particularly important. It has a number of places marked that both Alvar and Lady Cadence claim hold no significance, based on their own journeys through the city."

Sophie sat up straighter. "Do you think they could be the Panakes?"

"We're not ruling out any possibilities," Mr. Forkle said carefully. "But legends can be misleading. Think of the human legends about elves—there are seeds of truth, of course. But not enough to treat as a valid theory—but we'll get to that later. First we must let the Council know it's not safe to move Silveny."

"I'll take care of it," Granite said as Sophie asked, "Why can't they move her? She's pregnant, not sick."

"Ah, but pregnancies are fragile things," Mr. Forkle said. "They'd need to sedate Silveny for transport, and the drugs could harm the baby—not to mention the stress Silveny would feel while adjusting to her new home. Even in an ideal case, a move will be a huge change. And a case like this, with a species we literally have *no* experience with when it comes to childbirth, I have no doubt the Council will decide it's too dangerous."

"Can I tell Alden you'd be willing to use your telepathy to check on Silveny and give reports to Councillor Oralie?" Granite asked, pulling a dark leaping crystal from his cape.

"Of course," Sophie said. "And wait—you're going to see Alden?"

"In some form," Granite agreed.

"Can I go with you?" Biana asked, appearing in the corner.

"Ah, Miss Vacker," Mr. Forkle said. "Getting good at vanishing, I see."

"I fooled Calla this morning," Biana said proudly. "I finally figured out how to feel the pollen and keep it off my skin. But you're ignoring my question. Can I go?"

Granite shook his head. "Your father is being monitored too closely. Besides, I can't have you learning one of my identities."

"Couldn't we just hail Alden later and ask him who visited him?" Sophie asked.

"Do you think I'm brand new at having an alternate identity?" Granite leaped away before Sophie could answer.

Biana stared sadly at her feet, and Sophie knew how she felt.

"Do you want to use my Spyball to see your dad?" she offered. "You can't talk to him, but you can see how he's doing."

"Wait—if we watch through the Spyball, would we see the real Granite?" Biana asked.

Mr. Forkle sighed. "You kids think we're such amateurs. The answer to any of your theories is: No—it's not that easy. Besides, I have something else for all of you to do today. We've made arrangements with King Enki for the twins to live in Ermete's former residence. He's one of the dwarves we lost in the battle on Everest, and he had no family to inherit his possessions. Dwarven residences are different from ours, but your friends will adjust. And they'll be safe and have plenty of food."

"Wow. That's . . . really great," Sophie said, though living in a dead dwarf's house sounded mildly depressing. But it couldn't be worse than living in Wildwood.

"Good. Because you'll be the one telling them." Mr. Forkle removed a special pathfinder from his cape. The yellow crystal at the end was barely larger than the wand's point, and it only had a handful of facets carved into it. "This will take us to the Neutral Territories," he explained, adjusting the crystal.

Sophie was about to reach for his hand when she realized her mistake.

"Hang on," she told him, racing for the stairs. "If we're going, we're *all* going."

# FIFTY-THREE

"STOP!" TAM SHOUTED FROM ACROSS the river as he stretched out his arms and pulled every shadow toward his grasp.

"It's okay!" Sophie promised, running ahead of the others. "They're with me."

Tam flicked his wrists, launching the shadows across the water. "I never said you could bring people here."

"We mean you no harm," Mr. Forkle said calmly. "There's no need for your darkness tricks."

"It's not a trick," Tam said. "Unlike your disguise. And you don't come any closer unless I take a reading of all of you."

Keefe scrambled away from the shadows. "Uh, forget that."

"It doesn't hurt," Sophie told him. "It just feels really cold."

"I don't care. It's not happening," Keefe insisted.

"The only people who refuse readings are those with darkness to hide," Tam told him.

"Or maybe I just don't want some creeper putting his shadow in my brain," Keefe snapped back. "Especially a dude with silver tips on his bangs. What'd you do, melt down the buckles on your Exillium uniform and dip your head in?"

"My registry pendant, actually. I melted down the chain after I ripped off the crystal and threw it in my father's face. Now if I ever face him again, he'll see exactly how little I miss living in his glittering prison."

Keefe looked away, for once without a snappy comeback.

"I think we've gotten off track," Mr. Forkle said. "I appreciate your wariness, Mr. Song, but—"

*"How do you know that name?"*

"Relax. I know your name because I'm careful—like you appear to be. I don't visit someone I haven't investigated."

Tam snorted. "All you know are the Council's lies."

"I assure you, I searched well beyond the registry's files. Which is why I know that your sister was banished after she flooded part of Atlantis—even though it was your parents' fault. They should've known better than to bring a fledgling Hydrokinetic under the ocean. It's like bringing a Guster into a hurricane and expecting them to leave the wind alone. I also know that your father tried to convince people you were a year older than Linh, but you and your sister refused to go along with the lie. I know you scored off the charts on your entrance exams to Foxfire, but your sister scored even higher. And yet your performance at Exillium has been mediocre at best. You refuse to apply yourself during the skill lessons, and you've broken several bones due to careless risks. I've also met your father several times. Can't say I was impressed."

Tam's jaw fell and he lowered his arms, all trace of his shadows vanishing. "I've never heard anyone speak ill of my father."

"Then you haven't been talking to the right people," Mr. Forkle said. "Do not make the mistake of assuming all adults are like him. Now, where is your sister hiding?"

Tam hesitated a second. Then waved his hand, and the shadows around a clump of trees shifted to reveal Linh.

"Wow, that's like an antivanish," Biana said. "How did you do that?"

"We can trade ability secrets another time," Mr. Forkle interrupted. "At the moment, I have a proposition for the Song twins. Shall we?"

He pointed to the river dividing them.

Linh swept her arm and raised the water into an arch before taking her brother's hand and guiding him forward.

"Wow," Fitz breathed, and Sophie hoped he meant the river trick—but it was hard to tell with the way he was staring at Linh.

Dex seemed equally stunned as the twins crossed under the river and Linh set the water down for its normal flow. The only boy who didn't look impressed was Keefe—but that was probably because he was too busy glaring at Tam.

"So who are you guys?" Tam asked, frowning as he studied Mr. Forkle's ruckleberry wrinkles.

"This is Mr. Forkle," Sophie said. "He . . . takes a little getting used to. And these are my friends, Dex, Keefe, Fitz, and Biana."

Linh bowed shyly and introduced herself.

"I really love your hair," Biana told her.

Linh pulled at the long strands, brushing the silver tips against her palms. "Mine is less of a protest than my brother's. I melted my pendant to remind myself what happens when I lose control."

"Enough about our hair," Tam said. "Why are you here?"

"To make you an offer." Mr. Forkle turned to Sophie, and she explained about the arrangements the Black Swan had made with the dwarves.

"What's the catch?" was Tam's first question.

Mr. Forkle's lips curled with half a smile. "There is none. King Enki and I have everything arranged. All he asks is that you respect his laws while you live there—which are really no different than elvin laws, except perhaps slightly *less* restrictive."

Tam blinked several times. "Why are you helping us?"

"Because someone *should*." Mr. Forkle stepped closer, his wrinkled features softening. "I make a point of trying to right the wrongs I see in my world."

Linh wiped her eyes. "This is far more than we ever could've expected."

"It still seems like there has to be a catch," Tam mumbled.

"There isn't," Sophie promised.

"Please," Linh whispered to her brother. "I can't stay here any longer."

Her eyes roved to the dying Wildwood Grove, and fresh tears welled.

Tam sighed, tugging on the ends of his bangs. "I guess we could give it a try."

"A wise decision," Mr. Forkle told him. "If the arrangement doesn't suit you, we can find another. Do you need assistance packing up your tents?"

Linh shook her head. "We always keep everything gathered in case we have to flee. Give me five minutes."

She raised the river again, earning yet another "wow" from Dex and Fitz as she ran for the grove of trees.

"So," Tam said, circling Mr. Forkle. "I'm assuming Sophie told you everything I told her yesterday?"

"She did. It made me wish I'd spoken to you and your sister the last time I was here."

Tam froze. "When was that?"

"Several weeks ago, when I came to investigate the plague. I'm afraid my search was no less hasty than the Council's—a mistake I intend to correct."

"But I don't remember seeing you," Tam said.

"That's because I didn't want to be seen. One cannot live the lives I lead without mastering the art of hiding."

Tam glanced at Sophie. "You're right. This guy's going to take some getting used to."

"It's worth it though," Sophie said.

"I hope so." Tam's shadow fell over hers, and he shadow-whispered, "I'm trusting *you.* I don't care about me, but if something happens to Linh . . ."

*I promise, we're only trying to help,* Sophie transmitted.

Keefe let out a sigh that sounded more like a groan. "And I thought secret Telepath conversations were the worst. Just so we're clear," he told Tam. "*I'm* the president of the Foster fan club. And we're closed to new members."

Tam's cheeks flushed. "Uh . . . not sure what that's about but . . . no worries there—no offense!" he told Sophie.

She noticed he stole a quick glance at Biana after he said it.

Sophie couldn't decide if she should feel relieved or insulted. She was saved from having to decide by the river rising again.

"Wow," Dex and Fitz whispered, right on cue.

Linh crossed the riverbed carrying two small bags and a long cylinder, with poles sticking out of one end.

"You won't need the tents," Mr. Forkle told her.

"I hope not," Linh said, "but I'll feel safer knowing we still have a backup plan. Plus, we try not to leave a trace of anywhere we've lived."

474

"You're going to wash the campsite, right?" Tam asked her.

Linh nodded and raised her arms, gathering a storm over their former home. As soon as the clouds were in place, she clapped her hands and the storm burst, raining so hard the trees bent.

The rush of water flooded the river, but before it overflowed Linh waved her hands, wiping out the storm even faster than it had formed.

"Impressive," Mr. Forkle told her. "You show more control than you realize."

"I've learned to create fixed points," she said. "Tiny drops of steady among the chaos. They give me something to focus on and help me to keep a tighter hold. But the more water there is, the more it slips beyond my control."

"Of course," Mr. Forkle said. "Water is an element, no less volatile than fire or air. All you can hope for is exactly what you're achieving—victory within limits. I know someone who might be able to help."

"Who?" Sophie asked.

"Let's not get ahead of ourselves." Mr. Forkle reached into his pocket and pulled out two simple chains hanging with a tiny piece of magsidian shaped like a star. "The dwarves gave me these. They will take you to your new home and signal that you have permission to be there. Keep them safe, and never take them off. King Enki said he'd have provisions sent to you this afternoon. If there's anything you're missing, bring

Miss Foster a list to Exillium and I'll make sure you get it."

"You're not coming with us?" Linh asked as she looped her pendant around her neck.

"No. These are your lives. We won't interfere."

Tam looked relieved until Mr. Forkle added, "But before you go, I do have a request for Mr. Song."

"*There's* the catch!" Tam said, as if his world finally made sense. "And don't call me that."

"Is Mr. *Tam* acceptable?" Mr. Forkle asked. "I prefer to keep things formal. And it most definitely is *not* a catch. You're free to leave right now if you'd like—that is your choice. But I hope you'll consider my request and read the shadowvapor of the Wildwood Grove."

"You want me to do a reading on a bunch of sick trees . . . ," Tam said slowly.

"Assuming you're willing," Mr. Forkle agreed.

"I can already tell you it'll be off the charts," Tam told him, "since, y'know, the trees are dying."

"That *is* what one would expect from a plague. But as I said before, I plan to improve upon my previous investigation. This time I intend to be incredibly thorough."

Tam shrugged and stretched out his shadow, letting the darkness cover the grove in a smoky blanket.

"I don't understand," Tam said as the seconds ticked by.

"So it *is* as I thought," Mr. Forkle said. "Thank you—you've been very helpful."

"Wait," Tam said as Mr. Forkle pulled out his pathfinder. "How did you know I wouldn't feel anything?"

"I didn't. But I'd hoped that would be the result."

"Why?" Sophie asked. "What does that mean?"

"It means the plague feeds off shadowvapor. And hopefully we are one clue closer to a cure."

# FIFTY-FOUR

**Y**OU WERE RIGHT," FITZ SAID AS they climbed the stairs to their tree houses. "I *do* like the twins."

"So do I," Dex agreed.

Mr. Forkle had left to update the physicians in Lumenaria on their findings about the plague. Sophie *tried* to feel his optimism, but she couldn't quite get there.

Knowing more about how the plague worked *was* a good thing. But it still didn't feel like *enough*.

"Someone needs to tell Shade Boy the role of Troublemaker with Daddy Issues is already filled," Keefe mumbled, pulling her back to their conversation.

"You could've told him that when you warned him about the Foster fan club," Biana suggested.

"Or not," Sophie jumped in. "Seriously, why don't you like Tam?" she asked Keefe.

"What's to like?" He pretended to flip imaginary bangs, deepening his voice before saying, "The only people who refuse readings are those with darkness to hide."

His impersonation was spot-on. But Sophie could hear a trace of something deeper behind the tease—the same thing she'd seen on Keefe's face when he'd refused Tam's reading.

He'd turned into the boy in the boobrie dude's tent again—scared and angry and lost.

"I think you'll change your mind when you get to know him," Sophie said. "It sounds like you guys have a lot in common."

They'd reached the tree houses by then, and Granite was waiting in the girls' common room, along with Della, who looked wrung out after another visit with Prentice.

"The Council has decided to keep Silveny's pregnancy secret," Granite told Sophie. "And they've accepted your offer to help them communicate. In fact, they gave me some questions they'd like you to ask her today, so Vika can prepare before she visits."

"Vika *Heks*?" Sophie asked, her nose crinkling when he nodded.

The last time Vika had been around Silveny, she'd tried to tie the alicorn up and drag her to her family's unicorn preserve. But . . . much as Sophie hated to admit it, they probably were going to need Vika's help. The Heks family had been breeding unicorns for centuries.

Sophie sent out a call for Silveny, and within a few seconds her mind filled with Silveny's exuberant greeting. Silveny confirmed that she hadn't told anyone about the baby—not even Greyfell, which earned her a lecture about telling the daddy. She also said she was two weeks pregnant, and that the baby would arrive in forty-two weeks, during the blue moon. She then spent the rest of their talk begging for swizzlespice, and complaining about her new pasture.

Apparently the Council had moved the alicorns away from the normal equestrian area and set them up in a much smaller meadow with blue grass that Silveny found scratchy and sour. Sophie promised to find out if there was anywhere else the alicorns could live—and to get her a double shipment of treats. And while Silveny was *not* thrilled about a Vika visit, she perked up when Sophie gave her permission to drag Vika through the mud like she had the last time.

The next step was hailing Councillor Oralie to give her the update. Sophie's stomach twisted as she gave the command to the Imparter.

Oralie wasn't alone when she answered. Councillor Terik stood behind her and explained that he'd been assigned to monitor the conversation, to make sure no treasonous activities were happening.

Sophie studied their faces, wondering if she was speaking to the same Councillors who Tam had overheard in Wildwood.

The idea made her insides twist even tighter.

"Is something wrong?" Oralie asked.

Sophie started to nod, but then her mind flashed to the night Oralie risked everything to give her Kenric's cache.

Terik was also one of her few steady defenders.

"I'm just worried about the gnomes," she said. "I don't understand how this happened."

"Neither do we," Terik murmured—and there.

Right there.

Sophie saw the fear, mixed with a tiny bit of shame.

It only lasted a fraction of a second.

But it had definitely been there.

Which must mean the Council really *had* known—not that Sophie could prove it. And she was sure if she did, they'd claim they had reasons.

Mr. Forkle had said the same, but . . . could any excuse be good enough for blindsiding the gnomes?

"Did you hear me?" Councillor Terik asked, reminding her she was supposed to be listening.

"Sorry, what was the question?" Sophie asked.

"I asked how things are going at Exillium."

"Oh." She bit her lip. "Do you really want to know?"

"If we must," Terik said, and the sigh in his voice made Sophie snap.

Even if the Council did have a reason for keeping the plague secret—there was *no* excuse for the neglect Sophie saw every day at Exillium. So she told them about the physician's lack of supplies, and how threadbare all the tents and mats and towels were, and how meager the food was at lunchtime, and how the Coaches were forced to rely on fear and suffocating rules to keep control without enough help.

"You build entire cities out of jewels and live in glittering castles," Sophie said, "but you can't spare any medicine or food for a group of kids who are smart and talented and would try way harder if they weren't constantly being told they're worthless? What's the point of having the school in the first place? It could be a valuable rehabilitation center if you supported it. But you're letting it go to waste."

Silence followed her outburst, and Sophie braced for a lengthy lecture.

Instead Oralie whispered, "You're right. Exillium was originally created to be a center for alternative learning. I'm not sure how we lost sight of that, but . . . not anymore. Give me a list of everything they need, and I'll get it—you have my word."

"Just like that?" Sophie asked.

Oralie nodded. "Thank you for opening my eyes. Kenric would be so proud of you."

The name felt warm, and it relaxed Sophie's nerves, untangling some of her knots.

Kenric would've known about the plague, too. But he'd also been a good person—she was absolutely certain of that.

So maybe finding the truth would show her how he was able to be both.

"I've been thinking about legacies," Calla said when she found Sophie outside the next day, letting Iggy have a few minutes of bug hunting time.

Iggy had nearly ruined the replacement monocle pendant the Black Swan had given Biana—so Sophie had taken over imp babysitting for the day.

"Legacies," Sophie repeated, the word sour on her tongue.

Weren't legacies what people talked about when someone died?

"I'm not despairing, if you're worried," Calla said. "And obviously I don't have the plague. Still, I find myself wondering what I would leave behind, should the worst happen."

Her eyes dropped to Sophie's moonlark pin, and the necklace gained about a million pounds of pressure.

"I'd like to share something with you," she whispered. "Will you let me?"

"I . . . of course," Sophie said. "But only if you promise this doesn't mean anything."

"Being prepared is never a bad idea," Calla told her. "No

matter what happens, I won't be here forever. And when I think of what I want to be remembered for, it comes down to two things. You. And my starkflower stew. So what better legacy could I have than to combine them?"

"You're not planning on cooking me for dinner, right?" Sophie asked.

Calla laughed, and Sophie got a glimpse of why Keefe hid behind humor. Telling the joke had knocked loose the lump in her throat.

She followed Calla into the forest to a wide, bulbous tree dripping with flowering vines in every imaginable color. Nestled up against it was a small cooking area.

"Is this where you live?" Sophie asked as Calla started a fire within a circle of stones.

"I *live* among the forests. But this is where I rest."

She hung a silver cauldron over the flames and brought Sophie a basket of vegetables. Some of them Sophie recognized. Most she didn't. But Calla showed her how to slice them and add them in a specific order.

The air filled with familiar scents—caramelizing onions, simmering garlic, spicy peppers—and deeper earthier fragrances that made Sophie's mouth water.

"Gnomes don't eat much," Calla said, ladling in water in slow intervals. "But when we do, we want it to count."

She disappeared into her house and returned carrying two baskets, one overflowing with fresh herbs, the other filled with vials of colored powders. She made Sophie memorize each one, and the order it was added in. By the time she was done Sophie's stomach was growling.

"Final ingredient," Calla said. "The most important one."

The starkflower could've won the prize for ugliest flower, between its curled, shriveled black petals and gray speckles.

"For centuries we ignored them," Calla said. "But one day a blossom landed in my cooking pot, and this happened."

She dropped the flower into the stew, and Sophie watched as all the color leeched out in streams of shiny black.

"Shadowvapor," Calla explained, fishing out the blossom with the ladle to show her how it had turned gleaming white. The petals had also plumped, making the flower lush and hearty.

Looking at the pristine, shadowvapor-free flower reminded Sophie of the gleaming leaves of the Psionipath's shielded tree.

Had it looked so bright and healthy because the plague was feasting on its shadowvapor?

"You look pale," Calla said. "Are you feeling okay?"

"Of course," Sophie promised. "I'm just getting hungry."

She tried to smile as Calla served up heaping bowls of stew for everyone, and even remembered to invite Calla to join them for dinner.

But all she could think about was that she'd had the person causing all this pain trapped in a force field right in front of her.

And she'd let him get away.

# FIFTY-FIVE

LET'S SEE WHAT TORTURE EXILLIUM has for us today," Keefe said as they arrived on top of a blustery mesa. The desert basin below was nothing but cactus and scrub brush—no sign of the plague.

They made their way to the campus, and Sophie barely recognized the place.

New tents.

New mats.

Shiny new tables filled with . . .

"Is that breakfast?" Fitz pointed to the platters heaped with pastries covered in pink jam.

"Yes," a voice said behind them, and they turned to find

Sophie's purple Coach. "We'll be starting each day with a meal. And our lunch supply has vastly improved as well. I've also been told that six new Coaches are being chosen to assist us, as well as a team of goblin bodyguards for protection. Plus this." She held up her new pendant—a leaping crystal with three glittering facets. "Our access to the Lost Cities is limited, but we as Coaches are no longer completely banished, to give us a better channel of communication. It appears the Council has decided to pay more attention to our program."

She leaned closer to Sophie and added, "And I hear we have you to thank, Miss Foster."

"You know my name?" Sophie asked.

"It will be impossible to forget a Wayward with friends on the Council—especially one who triggered these changes. I've never seen anything like it in all the years I've been here."

"How many years is that?" Sophie asked, taking her small opportunity.

"Coming up on fifty. Seems too long, doesn't it?"

Her Coach let out a wistful sigh, and Sophie tried to sound casual as she asked, "So does that mean you were one of the Coaches who ejected a rebellious Psionipath a few years ago?"

Her Coach's back straightened. "Why?"

"I need to find him." She moved closer and whispered. "He's involved with what's happening to the gnomes."

Her Coach didn't move.

Sophie wondered if she was still breathing.

"You know who I'm talking about, don't you?" Sophie asked.

"I might," her Coach whispered. "But he was ejected. That's where my knowledge ends."

"What about his name?" Sophie pressed. "You know mine now. Did you know his?"

"I'm sorry," her Coach said. "I can't help you."

"Do you know someone who can? Maybe the other Coaches?"

"I can ask them. But I wouldn't get my hopes up."

"I have to," Sophie told her. "Hope is all we have left."

When she got home from Exillium, Sophie used the afternoon to study the maps Lord Cassius had found. She hadn't told Keefe where they came from—and she didn't want him asking too many questions—so she hid in her bedroom and spread them across the floor.

There were maps of the Neutral Territories in the mix, along with maps of the Forbidden Cities and the Lost Cities. The Neverseen clearly had their eyes on everything.

Sophie focused on the Neutral Territories, hoping she could find a pattern between the plague locations. Maybe then she'd be able to guess where the Neverseen would strike next.

She rearranged the maps so she could see where everything was in relation to each other, and started with Wildwood. From there she moved to Brackendale, where they'd found the Psionipath's tree. Next was Merrowmarsh, which Gethen had thought would be the next place. As far as Sophie knew, nothing had happened there, but she decided to count it anyway and assume the Neverseen's plans had changed because the Black Swan posted a dwarven guard. After that was the Strixian Plains, where the family of infected gnomes had been found, and then the Starkrial Valley, where Physic's apothecary had been closed because of the plague. Then Bosk Gorge, where Sophie had found the gnome. That was where the plague seemed to be spreading faster, so had the Neverseen changed something there—maybe to make up for the time they'd lost with Merrowmarsh?

Or, Elwin had said the gnome had burns as part of his injuries. Could he have done something to the force field to unleash the plague earlier?

After hours of plotting and arranging, all she really knew was that the plague seemed to be heading west. But there were dozens of Neutral Territories to the west of the last strike, so she was going to need more information to pin it down.

"This is quite a project," Calla said from her doorway. She held up a plate heaped with food. "You missed dinner."

Sophie glanced out her window, realizing the sun had almost set. She hadn't noticed how dark her room had gotten—maybe her Exillium night vision training was helping.

"Thanks," she mumbled, turning back to her maps.

"Take a break," Calla insisted, handing Sophie the plate. "All of this will still be here in a few minutes."

Sophie wished it wouldn't be.

Why couldn't it solve itself and go away?

Calla sucked in a breath and unrolled one of the maps sitting half exposed on the floor. "This is the closest I've ever come to seeing Serenvale."

Sophie glanced over Calla's shoulder and studied the map of Ravagog, with its jagged lines and blank, unmarked spaces.

"You never lived there?" Sophie asked.

"I'm too young. By the time I was born, the ogres had taken over. But I still hope to go there someday."

"Really?" Sophie asked. "Wouldn't it be hard to see how much the ogres have ruined it?"

"Yes," Calla said. "But there has to be *something* left. So if I ever found the hidden path, I would take it."

"You mentioned that before," Sophie said. "Is there really a hidden path into Ravagog?"

"It depends on who you ask. There's a legend among my people of a secret tunnel back to our homeland, a tunnel that can only be found by those willing to 'embrace the heartache.' I don't know what the riddle means, but I've always dreamed I would someday solve it. I'm sure the path is treacherous—and I know it would only cause me sorrow. But I have to believe it's out there, nestled in the lonely earth, waiting for me to try to find the Panakes."

The rest of the week was full of changes, but they only seemed to happen at Exillium. The Coaches started using their names—

the purple Coach was named Coach Rohana, the blue Coach was Coach Bora, and the red Coach was Coach Wilda—and Waywards were encouraged to do the same. They started working with partners or in groups, which made the lessons much more manageable. And at the end of the lesson on Friday, masks and hoods became optional.

"Never thought I'd see the day," Coach Rohana murmured to Sophie as the Waywards tossed their masks into the ocean.

Sophie turned to study her Coach, who had creamy brown skin and straight, shiny black hair.

"Do all of these changes make you nervous?" Sophie asked.

"Of course. Change always has rewards *and* costs. But, it will be nice to have more interaction with the Waywards—most of them, at least."

"I'm guessing you never found out anything about the Psionipath I mentioned?"

Coach Rohana sighed. "Actually, I did. I found his list of transgressions, and it was far longer than I'd remembered. He's not someone you want to encounter."

"But I have to," Sophie told her. "Please, if there's anything else you know . . ."

Her Coach stared into the distance, her expression both weary and wary as she whispered, "His name was Ruy Ignis."

# FIFTY-SIX

"R UY IGNIS," DEX SAID, TAPPING ON
the screen of the Dexified Imparter, where
he'd stored all the Exillium records he'd
stolen. They'd met up in the boys' common
room to see what they could learn about the Psionipath.

Dex handed the gadget to Sophie and she memorized every
detail of Ruy's file—not that it was much to go on. His parents
both worked in Mysterium, but they'd been the ones to turn
Ruy in to the Council, so it seemed unlikely he would be in
touch with them. And his location was listed as "banished and
ejected."

"I wonder if my brother knew him," Fitz said, reading over
her shoulder. "He's a year older than Alvar, so he probably was

a Level ahead at Foxfire. But they still would've crossed paths during PE and stuff."

"Do we have a way to reach Alvar and ask him?"

"My mom might," Fitz said. "Huh, it looks like Ruy got expelled when he was a Level Four, not long after he manifested."

The file didn't say what Ruy had done, just the "proven unstable and unfit for society," they'd seen before. But at the very end of the record Sophie noticed two words she hadn't seen before:

*Actions irredeemable.*

"What do you think that means?" Dex asked.

"It is not a phrase the Council marks someone with lightly," Mr. Forkle said from the doorway. "Whom are we discussing?"

Sophie explained what she'd learned from her Coach, and Mr. Forkle stroked his chin. "I'll have to pool my resources to uncover the specifics of Mr. Ignis's crime. But his past is unlikely to lead to his present location."

"It's still important to know as much about our enemies as possible, right?" Sophie asked.

"Indeed," Mr. Forkle agreed. "But for the moment, I need you to focus on your Cognate training. As this situation continues to unravel, it's more important than ever that the two of you reach your greatest potential. And currently, you're progressing slower than we'd hoped."

"Hey, I was almost dead for a week!" Fitz argued. "And we've worked through a ton of trust exercises."

"You have," Mr. Forkle agreed. "But therein lies the problem. Few people think of trust as an emotion. They prefer to view it as a force they control. But in its basest form, trust is as involuntary as sadness or anger or fear. A newborn child instinctively trusts its parents. Sophie's mind instinctively trusts mine—and now yours as well, Mr. Vacker. So what does that tell us?"

"That Foster has questionable taste in Telepaths?" Keefe guessed.

"No, Mr. Sencen. It's that emotions affect our telepathy in powerful ways. Joy gives us strength and confidence. Love pushes us to try harder and never give up. Fear clouds our judgment or holds us back. Sorrow strips us of our energy and hope. Anger makes us reckless, or too aggressive. And we cannot fully control these forces on our own—but Cognates can, if they learn to recognize each other's emotions."

Keefe snorted. "Definitely not Sophitz's strong suit."

"I agree," Mr. Forkle said. "Which is why I created a new exercise. I should've been diversifying your lessons earlier, to include a range of emotions beyond trust. We must make up for lost time today."

"What about the rest of us?" Biana asked as he led Sophie and Fitz toward the stairs.

"Wraith should be here to train with you within the hour,"

Mr. Forkle told her. "And Blur is coming to take a look at that database contraption of yours, Mr. Dizznee, to see if he can find a way to integrate those stones internally. And Mr. Sencen—"

"Oh, let me guess," Keefe interrupted. "Another *exciting* day of reading?"

"Actually, I'd like you to assist with Miss Foster's and Mr. Vacker's training. Your skills as an Empath will be invaluable."

Biana giggled.

"What?" Fitz asked.

"Oh, nothing," she said. "The three of you training together and working with emotions? I don't see how *anything* could go wrong there."

Mr. Forkle brought them to a cave filled with enormous glowing blue mushrooms and walls covered in twinkling glints of purple. Sophie felt like Alice in Wonderland as she sat on a toadstool as big as a table.

"What is this place?" she asked.

"Gora and Yuri's fungus garden. That musty scent you're smelling comes from the mold on the walls. Breathing it in can make emotions feel more potent."

"Fun as it sounds to have a fungus rush," Keefe said, bouncing on his toadstool, "why do I have to be here for this?"

"To ensure their interpretations of their emotions are accurate. And the mold's effect is incredibly subtle. All it does is clear the mind of other distractions." Mr. Forkle turned to

Fitz. "Do you remember how to find Miss Foster's emotional center?"

"I think so."

Keefe laughed. "Annnnnnnnd, the Foster panicking begins."

"I'm not *panicking*," Sophie told him, with a very unconvincing squeak.

She ignored Keefe's laugher as she gave Fitz permission to enter her mind.

Several uncomfortable seconds passed before Fitz said, "Okay, I think I'm there—and whoa, it's even more overwhelming than last time."

"Sorry," Sophie mumbled, wanting to hide under her giant mushroom.

"Powerful emotions are an asset," Mr. Forkle told her. "Especially for this. And now I must lead you to the same point in Mr. Vacker's consciousness. Try to follow my lead and memorize the trail."

The "trail" was a thread of warmth winding deep into Fitz's mind. It ended in a patch of darkness that hummed with energy.

*Push through,* Mr. Forkle transmitted, and Sophie gasped as she obeyed. She'd studied fractals in her human math classes, but she'd never been surrounded by a 3-D version. Every color. Every pattern. Every style and shape were woven together into something both breathtaking and completely overwhelming.

"It takes some getting used to," Mr. Forkle said. "But what you're seeing is a visual representation of each other's moods."

"So, does that mean if I do this . . ." Keefe tickled Sophie's neck.

"GAH—everything just went supersonic!" Fitz said.

Sophie snatched Keefe's wrist as he reached to tickle her again. "Don't. You. Dare."

"Whoa, now everything's red and ripply," Fitz said. "Is that because she's angry?"

"Precisely, Mr. Vacker. Every time her emotions shift, the patterns and colors will change. And with practice, you'll learn to interpret what you see."

"Okay, but . . . can't they just say, 'Hey—I'm feeling this'?" Keefe asked.

"People aren't always honest about their feelings—even with themselves," Mr. Forkle told him. "Plus, many telepathic assignments involve stealth and secrecy. So for this exercise I'm going to need you both to forget everything around you. Let the world drop away, leaving only you two."

Keefe sighed. "Just tell them to stare into each other's eyes and they'll be good."

"None of that, Mr. Sencen. From this moment on, you have one job and one job only: to judge their translations of the various emotions I'll be triggering."

"Triggering how?" Sophie asked.

"You'll see soon enough. And you'll guess first, Miss Foster. For this to work, Mr. Vacker, it's crucial that you not react externally. No yelling or thrashing or screaming or—"

"Uhhh, what are you going to do to me?" Fitz asked.

"Nothing you won't survive. Consider it an exercise in self-control. And try not to listen to his thoughts, Miss Foster. Study only the changes in his emotional center and make your deduction. We begin now."

Sophie closed her eyes and focused on the colors weaving around Fitz's mind. She was about to ask if she was missing something when the pattern exploded into a swirl of pale blue tendrils. The color felt too bright to be sad, but also too wild to be peaceful.

"Tension?" she guessed.

"Kinda close," Keefe told her.

The laughter in his voice made her wonder what had happened to poor Fitz.

She tried to think of other emotions as his mind turned electric blue.

"Shock?" she guessed.

"That counts," Keefe said. "Though the best answer would've been 'surprise.'"

"Is that an emotion?" she asked.

"Indeed it is," Mr. Forkle said. "One of the most common emotions you'll experience as you navigate someone's mind—hence why I chose it as our starting point."

"Can I talk now?" Fitz asked. "Because that was seriously disgusting!"

Sophie opened her eyes and tried not to laugh when she saw

red fruit smashed all over Fitz's face. He wiped his cheeks on his sleeves, but that only smeared the pulp.

"I think I'm going to like this assignment," Keefe said. "What else can we fling at Fitz?"

"Nothing for the moment," Mr. Forkle told him. "It's his turn to interpret. Everyone close your eyes. And remember, no cues of any kind, Miss Foster."

Sophie counted the seconds, bracing for the worst—and when nothing changed, she opened her eyes and found Mr. Forkle with his finger over his lips in a "shhh" sign.

"Um . . . confusion," Fitz guessed.

"That works," Keefe said. "It started as anticipation, but then it shifted."

"Very good," Mr. Forkle said. "And well done, Mr. Sencen. I wasn't sure you'd recognize confusion. It's one of the more challenging emotions for Empaths."

"Maybe on other people," Keefe said. "But on Foster it's easy. Why are her emotions so much stronger?"

"Honestly, I'm not sure," Mr. Forkle admitted. "I suspect it stems from the combination of her inflicting ability and her human upbringing. But it was one of the surprises of her development. Much like her teleporting. Okay, Miss Foster, it's your turn to guess again."

She closed her eyes and watched as the lines of color in Fitz's mind blossomed to a snowflake of purple.

"Pride?" she guessed.

Keefe laughed. "Wow, add more fail points to Sophitz."

"Quiet," Mr. Forkle told him.

The brightness in Fitz's mind dimmed, and the pattern seemed to melt into a swamp of murky gray green.

"Disappointment?" she tried.

"Now it is," Keefe said. "Before it was jealousy."

"Jealousy over what?" Sophie asked.

"Is it my turn to guess?" Fitz said, changing the subject.

Fitz guessed Sophie's next emotion: embarrassment from Mr. Forkle giving her a big hug. And Sophie guessed right when Fitz panicked after Mr. Forkle placed an especially hairy spider on his knee. They nailed the next few as well: stress, joy, and bravery. And the more they practiced, the more Sophie could sense their minds syncing. Eventually she could actually *feel* the emotion as Fitz experienced it, not just see the change in color and pattern.

"Remarkable, isn't it?" Mr. Forkle asked.

"Kind of," Fitz said. "It's cool to feel what she's feeling. But I still don't see how this helps with telepathy."

"Then stand up," Mr. Forkle ordered. "Both of you. And put your hands on my temples. Don't think. Just feel your way through my blocking—*if* you can."

They stretched out their minds, and Fitz's consciousness seemed to merge with Sophie's as they moved almost like a dance, sweeping around barriers and sidestepping defenses. When Sophie's excitement bubbled up, Fitz's steadiness slowed her down, saving her from pushing into a trap. And when Fitz grew too impatient, Sophie was there to calm his mind before he rushed the wrong direction. They ducked and dipped and scuttled, until they reached a swarm of cold currents dragging them up while Sophie's brain told her to keep fighting down.

Fitz struggled with her, and they'd almost fought their way through when she remembered what Mr. Forkle had told her about her abilities being *deceived* when she'd tried to read his mind before.

Maybe Fitz's confidence made her more daring—or maybe she was crazy—but she told Fitz to let the cold currents drag them up and away, against their instincts.

When they did, they crashed through a prickly barrier and . . .

. . . Mr. Forkle's thoughts filled their minds.

"WE DID IT!" Fitz shouted as Mr. Forkle scrambled to shut them out.

Sophie didn't feel like celebrating.

A second later, Fitz's smile collapsed as his brain processed what they'd both seen.

Sophie tried to warn him not to say anything—but he was already wheeling on Mr. Forkle to ask, "Why have you been meeting with Lord Cassius?"

# FIFTY-SEVEN

**Y**OU'VE BEEN TALKING TO MY dad?" Keefe shouted, his voice slicing around the cave.

Mr. Forkle mumbled something about not planning the exercise carefully enough, before he told Keefe, "Your father reached out to us after he found those maps in your mother's possessions—"

"Wait—those were hers?" Keefe's eyes narrowed at Sophie. "Why didn't you tell me?"

"I agreed to the meeting," Mr. Forkle jumped in, "assuming he'd either found something else, or wanted an update on you."

"Yeah, I'm sure he's been real worried about me," Keefe muttered.

"Actually he has," Mr. Forkle promised. "And he was incredibly relieved to know you're safe."

Keefe shook his head and turned back to Sophie. "I can't believe you knew about this."

"Only some of it," she promised. "I didn't know they'd met up in person."

"I didn't tell you that part," Mr. Forkle agreed. "I knew how you would feel about it."

"Why?" Keefe asked. "What did he want?"

Sophie could tell bad news was coming. She could feel it in the pit of her stomach, a sour bubbling and churning.

Still, she never would've guessed Mr. Forkle would say, "He asked to join the Black Swan."

"WHAT?" the three of them asked.

"Please tell me you laughed hysterically and kicked him out the door," Keefe begged.

"I told him we had many concerns about his trustworthiness."

That wasn't the same as a no—and Keefe definitely caught it.

"You're not actually considering letting my dad join, right?" he asked. "Because you realize that would be the dumbest decision in the history of dumb decisions."

"I know your father is a difficult person, Mr. Sencen. And I do *not* agree with his parenting methods. But there are ways he could be useful—"

"Unbelievable!" Keefe shouted. "Please tell me this isn't happening."

"Nothing has happened yet. We are far from deciding. But . . . it's not outside the realm of possibility."

Keefe laughed—a dark, angry sound. "You know what *is* outside the realm of possibility? Me staying here if you let him in."

"He wouldn't live here. He would maintain his identity in the Lost Cities."

"I DON'T CARE!"

"Keefe," Sophie tried.

He jerked away as she reached for his hand. "Uh-uh. You promised you weren't going to hide anything from me."

"I'm really sorry." She glanced at Mr. Forkle, knowing she was about to make everything so much worse. But if she didn't tell Keefe now, she'd never be able to tell him. "I was afraid if I told you, I'd have to show you your mom's note. They found it when they found the maps, along with a kit to make leaping crystals like the ones we use at Exillium. Mr. Forkle gave it to me and I was saving it until we knew more about what happened to her."

"That wasn't our deal," he snapped.

"I know. But I was worried about you. We've all been dealing with so much."

"So lying to me is better?" He rubbed his head so hard it looked painful. "Seriously, *what* is happening?"

"Perhaps we should leave this cave," Mr. Forkle suggested. "Away from the affect of the mold."

"I'M NOT MAD BECAUSE OF THE FUNGUS—I'M MAD BECAUSE YOU'VE BEEN LYING TO ME."

All Sophie could do was stare at her feet.

"Why didn't you tell me about this?" Fitz whispered to her.

"Dude, you don't get to ask that," Keefe told him.

"If you want to read the note we can go right now," Sophie told Keefe. "I have it hidden in my room."

Keefe shook his head. "Just tell me what it says."

"It says, 'Dear Keefe, I'm doing this for you. Love, Mom,'" Mr. Forkle told him when Sophie hesitated.

Keefe mouthed the words to himself, over and over and over. Finally he asked, "Doing *what* for me?"

"She didn't say." Sophie tried for his hand again and he jumped off his toadstool and backed away. "No—you lied to me."

"I know," Sophie whispered. "I'm sorry."

"That's not good enough!"

"Come on, it's not her you're mad at," Fitz said. "I know— I've been there."

"Have you? Because I seem to remember you having a bummer few weeks and then everything went back to perfect Vacker-land. So where's my perfect fix? Why does it just keep spiraling and spiraling and spiraling?"

"How can we help?" Sophie asked as he covered his face with his hands.

"Right now? You can leave me alone." He turned and stalked away.

The glowing mushrooms turned to a blur in Sophie's eyes.

Her tears felt cold.

Everything felt cold.

"Come on," Fitz said, draping his arm around Sophie's shoulders. That was when she realized she was shaking.

He'd only led her a few steps before Sophie stopped and turned back to Mr. Forkle.

"If you let Lord Cassius join the Black Swan, I'm out."

"Me too," Fitz said.

"It's not about who we *want* to work with," Mr. Forkle told them. "It's about putting aside differences for the greater good."

*"I don't care!"*

"I understand your anger, Miss Foster. I feel the same way every time I see Ms. Vacker sitting at Prentice's bedside. But I still let her sit there."

"My mom had nothing to do with what happened to him."

"I know that in my head, but not my heart. Emotion isn't logical. All I can control is how I act. Remember the oath you each swore when you joined us? You swore to do everything in your power to help your world. That includes relying on those we do not like, if they can help with something we need."

Sophie gave Fitz the note from Keefe's mom. He promised to slip it under Keefe's door if he didn't answer. Sleep felt impossible, so Sophie checked on Silveny, watching the alicorn's memories of when Silveny told Greyfell he was going to be a daddy.

The joy that sparked in Greyfell's eyes was one of the purest, most beautiful things Sophie had ever seen. It made her wonder what Lord Cassius had looked like when he discovered Lady Gisela was pregnant with Keefe.

Could a tiny bit of that spark have been there?

She hoped so.

She tossed and turned for another hour, then wandered to her window. She knew Keefe didn't want to talk to her, but when she saw his lights on she couldn't walk away.

It cost her three pairs of shoes to get his attention, and he refused to open the window. Fortunately, she'd prepared for that with a premade sign.

### I'M HERE.

Time seemed to slow down as Keefe stared at the words.

He didn't look at her as he turned away, and her heart crashed like stone. But he turned back a second later, holding his blanket and a pillow. No smile, but it was still an invitation.

Sophie raced to grab hers, and they both set up for another window slumber party, each leaning against the glass.

The distance between them had never felt so enormous.

But Sophie was willing to settle for "close enough."

# FIFTY-EIGHT

KEEFE WAS SILENT AT BREAKFAST, and the meal became awkward with a side of miserable. Dex and Biana were smart enough not to ask what was going on.

Keefe disappeared into his room the second he was done eating. The rest of them moved to the boys' common room to work. Dex was hammering tiny stone wheels—apparently he and Blur had decided that was the best way to add them to the Twiggler. Biana and Calla worked by the windows, testing to see how long Biana could fool Calla's eyes. And Fitz and Sophie plopped into the boulder beanbag chairs for another Cognate exercise.

The next assignment was called Trigger Cues, a trick to make them more efficient at probing memories. Apparently each elvin mind was filled with tiny threadlike trails, and Telepaths could learn to follow them to something called a "cue."

The more uncomfortable the trail felt to navigate, the more the person had tried to hide the truth at the end. Their assignment was to follow a difficult path and say the cue out loud. The shock of hearing it was supposed to trigger some sort of mental reaction that would uncover the secret to the other person.

Fitz let Sophie go first, and she chose a trail that felt like crawling through an itchy wool sweater. Waiting at the end were two words: Barcelona, Spain. When she spoke them, Fitz's mind filled with a boy's startled face—obviously a human boy, based on his clothes. He shouted, *"¡Imposible!"* and chased Fitz through the busy streets.

*That happened back when I was trying to find you,* Fitz transmitted. *I'd already ruled out the girl I'd gone to see, and I was getting ready to leave when I saw a group of kids kicking pigeons. One bird had a damaged wing and I was worried they were going to kill it, so I used telekinesis to lift it to safety. I didn't know anyone was near me. But that kid saw, and when I ran, he chased me, and he kept shouting things in a language I couldn't understand.*

*Wow, I can't believe how much you went through when you were trying to find me.*

*It was worth it.*

Her cheeks flamed, which was of course when Keefe came out of his room. He didn't acknowledge anyone as he plopped into one of the beanbag chairs near Sophie, but she could've sworn he muttered something about Sophitz.

"My turn?" Fitz asked.

Sophie nodded, imagining that all her most embarrassing secrets had trails lined with the safe, pretty things they were supposed to be avoiding. The trick might've worked, because the cue Fitz learned wasn't embarrassing—though it was the kind of secret she *should've* been guarding much harder.

"221B Baker Street," he said.

Her mind showed him a glass marble floating in a black void.

"Oh, is that how you retrieve the cache?" Fitz asked, then covered his mouth. "Sorry, didn't mean to say that out loud. And I didn't wreck anything by saying the words, right?"

"Nope, it only works with my voice."

Dex ended their conversation by jumping to his feet, screaming, "I DID IT!"

"You got the Twiggler to work?" Sophie asked, rushing to his side. "Does that mean you can use keywords now?"

"And all kinds of other things," Dex said. "Like, if I do *this*"—he spun the wheels he'd attached like knobs—"it pulls up all the files that have text blacked out. And right here"—he spun to the middle of the scroll—"it tells us what the drakostomes are. They're nematodes!"

"Are those some sort of frog?" Biana asked.

"They're parasites," Calla corrected. "Microscopic parasitic roundworms. I've cured many kinds from many forests."

The five friends looked at each other, knowing what that meant.

"What am I looking at?" Calla asked, leaning closer to the hologram. "This looks like an ancient scroll."

Dex nodded slowly, realizing their mistake the same moment as Sophie.

"Maybe we should—" she started.

But she was too late.

"Is this a transcript of the ogre treaty negotiations?" Calla asked. "Why is it talking about nematodes? I don't . . ."

Calla sank to her knees as the understanding washed over her.

"They knew?" she whispered. Her eyes locked with Sophie's. "*You* knew?"

"Not for sure," Sophie promised. "Not until right now."

Calla stumbled back, rushing for the stairs.

"Wait," Sophie called, chasing after her. "I know this is *huge*, but we need to think this through before we tell anyone. Once the news breaks, there's going to be chaos."

Calla's voice was as hollow as her eyes as she whispered, "The Council has wasted far too much time already. Now we're too late."

"YOU TOLD CALLA?" Mr. Forkle shouted, storming around the girls' common room.

"Not on purpose. Calla was here when Dex had the break-through," Fitz said.

"Oh, so it's my fault?" Dex asked.

"I didn't say that. I'm just saying that's how it happened," Fitz said.

"Plus . . . Calla has a right to know, doesn't she?" Sophie asked.

She couldn't stop picturing the betrayal she'd seen in Calla's eyes.

Mr. Forkle rubbed his temples. "I think it's important we try to remember that the Council still could have good reasons."

"Like what?" Sophie had to ask.

"Perhaps they didn't want the gnomes to live their lives under constant fear," Mr. Forkle suggested. "Or perhaps they worried what would happen if other species discovered the ogres held this powerful weapon? Don't you think someone else might try to get their hands on the drakostomes as well? It would put them in exponentially more danger."

Sophie sighed, no longer sure what to think.

"I must speak with the Collective," Mr. Forkle said. "We must *try* to prepare for the backlash."

"What kind of backlash do you think there will be?" Sophie asked.

"Like nothing we've ever seen."

He leaped away before she could ask any further questions, and when he returned hours later, she'd never seen him look so pale.

"The gnomes are gathering in Eternalia for a protest," he

said, sinking into one of the chairs. "The Lost Cities are in chaos."

"So what happens now?" Biana asked.

"Now we wait for the Council to respond."

Three endless days passed, giving everyone a glimpse of life in the Lost Cities without the gnomes. Fruit fell from wilting trees, bushes sagged, grass shriveled, gardens yellowed.

On the morning of the fourth day, the Council sent out scrolls informing everyone that they'd be giving a statement in Eternalia that afternoon.

"Can we go?" Sophie asked Mr. Forkle.

"Need I remind you that you have been banished?" he asked.

"So?" Dex said. "Give me five minutes in Slurps and Burps and I'll have us all unrecognizable."

"What are the odds of you actually staying here and obeying me?" Mr. Forkle asked.

"Soooo not gonna happen," Keefe said.

The rest of them nodded—even Della.

Mr. Forkle muttered a string of things that started with "you kids." But in the end, he pulled out a pathfinder with a dark crystal, adjusted it to a facet, and handed it to Fitz.

"Give me fifteen minutes to help Kesler prepare. Then use that to come find me."

# FIFTY-NINE

THE STREETS OF MYSTERIUM—ONE of the elvin working class cities—were eerily quiet when Sophie and her friends arrived.

The small, plain, identical buildings were closed up and dark, and the food stalls and vendor carts were all empty. Still, Della and Biana vanished, and Sophie, Keefe, and Fitz kept the hoods of their cloaks pulled tight around their faces as Dex led them to the only unique building in the whole city.

With its curved walls and twenty different colors of paint, the Dizznee's store looked like it had popped out of a nursery rhyme. A glowing sign read: SLURPS AND BURPS: YOUR MERRY APOTHECARY.

The door belched as they entered, and Sophie's stomach did a few quick flips.

Waiting for them at the entrance were Dex's dad and . . .

"Grady?"

Grady scooped her into his arms and she buried her face in his shoulder, giving herself ten seconds to soak up the hug before leaning back to study him. His blond hair was longer than she remembered, and his chiseled features looked a tiny bit sharper. But his eyes were bright and glassy with so much emotion it hurt her heart.

"I love you, Dad," she whispered.

"I love you too," he whispered back. "I've missed you like crazy."

From the corner of her eye she could see Dex giving his dad the biggest bear hug he could.

Keefe cleared his throat.

"Sorry," Sophie told him, wishing Keefe had someone to hug.

Dex let go of his dad too, and both father and son wiped their periwinkle eyes. Sophie had forgotten how much the two of them resembled each other.

"Well," Kesler said, straightening his white lab coat. "This is an amazing surprise."

"How did you know we'd be here?" Sophie asked Grady.

"Kesler hailed me after Mr. Forkle contacted him."

"I hailed your mom, too," Kesler told Dex, "but she wasn't

sure she could slip away. Plus, we didn't want to bring the triplets, since we know you can't stay. She said to give you this."

He pulled Dex in for another big hug, and Sophie noticed
Keefe cross his arms and shift away.

Kesler tousled Dex's hair, then frowned and stepped back,
"You're taller!"

"I am?"

Sophie tilted her head. "Whoa—he's right."

Dex had always been shorter than her, but now they were
the same height. He must've gone through a growth spurt over
the last few weeks.

"Don't go changing too much while you're gone, okay?"
Kesler made Dex promise. "And I know time is of the essence,
so I already gathered the elixirs I thought would work best."

He handed them each a small silver pouch filled with glass
vials.

"In case you're worried," he told Sophie, "yours are all
limbium-free."

Technically, Kesler was Sophie's uncle—though she never
thought of him that way. Just like she never thought of Dex
as her cousin. It was only by marriage—and adoption—so
it wasn't like they were actually related. Still, Kesler always
treated her like family.

"I didn't gather any for you," he told Della, "but I can if
you'd like."

"No, I prefer invisibility," Della said, vanishing.

"Wish I could hold my vanish for long enough," Biana mumbled. "These elixirs taste like feet."

"You're lucky," Keefe said, choking down one of his vials. "Mine tastes like armpit."

"The bad taste is intentional," Kesler told them. "To deter anyone from growing addicted to altering their appearance."

Sophie plugged her nose and downed her elixirs. He'd given her *Sea See*, *Absolutely Auburn*, *Freckle Juice*, and *Tanny Fanny*. She wasn't sure she liked the sound of the last one—and she definitely didn't like the taste. It was like drinking trash that had rotted in the sun for a couple of weeks.

"Should we be seeing a change yet?" Biana asked, pulling a mirror from her pocket.

"Usually takes about three minutes," Dex said, darting into the maze of shelves.

"What are you looking for?" Kesler called after him.

"You gave me boring ones!" Dex returned with seven vials and chugged them all.

Kesler shook his head. "You're going to regret that."

"Why?" Sophie asked.

"Let's just say too many appearance elixirs at once can be *unpleasant* when it's time to pass them. Another way we make sure no one takes them too often."

"Ew," Biana said, tilting her mirror another angle. "I still don't see anyth—EEP!"

She stumbled back as her dark hair turned red and coiled

into tight curls. Her teal eyes paled to ice blue, and her skin turned even paler, giving her a translucent glow.

"Wow," Sophie whispered, barely able to recognize her friend.

Fitz looked even weirder. His eyes had turned sky blue and his hair had turned dirty blond. He tossed the strands off his forehead and asked, "How do I look?"

"Like a wannabe me," Keefe said.

The edge to his voice made it hard to smile at the joke.

Keefe started to say something else, but a sneezing fit cut him off. When he finished, he had thick black hair covering his upper lip.

"You gave me a stache?" he asked, cracking an actual smile. He twisted the ends into points as his hair and eyebrows turned the same dark shade, and his skin took on a deep tan.

"You have to see yourself," Biana told Sophie. "You look a little like me."

"Ew, she's right," Fitz said with a shudder.

Sophie tried not to take the "Ew" personally as she checked her reflection. Her hair hung in dark, soft waves, and her eyes had turned aquamarine. Freckles dotted her nose and cheeks, and she had a deep tan to match Keefe's.

"How long will this last?" Sophie asked.

"Two hours at most. And the final twenty minutes can be hit and miss, depending on your metabolism. So I'd be away from any crowds before that happens," Kesler warned.

"They're not going there alone, right?" Grady asked.

The door belched. "No, they're going with me."

All eyes turned to find Sir Astin standing in the doorway.

"Whoa, so it really is him," Dex said. "I mean, I know you told us, but still."

"Him who?" Grady asked.

"This is Mr. Forkle," Sophie said. "One of his other identities."

Everyone squinted at the figure in front of them, trying to find any trace of Mr. Forkle in the pale blond elf.

"We need to split into two groups," Mr. Forkle-as-Sir-Astin said. Even his voice had shifted to the high whisper Sophie remembered. "There will be less chance of anyone seeing through our disguises if the size of our group does not match expectations."

"I'll take Fitz and Biana with me," Della said.

"That should work. Have your son transmit to either myself or Miss Foster if you have any problems."

*If you see Alvar, ask him about Ruy,* she transmitted to Fitz, hoping the Vackers would try for a covert family reunion.

Fitz nodded as Sir Astin asked, "Are we ready?"

"Almost," Dex said, then burped a huge belly-shaking burp that would've put Iggy to shame. He was still saying, "Excuse me," when his skin and hair turned five shades darker. His periwinkle eyes turned so deep blue they almost looked black, and muscles bulged in his arms and shoulders, stretching the fabric of his shirt.

"Okay, ready," Dex said, his voice at least an octave deeper.

Sir Astin rolled his eyes. "The Council's address will be starting soon. Della, let's have your group go first."

She took Fitz's and Biana's hands and glittered away, using the path Sir Astin created for them.

"Where are you taking Sophie?" Grady asked.

"I believe the Council set up their stage in the diamond plaza," Sir Astin said. "So I was thinking the ruby arches would be a safe place to tuck ourselves away."

Grady nodded. "I'll keep an eye on the guards."

"Thank you. And thank you for your assistance, Mr. Dizznee. Your generosity will not be forgotten."

"Just keep my boy safe and we're even." Kesler pulled Dex in for a final hug.

Sophie strangle-hugged Grady, wishing she'd gotten to see him for more than ten minutes.

Keefe stood there watching.

"I'm sure we'll see each other soon," Grady promised when Sophie pulled away.

She tried to believe him, giving one last smile as she took Sir Astin's hand and leaped to Eternalia.

# SIXTY

SOPHIE HADN'T BEEN TO ETERNALIA since the day Kenric died, when she'd stood with Alden and Fitz, watching the jeweled city melt in the Everblaze. She'd heard it had been rebuilt, but she'd assumed it would look patched together. Instead the new city shined brighter than the original.

Each new building was made from multiple jewels, and the colors were artfully arranged. It felt like walking through a world made entirely of stained glass. And yet, the breathtaking beauty felt *wrong*. A place blanketed with so much tragedy shouldn't be allowed to shimmer.

Sophie hid behind her dark hair as they entered a crowded square. Elves had gathered around a fountain with a statue in the center, resting under arching streams of colored water. Sophie's breath caught when she recognized the statue's face.

The sculptor had captured Kenric's toothy grin and the twinkle in his eyes. And yet, stone could never capture the warmth Kenric had radiated.

She studied the statue's features, trying to spot a similarity between his and hers—something to prove, or disprove, her theory. The slope of his nose looked familiar, as did the corners of his eyes, but it was too ambiguous to mean anything.

"Come along," Sir Astin said. "The protest is this way."

A river divided Eternalia, with the main city on one side, and the Councillors' twelve crystal castles glittering on the other. The Pures lined both shores, filtering the air and casting slender shadows. The shadows spread wider that day, from the hundreds of gnomes clinging to the towering trunks and balancing on the fan-shaped leaves.

More gnomes gathered along the river, lined up in neat rows like crops. They sang as one, demanding justice, their earthy voices echoing off the jeweled walls.

A row of goblins had stationed themselves in front of the gnomes, creating a blockade of rock-hard muscle. Sophie couldn't tell if they were trying to protect the gnomes, or stop them from entering the diamond courtyard where a stage had been set up for the Council. Either way, one goblin toward the center was the biggest, grayest, gobliniest sight for sore eyes ever.

"Sandor," she whispered, wishing she could tear through

the crowd and tackle him. But that would be the kind of crazy security risk he'd give her a never-ending lecture for.

Sandor didn't show any scars, and when he moved, she saw no sign of a limp. It seemed too much to hope that he could survive a fall like that with no permanent damage. But maybe Elwin was *that* good.

The crowd of elvin onlookers kept a safe distance from the goblins, stretching into the city and scattering among the jeweled buildings. Sir Astin led them to a ruby tower off to the side, with graceful arches lining the bottom floor that gave them enough shadows to hide in and still have a perfect view of the stage.

Sophie searched the crowd, hoping to spot Fitz. But she saw no trace of any of the Vackers. The only face she recognized was Jensi. He stood with his parents and an older brother Sophie had never seen before. Several guys with long greasy ponytails stood at Jensi's side, and Sophie wondered if that meant Jensi had gone back to hanging out with the group Marella had nicknamed the Drooly Boys. She wished she could catch his eye and give a small wave, but she knew he wouldn't recognize her.

"There's my mom," Dex said, pointing to a woman with amber-colored hair. She looked so much like Edaline, it took Sophie a second to notice Edaline standing next to her.

"I can't believe she brought the triplets," Dex said, laughing as the three wild-haired kids ran circles around Juline and Edaline.

"I guess everyone's here," Keefe mumbled. "Even *him.*"

Sophie followed Keefe's gaze to where his father stood with the goblin guards, ordering a small group of them to divide off and cover the stage.

"So he's back in charge of security," Keefe said, his voice as dark as his mustache.

"He regained his title recently," Sir Astin explained, "after those maps—and the guards he recommended—saved the alicorns from the Neverseen's latest attempt at capture."

"Wait—what?" Keefe asked, and Sophie was forced to tell him what little she knew.

"Great," Keefe grumbled. "Guess I can add that to the list of awesome things my mom is doing 'for me.' Or *was* doing for me. Or . . . whatever."

Sophie reached for his hand, hoping he wouldn't pull away. He twined their fingers so tightly it cut off her circulation.

"Don't look now," Dex whispered, "but I spy Stina."

Sophie followed the tilt of Dex's head. "Ugh—you have to be kidding me!"

Of all the people they could've ended up standing near, they *had* to wind up right by the Heks family? Stina had tamed her frizzy hair into a sweeping braid and wore a loose gown that made her look much more statuesque than gangly. But her scowl definitely hadn't changed.

"Is that Marella?" Dex whispered, pointing to a petite girl

next to Stina, leaning against an arch, unraveling one of the tiny braids in her long blond hair.

Marella had befriended Stina not long after her falling out with Sophie, and Sophie was sure she'd done it to spite her.

"We should be careful," Sophie said, pulling Dex and Keefe deeper into the shadows of their archway. "If any of them recognizes us, I'm sure they'll turn us in."

"I wouldn't be so quick to judge the Hekses—or Miss Redek," Sir Astin said under his breath. "The Heks family has proven there is more to them than we once thought. And as for Miss Redek, has she never told you about her parents?"

"No," Sophie admitted. Dex shook his head as well.

Marella gossiped about everyone except herself.

Sophie stole another glance at the couple standing with Marella. Her dad had wide ice blue eyes like his daughter, and her mom had the same unruly hair. They looked normal enough.

Sir Astin leaned closer. "Her mother suffered a traumatic brain injury when Miss Redek was barely a toddler. It's unclear exactly what happened—though many suspect an abundance of fizzleberry wine came into play. All we know is that Lady Redek fell off the balcony of their house and cracked her skull. Elwin did all he could, but some wounds cannot fully heal. At times her emotions get overloaded. I remember one conversation I had with her, she laughed, cried, and screamed at me in a matter of minutes. She drinks elixirs to manage it, but it still takes its toll on her family. In fact, young Miss Redek keeps trying to manifest as an Empath in hopes that she can help her mother gain further control. A couple of months ago we thought her mind had finally cooperated, but it turned out to be a misunderstanding."

"A couple of months?" Sophie whispered, realizing that synced perfectly with the time Biana manifested as a Vanisher.

That was the day she'd first noticed Marella not acting like herself—and not long afterward, her and Marella had their big fight. She'd thought Marella might've been jealous because she'd said once that she wanted to be a Vanisher too—but that must've been something Marella had made up to cover her secret. Now Sophie wished she could run over and apologize for not understanding. Or go back in time and be a better friend.

An immense fanfare reminded her why they were there, and her pulse sped as all twelve Councillors glittered onto the stage. Their jeweled cloaks and circlets glinted in the sunlight, but this time it didn't make them look regal. Compared to the gnomes in their overalls and grass-woven dresses, the Council looked frivolous and cold.

Oralie stood between Bronte and Terik, and Sophie could see the unease in their stance. Even Councillor Alina's confident smile was missing.

"Thank you for coming today," Councillor Emery said, his eyes focused on the gnomes. "As promised, we're here to answer your many questions. But we're going to start with the main one. *Why* were you kept in the dark about the plague? We did have a reason—one that was not actually *our* choosing. We kept the secret because your ancient leaders begged us not to tell you. In fact, it was their dying wish."

He paused to let the news rustle through the crowd. Even Sir Astin seemed surprised to hear it, and no one seemed to know how to react.

"Keeping our promise has been one of the greatest challenges we've ever faced," Emery continued. "But we felt it was important to honor the word we gave. We still feel it's important, which is why we must at least ask that you leave the matter here, trust that we're following the wishes of your leaders, and return to your lives."

Murmurs rose among the gnomes, swelling into angry shouts, and Councillor Emery held up his hands. "We assumed that would be your reaction. So be it. We'll provide the whole story—though it is not a happy one. It goes back five thousand years, to the time you lost your homeland."

Councillor Bronte stepped forward. "I was an Emissary when Serenvale was overthrown—newly appointed. In fact, Emissaries were a new thing for our world. I suppose that's not a detail you'd consider relevant—but what *is* relevant is that our hearts were broken when your refugees arrived in the Lost Cities. Their stories of famine and bloodshed inspired immediate action, and I was ordered to contact the ogres and make it clear that the only way to avoid war was to commit to a treaty. At first, the ogres cooperated, and agreed to meet under a truce. King Gowg—the ogre king at the time—even invited us to Serenvale. Councillor Fallon Vacker went with me, as did both of the gnomish leaders. But when we arrived, we began to see the depth of our dilemma. Serenvale had been destroyed. The Eventide river ran with polluted water, and the trees had all been torn from the ground. Even if the ogres surrendered the land, there would be nothing for your people to return to."

Angry shouts erupted among the gnomes, and Bronte paused to allow their rage before he continued.

"Our goal was still to negotiate peace," he said. "To ensure nothing like this would ever occur again. So with your leaders' permission, we continued our treaty negotiations. But the ogres refused to consider our demands. We were preparing to return to the Lost Cities, when King Gowg invited us to dine with him. He claimed it would be a chance to better understand one another. I cannot tell you how much I wish we hadn't agreed. The conversation was as horrible as the food, and he ended dinner with an ultimatum. He told us in three weeks we would see that he had the upper hand in these negotiations. We returned to the Lost Cities and prepared for an attack. But nothing changed and the deadline passed uneventfully. We were determining our next steps when we received word that your leaders had fallen ill."

Bronte's voice cracked, and he had to clear his throat several times.

"I'm sure you don't need me to describe their symptoms. It was the same plague we face now. And it had spread to their spouses, as well as the trees they'd taken up residence in. At first, we didn't understand the connection. We thought they'd encountered a new pathogen in our world, and we kept the quarantine quiet to avoid panic. The only gnomes who knew were the healers who worked with our physicians, searching for a cure. None of them could find the mysterious parasite. And then King Gowg paid Lumenaria a visit. That was the first time any of us heard the word 'drakostomes.'"

The word sounded heavier on Bronte's lips, as though it were a burden he'd been carrying for far too long.

"The drakostomes are an accident of nature," he whispered, and yet the sound still rang off the jeweled buildings. "A force that was never meant to be unleashed. Had your people not lost Serenvale, it's likely the plague would've remained undiscovered. But the ogres stole your homeland, tore down your beloved Panakes, and split open their bark."

A sharp gasp echoed through the crowd.

"Yes," Bronte told them. "The trees of your legends were real. And their fall unleashed the greatest danger your people have ever faced. We don't know how the ogres discovered the parasite—or how they infected your leaders—but King Gowg assured us he'd harvested enough to infect the entire gnomish population. He also insisted that there was no cure."

The crowd erupted, both elves and gnomes shouting in anger and grief and disbelief.

"That was our reaction as well," Bronte said. "But King Gowg claimed that the only substance able to resist the drako-stomes was the bark they'd once been preserved in. And he took quite a lot of delight in explaining that he'd burned every last piece of the Panakes in order to harvest the parasites."

Bronte let that sink in before he added, "That was when he gave us an ultimatum. We could surrender to his demands, and he would swear never to unleash the plague. Or we could sacrifice the entire gnomish species."

"It's important to note," Councillor Emery jumped in, "that the King's demands were surprisingly manageable. We assume that was because he feared war. He knew he would lose if he pushed us too far. So he made demands that would still give him the advantage, but that we would be willing to accept. The choice was clear, even if it still pains us all these centuries later."

"Our decision was made with the full support of the ailing gnomish leaders," Bronte added. "Their only request was that we protect the rest of the population. They asked us to house your people within our borders, knowing the Lost Cities were the only place the ogres would dare not tread. We promised that any gnomes who chose to live among us would be able to go about their lives any way they wanted. We have been incredibly grateful that you've chosen to assist us while you've lived here, and share your produce—but that was never a requirement. And it never will be. Our only desire is to shelter and protect your species."

Unease settled over the audience, no one sure what to say. Eventually a gnome braved the question no one else wanted to ask. "What happened to those infected with the plague?"

The Councillors reached for each other's hands, and a moment of silence passed.

"Our physicians never ceased searching for a cure," Bronte promised. "But they were unable to produce one. With their final breaths, your leaders made us swear never to tell anyone what had killed them. They didn't want your lives darkened by the shadow of the ogres' threat. And they didn't want any other creatures to discover the drakostomes existed, for fear they'd find a way to unleash them. Their only other request was that they be brought to Lumenaria to assume their final forms—a silent testimony to the ogres' atrocities. You know them well, though you likely have not realized. They asked us to call them the Four Seasons Tree."

The crowd's reaction to the news was a mix of shock, horror, and anger. But their shouts soon faded to cries of mourning.

"So is the Four Seasons Tree like a Wanderling?" Sophie whispered to Sir Astin. "Where some of their DNA gets incorporated into the seed after they die?"

"No, when gnomes meet their final end, they stand rooted

to their final resting place. They're plantlike in life, and truly plants in death."

"Please tell me every tree isn't a dead gnome," Sophie begged.

"Not every tree. But generally the most spectacular ones."

Sophie doubted she could ever walk through a forest without feeling sad again. Meanwhile, the crowd's grief seemed to be morphing into a single cry—a demand for justice so loud it shook the Pures. Sophie could see Councillor Emery fighting for control, but the crowd was whipping into a frenzy. Roots stretched out of the ground and pulsed with a thumping beat, fueling the gnomes' furious chants.

Finally another Councillor stepped forward—a male Councillor with a shock of black hair pulled into a ponytail. He cupped his hands around his mouth and made a sound like screeching tires and squealing children and yowling cats all competing to see who could be the loudest. It rippled through the air, leaving stunned silence in its wake.

"Thank you, Noland," Councillor Emery said as Noland reclaimed his place among the other Councillors. "Having a Vociferator in our ranks comes in handy. And we understand your anger. We hear your cries for action. But the fact is, a cure still has not been found. Over the centuries we've researched every parasite that ever affected a tree. And we've searched high and low for another Panakes. Both efforts have been unsuccessful. We did manage to create medicines that are slowing both the progress of the plague and easing the symptoms. But they're not enough to risk any action that might lead to further infestation."

"So those infected have no hope?" someone shouted, and Sophie could've sworn the voice was Calla's. "And the ogres get away with murder?"

"For the moment, the only answer we can give is 'yes,'" Emery said sadly. "We cannot punish the ogres for using this weapon without risking that they'll attempt an attack on those of you here in the Lost Cities. Even if we increase security, we know too little of how they spread the plague. And all it would take is one case to trigger an outbreak."

More angry shouting followed, and Sophie braced for Councillor Noland to unleash another sonic scream. But the ground in front of the stage rumbled first.

The goblins scrambled to regroup, forming a circle around an enormous brown beast crawling out of the earth.

King Dimitar, the ogre king.

# SIXTY-ONE

**K**ING DIMITAR LOOKED EVERY BIT as ridiculous as Sophie remembered, between his riveted metal diaper and his hairless gorilla-shaped body.

He also looked extra terrifying.

He wore no cape or crown—just a series of swirling tattoos across his forehead, and yellow stones set into his earlobes. But everything about him testified to his kingship. He moved with authority and confidence, as though he knew he could defeat the goblins towering over him without even needing his evil-looking sword.

If barbed wire were as thick as King Dimitar's head and sharpened to a wicked point, it would look a lot like his blade.

A single stroke likely wouldn't just kill someone, it would disembowel them.

"Oh, relax," King Dimitar said in his painfully familiar voice as the goblins pointed their curved swords at his chest. "If I wanted to kill you, you'd already be dead."

"And if your presence was welcome, we would've invited you," Councillor Emery countered.

King Dimitar smiled—a cruel curve made jagged by his pointed teeth. "You *accuse* me. That's invitation enough. If you're going to insinuate that my people are behind this plague—"

"Do you deny it?" Councillor Emery interrupted.

"I don't deny that the drakostomes exist. Nor that they are one of my favorite possessions. But tell me this: Have you found any signs of ogres at the sites of the infestations?"

The Council's silence made his smile stretch wider. "That's what I thought."

The gnomes resumed their cries, hurling insults and accusations. Councillor Emery called them to order before he told the king, "Evidence can be missed."

"Or it can never be left in the first place." He stalked closer to the goblins, forcing them back a step before turning to the crowd. "Your rebels came to me with this grand scheme for domination. I've simply sat back and watched it unfold."

"He's right," a new voice shouted from somewhere high above them.

Gasps echoed through the city as a black-cloaked figure waved from the roof of an amethyst and emerald tower. Even from that height, the white eye symbol on his sleeve taunted them.

"I wouldn't move if I were you," the figure told the goblins scaling the walls to arrest him. He snapped his fingers, and a sphere of neon yellow Everblaze sparked to life over his left hand. "You just rebuilt this city, didn't you?" he asked the Council. "I suspect you'd prefer not to do it again. Especially since this time I hardly think you can count on the gnomes to help."

King Dimitar laughed, picking bits of something Sophie didn't want to identify out of the jagged barbs of his blade. "Now you see my new strategy. I don't have to defeat the elves. You'll do that yourselves."

"Why?" Councillor Emery asked, his eyes focused on the Neverseen figure. "Why would you harm so many innocent gnomes?"

"Because sometimes you have to let things burn to let something better rise from the ashes." He tossed the fireball up and caught it with his other hand a split second before it would've ignited the building. "And let's not ignore the role you've played. We've been waiting for you to come forward, confess the secrets you've kept. We timed each release of the plague in careful stages—and look how many it took to get us here today. Even now, you only stand there because the gnomes pieced things together. That's become the elvin way, secrets and lies, while those who depend on you suffer in ignorance. But things don't have to stay that way!"

Sophie tried to think, but every time the flames flickered, her mind was paralyzed by memories of the jeweled buildings melting into glittering lava.

She was too lost in the past to ask the question Dex asked next—the question that changed everything: "There's no way to grow back a hand, right?"

The logic shattered her panic, and in the brief seconds of clarity she managed to realize, "That's not Brant."

In fact, now that her brain was catching up, she recognized the raspy tone of the figure's voice.

"No," she whispered. "It . . . it can't be."

But she knew it was, even before the figure pulled back his black hood.

"I'm tired of disguises," he said. "Tired of living like I'm the one with something to hide. Tired of letting you think I fear you. I stand before you now as the future of our world, every bit as unstoppable as my flames."

Sophie stared in horror at the face that was every bit as real as it was impossible.

Blond hair.

Slender features.

Cold blue eyes.

"Surprise," he said as Oralie screamed and Terik had to hold her back.

Somewhere in the chaos Sophie could hear King Dimitar laughing. But she was too shocked to feel anything.

Fintan had survived the Everblaze.

# SIXTY-TWO

**H**OW COULD HE BE ALIVE?" SOPHIE asked. "Alden saw the flames overwhelm him."

"Clearly there was some trick," Sir Astin whispered.

"Does that mean—"

"No." He cut her off before she could fully form the question. "Kenric is gone."

"So was Fintan!"

"Yes. But do you think Kenric would let us mourn his loss? Let that thought go—now. It will only distract you from our actual problem." He pointed to the roof, where Fintan stood, stroking the smoke around the Everblaze as if it were his pet.

It wasn't fair—if she had to have Fintan back, why couldn't she have Kenric, too?

But Sir Astin was right. Kenric would never let Oralie suffer. Just watching her thrash and flail and sob broke Sophie's heart.

Fintan turned to the goblins, who'd huddled up to work out a plan. "Remember, the only reason these flames aren't devouring this building is because I'm holding them back. If anything happens to me, this whole city burns."

"This is madness," Councillor Terik shouted at Fintan.

"No—it's called taking action," Fintan snapped back. "A new concept for you, I realize. I remember when I was a Councillor. Always sitting back, thinking we needed more time, more information, more thorough consideration. We claimed it proved our superior wisdom. But really? We were cowards. Afraid to make the hard choices and do what needed to be done."

"And what are you accomplishing by killing innocent gnomes?" Emery shouted.

"It's called getting your attention," Fintan said. "We have a plan—one I wish I could take credit for, but that's owed to our previous leader. It's a shame she couldn't be here to see her vision realized. In the end, she was a coward too. She wanted to think more. So I removed her to see the Lodestar Initiative through."

Keefe's hand fell slack in Sophie's, and she needed Dex's

help to keep him steady when Lord Cassius shouted, "What have you done to my wife?"

"Nothing more than she deserved," King Dimitar said, reminding everyone that Fintan wasn't the only monster among them. "And no more than I'd be willing to do to any of you."

"Is that a threat?" Councillor Bronte shouted.

"It's an end to the ridiculous charade we keep playing," King Dimitar told him. "Aren't you as tired of it as I am? You despise us every bit as much as we despise you. And were your minds not so pitifully weak, you would've attacked us long ago."

"And if you didn't know we could beat you, you would've attacked *us*," Councillor Emery snapped.

"For the moment," King Dimitar agreed. "But let's see what happens when we cut off your resources."

"Yes, let's," Fintan said, turning to the gnomes. "Everything the Council told you about the drakostomes is true—with the exception of one crucial detail." He paused to make sure he had their full attention before he added, "There *is* a cure."

King Dimitar reached into his metal diaper and pulled out a narrow test tube filled with a muddy liquid. Sophie wasn't sure which disgusted her more—where that test tube had been, or the fact that the ogres had withheld the cure all this time.

"You didn't honestly believe we wouldn't save some of the Panakes bark, did you?" King Dimitar asked the Council.

"So here's how this is going to work," Fintan told the gnomes. "You agree to our deal, and we'll give you the cure to save your ailing kinsmen. There *should* be enough time to save them—no thanks to the Council and their stalling."

"And what is your deal?" Councillor Emery asked.

"I'm not talking to you. This decision is entirely up to the gnomes. Are you listening?" he asked them. "I'm only going to say this once. We're willing to share the cure on a single condition. You must leave the Lost Cities and serve in Ravagog."

"The gnomes do not *serve* us," Councillor Zarina shouted.

"I love that you've managed to believe that lie after all this time. Perhaps you leave their chores to their discretion. Perhaps you tell them they can leave anytime. But they've been trapped by their ignorance, and those who dared to live beyond the Lost Cities had no knowledge of the danger of their situation. You also left them without a homeland, by your choice, not theirs, and *your* word that it was the request of their leaders."

"It was!" Bronte shouted. "Every decision we made was in an effort to protect your people. We can see now that there were flaws in our reasoning—but don't confuse the situation. The villains are not those who shielded you from the truths of these revelations. It's those who broke the treaty and unleashed the plague. Those who stand before you now ready to enslave you, not save you."

"It's true," Fintan told the gnomes. "Our offer isn't one of freedom. You *will* serve the ogres in Ravagog. But your loved ones will survive this infestation."

"I have a project for you," King Dimitar added. "One that requires your special talents. Serve me well and you have my word that I'll never unleash the drakostomes again."

"Why should we believe you?" someone shouted, and again, Sophie wondered if it was Calla's voice. "How do we know the cure is even real?"

"We're willing to prove it," Fintan said, nodding at King Dimitar.

King Dimitar flung the test tube toward the Pures, and the gnomes scrambled to catch it before it shattered.

"Test it," Fintan told them. "And as you watch it work, keep in mind that—by their own admission—the Council has tried to create a similar remedy for nearly five thousand years. They can't provide you with a cure. And you can't cure yourselves. We're the only ones who can help."

"You have one week to make your choice," King Dimitar added. "Either I will find you at the gates to Ravagog, ready to serve, or I will unleash the plague. And I wouldn't count on the protection of the elves. The distribution system is already in place. Hide here, and the drakostomes will contaminate the Lost Cities."

"A life serving the ogres is no life at all," Oralie shouted to the gnomes.

"Funny, I thought death from disease was far less of a life," Fintan corrected. "But as I said, it's your choice. You have a week."

With that, Fintan leaped away—but not before tossing his sphere of Everblaze at the Council. The silver stage burst into flames, and the Councillors scattered as the goblins rushed to pull them to safety. Others cried for the reserves of frissyn. Through the chaos, Sophie caught the briefest glimpse of King Dimitar laughing as he vanished into the ground.

"This was my mom's vision," Keefe said, shaking so hard Sophie knew he would collapse any second. His skin felt cold to the touch and his eyes looked glazed.

"What's wrong with him?" Dex asked.

"I think he's in shock." Sophie hoped that was all it was, but she couldn't help thinking about how Alden had looked after he first saw Prentice in Exile—when his mind first started to shatter.

Keefe had just seen his father. And King Dimitar pretty much confirmed his mom was dead. And Fintan had claimed that this horrible mess had been her idea. And thanks to Lady Gisela's note, Keefe knew she did it all for him.

"Keefe needs help," she told Sir Astin.

"I agree," he said. "Your disguises are also nearly gone. But it would be unwise to head straight to Alluveterre, in case the ogres are tracing any leaps."

"So where are we supposed to go?" Dex asked.

"With me," a sharp voice said behind them. "I can hide them at Sterling Gables."

Sophie spun around and found Timkin Heks. Her confusion morphed into disbelief when Sir Astin agreed.

"Wait," Sophie said as Timkin tried to take Keefe from her.

"It'll be okay," Sir Astin promised, holding a crystal up to the sunlight. "I'll meet you there as soon as I speak with the Collective."

He was gone before she could argue.

"Come on," Timkin said, dragging her, Dex, and Keefe toward his wife, who had a path already created for them.

"We can't leave Fitz and Biana," Sophie argued.

"Alden already took them away," Timkin said.

"And why should we trust you?" Dex asked, locking his knees to slow their momentum.

"Because Mr. Forkle isn't the only one with multiple names."

It took Sophie a second to figure out what he meant—and also who he could be.

She squinted at Timkin, trying to imagine him covered head to toe in white curly fur as she asked, "Coiffe?"

"Yes. Now come with me."

# SIXTY-THREE

TIMKIN BROUGHT THEM TO AN EXPANSIVE manor made of silver and crystal, surrounded by lush pastures filled with grazing unicorns.

"This is where you live," Sophie said, not sure what surprised her more—that she was at Stina's house, or that it was so bright and lovely. She'd always imagined the Hekses lived somewhere with blackened windows and crumbling walls, surrounded by gargoyles and craggy trees and a bunch of growling animals.

"We need to get him to lie down before he gets any paler," Timkin said, dragging Keefe toward the house.

Dex grabbed Sophie's arm. "Do you really think we can trust him?"

"He's Coiffe," she reminded him, still trying to wrap her head around it.

"But it's the *Hekses*," Dex said.

"I know. But . . . Fintan is alive. The Neverseen and the ogres are trying to force the gnomes into slavery. I think it's time to admit the world no longer makes *any* sense."

Dex couldn't argue with that.

So they followed their enemy into his house, which was decorated in pale blues and greens, like grass and sky. The furniture was plush, and the crystal walls were hung with family portraits. It wasn't as grand as Everglen, or as pristine as Havenfield, but it was the most homey house Sophie had encountered in the Lost Cities.

"Do you have an Imparter on you?" Timkin asked as he brought Keefe to the couch.

Sophie shook her head. "I left it back at Alluveterre."

"Fine, wait here," Timkin told them, "And don't touch anything."

Sophie dropped to her knees next to Keefe and tried to get him to look at her. "It's going to be okay," she said, taking his clammy hand.

Keefe didn't blink.

"This place gives me the creeps," Dex said, studying a humongous portrait of Stina on the wall. "Nothing about it makes any sense."

"*You* don't make sense," a snotty voice said behind them.

Sophie cringed, allowing herself one breath before she turned to face Stina—and found a fun bonus to put the cherry on top of the awkward moment.

Marella looked anywhere but at Sophie as she asked, "What's wrong with Keefe?"

"I don't know," Sophie admitted.

Keefe didn't seem to have a headache—which was a good sign. When Alden's mind broke, he'd clutched his head and cried out in pain.

But guilt affected people in different ways.

"Elwin will be here soon," Timkin said, stalking into the room, carrying a blanket. He froze when he noticed his daughter. "Where's your mother?"

"She stayed to make sure no one noticed you taking *them* away."

"Probably wise." Timkin draped the blanket around Keefe and placed his palm over Keefe's forehead to check his temperature. "I wish she'd kept you with her. I don't want you involved in any of this—"

"Why not?" Stina asked. "If *she* can be a part—"

"Unlike others in the Black Swan," Timkin interrupted, "I do not endanger children. Especially *my* children."

Sophie had seen the look on Stina's face many times, and fully expected a screaming match to follow. But after a second, she tossed her hair and stomped upstairs.

Marella turned to follow, and Sophie rushed to her side,

taking her chance before her former friend could walk away.

"I'm sorry for anything I said before I left," she mumbled.

Marella frowned. "Huh. I thought you were going to apologize for leaving without me."

"I . . ." Sophie didn't know how to finish her sentence. She'd never realized Marella would've wanted to go with her to the Black Swan. And . . . if she was being honest, she wouldn't have ever thought to include her.

She liked Marella—she did. But she didn't know her *that* well.

So she let Marella follow Stina upstairs, hoping Stina would be a better friend than she'd been.

"She's better off," Timkin said, echoing her thoughts.

"If you hate the Black Swan so much, why are you one of them?" Sophie asked.

"I don't hate the Black Swan."

Sophie snorted. "You've said nothing but horrible things about them."

"Yeah, I always figured you'd join the Neverseen someday," Dex added. "If you weren't part of them already."

Timkin smiled at that. "I'd wager you think anyone who dares not to like Miss Foster has allied themselves with evil. And truth be told, I still see no value in Project Moonlark. But our world needs change. And while I don't agree with all of the Black Swan's politics, I *can* agree that they're the best chance we have of surviving. So if that means spending my days pandering to a group of children who will surely never live up to the Black Swan's foolish expectations . . . so be it. I'm hoping to be proven wrong."

Sophie sighed, marveling at Timkin's gift to insult her in every possible way while still sounding logical. And she couldn't fault him for doubting her capabilities. She often doubted them herself. Plus, she remembered what Mr. Forkle had told her about their world needing checks and balances. Why shouldn't the Black Swan have similar voices of opposition?

She was spared from further musings by a familiar voice saying, "Look who's back in the Lost Cities again and already needing a physician house call!"

She rushed to hug Elwin, grateful for a friendly face. And as he patted her shoulders, she felt her knots of panic loosen. Elwin would fix Keefe. Everything was going to be okay—if she didn't think about the Neverseen and the gnomes and the million other catastrophes.

"Okay, let's tend to the runner up for Most Frequent Patient," Elwin said, turning his attention to Keefe. He flashed orbs of different color around Keefe's face to examine him.

As the minutes stretched on, Sophie forced herself to voice her worry. "Could his mind be breaking?"

"I can't tell," Elwin admitted. "That doesn't show up medically."

"Then I'll have to check," Sophie whispered.

"Is that safe?" Dex asked.

"If I survived the madness in Exile, I should be up for

this." Still, her hands trembled as she reached for Keefe's temples.

She braced for chaos and confusion, shards of memories and pockets of emptiness. Instead, Keefe's mind looked like a long, shadowy hall, leading to a single memory.

The scene was cracked and distorted, as if the memory had been repressed—or damaged. Keefe was only a kid, no older than five or six, and he'd climbed the endless staircase in Candleshade, following his mother's voice. He found her on the roof, standing in the moonlight, talking to two figures in black hooded cloaks. Keefe hadn't recognized the voice when the taller figure spoke. But Sophie did.

*Brant.*

"We need to move up the timeline on the Lodestar Initiative," he whispered.

"Why?" Lady Gisela turned to the other figure. "You said the girl had brown eyes."

Sophie's mind buzzed, realizing she had to be looking at the Boy Who Disappeared.

"But the real child is out there somewhere," Brant jumped in. "If Alden finds her first—"

"We're monitoring Alden closely," Lady Gisela interrupted.

"Not close enough," Brant argued.

The Boy threw out his hands. His words were garbled—damaged in the memory—but Sophie was pretty sure he said, "It's not easy to leave Foxfire."

"Then perhaps you should go to Exillium," Lady Gisela told him. "Ruy is having no problems there."

"You know I would draw way too much attention if I left," the Boy whispered.

The memory crackled too much to hear Lady Gisela's reply. Brant said something too, but the words mushed together—or maybe that was Sophie's brain trying to make sense of what she'd just learned.

The scene cleared as Lady Gisela said, "It's a good thing Fitz is close to my son's age. Perhaps they need to spend more time together."

At the mention of himself, Keefe stepped forward. "Mom? What's going on?"

Lady Gisela hid her surprise well.

"Nothing, baby," she said, opening her arms for a hug. "Why are you out of bed?"

Sophie couldn't decide what made her sadder: watching Keefe cuddle against his mom, or watching Lady Gisela turn to Brant and whisper, "Go get our Washer."

Washers were Telepaths with the ability to erase memories. That explained why the scene had blips and damage. Lady Gisela had it wiped from Keefe's mind.

But washed memories could come back. All it took was something to trigger it. Fintan mentioning the Lodestar Initiative must've been enough, and now Keefe's mind was fixated.

The memory started over, and Sophie watched it replay,

searching for clues she'd missed. One thing she knew for sure: Ruy—the Psionipath—wasn't the Boy Who Disappeared.

But that didn't matter at the moment. She needed to get Keefe back.

"He's remembered something his mom erased," she told Elwin when she pulled her mind back, "and now his brain is stuck on it."

"What did he remember?" Timkin asked.

Sophie stayed silent. Her trust in Timkin Heks only went so far.

"If that's the case, what his mind really needs is to rest long enough to reset," Elwin said, reaching into his satchel and pulling out a vial filled with deep purple serum. "This will knock him out for twenty-four hours, which should be enough time. I wouldn't leap him until he wakes up, though. He already looks a little faded. I'll give him something for that—don't worry."

"He can stay here," Timkin said.

"I'm staying with him," Sophie told him.

"I assumed."

Sophie helped Elwin prop Keefe up and pour the elixir on Keefe's tongue. Thankfully, Keefe swallowed it without a fight.

"I'll bring him to his room," Timkin said, lifting Keefe and heading for the stairs.

Sophie turned to follow, but Elwin blocked her, forcing her

to drink several elixirs while Dex endured a full checkup.

"Do you think Fitz and Biana will be safe at Everglen?" Sophie asked Dex.

"Of course they will," a stern female voice said behind them. "The Council has far larger problems than teenage runaways."

Vika stalked into the room, eyeing Sophie and Dex like intruders. She was tall, like her daughter, and her dark hair was slicked into a ponytail as tight as her features.

Sophie stood taller. "What's happening with the gnomes?"

"They're testing the cure. And then . . . who knows?" Vika undid her ponytail, letting her wild hair fall over her face. "Going to Ravagog is a death sentence for them. But so is staying here."

"You really think the ogres can unleash the plague in the Lost Cities?" Elwin asked.

"Assuming they haven't already," Vika said. "They could've done it today, while we all stood there watching. They've already done an excellent job of making us look the fools."

Sophie shivered as she realized that Vika was right. All the gnomes were gathered in Eternalia—it would've been the perfect chance to unleash the plague.

But she hadn't seen any sign of the Psionipath.

Then again, Fintan had made it sound like the force-fielded trees were just part of their timing system.

"For what it's worth," Elwin said, resting a strong hand on

Sophie's shoulders, "I think the ogres need the gnomes, and that's what they're really aiming for. King Dimitar said he had a project for them, remember? So I doubt they're infected yet, but I'd sure like to get my hands on that cure."

"Do you think we can make more from the sample they gave?" Dex asked.

"I'm sure the healers will keep a bit to try," Elwin said. "But I'm betting the Neverseen would have planned for that. I'm going to stop by Lumenaria after I leave here and see what's up. I'll be back to check on Keefe when the sedatives wear off."

Elwin was about to leap away, when Sophie ran over and whispered one additional request.

Elwin smiled. "Consider it done."

"What was that about?" Dex asked when Elwin was gone.

"Just . . . something that might help Keefe when he wakes up."

Mr. Forkle showed up later to take Dex back to Alluveterre. The Collective needed him to comb through the Lumenaria archive for any information on the Four Seasons Tree. He didn't have much of an update, though he said most of the gnomes had decided to leave for Ravagog if the cure worked.

"But they'll be slaves," Sophie whispered.

All Mr. Forkle said was, "We're working on alternatives."

He leaped away then, taking Dex and leaving Sophie alone at Sterling Gables with the Hekses, Marella, and an unconscious Keefe. She couldn't decide who was worse.

She stayed by Keefe's side, even though it meant sleeping

in a rather uncomfortable chair. Night stretched into morning, and Sophie began to realize how long twenty-four hours could *feel*. Vika brought her breakfast: sliced fruit that didn't taste ripe, a sour reminder of how different things would be without the gnomes in the Lost Cities.

"Can't you do some weird Telepath trick to fix him?" Stina asked when she checked on Keefe at lunchtime.

"Keefe's mind isn't broken," Sophie said. "But I do keep checking his dreams."

"Ugh, how creepy is that?" she asked.

"You can go now," Sophie told her.

Stina stalked away, and Sophie figured that would be the last she'd see of her. But Stina brought her dinner.

"It shouldn't be that much longer, right?" she asked as Sophie forced down a few bites of a purple root that was too mushy.

Sophie checked the time. "Should be about two hours. Any news on the gnomes?"

"My dad said the cure is working, so . . . that's good, right?"

"Yeah." Except it meant the gnomes really would be heading to Ravagog. She tried to imagine Calla serving King Dimitar, trapped in a land with no trees.

Stina sat on the floor and curled her long legs underneath her.

"Where's Marella?" Sophie asked to break the silence.

"She went home hours ago—nice job noticing."

"Um, I've been a little busy."

"Yeah," Stina said, "you always are. Why do you think she got sick of you?"

"Let's not do this," Sophie said. "I get it, you hate me. I don't get *why*, but—"

"You really don't know?" Stina interrupted, shaking her head. "The first time I saw you, you laughed at me. At Slurps and Burps, remember? You didn't even know me. And you didn't know Dex. But you sided with him, even though he'd turned *me* bald."

It had been a little more complicated than that, since Stina and her mom had been incredibly rude to Dex and Kesler. But Stina was right. Laughing at someone going through a hard time was never nice.

"I'm sorry," she told Stina. "I mean it. I am."

More awkward silence passed until Stina stood. "I still don't like you. But . . . I *could* change my mind if you find a way to fix this mess with the gnomes."

"Gee, no pressure there."

Stina shrugged.

She was halfway out the door before she added, "If you can't do it, I don't know who can."

# SIXTY-FOUR

**W**HEN KEEFE'S SEDATIVE finally wore off, Elwin declared him better. His cheeks had color again, and his eyes weren't glazed over, and he could even answer all of Mr. Forkle's questions.

But he *wasn't* better.

Sophie tried to get him to talk after Mr. Forkle brought them back to Alluveterre, but he closed himself in his room.

"It's not safe to talk to me," he called through the door. "Apparently I've been reporting on my friends for years."

"That doesn't matter," Sophie promised.

"Uh, yeah it does. For all I know, I'm the one who told the Neverseen that Fitz found you. Haven't you wondered how

Gethen knew to show up with that dog to try and grab you?"

"The only person who knew I found Sophie was my dad," Fitz said, joining Sophie outside Keefe's door. "I never told you."

"Okay, fine," Keefe said. "But I'm sure there were other times my mom had me spying on you."

"'Spying' implies intent, Keefe," Sophie reminded him. "You were used."

"Great. Because *that* makes it better."

He stalked away from the door and stopped responding when they called to him. Even when Sophie tried to give him the gift she'd asked Elwin to buy. She had to settle for leaving it in the hall outside his door. She hoped he'd find it later, and the fluffy green gulon stuffed animal would make it easier for him to sleep.

"The revelations of yesterday have bruised deep," Mr. Forkle warned her as she sulked to her room.

Sophie was more afraid they'd left a giant gaping wound that no amount of time could ever heal.

She kept replaying what she'd learned about guilt—how some elves reacted differently.

Based on what she knew about Keefe, she was pretty sure his response would be *reckless*.

"Going somewhere?" she asked from the shadows of the gazebo as Keefe tried to sneak down the stairs.

It was the middle of the night, and she'd been camped out for hours, waiting to see if her theory was right.

Sure enough, Keefe was there, fully dressed and carrying a satchel.

"So where are we going?" she asked, standing to show that she was dressed too.

"*You're* going back to bed," he said.

"I will if you will," she told him.

He shook his head. "I have to do this."

"Please tell me you're not honestly thinking of sneaking into Ravagog by yourself."

"Someone has to steal that cure. It's the only way to stop the plague *and* save the gnomes from slavery."

"I know," Sophie said. "But you can't do this by yourself. How are you going to get inside the city? And if you do get in—what then? You don't even know where you're going."

"I'll figure it out."

"Or you'll get yourself captured—or killed. You can't leave without a plan."

"We don't have time for plans! We have a week."

"Then we'll have to plan quickly."

She crossed the room and grabbed the strap of his satchel, which felt unexpectedly light as she pulled it off his shoulder.

"The Neverseen have been planning this for *years*, Keefe. You can't defeat them with zero thought and . . ." She opened his satchel and smiled as she peeked inside, where a fluffy green stuffed gulon stared back at her. "Mrs. Stinkbottom will help you sleep, not defeat ogres."

"I know," Keefe mumbled.

She wished he would smile, or crack a joke, or do *something* Keefe-like—especially at the name Elwin had chosen.

All he said was, "I also have a melder in there. And some of those cube things Dex used in Exile."

"That's not enough to take on ogres, Keefe. *Ogres.* Remember what King Dimitar did to Sandor?"

"That doesn't scare me."

"It should. I know it terrifies me."

"That's why I'm going by myself."

"No, you're not. We're a team. We're stronger together."

He reached for his satchel, but she wouldn't let go.

"At least give me one day," she begged. "One day to come up with a better plan."

His sigh stretched so long it sounded painful.

"Fine. I'll wait until tomorrow night," he said. "Then I'm leaving."

"We need a guide," Sophie told her friends as they gathered around the breakfast table for a How To Break Into Ravagog brainstorming session. "And not a telepathic guide. An actual guide, who knows their way around the city. We can't afford to get lost."

They only knew two people who'd been to Ravagog: Lady Cadence, Sophie's former linguistics mentor, and Alvar, Fitz and Biana's brother.

"It has to be Alvar," Keefe said. "Lady Cadence is scarier than the ogres."

Sophie agreed.

"Did we ever find a way to contact Alvar?" Sophie asked Fitz and Biana.

"I did," Della said, appearing in the corner of the gazebo, next to the pile of underripe fruit they'd picked for breakfast. "He didn't remember the boy you'd asked about. I forgot to tell you."

"I thought you were with Prentice," Biana said.

"I was on my way. Then I heard five of the people I care about most in this world talking about sneaking into the ogre capital. So I figured I should stick around and make sure you don't do anything crazy. And before you start to argue"—she held out her hands to silence them—"I'm not going to try to stop you. I knew when I followed you to the Black Swan that there would be times, like right now, where I'd have to stand by and watch you take huge risks. It's *not* easy. Part of me wants to barricade the doors and keep you safe until you're at least three hundred years old. But . . . I trust you—all of you." Her eyes lingered on Keefe. "And I know the incredible things the five of you can do. So I'm not going to talk you out of this. I'll even ask Alvar to help. But I need you five to promise you won't run off until you've discussed your plan with the Collective. I don't care if you think they'll try to stop you. You're strongest when you all work together."

Della left after they agreed—though Keefe didn't sound very convincing—and Sophie looked at her list of problems they hadn't solved. "Okay, so assuming Alvar is our guide, we need to figure out how we stay hidden."

"That's easy," Biana said, vanishing.

Fitz rolled his eyes. "What about the rest of us?"

"And how do you know the ogres aren't like the gnomes and have a way to see you?" Sophie asked. "Even if they can't, they'll be able to smell that we don't have a Markchain."

A Markchain was a silver necklace housing a tiny ecosystem of bacteria, and it served as a hybrid between the elvin registry pendants and the dwarves' magsidian. The scent made it clear to any nearby ogres that the person with the Markchain had permission to be in their city.

"Maybe Lady Cadence would let us borrow hers," Fitz said.

Sophie made a note of the suggestion, even if she couldn't imagine Lady Cadence agreeing. "We're going to need disguises, too. In case we're spotted. I still have the Neverseen robe I used when we went to visit Gethen."

"I have mine, too," Keefe said. His voice hid a slight quiver.

"Okay, so that's two. We'll have to find a way to make three more. And he had the Neverseen symbol on his arm, too—maybe we should add that. In fact, maybe we should try to re-create his whole outfit. He had this fitted vest that looked almost military style. The ogres probably don't know *all* the members of the Neverseen, so the harder we work to get the details right, the better chance we have of them letting us go if we get stopped." Sophie made another note, and drew a quick sketch of Gethen's vest, wishing she had Keefe's artistic skills.

"So, just to recap," Dex said, setting down the gadget he'd been tweaking. "We *might* have a guide. And we *might* have one Markchain. And we *might* have a way to make disguises. And I *might* be able to make enough weapons in the next, like, five hours. Anyone else see the problem?"

"Yeah, this is why I should go by myself," Keefe said.

The suggestion was met with a resounding, "No!" But Sophie knew Keefe wasn't going to listen. If she didn't figure something out, he *would* go alone.

"No, the *problem*," Dex said, "is that we still haven't figured how we're getting into the city. I'm guessing teleporting is out?"

"I remember Alvar saying the city is surrounded by force fields," Fitz said. "Who knows what they'd do to us as we tried to pass through."

"Maybe Alvar knows a secret entrance," Biana suggested.

"Maybe," Sophie agreed. But she doubted it.

"I know the way," Calla said from the staircase, making Sophie drop her pen midnote. She hadn't seen Calla since

Calla had left to tell the other gnomes the truth about the dra-kostomes.

Calla gave her a reassuring smile as she moved to Sophie's side. Her gray eyes were rimmed with red, and Sophie couldn't tell if that was from exhaustion or crying. But Calla's voice was confident when she told them, "I know how to get into the city."

"How?" Sophie asked.

Calla was about to answer, when she noticed the pathetic pile of fruit they'd gathered. She picked up one of the pieces, tracing her fingers sadly over the peel before setting it down and shaking her head. "One problem at a time," she whispered.

"What do you mean, you know the way?" Dex asked, getting back to the subject.

"I mean there's a secret path into Ravagog," Calla said. "I finally solved the riddle. All the songs said to 'embrace the heart-ache,' and now that I know the truth about our past, I know what the words mean. Our leaders would've known we'd never give up on our homeland, and made the way back for us to return. If I sing the song of the Four Season's Tree and embrace their heartache, their roots will open a tunnel to the ogre city."

"Does that mean you have to come with us?" Biana asked.

"I don't *have* to. I want to."

"But it's dangerous—especially for you," Sophie warned.

"I know the risks. But I will see my homeland, however lost it is. And I will take back freedom for my people."

Sophie could tell there would be no arguing the point, and

made a note that they'd need to make another Neverseen robe for Calla.

"Okay, so that's progress," she said. "But I feel like we still need a better plan for how to stay hidden."

"I might be able to help with that," Mr. Forkle said. "No need to hide that paper, Miss Foster," he added as he made his way to the table to join them. "I know what you're planning."

"You're not going to try to stop us?" Fitz asked.

"I doubt I could even if I tried. Plus, I learned from the mistakes in Exile"—his eyes strayed to Fitz—"that it's far better if we coordinate our efforts." He took her list and scanned it. "I assume your mother is working on reaching out to Mr. Vacker?"

Fitz nodded.

"Good. I'll have Granite talk to Lady Cadence about the Markchain. Perhaps she knows how to amp up its aroma to better cover a group of nine."

"Nine?" Sophie asked, doing a quick mental head count. With Alvar and Calla she only had them at seven. "Who are the other two?"

"Two elves with incredibly powerful abilities, who should solve many of these problems you're tackling. The trick will be convincing them to help."

"Who?" Fitz asked, but Sophie had already guessed.

It looked like she'd be dragging Tam and Linh into danger after all.

# SIXTY-FIVE

T HAT'S A LOT OF INFORMATION TO GET IN five minutes," Tam said, staring at the curved ceiling of the small den.

Their dwarven house looked like a clump of bubbles inside the earth, with tiny round rooms that somehow felt cozy, not claustrophobic. Maybe it was the subtle glow from the flecks of lumenite peppered through the walls. Or the way the stone furniture had been hand painted with intricate patterns of lines and dots. But even with Mr. Forkle filling a large portion of the space, Sophie didn't want to leave.

Or maybe that was because she knew her friends were back in Alluveterre working with Calla to arrange the supplies they'd need. Once Tam and Linh were on board—*if* Tam and Linh were on board—they would be departing for Ravagog that evening.

Part of her wanted to lock everyone up to keep them safe. But then the gnomes would die—or end up King Dimitar's slaves. And knowing Keefe, he'd find a way to sneak off on his own.

Teamwork was the best option—but she'd made Mr. Forkle promise he'd be upfront with Tam and Linh about all the risks.

"So . . . if I'm understanding this correctly," Tam said, "you want us to take a secret tunnel into Ravagog to steal the cure from the King?"

"It might not be directly in King Dimitar's possession," Mr. Forkle said. "We're actually not sure where he's keeping it, or what kind of vessel it will be contained in."

"Oh good," Tam said. "And here I thought it was going to be impossible."

"Nothing is impossible with the right team," Mr. Forkle told him. "That's why we need your help. Your shadows can keep everyone hidden."

"I wouldn't be so sure," Tam said. "I've never covered more than two people."

"But I can add mist to thicken the shadows," Linh reminded him. "It may not work under close scrutiny, but it will hide us from a distance."

"There's always going to be *some* danger," Sophie added quietly. "But some risks have to be taken."

Tam brushed his bangs out of his eyes and paced the ten steps the floor allowed. "Here's what I don't get. You said the gnomes can already tell the cure is working, right? So why did the ogres give a whole week for them to decide?"

"I've been pondering that question myself," Mr. Forkle said. "And I suspect the deadline is strategic. It's possible King Dimitar is hoping the Council will send in goblin forces, and he'll finally have his war. More likely though, the Neverseen is hoping we'll attempt something like this."

"You think this is a trap?" Sophie asked, her voice too loud in the small space.

"Quite simply . . . yes," Mr. Forkle said.

"Then, uh, why would you walk right into it?" Tam asked as Sophie's mind exploded with new worries.

"We're not," Mr. Forkle said. "We're taking advantage of their distraction. They'll be so focused on what they *assume* we're going to do that they won't be prepared for us to go a different way. That's why it's so important that we have you and your sister on the team. Your unique, unexpected abilities will give our strategy the advantage we need."

"Right, but—" Tam started to argue, but Linh stepped forward.

"I cannot speak for my brother," she said, "but I will go. The gnomes at Wildwood took care of us for years. I'm honored to have a chance to help."

"I guess that means I'm in too," Tam said. His eyes latched onto Sophie as he added, "Don't make me regret this."

"Oh good, Bangs Boy decided to join us," Keefe grumbled as Sophie and the others returned to the girls' tree house.

Tam didn't seem to notice the insult, too distracted by the leaves flying everywhere as Dex tested one of his Sucker Punches against the shrubbery chairs.

Sophie, meanwhile, was focused on a familiar face. "Alvar!" she said, rushing over to give him a hug. She realized halfway there that her friendship with the eldest Vacker sibling hadn't really reached the hugging stage—but she was too committed to abort.

Fortunately, Alvar laughed and set down the scroll he'd been reading to hug her back.

"Always good to see the famous Sophie Foster!" he said.

Alvar had the Vacker accent and the Vacker insane good looks, though he was more meticulous about his appearance. His dark hair was perfectly gelled, and his clothes never had a speck of lint or a wrinkle. He also had his mom's cobalt blue eyes instead of teal.

"Thanks for coming to help us," Sophie told him.

"How could I not? Apparently I'm the only member of my family not helping the Black Swan."

"Remember when you didn't think the Black Swan existed?" Biana asked her brother. "You and Dad used to fight about it all the time."

Now that Biana mentioned it, Sophie remembered that too. "But wait, Fitz said you used to go out looking for me. Why would you do that if you didn't think the Black Swan existed?"

Alvar laughed. "I was wondering when you guys were going to call me out on that. Honestly? I did the Sophie Search just to keep my dad happy—and because it was fun to sneak to the Forbidden Cities. It was probably good that Fitz took over. I'm sure my biases affected my search. I visited each girl expecting *not* to find an elf. All I needed was one detail to prove I was right, and I was out of there. I never could've looked past your eye color."

"I almost didn't, either," Fitz admitted. "As soon as I saw the brown, I thought I should leave. But . . . there was something about her. The way she kept herself separate. The way she was so much smarter than her teacher. And other than her eyes, she definitely looked like an elf."

Sophie was fairly sure he'd just implied she was pretty— and had to look away to hide her grin.

"So you really lived with humans?" Tam asked.

Sophie nodded. "It's a long story."

"One we do *not* have time for," Mr. Forkle added.

"I don't think we've met," Alvar said, turning to Tam and Linh. "New recruits?"

"More like temporary assistants," Mr. Forkle corrected. "Much like yourself. We would never expect any of you to swear fealty with so little information."

"But now we've seen your secret hideout," Alvar teased. "How can you keep us away?"

Mr. Forkle didn't return the smile. "I dare you to find it again."

"What if we *want* to join?" Linh asked, ignoring her brother as he elbowed her.

"That's something we could discuss," Mr. Forkle said. "*After* this mission. For the moment, we must stay focused. How is our progress?"

"Sucker Punches are almost done," Dex said. "Then I'll make as many of these as I can." He held up one of the cube-shaped gadgets he'd used in Exile.

"The cloaks are also finished," Calla said, pointing to a stack of black robes. "I'm still assembling the rest of the outfits."

"We're wearing disguises?" Linh asked.

"As an added precaution," Mr. Forkle agreed. "In case there are moments you and your brother cannot keep everyone hidden, it's best for you to blend in."

"They're hiding us?" Alvar asked. "What are their abilities?"

"I'm a Hydrokinetic," Linh said. "And my brother is a Shade."

Alvar scratched the back of his head. "Huh. That definitely changes things up."

"Why?" Keefe asked. "How do we know his little Shade tricks are even going to work? What if the ogres can see through them like Calla can see through the vanish?"

"They can't," Alvar said. "I used to sneak around the city all the time—but wait, gnomes can see us?" He disappeared and tried the *how many fingers am I holding up* test. "Whoa. Total mind blow."

"I know how to get around it," Biana said smugly.

"What's the secret?" Alvar asked as she vanished to prove it.

"Like I'd tell you!" She shoved her brother as she reappeared. "Honestly, though, you kinda have to figure it out yourself. I've been trying to teach Mom, but she still can't do it."

"Can you see Tam?" Sophie asked Calla, getting back to the bigger worry.

Tam gathered the shadows and faded from sight. A faint outline remained, but Sophie had to really look for it.

"My eyes see nothing beyond yours," Calla said. "The glints of life ignore him."

Keefe snorted. "How does it feel to be rejected by dust?"

"Pretty good, actually," Tam snapped back, "since it means I can survive this mission. Can you?"

"Yes," Mr. Forkle jumped in, "with your help." He eyed both boys. "Whatever differences the two of you have must be settled immediately. You're a team now. It's time to start acting like it."

"That'd be a whole lot easier if he'd let me take a reading," Tam said. He pointed to Alvar. "I'd like to do one on him, too."

Keefe rolled his eyes. "Forget it, dude."

"That's twice now you've refused. Do you really have that much to hide?" Tam asked.

"Hey, I'm not up for it either, and I'm not hiding anything," Alvar jumped in. "You want to know something about us—ask."

"Okay," Tam said, glaring at Alvar. "Why should I trust you?"

"Because I'm the only one here who knows the back paths of the city. It'd be easier if I knew exactly where we're going, though. I can think of several places they might keep the cure."

"Choose the one that would be the most obvious," Mr. Forkle said.

"Mr. Forkle thinks this is a trap," Sophie explained. She did her best to convince them it was the advantage Mr. Forkle believed, but they all looked a lot more fidgety, and she didn't blame them.

"That . . . complicates things," Alvar said, going back to studying the scroll he'd set aside. It turned out to be the map of Ravagog from Lady Gisela's possessions. "Does anyone have any idea which side of Ravagog this secret tunnel is going to bring us to?"

"Side?" Linh asked.

"Ravagog is separated by the Eventide into two parts," Fitz explained. "Half the city is underground, the other half is carved into the mountain."

"It's cute how he repeats things I've taught him like he's an expert, isn't it?" Alvar asked—and with that joke, Dex officially jumped on board Team Alvar. Even Keefe cracked a smile.

Tam still looked wary, and Sophie could see his shadow crawling closer to Alvar.

"Seriously, guy," Alvar said, scooting his chair away. "Respect people's boundaries. You don't see the Telepaths poking around everybody's heads, do you?"

"No, you do not," Mr. Forkle agreed. "Though Shade readings are far less intrusive than telepathy."

"Whatever," Keefe said. "Can we go now? We're losing time."

"We're going tonight?" Tam asked. "Wouldn't a night raid be exactly what they're expecting?"

"It's still safer than broad daylight," Keefe argued.

"Not for me," Tam said. "I can control the shadows at any time. It's safer to go when they're not on alert."

"I actually agree with Mr. Song," Mr. Forkle said after a long minute. "That will also give you a few hours of rest before a very long day."

Sophie could see the fury in Keefe's eyes and slipped to his side, leaning in to whisper. "It's only a few more hours. Please wait with us."

"I could be back with the cure while the rest of you guys are still sleeping."

"Or you could be dead," Sophie reminded him. "Please don't make me beg."

Keefe let out a sigh. "Fine. I'll wait until dawn." His eyes found hers as he whispered, "For *you*."

Sophie didn't know what to make of the last part, but her heart flipped to hummingbird mode.

Mr. Forkle cleared his throat. "I suggest you all head to bed. Is anyone willing to share their room?"

"Of course," Sophie said, quickly adding, "I meant with *Linh*."

"I guess I'll take Alvar with me," Fitz said.

"Actually, I'd rather bunk with Keefe." Alvar turned to the group and whispered, "Fitz is a cuddler."

"You can have my room," Dex told Tam. "I'm going to stay up tweaking the wiring on these cubes—"

"No, Mr. Dizznee, you're going to rest," Mr. Forkle interrupted. "You *all* are. Even you," he told Calla, "at least take a few minutes."

"I cannot rest while my people are suffering," Calla argued.

Mr. Forkle decided not to argue. He shooed everyone else to their rooms, and Linh dozed off as soon as her head hit the pillow. But Sophie tossed and turned and tossed some more.

"You should be sleeping," Calla said when Sophie tiptoed out to the main room.

Sophie sank into the shrubbery chair across from her. "I know. But I can't rest while your people are suffering either."

Calla set down the vest she'd been sewing, which looked exactly like the one Gethen had worn. She'd made eight others, though one was purple and had ruffles along the edges.

"Biana designed her own," Calla explained. "I didn't fight her since she can vanish. Plus, her design is fairly clever." She lifted up the ruffles to show a row of carefully concealed goblin throwing stars.

Sophie traced her fingers over their shiny blades.

"You're afraid," Calla said quietly.

"Aren't you?" Sophie asked.

"Mine is a different kind of fear. I don't mind if something happens to me. But I fear for those I care about—especially you. I wish you would get the rest you need."

She moved behind Sophie, combing her fingers through Sophie's hair. "This was a trick my mother used when I was a little girl. Gnomish children must sleep when it's dark, but I was a restless child. I took the needs of the forest very seriously. So my mother declared this my 'tomorrow braid.' As she wove it, she'd tell me to imagine anything I feared being drawn out of my mind and folded into the braid. That way those worries were tucked away for the night, but still waiting to bounce back as soon as I unbraided my hair in the morning. It's why I still plait my hair—though now I do it to remember her."

Sophie closed her eyes and tried to imagine her worries twisting with each careful weave Calla made.

By the time Calla was done, she was asleep.

# SIXTY-SIX

**A**NY REASON WHY WE'RE NOT having the roots pull us to Ravagog?" Keefe asked as they fought through the cramped tunnel. "It would be way faster than walking."

"The same reason we didn't have the roots carry us to Exile," Calla said. The brief pause in her song made the tunnel close tighter, and it tightened further when she added, "Roots this old only have the strength to carry us one way, and the escape will be far more crucial."

She belted out the next verse to widen the tunnel again, and Sophie had to dry her eyes on her cloak sleeve. The lyrics officially won the prize for Most Depressing Gnomish Song Ever.

Now Sophie knew why the legends had warned of embracing the heartache.

Their Exillium skills came in handy, allowing them to see through the darkness and stay cool despite the stuffiness of the tunnel. Sophie channeled energy to her muscles to keep moving steady, but she still battled exhaustion, especially when the tunnel started to slope up.

The longer they walked, the more the roots narrowed, as if the Four Seasons Tree was stretching as far as it could reach. When the roots were no thicker than gossamer threads, Calla announced that the surface was right above them and asked if she should sing open an exit.

"Let me go out first," Alvar whispered. "I need to figure out where we are. As soon as it's safe, I'll come back and get you."

"I'll go with you," Biana offered.

"You should save your energy," he said. "And I should take the Markchain to cover my scent."

Sophie removed the silver pendant hanging from her neck and handed it to Alvar. She was still stunned Lady Cadence had agreed to loan it to them.

Tam had thought they shouldn't bring it, worried the scent canceled his concealment. But Alvar insisted they needed to camouflage their smell as well as their appearance.

Calla sang a deep, low verse, which sounded more ominous

than Sophie would've liked as the earth nudged open, letting in streams of greenish light.

"I'll be back as soon as I can," Alvar said, turning invisible. The only sign that he'd left was the shifting dust as he climbed out of the tunnel, and the rustling of the roots as Calla closed the earth again.

Fitz offered everyone water from a magsidian flask Mr. Forkle had given him, and Keefe guzzled the whole thing. Fortunately, the flask had been carved to draw moisture out of the air and refill itself.

"I wouldn't drink that," Linh warned. "There's something wrong with the water."

She gathered more and molded it into an orb hovering over her hand. It had a slight greenish glow that turned Sophie's stomach.

"Sorry guys," Keefe mumbled. "I would've saved some if I'd known."

"How much do you trust him?" Tam shadow-whispered in Sophie's ear.

*Alvar?* she asked.

"Him too. But I'm much more worried about your Empath buddy. He's hiding something. That's why he won't let me take a reading."

*He is,* Sophie agreed. *But I know what it is.*

Keefe probably wouldn't want her to tell Tam, but it was the kind of secret that couldn't stay hidden. *Keefe's mom was one of the leaders of the Neverseen.*

"What do you mean by 'was'?"

Sophie did her best to explain the situation. A long silence passed before he asked, "What do you think he'll do if he finds out his mom is still alive?"

"I know you guys are talking about me," Keefe said, making Sophie jump. "Care to fill me in?"

"I was asking her why the president of her fan club spends more time styling his hair than the girls do," Tam told him.

"Dude, you did *not* just insult the Hair."

Calla silenced both boys, reminding them that someone on the surface could hear them. After that, the waiting felt endless, especially since Keefe seemed determined to stare a confession out of Sophie. She closed her eyes and counted the seconds slipping away.

Eight hundred and twenty-two passed before Fitz said, "Alvar's been gone a long time."

"Do you think something happened to him?" Biana whispered. "I could go out and look."

"We shouldn't split up again," Fitz told her. "If we leave, we all leave together. But let's give him a few more minutes."

Another two hundred and thirty-three seconds went by before dust rustled above them. "All clear," Alvar whispered. "But hurry."

# SIXTY-SEVEN

OKAY, THIS PLACE IS WAY CREEP-
ier than I thought it would be," Keefe whispered as they crawled out of the tunnel and
into the underground section of Ravagog.

The city was silent, save for a steady low-frequency rumble
that felt like an itch under their skin. Glowing green moss
coated the dark stone walls, casting sickly light through the
enormous cavern beyond. The buildings were carved into the
humongous stalagmites and stalactites jutting from the floor
and ceiling like sharp, jagged teeth, with tufts of stagnant fog
swirling like rancid breath.

"Where are the ogres?" Fitz whispered, scanning the dark
windows pressed into the rock.

"We got lucky," Alvar said, appearing beside him. "This is the working end of the city, and right now it's naptime. That's why I waited a few minutes to come get you. They just went down for the count, and should be out for an hour."

"Ogre naptime?" Dex asked.

"Not as cuddly as it sounds," Alvar told him. "They basically push their workforce until they collapse. Then they let them rest just long enough to get back on their feet and drive them until they crash again. Their workers never get more than an hour of sleep at a time, and they keep working them until they have nothing left to give."

Sophie shivered, realizing that would've been her fate if King Dimitar had gotten to choose her punishment after she had tried to read his mind. And it was the life every gnome would endure if they didn't steal the cure.

"Hoods up," Alvar said. "We need to get to the other side of the river before the workforce wakes up."

Tam blanketed them with shadows and Linh added hints of mist—though she was surprised at how little control she had over the green fog. Their progress was slowed further by how closely they had to stick together, and how many twists and turns they had to make. The city had no streets or sidewalks, and there was no rhyme or reason to the jagged buildings. If Alvar hadn't been there to guide them—they followed Calla, since she could see him—they would've gone in circles.

Despite the confusing layout, Sophie couldn't help worrying

that things were going *too* easily. After all they'd heard about the dangers of Ravagog and the efficiency of its security, they hadn't seen a single ogre. Could *everyone* really be asleep?

Her question was answered when they reached the main bridge: cold metal and dark stones stretching across an enormous canyon. Pointed silver arches were scattered along the bridge, with fiery green orbs in their centers. It looked exactly how Fitz had shown her in his mind, with one dangerous exception.

At either side of the bridge, dozens of lumpy-faced ogres marched back and forth in a careful pattern, their massive barbed swords drawn and ready.

"Does the bridge always have that many guards?" Sophie asked.

"No," Alvar whispered. "It seems like they're expecting someone."

"Us," Sophie said. "They're expecting us."

The air turned colder as the reality settled over them.

Fitz cleared his throat. "So how do we get across?"

"I'm still working that out," Alvar admitted as he led them behind a stalagmite where they still had a view of the bridge.

"How thick can you make the shadows?" Sophie asked Tam.

"Not enough to get past that many guards—especially in this weird green light. And look at the pattern they're making as they march. There's no way all nine of us could slip past at the rate we move."

"And the bridge is the easy part," Dex said, pointing to the other side.

In the distance, the other half of the city had been carved into the mountain—a series of dark ledges jutting out of the rockface like bark mushrooms climbing up a tree. Each ledge was lined with metal columns and covered by metal awnings. Stone staircases netted the ledges together and wove around the misty waterfalls cascading down the mountain.

But before they could reach the city, they'd have to cross a stretch of empty dust land, without a single tree or rock or shrub to camouflage their shadows.

"I could go on my own," Alvar suggested.

"Uh, you're not the only Vanisher," Biana reminded him.

"And what do *we* do? Sit here and wait to get caught?" Fitz asked.

"We might be able to cross the water," Linh said. "And then I could call clouds from the waterfalls to obscure our shadows."

"Can you really control the river?" Tam asked. "That isn't normal water."

He pointed to the base of the steep canyon, where the river glowed with the same greenish tint as everything else.

"The ogres add an enzyme," Alvar explained. "It makes them stronger, but I'm pretty sure it's toxic for everyone else. The gates filter it out before the water flows into the valley."

Everyone turned to Linh, whose brows were pressed together.

"I can't part or lift the water, but . . . there might be a way. I need to get closer."

Alvar found a trail down the sheer slope, and after several precarious minutes—and many near falls—they reached the riverbed and ducked into the shadow of the bridge.

"No one can see us here," Tam promised as Linh moved to the water's edge. She waved her hands back and forth, whispering strange, swishing words.

"Assuming we find a way across," Sophie said to Alvar, "where exactly are we going?"

"I'm still deciding," he admitted. "It has to be in either the Armorgate or the Triad. The Armorgate is their military university. It has secret caverns deep in the mountain where they develop their weapons."

"That sounds impossible to break into," Sophie said, imagining something out of a spy movie with lasers and retina scanners and a million kinds of alarms.

"It is," Alvar agreed. "The Triad isn't any better. That's where King Dimitar holds court, in the most visible spot in the whole city. His best warriors are always at his side."

"That would be a better place for a trap," she realized.

King Dimitar would want something public, so everyone could witness his triumph.

"My shadows won't fool the ogres up close," Tam warned, guessing what she was thinking.

Sophie nodded. "We'd need a distraction."

A plan was piecing together in her mind—one far too insane to share until she'd thought it through. But she knew one thing, "I think the Triad should be our focus."

"Is she okay?" Dex asked, pointing to where Calla had her ear pressed against the ground, tears streaming down her cheeks.

Sophie crawled to Calla's side. "What happened?"

Seconds ticked by. Then Calla whispered, "I can feel them. The Panakes. They're still here."

# SIXTY-EIGHT

SOPHIE GLANCED DOWN THE RIVER, desperate for a glimpse of the miraculous trees. All she saw were dark, barren rocks.

"The trees themselves are gone," Calla whispered. "But traces of their roots remain. I can hear them singing. But I don't understand . . ."

She pressed her ear to the ground again, closing her eyes and humming a melody that felt both heartbreaking and hopeful.

"I found a way across!" Linh whisper-shouted, reminding Sophie where they were. "But I can't hold it for long."

Everyone rushed to the shore, where Linh raised her foot over the glowing river and stepped down.

"Follow my path exactly," Linh said as the water turned solid under her foot. "And do not lose your balance."

Sophie willed her clumsiness into submission as she stepped onto Linh's rippled footprint. The water felt springy, like standing on a trampoline. Keefe followed in her wake, then Biana, Dex, and Fitz. Tam coaxed Calla away from the ground and stepped out after her. Alvar was the last to cross, and his feet had barely touched the opposite shore when Linh sank to her knees, her skin as green as the river.

"I need a moment to catch my breath," she said.

"Take a minute—but only a minute," Alvar told her. "From here on out it's going to be a lot trickier, especially if we make it across the playa. Biana—make sure you stay vanished. Tam—do your best to shade the rest. Hoods up. No talking. Walk with purpose. The more you look like you belong, the more likely someone is to believe you if they spot you. And if our cover is blown—run. Use your abilities. Do whatever you have to do. If they capture you, there will be no getting out of here. Everyone clear?"

He waited for each of them to nod.

"Oh, and here," he said, returning the Markchain to Sophie. "Stay in the center of the group, so the scent is the most evenly dispersed."

Sophie clasped it around her neck as Alvar vanished, whispering for everyone to follow him. The path out of the canyon was steep and narrow, and they were out of breath when they reached the top. None looked shakier than Linh.

"Are you sure you can handle this?" Tam asked his sister as she reached toward the sky.

"The falling water has not been tainted." Linh closed her eyes, her brows pressing together. Mist curled off the waterfalls and gathered into two thick gray clouds, blocking the sun and casting shadows across the playa.

"You're pushing yourself too hard," Tam said, catching her when she collapsed.

"I know my limits," Linh promised, but her voice sounded ragged. And when she tried to stand, she fell over.

"We need to keep moving," Alvar said. "The ogres could find those clouds suspicious."

"I'll carry her," Fitz told Tam. "You need to concentrate on the shadows."

Tam reluctantly handed his sister over, and Alvar and Biana vanished again as everyone headed into the playa. They walked with slow, deliberate steps to avoid kicking up dust. Sophie kept her eyes trained on the mountain as the city came into better focus.

Metal pillars capped by green glowing fireballs illuminated the paths through the city, which were all zigzagging and narrow and treacherous. There would be no quick climb to the top, nor any way to avoid the busier parts of the city.

"That's the Triad," Alvar whispered, his arm blinking into sight long enough to point to the center of the mountain. A ledge jutted farther than all the others, stretching to a sharp point between two wide waterfalls.

They were too far away to see the throne or guards, but Sophie knew they were up there.

"You sure you want to do this?" Alvar asked.

She swallowed the bile on her tongue and nodded.

The more she thought about it, the more she had to accept that there was no way they could get the cure without being seen—and King Dimitar had to be counting on that. So if they could turn his expectation on its head with a trick, it might buy them enough time to get what they needed and get out alive.

"Okay," Alvar said, letting out a breath. "Now we head into the city."

He led them to a stairway on the far side of the mountain, and they climbed to the lowest level of Ravagog. Alvar had them pause at the top, pressing their backs against the rockface. Sophie couldn't tell if they were hiding or resting.

This level was a curved platform, about as wide as the bottom floor of the glass pyramid at Foxfire, and it was crammed with booths selling all kinds of foul-smelling things. Ogres bartered for better prices as the shopkeepers shouted to get their attention, the ogre language sounding blunt and clipped.

Sophie had never seen a female ogre before, and they were even harder to look at than the males. They wore only two narrow tubes of leather, one around their chest, the other their hips, leaving most of their warty skin on display. Brittle white hair grew from a single patch in their lumpy foreheads and stuck out like wild feathers, and their eyes had a strange milkiness to them. There were children too, playing with strange metal toys that reminded Sophie of pinwheels. They chased each other through the markets, laughing as they scurried around their mother's legs. The scene felt unnerving, but also incredibly normal. Families going about their daily lives. Sophie wondered if they even knew what terrible threats their king had made.

Fitz set Linh down and she called mist around them, thickening Tam's shadows before they tiptoed into the crowd. Their snail's pace went against all of Sophie's instincts, but it gave Tam time to adjust the shadows with every movement, and Alvar time to select the best path through the ever-moving ogres. Sophie was soaked with cold sweat when they reached the end of the market and started up another flight of stairs. But they made it. One down—*many* more to go.

The second level was narrower and blissfully ogre-free, though Sophie was sure there were plenty of ogres behind the massive barred doors heading into the mountain. They sprinted the whole way across, to yet another stairway, wider than the others, with jagged carvings on each step.

As they climbed, Sophie decided it was time to transmit her crazy plan. She started with Tam and Linh, since she had no idea what they would say. Naturally, Tam shadow-whispered that he thought she'd lost her mind. But both twins promised they'd help however she needed.

Sophie transmitted the plan to Fitz next, knowing he would have a *lot* of questions. They'd crossed another entire level—some sort of construction zone that time, filled with ogres in chains hammering at the mountain—before Fitz told her, *If that's what you think we should do, I trust you.*

Biana was easy to convince, as was Dex. Which meant it was time to stop stalling and ask Keefe. She almost changed her mind—the role she needed him to play would be the most dangerous thing any of them had ever done. But he was the only one who could pull it off.

*I was wondering when you were going to include me,* Keefe thought, the second her voice filled his mind.

*Oh, you're part of this,* she promised. *You're the most important part. But if you don't think you can handle it—*

*I can handle it,* Keefe interrupted. *Boss me, Foster. I'm in.*

He responded to the plan better than she'd thought. In fact, he almost seemed . . . excited.

*This isn't a game, Keefe.*

*No, but it's what I've been wanting to do for weeks. I got this, Foster. Trust me.*

*I do,* Sophie promised. *I wouldn't be asking if I didn't.*

She transmitted her plan to Calla next, and the tiny gnome nodded. Which meant she only had one more person to convince before things became *real.*

She waited until they reached the next level—another row of barred doorways, which was thankfully ogre-free—before she transmitted, *Can I open my mind to your thoughts?*

Alvar appeared at her side. "I don't like people in my head," he whispered. "Hazard of growing up with a telepathic father."

"Okay," she said, stumbling back a step. "I just wanted to tell you the plan."

"I thought the plan was to grab the cure and run."

"That'll be part of it," Sophie said. "We're also going to create a distraction—"

"*Bad* idea," Alvar interrupted.

"I know it's dangerous, but we need something to keep King Dimitar busy, so Fitz and I have a chance to probe his mind."

"WHAT?" Alvar's whisper was so loud it sounded screechy. "Are you crazy?"

"We have to try," she insisted. "There might be more to the Neverseen's plan than we realize, and this is our chance to find out."

Alvar shook his head so hard his hood slipped off. "You're changing too many things."

"No we're not. We're just taking every opportunity we get," Fitz whispered.

"Um, guys," Tam interrupted. "We're in the middle of *Ravagog*. All this debating is going to get us killed."

Alvar swore under his breath and pulled his hood back over

his head. "Fine. Let's keep moving. Transmit the plan to me and I'll do whatever you want."

Sophie glanced at her friends, who seemed as unsure as her. Her plan had needed Alvar to be a lot more committed than he sounded.

As they climbed the next flight of stairs, she made a last-minute amendment. Originally she'd been thinking Alvar could share Keefe's role, but she didn't know him well enough to trust him with that responsibility.

She transmitted the change to Keefe before telling Alvar, *All you have to do is stay invisible—and when it's time to run, guide us back to the tunnel. If you have a problem with that, let me know.*

He stayed silent.

They made their way up two more levels, one busy with ogres, the other mostly empty, until they reached a staircase by a waterfall.

"Next level's the Triad," Alvar whispered. "Last chance to see reason."

"We're doing this," Keefe said, his voice shaky.

He looked like the boy Sophie had seen in the physician's tent at Exillium, but that was who she needed him to be at the moment.

She turned to her friends, and one by one they all signaled to show they were ready.

Alvar sighed. "Let's hope nobody dies."

Sophie refused to let the warning shake her, as Linh blanketed them in so much mist it soaked their cloaks. Alvar took the lead, with Sophie right behind. Which meant she was the first to get a glimpse of the Triad.

The level had no railing. Just a sheer, deadly edge lined with cold metal pillars that supported the black metal awning overhead. The space was a triangle, and at the farthest point, a twisted tangle of metal formed a barbed throne, overlooking the entire kingdom. Perched proudly in the center, still wearing nothing more than his metal diaper, was King Dimitar.

A dozen ogre guards were lined up on either side of him, each one big enough to wrestle a bear one-handed. Resting at his feet was a small metal chest locked by a single round padlock, surely the cure, set out like bait.

It wasn't too late to turn back. They might even make it out of Ravagog safely. But they needed that box—and more than that, they needed the truth.

She took one steadying breath and gave her friends the signal.

Tam called more shadows as Dex scooped up Calla and everyone except Keefe locked hands. They levitated to the top of the metal awning, hoping the roar of the waterfalls covered the soft *thunk* as they touched down.

Keefe waited until they were all safely out of sight.

Then he threw back his hood and stepped out of his shaded hiding spot, shouting, *"I demand an audience with the king!"*

# SIXTY-NINE

SOPHIE WAS PRETTY SURE THE ELVES didn't have anything like the Academy Awards, but if they did, she would've given one to Keefe for his performance as the Desperate Runaway.

He managed to hide his anger and look both terrified and innocent as King Dimitar's guards swarmed around him.

"I'm unarmed," Keefe promised. "And I'm not here because of the Council. In fact, they banished me weeks ago."

"Bring him to me," King Dimitar ordered.

His guards dragged Keefe forward, the largest one pinning Keefe's hands behind his back with a single meaty fist.

King Dimitar scraped at his pointed teeth as he asked, "Do you know what happens to those who trespass in my city?"

Keefe bowed his head. "Most trespassers mean you harm. I'm just here for answers."

"So you're not here for this?" King Dimitar scooted the locked chest forward with his clawed toes.

"I don't know what's in there," Keefe said, "but it has nothing to do with me."

King Dimitar nodded at his guard, who lifted Keefe by his neck. "If you'd like to continue breathing, you'll tell me how you succeeded in entering my city."

"Kind of hard to talk when you're choking me," Keefe wheezed.

"Let him breathe."

The guard loosened his grip enough to let Keefe suck in a ragged breath.

King Dimitar repeated his question.

"Old gnomish or dwarven tunnel," Keefe rasped. "By the river. It collapsed as I crawled through."

Sophie had known Keefe was a brilliant liar, but she'd never fully appreciated his talent. He'd blended just enough truth to sell his story, and misdirected the ogres far away from the real tunnel.

"Put him down," King Dimitar said, and the guard dropped Keefe like trash.

Keefe collapsed to his knees and hacked and wretched. Each anguished sound twisted Sophie's heart.

*He'll be okay,* Fitz transmitted. *He's probably laying it on thick for sympathy.*

If that was Keefe's plan, it wasn't working.

"Elves are such weaklings," the King said, jumping down from his throne. "Your only asset is your mind—and I could crush your skull with my thumb."

"Maybe," Keefe said, rising shakily to his feet. "But you don't want to do that."

"Oh, I believe I do," King Dimitar said, wrapping a meaty hand around Keefe's head.

Keefe didn't struggle. He even sounded calm as he said, "Then you'll never know what I came here to tell you."

King Dimitar leaned closer, sniffing Keefe's neck. "I know you're not one of the rebels."

His claws shredded Keefe's black cloak, leaving him in his green cape, brown vest, black shirt with . . .

"Interesting," King Dimitar said, tracing a claw over the black Neverseen armband. "They claimed only their own knew this detail. And you do look familiar."

"Must be the family resemblance," Keefe said. "Which is also how I know about this." He pinched his Neverseen armband before covering it with his cape. "My mother is Lady Gisela."

The king didn't blink.

"Okay, maybe you know her better as the elf you tortured a few weeks ago, and had dragged into the mountains," Keefe told him.

"Oh, *her*." King Dimitar sounded so gleeful it made Sophie want to vomit. "The disappointment."

Tam shadow-whispered in Sophie's ear, "This isn't going well."

*Too early to tell,* she transmitted back, hoping she was right.

She didn't know how Keefe found the strength to stay so calm as King Dimitar circled him, studying him from all sides. "Please, King," Keefe whispered. "I came here to know if she's still alive."

"Of course you did." He tilted Keefe's chin up with a claw. "The question is, why would I tell you?"

"Because I can tell you a secret about the alicorns."

Sophie's hands curled into fists. It was what she'd told him to say—but she still hated it.

She knew Keefe would have to offer King Dimitar a secret he would actually consider valuable. And it couldn't be something that would cripple the elvin world, either. So, she'd chosen the secret she knew could only be kept for so long.

"Why do you think I have any interest in a pair of winged horses?" King Dimitar asked.

"Because you know the Council would do anything to protect them," Keefe said. "They care about them even more than they care about that." He pointed to the locked chest. "They know they can keep at least a few colonies of gnomes alive. But if you take the alicorns, they have no other options."

Now he had the King's attention, and Sophie hoped he'd be able to keep stalling long enough for the next phase of the plan.

*Ready?* she transmitted, slipping into Fitz's mind.

*Think this is going to work?* he asked.

*It has to. If he catches us, we're all dead.*

With that cheerful prospect, they locked eyes and stretched their consciousness toward King Dimitar.

*It'll feel soft,* she warned Fitz. *Almost smothering.*

*We can do this,* Fitz told her. *It's what we've been training for.*

Together they pushed into King Dimitar's mind, falling through a sea of feathers. It felt like they'd been plummeting forever, but then they crashed into a pillow stuffed with dandelion fluff and suffocated in the fuzz.

Someday Sophie wanted to understand why ogres' cruel, murderous minds felt like giant marshmallows. But for the moment, she just wanted to survive.

Fitz's consciousness stuck close to hers and they pooled their energy, bracing for King Dimitar to discover them.

Thirty seconds ticked by. Then a full minute.

When another minute passed, Sophie decided they were safe.

They couldn't transmit to each other without giving themselves away, but Fitz knew to follow her lead. She imagined the fractals of his emotional center and without even trying, a portion of her consciousness drifted there. The other portion of her mind waded deeper into the sweltering cotton candy.

Hopelessness swelled as the softness seemed to expand around her, but Fitz beat it back with a rush of confidence. And when his emotions turned weary gray, she boosted him with a rush of energy. Together, they balanced each other and kept pushing, pushing, pushing until finally, with a firm tug, Sophie peeled back the last veil of King Dimitar's mind.

Darkness lurked beyond—an inky pool of poison waiting to drown her.

Fitz sent her another burst of energy as Sophie plunged into the swamp of memories alone. She'd been in some sludgy minds before, but this was a boiling tar pit, and each bursting bubble unleashed a revolting memory.

Sophie had expected to witness evil. But nothing could've prepared her for the devastating truths she scooped out of the mire.

*Did you get it?* Fitz asked as she pulled their minds back to the eerie green light of Ravagog.

Sophie wanted to lie—spare him the heartache. But they were a team. He needed the truth. So she gathered what little courage she had left and transmitted, *The cure is a hoax.*

# SEVENTY

**D**OES THAT MEAN THE CHEST
*King Dimitar has is a fake?* Fitz transmitted.
*Yes,* Sophie said, feeling tears leak down
her face. But it was so much worse than
that. *It was all a lie, Fitz. There is no cure. The one they gave the
gnomes in Eternalia wasn't real.*

And even *that* wasn't the worst thing she'd discovered. But
before she could crush Fitz's spirit any further, she heard
Tam's shadow voice whispering in her ear.

"I hope you guys got what you needed, because your
boy is about to lose it. Biana's already on her way down for
retrieval."

Sophie couldn't decide which of those facts was more

terrifying as she looked down and found Keefe getting choked again, this time by King Dimitar himself.

"That's where I've seen you!" the king shouted. "You were with that foolish girl who thought she could get away with invading my mind. Is she here?"

And that—unfortunately—was the exact moment Biana chose to steal the silver chest.

The second the chest moved King Dimitar dropped Keefe and lunged, snatching Biana and shaking her until she appeared.

"Another one!" he bellowed, as Dex shouted, "EMERGENCY PLAN—GO!" and flung one of his cube gadgets at the king's feet.

King Dimitar scrambled back as the gadget exploded, and Sophie couldn't see through the smoke to know if Biana got away. More gadgets flew—smoke bombs, stink bombs, sound bombs—as Sophie and the rest of her friends levitated into the fray.

Fitz had Calla in his arms, but he set her down and charged into the smoke screaming, "Biana, where are you?"

"Over here!" Keefe shouted, Sucker Punching the ogre who was trying to grab both of them. The punches barely elicited a grunt from the ogre, but Keefe kept fighting anyway.

"Duck!" Linh shouted, and Keefe and Biana dropped to their stomachs as a stream of water blasted the ogre like a fire hose.

The ogre swayed off balance and toppled off the cliff.

"Don't worry," Sophie told Linh when she screamed. "Ogres can phase shift as they fall—you didn't kill him."

"TIME TO GO!" Tam shouted, running toward them with ogres lunging after him. He grabbed his sister's hand and ran full speed off the edge of the platform.

Fitz and Biana followed, carrying Calla between them.

"Come on, Foster," Keefe said, pulling her toward the edge.

"What about Dex?"

"Right behind you!" Dex threw a modified obscurer and whited-out the world.

"Next time warn us that you're going to blind us," Keefe said, clinging tighter to Sophie. "Nothing like jumping off a cliff you can't even see."

"I can see," Sophie said, pulling Keefe forward. "Jump right . . . now!"

They leaped together, and for a horrifying second Sophie couldn't concentrate enough to levitate. Keefe held her up with him until she got control. Her steps were shaky, but she remembered her Exillium training, and they put a good distance between themselves and the mountain. If only it were safe to teleport through Ravagog's force fields. Instead, they'd have to make it back to the tunnel.

"Are you okay?" she asked, noticing the bruises forming on Keefe's neck.

"I'll live," he said. "Well . . . assuming we survive *that*."

He pointed to where dozens of heavily armed ogres had

phase shifted to the dusty ground below. More ogres were swarming over the bridge, moving shockingly fast for such bulky creatures. They stormed the empty playa, waving their swords and snarling, waiting for their victims to land.

"Uh, Dex, I hope you have some of those exploding gadgets left," Keefe said, "because I'm not sure how much longer Fitz and Biana can carry Calla."

Dex flung two more gadgets, and he must've boosted his arm strength, because they launched to the other side of the bridge. Sophie worried it was a mistake, until one explosion created a crater near the bridge's first arch, and the other erupted with an ear-splitting screech that sent the ogres scattering away.

It stemmed the tide of incoming reinforcements—but they still had more ogres than they could handle. And Dex had to ruin the small victory by saying, "That was all I had."

"Then it's my turn!" Linh shouted, spinning in midair and thrusting her arms toward the mountain. Jet streams blasted out of the waterfalls, flooding the playa and washing the ogres over the edge of the canyon.

Before Sophie could celebrate, Fitz, Biana, and Calla collapsed into the crashing waves.

"Linh!" Tam screamed, and Linh whipped her arms again, sweeping the water back toward the mountain in a massive tidal wave.

Fitz, Biana, and Calla dropped into the mud, coughing the water out of their lungs.

Keefe, Dex, and Sophie landed as close as they could get, sinking up to their knees in the paste-thick muck. Tam set Linh down beside them.

"Wow," Keefe and Dex said—a "wow" Linh definitely deserved. Somehow she was holding the tidal wave steady, keeping it as a wall between the mountain half of the city and where they stood.

Across the canyon, the ogres stared at the wave with a mix of fear and fury, none daring to cross the bridge and risk getting washed into the river like their brethren.

"You guys okay?" Sophie asked, stumbling through the mud to help Fitz and Biana to their feet.

"I think so." Biana tore off her soggy Neverseen cloak and flung it away. Her clothes underneath weren't as muddy, and Fitz and Calla quickly copied her. Sophie did the same. Dex dropkicked his cloak across the soggy plain.

And then Biana asked the question Sophie hadn't thought to ask: "Where's Alvar?"

A moment of silence passed—followed by frantic shouting as they fanned out to search.

Sophie explained to a hysterical Biana that she was going to track Alvar's thoughts, when a deep laugh behind them sent them spinning around.

"Didn't mean to freak you guys out," Alvar said as Biana tackled him with a move that seemed more strangle than hug. "I just wanted to see if I'd figured out how to fool Calla's eyes. Looks like I have."

"Dude, now was *not* the time," Fitz said, and even Keefe nodded in agreement.

"Oh, relax. I also grabbed this!" He kicked at a pile of mud, revealing the silver chest.

He seemed so proud of himself, Sophie didn't have the heart to tell him the chest was useless. Plus, she knew what *was* in the chest, and it wasn't something she wanted the ogres having their hands on.

"Uh—are you guys forgetting that my sister is holding back a *tidal wave* over here," Tam yelled, pointing to Linh's trembling form. "She's not going to last much longer, so you'd better figure out how to get us out of this place before it crashes."

Sophie checked the other side of the canyon, where hundreds of ogres paced impatiently. "We'll never make it back to the tunnel," she said.

"Gee, you think?" Alvar asked. "But you're the girl with all the plans. I'm sure you'll figure out something."

"What if we let the tidal wave go?" she said. "Would it wash the ogres away?"

"The canyon is too wide," Linh said, her voice strained. "All it will wash away is the bridge."

"Then we'd *really* be trapped," Alvar said.

"Would we?" Sophie asked, turning to Dex. "I know it's not a gadget, but what do your Technopath senses say. Could we survive it?"

"Survive what?" Biana asked.

Dex knew. His eyes widened as his brain seemed to work the problem through. He nodded slowly. "Yeah . . . I'm pretty sure we would. Depending on where this river ends up."

"It's the same river we used to live by in Wildwood," Tam said.

"And the flood would be strong enough to break down the gates?" Sophie asked Linh.

Sweat poured down her face as she nodded.

Sophie turned to her friends. "What do you guys think? Linh can't hold on much longer."

"Just so I'm clear," Keefe said. "You're suggesting we unleash the tidal wave and destroy the bridge while we're *on* it, and hope the broken pieces smash through the gates without squishing us and carry us out of Ravagog like a raft?"

"Unfortunately . . . yes," Sophie said. "I don't see another option, do you?"

Everyone stared at the bloodthirsty ogres.

"I guess it's time for you to flood another city," Sophie told Linh. "And this time, let's destroy everything while you're at it."

# SEVENTY-ONE

**N**EED ME TO HELP?" SOPHIE ASKED Tam as he carried Linh toward the bridge.

"I've got her." But every time he lost his balance, Linh's concentration would falter and the wave would swell higher.

"Hang on, Linh," Sophie told her. "You can do this."

"I can," Linh said, gritting her teeth so hard they looked ready to crack. "There will be no flood until we're ready."

The ogres roared to a frenzy when Sophie's group reached the bridge. A few even crept to the first fiery arch, hovering near the crater Dex had made, eager to spill the first blood.

"Let's try to stay in groups through this," Fitz said. "No one should be alone."

Keefe hooked his arm through Sophie's, and Biana took his arm. Fitz stayed with Tam and Linh, helping hold Linh steady as she clung to the edge of the bridge and kept her eyes fixed on the wave. Dex, Calla, and Alvar made a small circle, the two boys each holding Calla with one hand and the silver chest with their other.

"Don't take any risks to save that thing," Sophie told them, pointing to the chest. "It's not worth it."

"Why not?" Alvar asked.

"Brace yourselves!" Tam shouted before Sophie could answer. "Linh needs to let the water go."

"Do it!" Sophie said, clinging to the stone railing.

With an anguished cry Linh lowered her hands and called the wave toward them. The ogres who'd crawled out onto the bridge scrambled back, but Sophie and her friends stayed locked in place, staring down the oncoming flood.

"It needs to hit us from behind," Dex shouted. "Otherwise we'll be crushed against the canyon."

"Working on it!" Linh said, screaming as she twisted her arms and curved the massive swell as much as she could.

For one surreal moment, Sophie and her friends stood, slack-jawed, clinging to anything they could grab hold of. Then the tidal wave crashed over them.

The bridge cracked on impact, splitting into two parts, showering them with green sparks as the flaming arches toppled. Dex's group was forced to split, and he dragged Calla with him to share the piece of bridge holding Tam, Linh, and Fitz. Alvar jumped with the silver chest onto the piece of rubble that Sophie, Keefe, and Biana clung to, right as it broke free and took off down the river.

Their debris dipped and ducked and thrashed through the white-capped water, rushing so fast the world smeared to a blur.

"So, um, not to freak you out more than you already are," Keefe shouted, catching Sophie's arm and dragging her back before a smaller wave could wash her overboard. "But . . . what happens when we go KABOOM?"

He pointed ahead, where the gigantic iron gates were growing larger by the second. Linh had seemed sure the force of the water and debris would break the gates open—but that didn't explain how they would survive the crash.

"Time for the famous Sophie Foster to come up with another brilliant plan and save us, right?" Alvar asked.

But Sophie was out of ideas. Even with all four of their minds combined, their telekinesis strength would never be enough to shove the gate open before they got there. And with the rushing wind and the panic pumping through their veins, Sophie didn't see how they'd ever be able to levitate safely away.

*Linh says to jump into the river,* Fitz transmitted from his raft. *She can cushion you in the water.*

Sophie could think of *many* things wrong with that plan, but she wasn't in a position to argue. "Linh says we have to jump!" she shouted, pulling the others to the edge of their rubble and leaping into the flood.

The water was freezing, but it had a strange burn too, like lemon juice in a cut, and the stinging pain made Sophie forget any of the tricks she'd learned in Exillium to hold her breath. The currents knocked the last of the air from her chest, and as the bubbles slipped toward the surface, Sophie followed, kicking her legs frantically, her lungs screaming, her vision dimming until her head broke through the water and she sucked in a grateful breath.

Keefe surfaced beside her and she clung to him. He held on tight and reminded her they had to get underwater for Linh's protection. Sophie had just enough time to fill her lungs with air before Keefe dove, pulling her under with him.

She forced herself to swim, ignoring the pain as bits of rubble pummeled them from all sides. She tried to remember that she owned the new record at Exillium for holding her breath—she just needed to slow her body down, slow her lungs down, slow her heart down.

An explosion blasted through the water, but as the storm of shrapnel hurtled toward them, it split down the center, half of it drifting over their heads, the other half below their feet. Sophie had no idea how Linh could control so many things at once, but she sent silent thanks for protecting them as they washed through the blast zone to safety.

"WE'RE ALIVE!" Keefe shouted when they surfaced again in the middle of the raging flood. "And so are Alvar and Biana! I can see them a few feet behind us."

"What about the others?" Sophie asked, kicking away debris before it smashed them.

"I can't see that far, but the gate's open now, so they should have a smooth ride. Plus, they've got Linh. She'll keep their raft steady."

"True," Sophie said. "You probably should've grouped up with them."

"Nah, I like my group better." He pulled her closer, just in time to miss a jagged rock.

The river rushed at a breakneck speed, waves tossing them back and forth, knocking them into flotsam. They clung to each other until the currents washed them into a bed of broken reeds.

Sophie waded out of the shallows, collapsing on the grassy ground and gulping as much air as she could.

"I think we made it," Keefe said, crumpling beside her.

Sophie stared at the sky—a red sunset so bold it felt almost violent. Still, she preferred it to the sour green light of Ravagog.

"Any sign of the others?" she whispered.

"I saw their chunk of bridge wash ashore a while back," Keefe said. "So I'm betting they're on foot now."

Sophie knew they should get up and search, but her body felt like it had been molded from mashed potatoes. The best she could do was lean her head on Keefe's shoulder, trying to stay warm in the chilly evening wind.

"Awwww, you guys look so cute!" Alvar said, stumbling toward them a few minutes later. "Sorry, didn't mean to interrupt cuddle time," he added as Sophie scrambled away.

Sophie was sure her cheeks were redder than the sky, especially when she realized Biana was there too. She pulled her soggy hair forward to cover her face. "It's cold here."

"It is," Biana agreed.

Sophie couldn't tell if the strain in Biana's voice was exhaustion or something else. She decided to change the subject. "Where are we?"

"Near Wildwood," Alvar said. "Which is good. I was hoping that's where we'd end up."

"Really?" Sophie asked. "Why?"

Alvar lifted the silver chest, which he'd managed to carry through all that chaos. "Seemed like a good place to bring this!"

His smile was so bright, Sophie couldn't look at him as she told him the truth. "That's not the cure. That's how the ogres were planning to get the plague into the Lost Cities. They wanted us to steal it and bring it there. Then when we opened it—poof! The plague would be our fault."

Alvar tested the lock on the chest. "Are you sure?"

"I saw the whole plan in King Dimitar's mind. He's also plotting to get rid of the Neverseen once he's done using them."

"He thinks *he's* using *them*?" Alvar asked.

"He's using everyone," Sophie said. "Letting us tear our world apart so he can crush the pieces to bits." Sophie shook her head. "We'll have to destroy that chest. And I don't know how I'm supposed to tell Calla there's no cure."

"I already know," Calla said behind them. Sophie scrambled to her feet to find Calla, Tam, Linh, Dex, and Fitz, shuffling closer. It should've been a moment of celebration—they'd invaded Ravagog and lived to fight another day! But the devastating realities cast a shadow far gloomier than any Tam could create.

"You know the cure is fake?" Sophie whispered.

Calla nodded, her eyes focused on what remained of the Wildwood Colony in the distance. "The Panakes told me. I finally understand their song. The cure lies in their blossoms, not their bark. But hope is not lost. I'll explain how later. Right now we should get somewhere safer. I'm sure the ogres will come after us."

"Yeah," Keefe said. "You guys realize we just destroyed Ravagog, right? What do you think that means? Like . . . did we just start a war?"

"*We* didn't start anything," Fitz said. "This whole thing was a trap the ogres set."

"Somehow I don't think King Dimitar is going to care about that," Keefe mumbled. He glanced at Sophie. "And I'm guessing you didn't learn anything about my mom?"

"I tried," she whispered. "But his mind was too fixated on the drakostomes."

"That has always been the ogres' problem," a frighteningly familiar voice said. "They always fail to see the bigger picture."

Sophie and her friends scrambled together as they turned to find Brant and Fintan walking toward them, each holding spheres of Everblaze.

# SEVENTY-TWO

I'M GUESSING THIS IS THE PART WHERE YOU
demand to know how we found you," Fintan said as Brant
moved to block their path from behind. The Everblaze
flamed brighter with their slightest movement, making
it clear that pain would follow any attempt at escape.

"You keep forgetting that this was our plan from the beginning,"
Fintan added. "Well—not the flood. You managed to surprise us
with that one. And you stopped us from infecting Brackendale
and Merrowmarsh. But the rest has gone like clockwork."

Biana stepped in front of Calla, shielding her from the
fire. "How could you do this to the gnomes? After everything
they've done for the Lost Cities?"

"To expose the Council's lies," Brant said. "Now everyone

knows how much they hide, and how little protection they truly give their people."

"Which accomplishes what?" Sophie asked. "All you've done is make people afraid."

"Indeed, Miss Foster," Fintan agreed. "And fear is the world's greatest motivator. Look at the power your group harnessed today as a result of your terror." His eyes roved to Keefe as he added, "That was your mother's mistake. She surrendered to her fear, and it cost her everything."

"Including her life?" Sophie asked.

"Interesting that the question does not come from her son," Fintan noted.

"That's because I don't care about her!" Keefe said.

Fintan smiled. "I suppose it wouldn't matter, then, if I told you she's currently locked in an ogre prison? And that your role in today's invasion surely earned her a death sentence?"

"You're lying," Keefe said, his voice cracking.

"Not this time," Brant told him. "We're the ones who sealed her in her cell."

"I suppose there's a chance we could barter her freedom," Fintan said. "But we'd need proper motivation."

Brant said something else after that, but Sophie couldn't listen. When he spoke, all she could see were his new scars. She'd thought his handsome features had been ruined before. Now they were *gone*.

One of his ears.

Parts of his lips and chin.

Most of his jet-black hair.

His face was more scar tissue than *face*. And that didn't include the mottled, veiny stump at the end of his right wrist where his hand used to be.

"Why, Miss Foster, you don't look happy to see me," he said, adding more flames to his fireball. "Didn't you swear you *would* find me again? I've been looking *so* forward to thanking you for my makeover. You too," he told Dex. "I have *excellent* things planned for you both."

"Forget it!" Tam shouted as a wave crashed over Brant, and Linh yelled, "RUN!"

They'd barely made it a step before a wall of fire erupted in their path.

"That's quite enough of that," Fintan said, curling the fire into a circle, closing them inside a cage of Everblaze.

"You can stop wasting your energy on water tricks," Brant told Linh. "You've complicated things enough already. Luckily, we've had eyes on you this whole time."

"What does that mean?" Sophie asked.

"It doesn't matter," Alvar said. "What do you want from us?"

The two Pyrokinetics shook their heads.

"I told you, Mr. Vacker," Fintan said. "The charade is over. I spent weeks in Exile. I let my mind be broken. I let them declare me dead. I'm not going to hide anymore. It's time you make your choice. Stand with us, or turn against us."

*"What?"* Keefe said as the walls of Everblaze flared brighter, painting everything in its eerie yellow glow.

Biana and Fitz stepped away from their brother.

"What does he mean?" Fitz asked.

"I *mean* that your brother is one of our longest standing members. Youngest to ever enlist—though he made a lot of mistakes back then. One especially big one."

Fintan's eyes flicked to Sophie, and his meaning sank in.

Dex held her steady as she wheeled on Alvar. *"You* were the Boy Who Disappeared?!"

The words seemed to shatter whatever remained of Alvar's facade. He smoothed his hair and shed his soggy cloak as he said, "Yes."

Rage-fire burned in Sophie's stomach, searing hotter than the Everblaze. "How could you?"

"You wouldn't understand," he said.

"Try me," Fitz told him.

"You *really* wouldn't understand," Alvar snapped. "You're the Golden Son. I had to *find* people who appreciated my talents."

"More like overestimated them," Brant muttered. "You had her right in front of you, and you walked away. Scratched her off the list."

"You want to compare mistakes?" Alvar snapped. "Ruy let both of them get away a few weeks back. And let's not forget the worst kidnapping in the history of kidnappings."

"NO!" Keefe shouted as Fitz and Biana backed away from their brother.

"You were there?" Dex asked, shaking so hard Tam and Linh had to keep him steady.

"Of course he was," Fintan said. "He helped plan it."

Sophie reached for Fitz, relieved when he didn't pull away. She had no idea how the Vackers were going to survive another family tragedy.

"How could you?" Biana asked.

Alvar's expression softened when he looked at his sister. "You'll understand, someday, when you see the Vacker legacy for what it is."

"In the meantime," Fintan said, "you're all coming with us. The seven of you have proven very useful. Especially you two," he told Tam and Linh. "Who'd have thought I'd find so much value in a pair of twins?"

And with that final insult, Sophie decided it was time for Plan C.

She transmitted a warning to her friends and reached for her Black Swan pendant. Fury and disgust fueled her as she held the glass in the fading sunlight.

A beam of white fire sparked to life, igniting the silver chest at Alvar's feet.

*"That,"* Fintan said calmly, "was a very dumb move."

But the flames wouldn't stamp out, and they ignored every command the Pyrokinetics shouted.

"If that's how you want to play," Brant said, ordering the wall of flames to tighten.

Sophie launched another beam of her own fire, and it parted the wall of Everblaze.

"Time to go!" she screamed, dragging her friends through the gap. Flames nipped at her skin, but she barely felt them.

"Is there a cliff nearby?" she asked Tam and Linh as they ran.

"No need," Calla said.

She belted out a song that made one of the withered trees bend down and tangle its branches around their feet. A quick *THWANG!* snapped the tree back, whipping them into the sky. They clung to each other as they soared higher and higher.

As soon as they started to drop, Sophie split a crack in the sky.

The last thing she saw was Alvar's pained expression as they slipped into the void and teleported away.

# SEVENTY-THREE

RADY AND EDALINE WEREN'T outside when the traumatized group appeared in Havenfield's pastures. But as soon as Sophie called for help, they came rushing out of the glittering crystal mansion.

Within minutes Elwin had arrived to treat any burns, cuts, scrapes, and bruises they'd picked up during their various escapes. But nothing could ease the shock that had settled over everyone.

No one wanted to answer the questions Grady and Edaline kept repeating. Even Sophie could only cling to her parents and let her silent tears soak their tunics. But when Alden arrived, looking equal parts worried and relieved, Sophie knew it was time to speak.

She held tight to Grady's and Edaline's hands as she gave a brief summary of the havoc they'd caused in Ravagog. The adults' eyes seemed to widen with each dangerous detail. Their fear turned to fury when she moved on to the further chaos with the Neverseen, and Sophie pulled Grady closer so he wouldn't try to go after Brant. Alden hailed the Council and asked them to send someone to extinguish the Everblaze and start cleaning up the toxins that would've leaked into the valley from the ogres' tainted river. Then he hailed Mr. Forkle-As-Sir-Astin and told him the Collective should gather at Havenfield.

Sophie decided to wait until everyone had arrived before revealing the devastating truth about the gnomish cure. But Alden deserved to receive the news about Alvar in the privacy of close friends.

"There's something else I have to tell you," she mumbled. "But first, I need you to promise that your mind is strong enough to handle it."

Alden glanced at Fitz and Biana before he nodded.

"Wait," Elwin said, handing Alden a vial filled with clear liquid. "This will take the edge off reality, if you need it."

"Surely the news can't be that bad," Alden said.

"It is," Biana whispered, reaching for her dad. "Alvar's part of the Neverseen."

The vial slipped from Alden's hand, hitting the grass with a soft *thud*. Elwin tried to hand it back to him, but Alden waved the elixir away. "You're sure?" he whispered.

"Positive," Fitz mumbled, tearing out chunks of grass by the roots. "He was also one of Sophie's kidnappers."

Alden wobbled as the words hit him, and Biana helped him sit on the grass. Elwin tried again to make him take the elixir, but Alden waved the medicine away, calling Fitz to come closer. The three Vackers clung to each other and cried.

Dex turned to Sophie with a look like, *Do something*.

Grady and Edaline looked just as helpless. Even Tam—who could've been smug, since he'd never trusted Alvar—wiped tears from his silvery eyes and held his sister's hand.

Keefe, meanwhile, wandered away from the group, sitting with his back pointed in their direction. Sophie joined him.

"Alvar was my hero," he whispered.

She reached for his hand, wondering how many betrayals Keefe could survive. "It's not your fault for believing his lies."

"It still makes me an idiot. Plus . . ." Keefe stared at the sky, which seemed too pink and peaceful as the sun slowly dipped below the horizon. "Last night, when Alvar slept in my room, he said I reminded him a lot of himself."

"He has good qualities too, Keefe."

"Yeah, but I don't think that's what he meant. I think he was trying to recruit me."

"They tried to recruit Jolie too, remember? All that means is he thinks you're talented."

"Maybe," Keefe said, still not looking at her. "He even told me to reach out to him if I ever needed anything. Said he thought of me like a brother."

"He's not *all* bad. No one is. That's what makes villains so scary. They're not as different from us as we want them to be."

"Villains," Keefe repeated, saying the word like it tasted sour. "And they think I could be one of them. Gethen even made it sound like my mom planned for it . . ."

"So? When have you ever done what either of your parents wanted you to do?" She'd hoped that would earn her at least half a smile, but Keefe shook his head.

"Are you worrying about what Fintan said?" she asked. "About your mom . . ."

"I don't care what happens to her."

He must've cared a little, though, because after several awkward seconds he asked, "What do you think Fintan meant about bartering for her freedom?"

"I don't know. But the Neverseen are never going to do anything to *help* us. It's all a trick, just like the cure. That doesn't mean we give up hope, though. There are lots of things we haven't tried."

"Like what?"

Sophie couldn't think of any, but she knew they existed. "We'll figure it out, okay?"

His shrug wasn't really an answer.

"Sophie?" Alden said, waiting for her to turn around. He looked pale, and the tight lines in his features added years to his face. But he didn't seem ready to shatter as he said, "I've often wondered how the Neverseen knew we'd found you. I never considered that I'd told Alvar when Fitz returned from San Diego. He used to be part of the search so I thought he deserved to know . . . I owe you a *huge* apology."

"No you *don't*," she promised, rushing over to give him a hug.

Fitz and Biana joined in, and after a moment she felt more arms add to the group as Grady, Edaline, Elwin—even Dex—held everyone tight. Sophie glanced to where Keefe sat alone and glared at him until he reluctantly got up and hugged his friends. Tam and Linh were the last to wrap their arms around the group, but they fit right in.

"What happened?" Della asked, sending everyone scrambling back.

She stood with all five members of the Collective, but Sophie could only focus on Della. She knew in a few seconds Della would go from worried to utterly devastated, and Sophie wished she could stop time so it wouldn't have to happen.

Alden cleared his throat. "There's much to discuss, my love. But we should go home."

Della shook her head. "Where's Alvar? What's going on—"

"It's not what you think," Alden interrupted. "He's . . ."

His voice faded away. Fitz and Biana couldn't seem to say it either.

Grady stepped forward. "Alvar has . . . lost his way. Like Brant. And Lady Gisela."

Sophie could see the moment of understanding dawn in Della's eyes. Grief turned to shock—then fury and confusion, all of the chaos spilling out in thick tears.

"No," Della whispered. "He wouldn't . . ."

"Oh, he would." Fitz's voice was black ice.

"Come on," Alden said, hooking his arm gently around his wife. "They can handle this one without us."

He turned to Mr. Forkle, who nodded gravely.

"If it helps," Granite said quietly, "this changes nothing for us. We trust your commitment implicitly—same for Fitz and Biana. Whenever—if ever—you're ready to return to our cause, there will always be a place."

Except now they'd be working to capture their *son* and *brother*, Sophie realized.

And when Fitz and Biana had fought the Neverseen on Mount Everest, there was a good chance they'd been fighting Alvar without realizing it.

But Keefe was facing that too, and he was doing okay. Ish.

Now they could band together, once they recovered from the shock of it.

Fitz took his dad's free hand, Biana clung to her brother, and the four Vackers leaped away as a family.

"The Council is on their way, I assume?" Mr. Forkle asked Grady.

"Oralie said they were going to make sure the fire was contained in Wildwood before they came here," Grady said.

At the mention of the devastated colony, all eyes turned to Calla, who was leaning against a tree, her ear pressed to the bark.

"There is so much life here," Calla whispered, her eyes turning to the pastures. "More than I've felt anywhere."

Havenfield was one of the rehabilitation centers for the Sanctuary, so the expansive grounds were divided into pastures for all manner of impossible creatures.

"This is where you live?" Calla asked Sophie.

"When I'm not banished," she said, forcing a smile.

Calla turned to the rows of bulbous trees in the distance, where the Havenfield gnomes normally lived. "I like it here. This will be good."

"What will?" Sophie asked.

"I'll explain when the Council arrives," Calla promised.

She stood to wander the grounds, humming to the various trees, and the adults murmured among themselves, discussing things Sophie couldn't make herself pay attention to. She sat with her friends, the five of them lost in their own worries as the sky faded from sunset to twilight.

The evening star had just risen when the Council glittered into the clearing.

"Still wearing disguises?" Councillor Alina said, frowning at the Collective.

"We would love to work with you openly," Granite told her. "You're the ones who've denied us the privilege."

Councillor Emery held up his hand, silencing Alina before she could respond. "We have more important things to discuss than our divisions."

"Indeed we do," Mr. Forkle said. "I assume you know about Ravagog."

"We've seen the damage," Councillor Emery agreed.

He didn't sound furious. He sounded *impressed*.

Still, Sophie had to ask, "Does this mean we're going to war with the ogres?"

"It's *possible*," Councillor Emery warned. "But too early to tell. You have dealt King Dimitar a heavy blow. You've demolished Ravagog's gate and removed the only bridge connecting his city. Our goblins are already forming a perimeter around the city to remind the ogres that we are far more prepared for battle than they are at the moment. And now that the king has lost his secret weapon with the drakostomes, our hope is that he will finally negotiate a real treaty—one that gives us the level of control we expect."

"This is assuming, of course, that they truly *have* lost their secret weapon," Councillor Terik chimed in.

All eyes shifted to Calla.

She finished the song she'd been humming and took a slow breath, keeping her shoulders square. "The ogres' cure was a fake," she said, allowing them a second to process. "But it doesn't matter. *I* will be the cure."

# SEVENTY-FOUR

**W**HAT EXACTLY DOES THAT mean?" Elwin asked Calla. "How can you be the cure?"

"Because I know what the Panakes are," Calla said. "The legends called them the Brave Ones and I never understood why. But their roots sang of a life given freely. That's where the healing comes from. The blossoms sprout from the sacrifice."

"Anyone else confused?" Dex asked.

Sophie definitely was.

But she didn't like the word "sacrifice."

She ran to Calla's side, grabbing her green-thumbed hands. "Please tell me you're not sacrificing yourself."

Calla stared at the pastures, her eyes both sad and dreamy. "I'm old. I've enjoyed thousands of years on this earth. And now I'll enjoy thousands more in a different form."

"But—"

Calla placed her finger on Sophie's lips. "You can't change this, Sophie. Do not try."

"So you're saying the Panakes were gnomes," Councillor Emery said, breaking the silence.

"Brave Ones who choose to shift their form," Calla agreed. "Their sacrificed life energy nourished the Panakes to give them the power of healing."

"Fascinating," Councillor Terik whispered.

Bronte shook his head. "All this time, we never realized the cure was within our control."

"What control?" Sophie asked. "She has to *die* for this. Calla, you can't—"

"I must," Calla interrupted. "Don't tell me you would not do the same, if you could save your friends."

Tears gathered in Sophie's eyes, spilling down her cheeks. "But you're my friend too."

Calla smiled. "I know. And I do this to help *you*, as well." She turned to the Council, her gray eyes hardening. "Remove the banishment from these children—all of them. Even the two who've left. They saved my species. I wouldn't know this path to the cure without them."

"I agree," Councillor Bronte said, ignoring Councillor Alina's huff. "It is time we start correcting our past errors."

The Councillors murmured among themselves, but Sophie couldn't listen. She was too busy trying to think of a way to change Calla's mind.

She only paid attention when Councillor Emery called, "All in favor?"

All twelve Councillors raised their hands.

Grady and Edaline rushed to hug Sophie, scooping up Dex and Keefe in the process. Sophie pulled away, not ready to celebrate.

"Calla," she started.

"This was my choice," Calla interrupted. "I made it willingly. And it cannot be undone. I've already let my final song settle into my heart. There's no stopping the shift now."

Elwin made his way over, flashing colored orbs around Calla. "She's right. It looks like everything inside her is slowing down."

"How long do you have?" Grady asked, holding Sophie steady as everything spun too fast.

Calla stared at her hands, where the green coloring was already spreading beyond her thumbs. "Sometime tonight the final shift will happen, and by morning you'll find my tree."

"Morning," Sophie repeated, her voice breaking.

That was too soon. Everything was happening so fast—she couldn't . . .

"Hey," Keefe said as Sophie pulled away from Grady. He took her hands. "It's okay."

"How is it okay?" she yelled. "Calla's *dying*."

"I'm *changing*," Calla corrected. "And I don't mind—see?"

She offered Keefe her hand, and he placed his palm over hers and closed his eyes.

"She really does feel at peace," he said.

"I am." Calla wiped Sophie's tears. "Please don't cry for me. This is my happy ending. How many get to choose their last breath, and make it for the good of everyone?"

"But I'm going to miss you so much," Sophie cried.

"And when you do, you can come sit under my tree." Calla turned to Grady and Edaline. "I have one favor to ask. I must set my roots down somewhere. And the earth feels peaceful here."

"Of course," Edaline whispered. "Our home is your home."

"Anywhere you'd like," Grady added. "Even if you want the middle of a pasture."

Calla pointed to a small hill overlooking the other pastures. Sophie knew if she stood there, she could see the ocean.

"That will be my place," Calla said, "from this day forward."

"We'll make sure your Panakes is nurtured and protected," Grady promised.

"No," Sophie said. "There has to be something I can do—"

"There is," Calla interrupted. "You can listen to my songs. And you can make starkflower stew and pour a bowl into the ground to share it with me. And you stay my brave moonlark, always."

She reached for Sophie's allergy remedy necklace, planting a kiss on the pin.

Then she pulled Sophie close for a final hug.

"You must go now," Calla whispered. "I don't want you to witness the shift. Go inside—all of you. Please."

Everyone watched in silence as Calla climbed the hill—her hill. The last place she would ever stand.

"Go," she said again, planting her feet firmly in the center. "Let us all find rest."

She closed her eyes then, swaying with the breeze. The faintest hum of her melody drifted through the night, turning the air restful. Singing of the coming dawn.

"Goodbye," Sophie whispered, so softly she was sure Calla couldn't hear her.

Calla opened her eyes. "Farewell, Sophie Foster."

# SEVENTY-FIVE

THEY MOVED OUT OF CALLA'S SIGHT, near a pasture filled with grazing griffins. The Council left quickly, promising they'd return in the morning to check the Panakes.

Elwin vowed to come as well, in the hopes that there'd be blossoms ready to harvest. None of the gnomes in Lumenaria were showing red yet, but the sooner they got the cure, the better.

"What about you?" Mr. Forkle asked Tam and Linh. "I can bring you to your family. Or, we have two tree houses that now have vacancies—regardless of whether you join our order."

The twins exchanged a glance.

"If you mean that," Linh said, "we'd like to take your offer."

"Someday we'll face our family," Tam added. "But not until we're ready."

"Fair enough," Mr. Forkle said. "And what about you, Mr. Dizznee? I'm assuming you'll be going home?"

Dex nodded. "Unless Sophie needs me."

Sophie choked down the lump in her throat. "Give the triplets a hug for me."

Dex hugged Sophie first, telling her to hit her panic switch if she needed him. She promised she would as he glittered away.

"Which leaves you," Mr. Forkle told Keefe. "You can stay with Tam and Linh. Or I'm sure Alden has a place for you at Everglen."

"We have one here as well," Grady said.

"Wow, didn't see that coming," Keefe told him. "And thanks. But . . . I'm going back to Candleshade—and there's no need for that tidal wave of worry you're hitting me with, Foster. I'll be fine."

"Fine?" Sophie repeated, remembering Keefe's epic freakout when he'd found out the Black Swan were considering letting his father join their ranks. "You can't go back there, Keefe. You hate it."

"I do," he agreed. "But I can't keep running from who I am."

His voice hitched on the last words, and he wouldn't look at her as Mr. Forkle created him a path to Candleshade. When he glittered away, she caught a glimpse of the scared angry boy she was starting to know too well.

Part of her wanted to chase him, drag him back to a better place. The other part of her couldn't handle any more drama that day.

"I'll see you tomorrow," Mr. Forkle told her. "And I'll send your belongings within the hour. I know there's a certain blue elephant you cannot sleep without. As well as a troublesome imp!"

Sophie mumbled her thanks, but sleep was out of the question. How could she sleep when she knew Calla was out there, changing?

"Come on, kiddo," Grady said, wrapping his arm around her. Edaline did the same, and they walked inside arm in arm.

Sophie studied Havenfield's living room, with its crystal walls overlooking the ocean and its wide curved staircase, trying to feel like she was truly home. Edaline made custard bursts while Sophie showered and changed, and she was glad to be wearing nonfurry pajamas. But even with Ella in her arms and Edaline rubbing her back, her bed felt weird.

Her room felt weird.

Everything was wrong.

When her parents finally left, she squeezed her eyes tight and stretched out her mind to Silveny.

*FRIEND!* the alicorn transmitted. *SOPHIE! FRIEND! VISIT!*

Sophie only had one question.

*Safe?* she transmitted.

*SAFE! SAFE! SAFE!* Silveny agreed, and Sophie felt her shoulders relax. She hadn't forgotten the secret Keefe had shared with King Dimitar.

Tomorrow, she would have to ensure Silveny stayed safe—permanently.

Calla's Panakes tree was the most exquisitely beautiful tree in the history of beautiful trees. It stood stately and elegantly on its hill, with long sweeping branches floating on the ocean breeze. The tree reminded Sophie of a weeping willow, but it didn't make her sad like she'd thought it would. Somehow, the tree felt hopeful—and friendly.

It might've been the braided bark, which reminded her of Calla's plaited hair. Or the way she could hear soft whispers in the rustling star-shaped leaves. Most likely, though, it was the colorful blossoms. Thousands of them—maybe millions—turning the branches into garlands of silky fluff.

The flowers changed colors in the shifting sunlight, sometimes pink, sometimes purple, sometimes blue. Their indescribably sweet scent made Sophie's head feel clearer, her heart lighter. She had no doubt they truly could heal anything.

The Council invited all the gnomes to come to Havenfield to gather the petals. And while there were definitely tears, there was also a bittersweet celebration. Every one of the gnomes knew the sacrifice Calla had made for them and vowed to honor her memory. Grady and Edaline invited them to visit the tree any time they wanted, and the gnomes joined hands and circled Calla's tree, singing a song of love and gratitude.

With each powerful lyric, Calla's tree grew taller, and new blossoms sprouted to replace those that had been harvested.

The Council arrived later, quieting the celebration by reminding the gnomes that they now had a choice: They could remain in the Lost Cities, or they could start a new homeland.

"The ogres hold no threat over your species any longer," Councillor Emery assured them. "So if you'd prefer to establish a world of your own, we'll do all we can to support you. The Neutral Territories hold many beautiful places, and once we eradicate the plague, you would be welcome to any of them. We'd also provide any help and protection you require."

Stunned silence followed.

"You don't have to decide today," Councillor Emery told them. "We realize this is a rather large decision."

The gnomes didn't need the extra time. They all spoke in unison, shouting, "We choose to stay in the Lost Cities. Our lives are *here*—and they have always been happy. All we ask is that you promise there will be no more secrets."

"Agreed," Councillor Emery promised.

"And for the record," Councillor Terik added, "we're honored you've chosen to stay. Please don't ever think of yourselves as our guests. The Lost Cities are your *home*."

That triggered a huge eruption of cheers, followed by celebratory songs as the gnomes called roots to carry them away to their regular residences. Grady and Edaline tried to convince the Havenfield gnomes they should take time to rest, but the gnomes were itching to get back to work. Within hours, the animals were bathed, the pastures looked pristine, and they'd built a gorgeous fence around Calla's Panakes tree.

By evening it almost felt like Sophie had never left Havenfield. The Council even gave her a shiny new registry pendant.

But when Edaline offered to clasp it around her neck, Sophie hesitated. The Council had yet to prove they were truly going to work with her. She had one demand—one she knew they would resist. She had to make sure they'd agree to it before she committed to her return.

Grady didn't ask questions when Sophie asked him to arrange a meeting with the Councillors at the Sanctuary. He did insist that he and Edaline join her, but she'd wanted them there anyway. She also asked Keefe to meet her there, but decided not to bother the Vackers. They were dealing with enough at the moment. And Dex, Tam, and Linh weren't really involved.

Keefe was the first to arrive outside the humongous snow-covered gates in the shadow of the great mountain. The smile he greeted her with definitely wasn't convincing. She noticed he wasn't wearing his registry pendant either.

"So what's with all the vagueness and mystery?" he asked.

"I'll explain when everyone gets here."

Keefe nodded, but his eyes strayed to the sun, like he was checking the time.

"Do you need to be somewhere?" Sophie asked.

"Still worrying about me, I see," he said. "I guess it's good to know the Mysterious Miss F. hasn't gotten sick of me yet."

"I'll never get sick of you, Keefe."

"We'll see."

She noticed he hadn't actually answered her question.

Before she could press him, he reached into his pocket and handed her a small blue-velvet pouch. "By the way, um . . . this is for you."

Sophie's cheeks warmed, despite the biting cold. And when she poured the pouch's contents into her palm, she found a long necklace, each bead painted with a different flower.

"This is the one you made for your mom," she said, tracing her fingers over the stunning beads. The intricate details he'd given each blossom made them look like photographs.

"Yeah," he mumbled, fussing with his hair. "I know you already have a ton of necklaces and stuff, but . . . I wanted you to have it."

"You're sure you don't want to keep it?"

He shook his head.

He still wasn't looking at her, so she leaned closer and whispered, "She's not gone yet, Keefe."

"I know. But either way, it's yours now. I even made you a new bead."

He showed her one in the bottom center, slightly larger than the others, and decorated with . . .

"Is this a Panakes blossom?" she asked, squinting at the lacy pink, purple, and blue flower he'd painted. He'd set a tiny crystal on the largest petal, like a sparkle of dew. "How did you know what they looked like?"

"I stopped by around sunrise to see Calla."

"Why didn't you wake me up?"

He shrugged. "I didn't want to interrupt your Ella cuddle time."

"So . . . you just sat outside by yourself? For how long?"

"Not that long. It wasn't a big deal. I was heading home from a thing and decided to check on Calla on a whim."

"A thing . . . ," she said slowly, waiting for Keefe to elaborate. When he didn't, she told him, "If you hate being at Candleshade, Keefe, you don't have to stay there."

"I know. I probably won't. Aren't you going to put that on?" he asked, changing the subject.

The beads felt cool on her skin as she slipped the necklace over her head. "How does it look?"

Keefe's smile looked more sad than happy. She wanted to ask if he was okay, but she could see Edaline giving her one of those *isn't that the CUTEST?* smiles straight out of every teenager's nightmares.

"Thanks," she mumbled, tucking her hair behind her ears. "It's really beautiful."

Keefe shrugged. "It's nice to see someone finally wearing it."

"Well, you'll be seeing a lot of it. I'm going to wear it every day." She hoped that would earn her a smile, but Keefe's eyes returned to his feet. He seemed almost . . . nervous. His palms even looked a little sweaty.

The Council arrived then, ending the uncomfortable moment—though they brought their own tension to the mountain.

"Just because you've been pardoned, Miss Foster, doesn't mean you get to demand our attention," Councillor Alina snapped.

"Tell us, Miss Foster," Bronte said. "Why have you called us here?"

Sophie reached for Keefe's hand, needing his support as she stared into the faces of the twelve Councillors and said, "I want you to set Silveny and Greyfell free."

# SEVENTY-SIX

AT FIRST THE COUNCILLORS laughed, assuming Sophie was joking. But when the punch line never came, they switched to shouting and arguing.

Sophie stood in silence, waiting for one of them to get to the right question. Oralie was the one to finally ask it.

"Why?"

"We had to tell King Dimitar that Silveny's pregnant," Sophie said, causing a whole lot more yelling and arguing. "It was the only way to sell the lie we used to distract him. So he knows. And I'm sure he's going to go after the alicorns even harder, now that he doesn't have the drakostomes. It's only a matter of time before he finds a way to break into the Sanctuary. They're getting closer each time."

"So we move the alicorns," Councillor Terik suggested.

"To where?" Sophie asked. "Some tiny underground cavern where Silveny and Greyfell will be miserable? How will that be good for the baby?"

"We also don't know if the Neverseen have any other spies helping them," Grady added. "They've been pretty good at hiding right under our noses."

"And how is it safer to release the alicorns and leave them completely unprotected?" Councillor Emery asked.

"Because they can teleport," Sophie reminded the Council. "Why do you think it took you so long to find Silveny? The only reason she let me catch her was because she *chose* to come to me—and it took tons of convincing to prove to her I was safe. I'm sure she'll be even more careful now that she has a family to protect. And the ogres can't steal her if they don't know where she is."

"Her reasoning does have its merits," Councillor Clarette said quietly.

"How?" Councillor Alina demanded. "This world is too dangerous."

"The alicorns survived for thousands of years on their own," Bronte argued.

"Yes, and Greyfell very nearly didn't," Councillor Emery

reminded him. "We've all seen his scars—and those happened decades ago, before humans built their weapons of mass destruction."

"They'll also have ogres hunting them this time," Councillor Alina added. "And the Neverseen."

"Not if we make them think the alicorns are still in the Sanctuary," Edaline suggested. "They'd never expect us to set them free. So let them keep their focus on the wrong place."

"And Sophie can transmit to Silveny and check to make sure she's okay," Oralie added.

"Silveny can also transmit to me if she needs anything," Sophie agreed.

Councillor Emery frowned at the other Councillors. "It appears we have much to discuss."

"We can't wait too long," Sophie told them. "King Dimitar might already be planning something. We have to let them go before it's too late. There's no way to completely guarantee the alicorns' safety. Just like we couldn't truly protect the gnomes. So maybe we have to trust that other creatures can take care of themselves. Calla was the one who saved her people, wasn't she? Not us."

She could see several Councillors nodding. But not enough, so she added one more thing. "Believe me, I *don't* want to let Silveny go—or Greyfell, or the coming baby. I just lost Calla. I can't lose them." Her voice cut out and she cleared her throat. "But I want them safe more than I want them close. I want to know they can run away if they need to, not be trapped under a mountain like sitting ducks."

Councillor Emery sighed. "Give us a moment."

He closed his eyes to moderate the telepathic debate.

Minutes ticked by and Sophie tugged on her eyelashes. After all she'd been through, she deserved a nervous habit.

"I can't believe we're going to do this," Emery eventually announced. "And we do so only if you agree to our conditions."

"You must check on Silveny daily," Bronte jumped in, "and give us a report so we know what's happening. And if any of us see any signs that this new arrangement is too dangerous, you must do everything in your power to help us bring the alicorns back to the Sanctuary."

Sophie glanced at Keefe, glad to see him nodding. Grady and Edaline seemed to approve of the plan as well.

"Deal," she told the Council.

She tried to celebrate the victory—cling to it as proof that she and the Councillors could work together. But a wave of sadness tried to drown her when Councillor Emery hailed Jurek and told him to bring the alicorns.

All too soon the massive gates swung open, and the blast of bright sunlight made Sophie's eyes burn. Or maybe that was her tears when she spotted the two glittery winged horses galloping toward her.

Her head filled with an endless stream of *SOPHIE! SOPHIE!*

*SOPHIE! KEEFE! KEEFE! KEEFE! VISIT! VISIT! VISIT!*

*Yes—I'm here!* she transmitted as a familiar tall figure with long dreadlocked hair approached.

Jurek held the alicorns with thick golden ropes tied loosely around their necks. He didn't smile as he bowed to the Council. "I'm hoping I misunderstood your instructions."

"So am I," Councillor Emery said.

Silveny trotted closer, nuzzling Sophie's shoulder. The female alicorn had always been stunningly beautiful, between her gleaming silver wings, wavy silver mane, and the swirled silver-and-white horn in the center of her forehead. But she seemed to be benefitting from that famous "pregnant glow." Her fur looked almost opalescent, and her brown eyes shined.

Greyfell looked far less excited. Sophie could see the tension twitching in every muscle of his body. And his blue-tipped wings kept flapping nervously.

*It's okay,* Sophie transmitted. *Trust. Friend.*

Greyfell whinnied, but he kept right on twitching. Silveny, meanwhile, had switched to nuzzling Keefe, and had finally coaxed a real smile out of him.

"Hey there, Glitterbutt," he said. "Glad to know you missed me."

*KEEFE! KEEFE! KEEFE!*

Sophie choked back a sob as she realized this could be the last time she ever saw Silveny. The alicorn could ignore her transmission, or fly so far away she couldn't reach her, or . . .

worse things she was trying very hard not to think about.

*SAD?* Silveny asked.

*Yeah,* Sophie admitted. *But it's going to be okay.*

She willed the words to be true as she did her best to explain to Silveny and Greyfell what was about to happen. They didn't seem to understand, until she told Jurek to untie the golden ropes, leaving the alicorns able to fly away if they wanted.

*Free,* Sophie told them. *Fly free.*

Silveny glanced back at the Sanctuary. *STAY?*

Sophie shook her head. *You guys will be safer on your own.*

*STAY,* Silveny repeated. *SOPHIE. FRIEND.*

*Safe is more important,* Sophie promised. *You need to protect your baby.*

The final word ended Silveny's resistance.

Greyfell stretched his wings and stared at the grayish blue sky. It wasn't as beautiful as the rainbow sky inside the Sanctuary, but it was the first real sky Greyfell had seen in decades. Sophie watched his brown eyes glint and knew she was making the right choice. The alicorns deserved to be free. They could take care of themselves.

She brushed her fingers down Silveny's nose and patted Greyfell's side. *Better get going before the Council changes their minds.*

Silveny nuzzled her again, releasing a whinny that broke Sophie's heart. Then she flapped her wings and launched into the sky.

Greyfell followed immediately, and they circled above, climbing higher and higher with each rotation.

"Let's hope this isn't a mistake," Councillor Terik murmured.

Sophie was making the same wish.

Keefe's hand reached for hers, and together they watched the alicorns dive, racing toward the ground so fast they split the sky.

Right before they disappeared, Silveny transmitted, *SOPHIE. FRIEND. ALWAYS.*

But the best words were her last two: *VISIT. SOON.*

# SEVENTY-SEVEN

**S**O WHAT NOW?" KEEFE ASKED AFTER the Councillors had leaped away and Jurek had closed the Sanctuary's gates. "You off to Everglen to check on the Fitzter?"

"I thought I'd give them a little space." She'd probably hail him later to make sure he was okay. But she knew they'd need some time. "This is a family thing, y'know?"

"I guess." Keefe kicked a pile of snow, sending it scattering. "So you're going back to Havenfield, then?"

"Yeah. Why, what are you up to?"

"Nothing," he said—a little too quickly.

"So . . . do you want to come over, then?" she asked, fidgeting with the necklace he'd given her. "I thought I might try to make starkflower stew to give to Calla's tree—and I know that sounds *super* exciting, but . . . you could make fun of me. And then you could stay for dinner, and—"

"Foster, you don't have to take care of me."

"Maybe I just like you," she said—then realized how that sounded. "I'm just . . . worried about you."

Keefe stepped closer. "I know. It's one of the things I like about you."

Her stomach filled with fluttering things, which flitted around even more when she noticed how close they were now standing. The toes of their boots were almost touching, and his breath felt warm on her cheeks.

Someone cleared their throat, reminding them they weren't alone. When Sophie turned, she found Grady glaring and Edaline smiling that goofy smile again. She couldn't decide which was worse.

"We're heading home—" Grady started.

"But you don't have to leave with us," Edaline finished. "Just make sure you let us know where you are if you decide to go somewhere."

Grady started to say something else, but Edaline created a path of light and whisked him away.

"That was weird," Sophie mumbled, sure her face was bright red.

"Yeah," Keefe said, his cheeks flushed too—but that was probably from the freezing wind.

"So you really don't want to come over?" she asked. "Even for a little while?"

"I . . . can't. But you should go to Dex's. Or go hang with my buddy Bangs Boy."

"Still refusing to call him Tam, huh?"

"Some things should never change."

"What about *you*?" Sophie pressed, wondering why it seemed like he was trying to get rid of her. "Where are you going?"

"What makes you think I'm going anywhere?"

"I don't know. You're acting really weird. You keep avoiding the question—don't think I haven't noticed."

"I'm fine," he promised.

"That's *still* not a real answer."

He reached up and mussed his hair. "Don't worry about it, okay?"

"What's that supposed to mean?"

"Nothing, I swear. I meant . . . I'm dealing with something right now."

"You're really worrying me now, Keefe. What is it?"

Keefe looked away. "I'm just going to see someone. It's not a big deal."

"Can I go with you?"

He shook his head. "Please forget it, okay?"

She watched him shuffle from foot to foot, his fingers twitching, twitching, twitching. "I don't know what you're up to, Keefe—but you promised you'd let me help."

"I know. But this is something I have to do by myself. It's fine, though, I swear. It's all going to be fine."

He sounded like he was trying to convince himself.

"Remember when we were at the Black Swan's ocean hideout, and you ate the drugged cookie and left me all alone with Silveny?" he asked. "I trusted you. I'm just asking you to do the same."

"I seem to remember almost dying that day . . ."

"And I'm saving the near-death experiences for you and Fitz. I like being alive." He stepped closer then, so close she could count the snowflakes in his eyelashes, which were much longer and darker than she'd realized. "Please just trust me, Sophie."

She chewed her lip. "You'll hail me later and let me know you're okay?"

"I'll hail you as soon as I can."

That wasn't the answer she'd been looking for, and it definitely added to her worries. But she couldn't think of anything else to say except, "Okay."

He grinned at her then, a real Keefe grin, and she let herself believe she was making the right decision.

She managed to stay convinced as they said a quick goodbye—even as she pulled out her home crystal and held it up to the light.

But then she noticed the crystal in Keefe's hand and realized it was pale yellow—the same color as the crystals that went to the Neutral Territories.

Without thinking, she lunged and grabbed Keefe's shoulders, letting the light carry her with him as he glittered away.

"WHAT ARE YOU DOING?" Keefe yelled as they reappeared by a bloodred lake, surrounded by stark, misty mountains.

Sophie recognized it from the memory she'd seen in Mitya's mind. "I should ask you the same question. Are you serious right now? Were you actually thinking of breaking into an ogre prison by yourself?"

"Go home, Sophie."

"I'm not leaving without you."

He grabbed her home crystal pendant and tried to hold it up to the light, but she wrestled the pendant away.

"Please," he begged. "You have to get out of here."

"So do you!"

"I can't."

Round and round the arguing went, and Keefe lunged for her home crystal again. It flew out of her hand, splashing into the red lake.

Keefe was shaking now, tearing through his pockets, searching for another crystal.

"You don't have your home crystal with you?" she asked. "How were you planning to get back?"

"He wasn't," a familiar voice said behind them.

Sophie studied Keefe's face, noting that he didn't look the least bit surprised as she turned to find Alvar, Fintan, and Brant.

# SEVENTY-EIGHT

THIS IS A TRAP, SOPHIE REALIZED.
But it didn't seem to be the Neverseen's doing.
Somehow, some way, Keefe had set this up.
So what was his plan?

*And why hadn't he told her?!*

"I must say"—Fintan raised his hands, ready to call down flames—"you've really outdone yourself, Mr. Sencen. Miss Foster is an excellent addition to our bargain."

Keefe jumped in front of Sophie. "She's not supposed to be here."

Brant's scarred smile crawled straight out of Sophie's nightmares. "Then we'll consider her an excellent bonus."

Sophie hadn't noticed that Alvar had vanished until she felt his arms wrap around her. She screamed and thrashed and kicked, but he was too strong. He pinned her arms behind her with one hand while he ripped her Black Swan pendant off her neck and tossed it to Brant.

"Let's leave the fires to the professionals, shall we?" Brant asked as he crushed the monocle under his heavy black boot. "I'll take yours, too."

Keefe jerked away as Brant yanked the pendant off his neck.

"Must we really do this again?" Brant asked, snapping his fingers and creating a sphere of Everblaze.

"Not if you let her go," Keefe said.

"I'm finding it rather hard to believe your commitment," Fintan told him. "Surely you've realized that switching sides means betraying your friends."

Sophie's stomach switched to vomit mode. "What is he talking about, Keefe?"

"You can't guess?" Brant asked.

She was developing some terrifying theories—but none of them made sense. Or they didn't until Fintan asked Keefe, "Where's the cache?"

The only way they would know she had the cache was if Keefe had told them. He must be running the same trick she'd had him use on King Dimitar, offering something the Neverseen wanted in order to get information.

But what kind of information?

And then she knew.

*There are better ways to save your mom,* she transmitted to Keefe. *Let's get out of here and we'll figure it out together.*

Not that she had any idea how they were going to get away. Her home crystal was gone, and Keefe didn't seem to have one either. But the mountains weren't *that* far away. If they made a run for it they might be able to get high enough to teleport—assuming she could get out of Alvar's viselike grip.

"We should finish this at the hideout," Alvar said, as if he knew what she'd been planning. "Ruy will be wondering where we are."

"Not until he proves he can deliver the item," Fintan said. "Show us the cache."

"Let her go first," Keefe snapped back.

"There you go again, making it hard to trust you. So let's make this easier." Fintan shoved Keefe to the ground and grabbed Sophie from Alvar. He squeezed her arm so hard she wondered if the bone might snap.

Everblaze erupted in his free hand and he held the flames under Sophie's nose. "Give me the cache," Fintan said, "or I'll start giving her scars like the ones she gave Brant."

"Okay," Keefe said, stumbling to his feet. "I'll get it right now."

Sophie was trying hard to think of a way to help him out of his bluff when she heard the sound of her voice saying, "221B Baker Street."

The cache dropped into Keefe's palm with a *plop*, and Sophie's jaw fell.

"How did you . . ."

Keefe wouldn't look at her. "I pieced it together after I heard you training with Fitz. And mimicking's easy."

"Give it here," Fintan ordered.

*Don't do it*, Sophie transmitted.

Keefe kept his focus on Fintan. "You'll honor the rest of our deal?"

"*If* you prove your loyalty," Brant snapped.

"I brought the cache—what more do you need?" Keefe asked.

"You haven't actually given it to us," Fintan reminded him. He pointed to Alvar, who was the only one with free hands.

Sophie couldn't breathe when she saw the look on Keefe's face. There were so many emotions stretched across his features: Pain. Sorrow. Regret.

But the worst was shame.

"Don't do it," she begged. "That cache could destroy everything."

"That's the point," Fintan agreed. "Three seconds, Mr. Sencen, then things get ugly."

Sophie couldn't fight back her sob as Keefe handed Alvar the cache. She tried to grab it telekinetically, but Alvar's grip was too tight. And as soon as he had it, he leaped away.

*Gone.*

"*Now* we're getting somewhere," Fintan said, still holding the flames under Sophie's nose. "But you still have one more test before I'll trust you. And since the strongest bonds are created with fire . . ."

Brant smiled and picked up the bent frame of Sophie's ruined monocle pendant. He passed the dented metal through the flames of Everblaze, then offered it to Keefe. "Brand her a traitor and maybe we'll believe your commitment."

"Why are you doing this?" Sophie asked as Keefe took the red-hot pendant. "How can you join them after everything they've done?"

Keefe's eyes stayed focused on the brand. "I can't pretend I'm who you want me to be anymore."

"What does that even mean?" she screamed.

Keefe's voice was choked now, but Sophie was too angry to cry.

"It means I got more memories back," he said. "I'm not like you. You were made to be the hero. I was raised to be something . . . else."

He reached toward her face, and she braced for searing pain. But all he touched was the necklace he'd given her. "I wanted you to have this before I left," he whispered. "I thought it would be good for you to have something to remember me by. In case someday . . ."

"I'm growing impatient, Mr. Sencen," Fintan warned.

"Give me a second!" Keefe traced his fingers over the beads, lingering on the one he'd made. "I know why my dad hated it now. It looks like our Exillium necklaces, doesn't it? That's why my mom must've liked it. She knew I was meant to be the outcast. You keep trying to fix everything, Sophie. You even fixed Exillium. But you can't fix me."

His eyes met hers then, and they held some sort of plea.

He glanced to his left, and she followed his gaze, spotting the faintest trace of a light path, glinting out of the tiny crystal on the new bead he'd painted for her.

"You understand, right?" Keefe asked.

"No." But she did. Sort of.

*Come with me,* she transmitted.

"I have to do this," he said. "Please don't hate me."

Their eyes met again and he nodded toward the faint trail of light he was still holding in place.

Sophie swallowed hard, wishing there was something—anything—she could do to take him with her. But her only choice was to channel the full force of her mental strength and twist free of Fintan's iron grasp. She fell toward the path, taking one last look at Keefe's anguished face as the light he'd created for her pulled her away.

# SEVENTY-NINE

I THINK WE NEED TO GO THROUGH THIS ONE more time," Mr. Forkle said, pacing across the petaled carpet of Sophie's Havenfield bedroom. The rest of the Collective stood near the doorway, and Grady and Edaline sat with her on the bed.

They'd wanted to hail Elwin, but Sophie wasn't injured— unless crushed hearts counted.

The path Keefe had made for her had brought her straight home, erasing any doubt that he'd wanted her to escape. He'd probably used his mom's crystal-making kit when he painted the bead. But none of that changed the fact that he'd given the Neverseen the cache—using her voice. And that he'd clearly arranged the whole meeting.

If she hadn't followed him, he'd still be with the Neverseen right now.

He'd still be a traitor.

The word made her dizzy and nauseous and ache in places she didn't know could hurt. And it only got worse as she recited the story from the beginning again.

Grady's hands curled into white-knuckled fists. "I knew we shouldn't have left you alone with that boy!"

"If it makes you feel any better," Sophie mumbled, "he didn't want me there either."

"Which *is* significant," Granite jumped in. "He clearly never meant to put Sophie in danger, and he took quite a risk getting her out of there."

"What do you think the Neverseen will do to him?" Sophie whispered. "They'll have to know he helped me."

"Perhaps not," Mr. Forkle said quietly. "Mr. Sencen has always had a talent for spinning convincing stories and excuses."

"You mean *lying*," Grady corrected, the word dripping with bitterness.

"It's a trick we've all been forced to rely on at times," Granite reminded him, gesturing to his rocky disguise. "I understand the disappointment you're feeling—"

"I'm more than disappointed!" Grady snapped. Edaline took his hand, trying to calm him.

"I know," Granite tried again. "But right now, our focus should be on developing our contingency plan."

"What do you mean?" Sophie asked.

"Mr. Sencen knows quite a lot about our organization," Mr. Forkle said, "including the location of Alluveterre, and my identity as Sir Astin, as well as the Hekses involvement."

"You don't think he'd tell the Neverseen that, do you?" Sophie asked.

"We have to prepare for the possibility." Granite turned to Blur, Squall, and Wraith. "Can you increase security at Alluveterre? And explain the situation to Tam and Linh, and Vika and Timkin?"

"Sophie will need extra security as well," Mr. Forkle added. "All the children will."

"We'll take care of it," Blur said.

"I'd like to hear your plan," Grady told him. "Keefe knows far too much about Sophie for us to treat this lightly."

"He wouldn't hurt me," Sophie insisted.

Grady shook his head. "He already has."

The words loomed over her as Grady followed Blur, Wraith, and Squall out of her room. Edaline started to follow, then turned back and hugged Sophie tight.

"We'll figure this out," she promised. "Everything's going to be fine."

"Fine" didn't sound nearly as comforting as Edaline probably wanted it to. But Sophie still told her, "Thanks."

Edaline hugged her again, then left Sophie alone with Mr. Forkle and Granite. Somehow the smaller group made it easier for her to ask the question she couldn't get away from.

"Do you think Keefe is *bad*?"

"'Bad' is a relative term," Mr. Forkle said. "All I can say is that he's become very reckless."

"So you think his guilt made him do this?" Sophie asked.

"I think he's desperate for answers we cannot give him," Granite said. "And this is the path he has chosen."

"But how is this a path?" Sophie asked. "The Neverseen will never trust him unless he convinces them he's one of them."

"And therein lies the recklessness," Mr. Forkle agreed. "It will be up to Mr. Sencen to decide his level of commitment."

Sophie's mind flashed to what Fintan told Keefe during their confrontation.

*Surely you've realized that switching sides means betraying your friends.*

Was that why Keefe had given her the necklace?

She stared at the bead he'd made. The tiny crystal she'd used to escape had dissolved—but it *had* been there.

And it had saved her.

But he hadn't known she'd be following him that day, so he must've made the bead for "just in case."

It helped thinking that, imagining Keefe trying to preplan for any possible dangers. Except . . .

He'd only made *one* bead.

"And you have no idea what he meant," Granite said, "when he mentioned that he'd regained memories his mother had erased."

Sophie shook her head. "All he said was that he was raised to be something else."

"Likely another part of this Lodestar Initiative," Mr. Forkle said. "We'll have to increase our efforts to learn more about it. Perhaps I should pay Gethen another visit."

"I'm going with you," Sophie said.

His mouth started to curve with a "no," but at the last second he changed it to, "Of course. I'll speak with the Council to arrange it. In the meantime I urge you not to make rash decisions. Don't be too quick to give up on your friend. But do not trust him blindly, either."

"What about the cache?" Granite asked, unleashing a whole new set of worries. "The Council won't be happy to know Sophie has lost it."

"We must recover the cache—quickly," Mr. Forkle said, "before the Council discovers it's missing."

"You mean we're not going to tell them Keefe stole it?" Sophie asked.

Mr. Forkle sat next to her on the bed, his bulky weight making her lean toward him. "This isn't the first time we've had to keep secrets from the Council. And it likely won't be the last. If the cache remains missing too long, we'll inform them. But to tell them now would only be a distraction."

"How are we going to get it back?" she asked.

"I'm still working on that," Mr. Forkle said. "But hopefully, with the right planning, we can recover everything we've lost."

The glint in his eyes made it clear he wasn't giving up on Keefe either.

"Sounds like she'll need a good bodyguard," a high-pitched squeaky voice said from the doorway.

Sophie jumped out of bed and sprinted across the room, throwing her arms around Sandor. She didn't mind at all when he lifted her off the ground, or the noseful of musky goblin scent.

"I'm not hurting you, right?" she asked, realizing how tight she was squeezing—even if it was hard to imagine hurting so much rock-hard goblin muscle.

Sandor laughed. "No, Miss Foster. I've never been better."

He set her down and turned to Mr. Forkle, informing him of the new security protocols Grady and the rest of the Collective had agreed upon, which included bodyguards for Fitz, Biana, and Dex, as well as regular observation of Everglen and the Hekses' house. The best news was that Sandor would resume his supervision of Sophie.

Sophie tried to listen to the rest, but she kept staring at the bead in Keefe's necklace. He'd chosen a Panakes blossom, which Calla had said could heal anything.

As she stared longer at the intricate flower, she noticed tiny letters painted into one of the petals—the same petal that had hidden the crystal that saved her.

*Trust me.*

Mr. Forkle cleared his throat, reminding her she wasn't alone.

"You're *not* alone," he said, making her wonder if he'd been eavesdropping on her thoughts. "And I think it's important for you to know that as you enter this next phase in your life. You're back in the Lost Cities. Back under the watchful eye of the Council. Returning to the routines of Foxfire. And I'm sure everything that's happened will make you question who's truly on your side. So I think it's time to finally answer a certain question you keep asking, don't you, Granite?"

"I do," Granite said, though he sounded wary.

They each pulled a small vial from their cloak pockets. Sophie didn't recognize the green liquid in the bottle Granite held. But she definitely recognized the callowberries in Mr. Forkle's hand.

She gasped as he popped one into his mouth and swallowed. Granite coughed and spluttered as he downed his elixir. For five seconds nothing happened. Then their bodies started shifting and shrinking. The process looked painful as their features tightened and twisted into their rightful places.

Sophie tried to guess which faces would soon stare back at her, but when the shift was complete, she discovered how wrong she'd been.

"You?" she whispered, not sure which of them stunned her more.

Mr. Forkle had turned into the tall, black-haired Magnate Leto, her Principal at Foxfire.

And Granite's rocky features had dissolved into the

olive-toned complexion and blond hair of Sir Tiergan, her telepathy Mentor.

"Yes," they said, looking both proud and shy.

"The surest way to protect you was to be in your life," Tiergan told her, "even if it meant resorting to deception."

"So that means . . ." She couldn't finish the sentence, her mind splitting in too many different directions. All the times Sir Tiergan had helped her or guided her, all of Magnate Leto's strange looks and probing questions.

It seemed so obvious now—but also so impossible to wrap her head around.

"Is anyone who they really say they are?" Sophie asked, sinking back onto her bed.

"Yes," Magnate Leto—Mr. Forkle—whatever she was supposed to call him—told her. "You are, and always will be, Sophie Foster."

"And we will continue to watch over you. Which is why we've chosen to reveal ourselves. We want you to know that you're never alone," Granite-as-Tiergan said. "We're always here in one form or another. All you have to do is trust us."

That was what Keefe was asking for too, along with the final words he'd said to her.

*Please don't hate me.*

The request had never felt more impossible. But Sophie decided in that moment that she was going to grant it. She may not understand what he was doing. But she couldn't hate Keefe.

"There's the determination I've come to know so well," Mr. Forkle-as-Magnate-Leto said with a smile. "So let me leave you by sharing some encouraging news as well. Something to prove we *are* making progress. We have a long road ahead of us, with many challenges on the horizon—"

"This is supposed to be encouraging?" Sophie interrupted.

Mr. Forkle-as-Magnate-Leto sighed. "You kids are so impatient."

Sophie smiled at his familiar phrasing and motioned for him to continue.

"As I was saying," he said, "the tides are turning in our favor. Our losses have been small, and our gains have been great. Especially since Mr. Tam agreed to a favor this morning." He paused to smile at Granite-Tiergan before turning back to Sophie. "As of this morning, Prentice is awake."

# ACKNOWLEDGMENTS

Okay, I know you probably started reading this secretly hoping it was the beginning of Book #5, but alas. IT WILL BE WORTH THE WAIT, I PROMISE. ☺

(Unless you're one of my future fans, reading this when the book is already out—in which case, why are you still here? Go get Book #5!)

This is why I love you guys so much. You make me wish I could write even faster, so there'd never be a delay between books. But since I haven't manifested that ability—and have yet to find a TARDIS—thank you for your patience and enthusiasm and devotion and letters and fan art and cupcakes and all the other incredible things you do to prove that I have the Best. Readers. EVER.

This series also wouldn't exist without the constant guidance and support of Team Shannon! (Shhhh—they don't know I call them that!)

Laura Rennert, can you believe this is our sixth book together? I'm running out of clever ways to thank you! So I'll just hand you some tea and say, "Here's hoping for many more books to come!" I also must thank everyone at Andrea Brown Literary, as well as Taryn Fagerness, for spreading the Keeper love worldwide. And to my foreign publishers, thank you for everything you do to share these stories with your readers.

Liesa Abrams, this is our sixth book together too. Somehow, I keep winning the editor lottery! Thank you for your constant, tireless energy and for helping me mold this story into the book it needed to be. *sends you all the gluten-free cupcakes and cookies* I also want to thank everyone at Simon & Schuster for the love they show this series, especially Mara Anastas, Mary Marotta, Katherine Devendorf, Emma Sector, Carolyn Swerdloff, Teresa Ronquillo, Jennifer Romanello, Ksenia Winnicki, Lucille Rettino, Michelle Leo, Anthony Parisi, Betsy Bloom, Matt Pantoliano, Amy Bartram, Mike Rosamilia, and the entire sales team. Plus an enormous THANK YOU to Karin Paprocki, for continuing to outdo herself with my covers, and to Jason Chan, for his jaw-droppingly gorgeous artwork.

Thank you, Sara McClung, for stepping in with a sanity-saving (and game-changing!) brainstorming session when I needed it most. I could never write a Keeper book without you. Tremendous thanks also go to Victoria Morris, for being the voice of encouragement and reason that guided me through the final push. And thanks to Kari Olson, for being the one I go to with All The Questions (even if your answers often unhelpfully involve Keefe and kissing).

Special thanks also go to Amélie Mantchev, Barbara Sutherland, and Kerry Sutherland, for being my incredible fact-checkers and helping make sure I'm keeping my details straight. Now I can blame you guys if there are any mistakes. (I kid, I kid!) You guys rock!

I also have no idea what I'd do without the amazing authors I turn to for advice, motivation, commiseration—whatever I need to survive this hectic business. Thank you, Erin Bowman, Zac Brewer, MG Buerhlen, Lisa Cannon, Christa Desir, Debra Driza, Nikki Katz, Lisa Mantchev, Ellen Oh, Andrea Ortega, Cindy Pon, CJ Redwine, James Riley, Amy Tintera, Kasie West, Natalie Whipple, and Sarah Wylie. I'm probably forgetting some of you—hazards of deadline brain—so if I have, know that I'll forever kick myself for leaving you out!

And I will seriously never be able to properly thank the many teachers, librarians, bloggers, and booksellers who've helped this series grow, especially Mel Barnes, Alyson Beecher, Katie Bartow, Lynette Dodds, Maryelizabeth Hart, Faith Hochhalter, Heather Laird, Katie Laird, Kim Laird, Barbara Mena, Brandi Stewart, Kristin Trevino, Andrea Vuleta, and *so* many others. I could add another hundred pages if I tried to thank you all—and my publisher would probably strangle me—so if you're not mentioned, please know I adore you and am forever grateful.

Finally, to my parents, thank you for your never-ending support, for your determination to get Keeper in the hands of every single kid, and for the steady supply of home-cooked food during the crazed deadline days when the mere thought of *more* take-out made me want to hide.

Turn the page for a sneak peek at

# KEEPER
## OF THE
# LOST CITIES

Book 5: **LODESTAR**

**T**HIS IS A SECURITY NIGHTMARE!" Sandor grumbled, keeping his huge gray hand poised over his enormous black sword.

His squeaky voice reminded Sophie more of a talking mouse than a deadly bodyguard.

Several prodigies raced past, and Sandor pulled Sophie closer as the giggling group jumped to pop the candy-filled bubbles floating near the shimmering crystal trees. All around them, kids were running through the confetti-covered atrium in their amber-gold Level Three uniforms, capes flying as they caught snacks and bottles of lushberry juice and stuffed tinsel-wrapped gifts into the long white thinking caps dangling from everyone's lockers.

The Midterms Celebration was a Foxfire Academy tradition—hardly the impending doom Sandor was imagining. And yet, Sophie understood his concern.

Every parent roaming the streamer-lined halls.

Every face she didn't recognize.

Any of them could be a rebel.

A villain.

*The enemy.*

Sandor watched Sophie tug on her eyelashes—her nervous habit, back in full force. "Nothing is going to happen," he promised, tucking her blond hair behind her ear with a surprisingly gentle touch for a seven-foot-tall goblin warrior.

It definitely helped having Sandor back at her side—especially after almost losing him during the battle on Mount Everest. And Sandor wasn't the only goblin at Foxfire anymore. Each of the six wings in the main campus building had been assigned its own patrol, with two additional squadrons keeping watch over the sprawling grounds.

The Council had also added security throughout the Lost Cities.

They had to.

The ogres were still threatening war.

And in the three weeks since Sophie and her friends had returned from hiding with the Black Swan, the Neverseen had scorched the main gate of the Sanctuary *and* broken into the registry in Atlantis.

Sophie could guess what the rebels had hoped to gain from the elves' secret animal preserve—they obviously didn't know that she'd convinced the Council to set the precious alicorns free. But the registry attack remained a mystery. The Councillors kept careful records on every elf ever born, and no one would tell her if any files had been altered or stolen.

A bubble popped on Sophie's head, and Sandor caught the box of Prattles that had been hovering inside.

"If you're going to eat these, I should check them first," he told her.

Sandor's wide, flat nose scented no toxins in the nutty candy, but he insisted on examining the pin before handing them over. Every box of Prattles came with a special collectible inside, and in the past, the Black Swan had used them to send Sophie messages.

He fished out the tiny velvet pouch and Sophie caught herself clutching her allergy remedy necklace. She still kept the silver moonlark pin that Calla had given her attached to the cord—a reminder of the friend she'd lost, and a symbol of the role she needed to figure out how to play.

"Looks like we're good," Sandor said, handing her the small boobrie pin—a strange black bird with bright yellow tail feathers. "Can't imagine *that* means anything important."

Sophie couldn't either. Especially since the Black Swan had been annoyingly silent.

No notes. No clues. No answers during their brief meetings.

Apparently they were "regrouping." And it was taking forever.

At least the Council was doing *something*—setting up goblin patrols and trying to arrange an ogre Peace Summit. The Black Swan should at least be . . .

Actually, Sophie didn't know what they should be doing.

That was the problem with having her friend join the enemy.

"There you are!" a familiar voice said behind her. "I was starting to think you'd ditched us."

The deep, crisp accent was instantly recognizable. And yet, the teasing words made Sophie wish she'd turn and find a different boy.

Fitz looked as cute as ever in his red Level Five uniform, but his perfect smile didn't reach his trademark teal eyes. The recent revelations had been a huge blow for all of her friends, but Fitz had taken it the hardest.

Both his brother and his best friend had run off with the Neverseen.

Alvar's betrayal had made Fitz wary—made him doubt every memory.

But Keefe's?

He wouldn't talk about it—at *all.*